WHITE LIGHT

By K. E. Anker

Published by Katy Anker © 2019

For Laura and Rachel,

without whom this story would still be unfinished.

Chapter 1: The Beginning

Thomas already wanted the ground to open up and swallow him whole, and they hadn't even got there yet.

The car had been crawling along the M6 towards the Lake District for hours now and, if Daniel's falsely cheerful voice piped up suggesting that they stop in another fucking service station to '*grab a bite to eat and stretch their legs*' , Thomas was actually going to tuck and roll out of the car. To put it mildly, he needed to get out of the car yesterday. To put it *harshly*, Thomas wanted to use Henry's lighter to set fire to himself.

"I can practically feel the loathing rolling off of you, Tom, and it's obscuring my vision," Henry said mildly as they finally - *finally* - left the motorway behind… not that the A590 was much better but still, Thomas would take the small victories where he could get them.

"Won't be too much longer now, Tom," Daniel lied kindly, twisting in the front seat to smile at the older man with his kind blue eyes, his lip-ring glinting in the sunshine. The three of them had been crammed into the car for what felt like most of Thomas's adult life - which, admittedly, had only been three years - and, as the fifth hour of driving finally dawned, Thomas gave up, relaxing back in his seat.

They'd left their homes in London at six o'clock that morning, stowing the last of their belongings in the removal van and agreeing to meet it up north later that day, after they'd had time to pick up the door keys from the estate agent. Honestly, if Thomas had been tired this morning, he was *exhausted* now, his green eyes bleary as he noticed that there was fortunately a lot less traffic on this road. He let out a low breath he hadn't even realised he'd been holding as his overheated cheek fell to rest against the cool glass. Fields and woodland flew past through the window as Henry's car carried them on, and Thomas stretched out his bad leg as best he could in the cramped space, wincing a little at the pain he could feel.

"How's your sciatica, Tom?" Daniel asked from the front passenger seat, almost like he knew what the older man was thinking. Thomas looked up at the blond man slowly, aiming to keep his expression blank and free of pain although he probably just looked unfriendly. Daniel grimaced and Thomas immediately felt bad.

"You worry too much," the older man said, forcing a huff of laughter as he awkwardly dragged his fingers through his freshly-dyed red hair. "Don't stress about me, okay? I'm fine."

Thomas was lying of course.

Ever since the car accident a few years earlier, he'd never been the same. A disc had slipped in Thomas's spine when his father's car had ploughed into him on his walk home from college and, once he'd woken up in the hospital two weeks later - unable to move and half-blind with pain - his assailant had been sitting right there at his bedside with his arm wrapped around his wife and cold fury in his eyes.

Despite Thomas being certain that his injuries had been caused by his father, Peter Barnes's car had mysteriously 'vanished' while his son was still in a coma and no one had ever been able to prove it had been him due to the lack of evidence. Of course, who was going to believe Thomas's story anyway?

Even when he was considered recovered enough to view things 'sensibly', no one really took his claims seriously. It was the word of a deeply troubled and mentally unstable teenager against that of his outwardly loving, hard-working estate agent father who would never dream of hurting his family… at least in any way that could be pinned on him.

His mum was too afraid to speak out and Thomas didn't want to hurt Diane by forcing her to choose between them, and the solitary police officer who had been sent out to investigate the hit and run didn't believe him either. No one did… no one but Henry and Daniel, and Thomas's grandpa. The red-haired man was convinced even his two best friends had started to doubt him in the end, growing wary of him and his mood swings in a way they never had been before (although, with hindsight, that could just have been his paranoia talking).

Only Thomas's grandpa had believed him entirely.

Old Ken Barnes had listened to his grandson when no one else would.

"Tom?" Daniel asked softly and the red-haired man jerked in shock, mortified when he realised his tired green eyes were welling with tears. Henry's tanned hands were white-knuckled on the steering wheel as they passed over the River Kent and Thomas swallowed roughly past the lump in his throat.

"I'm fine," he whispered, staring down at where he'd bitten his fingernails painfully short as he forced the tears back. "Just… remembering. That's all."

Henry's dark brown eyes were fixed sadly on his childhood best friend in the rear view mirror but Thomas couldn't look at him… couldn't bear to see the inevitable *kindness* there that only made him feel worse. It was sunny outside the window but the warmth didn't seem able to permeate the car. Thomas felt cold as he slumped there against the seat.

"Were you thinking about your grandpa?" Daniel asked softly and the older man shrugged, the movement jerky and painful as his back ached.

"Sure," Thomas sighed, deciding it was easier to tell a half-lie than the truth. Nobody wanted to hear about how much Thomas hurt. Nobody wanted to hear about the sickening mixture of pain and numbness that had been radiating through his sciatic nerve ever since that fateful day of the accident, or the awful tingling sensation in his left leg and lower back that kept him awake at night, or the fact that he couldn't lie down with his legs flat on the mattress anymore or he might not be able to stand up again. Nobody wanted to hear that his left calf muscle, and the muscles in his foot and ankle were so weakened that he struggled to run anymore… that sometimes he struggled to *walk*.

His two best friends already knew how broken he was.

What would reminding them now achieve besides ripping open old wounds better left untouched?

Thomas's pride had combined with his stubbornness years ago, around the time the twenty one year old had vowed never to let on how awful he sometimes felt. It was why he hated using his cane when it hurt too badly to put weight on his leg. It was why Thomas had chosen to drop out of college instead of facing his classmates feeling like a cripple. It was why he had learnt to cry silently when he was still a kid. He couldn't stand people thinking he was weak. He *hated* it.

Daniel was watching the red-haired man so unhappily that Thomas had to look away, had to force himself to focus on something - *anything* - else… anything but the pain he had caused on his best friend's face.

The first thing Thomas's gaze settled on was the spell jar in his lap. His mum had slipped it to him through the open car window when they'd left that morning, a remnant of her dabbles in witchcraft during college. As far as he knew, Diane didn't practice much anymore so it always sent something warm and soft unfurling in Thomas's chest when she gave him something like this.

'*Something to remember her by,*' the little voice in his head whispered nastily. Thomas pressed his lips together so hard they went bloodless, fighting to ignore it because he hated that voice so much… hated that it always whispered the things that scared him most.

He'd talked to his counsellor Linda about it before; told her that he found it so hard to control his thoughts sometimes that they felt like they were burning him up from the inside out and... god, now that he was remembering her with her kind eyes and greying hair, a lump was rising in his throat all over again because... fuck, he didn't know how he was going to *cope* without Linda's support. She'd assured him that he'd be fine so long as he followed the exercises they'd gone over together and made sure he didn't bottle things up but... Thomas was fairly certain those were both easier said than done. He didn't think he was ready at all.

'Focus on the jar,' he told himself desperately. *'Focus on your breathing and calm down. You're not allowed to freak out in the car with Hal and Danny.'*

Thomas forced his damp green eyes open cautiously, letting out a quiet relieved breath when he realised that the younger two men were now watching the road ahead as Henry guided the car onto the A591. They glided over the tarmac in silence, flying past Sizergh Castle so quickly that Thomas barely caught a glimpse of the medieval fortress through the thick woodland edging the road.

The spell jar grew sweaty in his palm as he gripped it tightly, contemplating living in a place as strange and wild as this. Thomas was used to kebab shops and grotty little newsagents that seemed to sprout out of the cracked pavements on the backstreets of north London. His current surroundings were about as far from that world as it was possible to get because everything just seemed so ancient and strange here. It was all so much *bigger* than he was used to, with mountains on the horizon and thick forests stretching out around him.

Thomas was so glad his mum had given him the spell jar now; it was something familiar and comforting to hold onto when his heart felt like it was about to beat right out of his ribcage.

His throat thickened as he lifted the jar closer, twisting it in the warm light filtering in from outside so that the glass glinted in the sunshine. There was a little piece of paper tucked into his pocket - handwritten in his mum's delicate script - that detailed all of the ingredients and intentions gathered in the jar but, over the course of the morning, Thomas had already memorised them.

Diane had used sea salt for protection, black pepper to banish negativity, ginger for adventure and new experiences, sage for cleansing and purification, and cumin to promote peace and tranquillity. The ingredients had been layered neatly inside the tiny jar and Thomas's heart beat a little calmer as he focused on it, breathing slow and deep the way Linda had encouraged him to whenever he got panicky during one of their sessions. Thomas rubbed the pad of his thumb gently over the white wax his mum had used to seal the jar, pressing his lips to it silently.

The white symbolised hope, protection, and peace, and Thomas had possibly never missed his mum more than he did in that moment. She loved him more than anyone alive and, despite how bitter the twenty one year old might have felt at the prospect of fleeing his past (and her with it), he never forgot that. He loved her too.

Diane had insisted he join Henry and Daniel in an effort to keep him safe, just like she'd lovingly crafted this jar. Thomas had seen it in her tear-filled eyes when she'd carefully passed it through the open car window to him - the same green eyes she shared with her son – and gently pressed a kiss to his forehead.

"Such sad eyes," she'd whispered when she'd drawn back to look at her only child, laying her palm lightly against his pale cheek. "Keep yourself safe for me, Tommy, until I see you again. This isn't the end; do you hear me? It's the beginning."

Remembering those words now made Thomas feel a shadow of his former hope, a sliver of the excitement he had felt when he'd first agreed to move up here with his two best friends and Thomas held onto it with everything he had, sheltering the spark in his chest just like Henry and Daniel were doing as they tried to stay optimistic.

Henry had wanted to leave his overprotective home for as long as he could remember and, when he'd chosen to study the work rangers did in the Lake District for his geography project during secondary school, it was instantly all he ever wanted to do. Moving to Cumbria to become a field ranger in his favourite place on the planet was the dark-haired man's dream and there had never been any question of Daniel following Henry there.

The blond man would have done anything to get away from his homophobic family - not that Thomas could blame him for that - and chasing the affection Henry so willingly bestowed upon him had always been Daniel's favourite thing to do. He'd been in love with Henry from day one and he would have followed him anywhere.

Thomas was just along for the ride.

"How much further is there to go?" the red-haired man asked curiously, glancing out of the window and trying to work out whereabouts they were. He'd just seen a sign stating that a place called Kendal was two miles away but it meant nothing to Thomas. He'd never been in this part of the country before, not even when his two best friends had come to visit the new house a few months previously (although Thomas used the word '*new*' sparingly; the house might have been renovated recently but it had been up in the Fells for *years*).

Henry and Daniel had had to go on the visit without Thomas - not that they'd been too upset by that as they'd probably used the experience as some sort of Big Gay Road Trip Of Unresolved Sexual Tension - but Thomas had been disappointed, mostly in himself. He'd been in too much pain at the time to even leave the house so sitting trapped in a car for well over twelve hours there and back would have been excruciating, not to mention impossible.

He wished that had been the only occasion his sciatica had prevented him from enjoying but it just wasn't the case. There'd been the holiday to Belgium last year and the Disneyland Florida trip two years before that, and there were the smaller things too; the nights going to bars and those stupid pub quizzes Daniel loved, and that one Christmas where Henry wanted them all to go ice-skating together but Thomas had to sit on the benches and watch. His sciatica flared up every now and then - sometimes for a reason, mostly out of nowhere -

and Thomas grew bitterer with every explosion of pain... with every missed opportunity that held him back.

Thomas didn't want to have to rely on strong painkillers and a fucking walking stick in order to leave the house on his bad days.

He wanted to go outside and feel the sun on his skin without pain just like everyone else did.

"There's still around forty miles to go," Henry said and it took Thomas a moment to remember that he'd even asked a question in the first place. "We should be there in about two hours unless we stop for lunch now." Henry's dark eyes met Thomas's in the rear view mirror and he smiled hopefully, apparently perking up at the mention of food. "Should we stop now or eat later?"

Thomas pulled a face as he considered this. They'd stopped for a large fry-up that morning which had been just the right side of greasy but Thomas was flagging now and he definitely wouldn't say no to a cheese sandwich. Daniel seemed to agree.

"I think we should find a pub somewhere to stop," the blond man said after a moment's thought. "We're not going to have the kitchen set up when we get there later so we might as well have our main meal now." Daniel glanced back to shoot Thomas's bad leg another worried glance. "I don't think it would be a bad idea to get out of this car anyway."

"I agree," Henry said, stifling a yawn although his tired eyes were already scrutinising the nearest road sign as he tried to find a place for them to stop. "My butt's falling asleep. I won't be able to get out of the car at this rate."

Daniel rolled his eyes fondly as he reached across the gearshift to lay a comforting hand on the tanned man's arm, for once forgetting his concerns for Thomas in the face of doting on Henry which was something that Daniel took very, *very* seriously.

"We should stop now," the blond man said gently, making Henry's lips curve into a hesitant smile. (Thomas just hoped they didn't start giving each other The Eyes as they so often did when they got lost in each other's gazes; otherwise the car might end up wrapped around a tree, and them with it.) "You've been driving for hours, Hal. You deserve a rest."

Thomas mimed pretending to be sick in the back of the car but, when no one gave him any attention, he gave up with a little huff and settled back in his seat to see where they would be stopping for food.

In the end, after a scenic drive through the Lyth Valley and an irritatingly bumpy ride along a winding lane called Underbarrow Road, lunch came to them in the form of a pub called The Black Labrador. Henry's whole face lit up when he saw it, presumably because he loved dogs so much, and Daniel was practically giving the dark-haired man heart eyes as they climbed out of the car together, relishing in stretching their legs and breathing in the fresh air. It took Thomas a little longer to join them, his face paling at the pain he could feel rocketing down his leg as he struggled to straighten up once he made it outside.

The pub garden was reassuringly busy as Daniel led the way excitedly inside. Thomas turned down the arm Henry hesitantly offered him with an embarrassed shake of his head and, gritting his teeth, the red-haired man followed his two best friends into the pub. It was nice inside, cool and shady, and as rustic and traditional as Thomas had imagined. Daniel sighed wistfully at the sight of the comfortable-looking room.

"I hope I can get work in a nice place like this," the blond man said quietly, his blue eyes darting about as he took in the blazing log burner and the dark wood of the bar gleaming where it had been polished to a shine. "What about you, Tom?" Daniel asked, looking so enthusiastic that - for just a moment - he was untouched by the years that had passed since they'd first met him. Standing there illuminated in a beam of sunlight, he looked just like the excited boy Thomas and Henry had befriended that day in their drama class when they were fourteen years old.

"Would you consider working somewhere like this?" Daniel asked and Thomas blinked as the illusion broke. There was the Daniel he knew and loved now, with his neat blond hair and the laughter lines just beginning to crinkle the skin around his sky blue eyes.

"Maybe," Thomas mumbled, not wanting to rain on Daniel's parade by telling him how unlikely it was that he'd be able to work somewhere that required him to be able to move around with ease. "You'd be great though, Danny," the red-haired man said sincerely. "I know you would."

Daniel smiled so wide that his blue eyes crinkled and, when Thomas shot a quick look towards Henry, the dark-haired man was watching Thomas with something like relief. It made the red-haired man feel guilty. He knew he could snap at the people he cared about most when he was feeling anxious or vulnerable but he couldn't believe that even being passably pleasant was cause for surprise.

God, how could Henry and Daniel put up with him if he'd really grown that prickly?

Thomas didn't know what he'd done right to deserve best friends like them.

The metaphorical raincloud that had momentarily dissipated during the car ride up north gathered like a storm around Thomas's head and, by the time their meal had ended and they'd bundled back into the car again, he was back to feeling tense and defensive. The pain growing in his leg was shooting down into his foot and Thomas gritted his teeth against it, pressing his head back hard into the seat in an effort to distract himself as Henry guided the car out onto the road.

Daniel started up a half-hearted game of 'I Spy' as they were driving past Burneside and Staveley but it wasn't until the A591 took them across the Troutbeck Bridge and Henry started singing 'Accidentally In Love' by Counting Crows in a deliberately tuneless way that Thomas finally cracked a smile.

"There's that grin we love!" Henry cheered from the front seat, his chocolate brown eyes twinkling as Daniel smiled at Thomas over his broad shoulder. "We missed it, Tom. You gotta smile more often."

"I'll see what I can do," Thomas muttered but he was still smiling a little bit as the car travelled through Ecclerigg. Windermere Lake was hidden behind the trees, only evident in the glimpses of blue water glinting in the early afternoon sunlight when Thomas glanced back. The A593 took them over the River Brathay and the red-haired man watched the quaint little houses passing them as the sunlight dappled down through the trees. He hoped their house looked like this; it was hard to see in the pictures Henry had shown him since the sun had already been going down by the time the pair of them had arrived but he'd caught a glimpse of red brick and a dark slate roof. Thomas hoped it held at least some of the charm that these houses passing now did.

The car climbed noticeably higher when they passed through Little Langdale and Thomas's palm pressed flat against the window as he peered out at the wide blue lake they were passing. Thomas could see the mountains rising in the background, the sheep grazing in the fields by the road as the car twisted carefully through the Wrynose Pass.

After that, the journey grew more frustrating. It took almost an hour to reach the Hardknott Pass after they got stuck behind not one, not two, but *three* tractors. Thomas was grumpy again and even Daniel looked vaguely surly now, and Thomas could tell Henry was getting pissed off too because his shoulders were tense and his dimples hadn't been visible in well over half an hour, an anomaly that was almost unheard of. It reminded Thomas vaguely of their last year at secondary school when all of them had been trying (and failing dismally) to revise for their maths GCSE. They'd been collectively annoyed then too.

"There's a Roman Fort over there," Thomas said from the backseat, attempting to break the tension as he pointed half-heartedly towards the ruins. Daniel shot him a mildly dirty look.

"I don't care about a Roman Fort," the blond man said sulkily. "What I *care* about is finding a toilet as soon as possible."

"Then why didn't you say something sooner?!" Henry grumbled as they drove alongside the River Esk, shooting the blond man a scowl that still managed to look vaguely fond. "I told you not to drink all those apple juices in the pub! Fruit juice isn't even thirst quenching, Daniel! It's hot today!"

"I drank it for the vitamins, Henry! The *vitamins*! Something you'd know about if you actually took those multivitamin tablets I keep buying you! They'd make your hair look healthier."

"My hair's fine, thank you *very* much!"

Thomas rolled his eyes as he watched the two of them bickering like an old married couple but he had to admit that it helped distract him from how bored he was. By the time they'd finally stopped fighting - and Henry had grudgingly stopped the car so that Daniel could pee behind a bush - they were already driving along Bowerhouse Bank, just half an hour from their destination if they didn't get stuck behind any more slow-moving agricultural vehicles.

The ground was rising beside the road now, rocky and craggy as the blue sky darkened when the sun slipped momentarily behind a cloud. An apprehensive silence filled the car when they crossed Santon

Bridge and it felt almost as though the three of them were finally feeling the weight of their decision to move here. Thomas could feel the hairs on the back of his neck rising and he shivered at the tension he could feel saturating the car as they headed towards the village of Nether Wasdale. There were no other vehicles in sight now.

Once they were out the other side, the trees edging the right side of the road dropped sharply beneath the metal barrier as they climbed carefully higher, the land falling away into a steep hill that led down to Wast Water Lake. Illgill Head rose up behind it, the mountain peak reflected in the miles of rippling water as Henry guided his car along beneath the canopy of trees. The roads were unnamed now, dark and dappled with shadows as, all the while, the rocky ground rose around them, carrying them with it.

When they finally broke through the trees, the sudden sunlight blinded them and Henry stamped hastily on the brakes, keen not to swerve off into one of the low stone walls that edged the road. Thomas blinked to clear his vision, his hand falling to rub at his aching leg unconsciously as his emerald eyes drank in his surroundings, growing rapidly wider as he saw Scafell Pike rising colossally in the distance, the tallest mountain in all of England.

"This is it," Henry could be heard breathing as he carried them onwards towards the small hamlet of Wasdale Head, apparently unaware that his words were audible. "I made it."

Thomas's breath caught in his throat as he looked outside, turning his head frantically in an effort to take everything in as they wound through the valleys, climbing higher and higher. All Thomas could see for miles around were fields and great expanses of rock as the mountains towered into the sky, and it sent his heart racing in his chest as he curled his fingers desperately around the spell jar in his sweaty palm, the last trace of home he had left.

They had to drive around Scafell Pike to reach the hamlet and Thomas's eyes almost felt like they were going to roll out of their sockets as he gazed around him in shock. He'd had no idea how remote it was going to be living here and this realisation only sank in further when they finally reached what passed for a main road in Wasdale Head. It was little more than a dusty track winding through tiny buildings surrounded by muddy fields and the occasional wind-battered tree. The sun shining through the clouds made the long grass look like rippling waves and the red-haired man's eyes widened at how beautiful Wasdale Head looked in the sunlight.

"This is just like being in the Shire," Thomas mumbled unthinkingly, unaware that Henry and Daniel were grinning at him from the front seat, apparently relishing in his reaction the first time he saw where they would be living. "Except, y'know, if the Shire had its own mountain range or something."

"You could've just said the Misty Mountains instead," Henry pointed out as he finally drew the car to a stop in front of the Barn Door Shop. It was a small white-painted building selling outdoor gear, presumably for the numerous tourists arriving to go camping and try climbing the nearby mountains, but Thomas barely noticed as he rolled his eyes at his best friend's comment.

"Nerd," he said firmly.

"Muggle," Henry retorted.

"You're crossing your franchises," the red-haired man said. "Anyway, am I allowed to say '*finally*' now? Are we here?"

There were people in brightly coloured anoraks passing their car on the narrow street and Daniel watched them curiously as they disappeared into Ritson's Bar, tucked away behind the Wasdale Head Inn. It was the establishment he was hoping to work in and Thomas watched the blond man with soft eyes for a moment before he turned to Henry as he answered him.

"Almost," the dark-haired man said. "I just need to pop into the Inn to collect the keys from the estate agent and then we can get back on the road." Henry rubbed the back of his neck uncertainly but his face was alight with excitement now as he stared around at the place he'd always wanted to live in... this strange new green world that Thomas didn't know quite how to process. "The estate agent said Wasdale Head was a 'sprawling agricultural hamlet' and she wasn't kidding. Our new place is another half-mile away, through the other side of the hamlet. The house is in a much smaller place; it's got a different name too I think. We need to go higher to reach it."

Thomas gulped nervously when Henry bid them goodbye and bounded over towards the Inn, wrapping his arms around himself as though his jumper wasn't *quite* enough to keep him warm against what seemed to be a perpetually cold wind. When he'd finally disappeared into the building, Daniel dragged his eyes away to give Thomas a wan smile which didn't quite reach his damp blue eyes.

"You okay, Danny?" the red-haired man asked softly. Daniel pressed his lips together when he heard how gentle Thomas's tone was but he reached for his best friend shakily, looking relieved when Thomas tangled their fingers together without a second thought.

"I… I think so, yeah," the blond man murmured after just a moment too long. Thomas rubbed his thumb over Daniel's knuckles comfortingly.

"You don't look sure," Thomas pointed out gently. "Do you… do you regret saying you'd come here? Are you… scared?" '*Like I am*,' the little voice added bleakly and, for once, Thomas didn't resent it because it was true. Being here – so far away from his mother and everything he knew – was terrifying.

"Not really," Daniel said after a moment of hesitation. "This will make Henry happy and you needed a clean break too… and it's hardly like I have anywhere else to go, is it? My parents wouldn't have me back if I begged them and my brothers are the same." Daniel's usually-calm expression faltered with pain and Thomas tightened his grip, his own discomfort forgotten in the face of the blond man's grief.

"I'm sorry, Danny," he whispered as more tourists passed by outside the car, their laughter and voices strangely muffled through the windows. "I'm so sorry."

"*I'm* not," Daniel insisted and it bothered Thomas that he couldn't tell whether the younger man was being honest or not. "It'll be easier out here. A fresh start with my two favourite people on the planet. I can't think of anywhere I'd rather be."

'*Henry's bed*,' the little voice whispered but Thomas didn't say it. He didn't want to see Daniel hurting.

"I think you're right," the red-haired man said instead, hoping beyond hope that his words were true. "Although, I have to admit, there's a lot less here than I thought there'd be. Like… how do we eat?"

"The same way you always do, Tom," Daniel said with glittering eyes. "You put a fork in one hand and a knife in the other - or do you just prefer eating with your fingers? I can never tell."

"Shut up!" Thomas complained but at least he was smiling, the little voice silenced for now. "I mean getting groceries, you loser! Do we get them delivered all the way out here or…?"

"I doubt it," the blond man said, nibbling his bottom lip worriedly although he seemed to be thinking hard. "I looked it up last night though. If I remember rightly, there's a Sainsbury's about an hour away in a place called… I think it's Cockermouth?" Daniel paused for Thomas's predictable snort of laughter before continuing. "That's the closest supermarket to us. I guess it wouldn't be the end of the world if we had to go there to pick up our groceries."

"There was a Tesco express round the corner from me back home," Thomas said glumly and Daniel rolled his eyes at him.

"There were also takeaway food places," the blond man pointed out. "Your world is changing, Tom."

"Oh, the horror!" the red-haired man cried dramatically. He sobered after a moment though, pulling a face. "An hour is pretty far though.

You better not forget to buy toilet rolls or something." Daniel stuck his tongue out and Thomas responded by copying him like the immature child he was. "I hope Henry enjoys spending all of his fancy new ranger wages on fuel."

"You're hilarious, Tom," Daniel said dryly. "You see, we live in the Lake District now. It's kind of an expectation that we're probably going to use a lot of petrol."

"Henry's vehicle's emissions will single-handedly destroy this planet, Daniel."

"Very funny, Tom, but I think Trump is going to do that first."

"What's Trump done now?" Henry asked as he climbed back into the car with them, bringing with him the cold smell of the air outside as he spun their new door keys around his index finger triumphantly.

"Oh, just existed," Thomas said with a shrug. "Did the estate agent tell you the name of the place we're going then, Hal?" he continued sarcastically. "Because it'll be pretty hard to find it if the only directions we have are '*higher*'. It wouldn't be very helpful either. I mean, how on earth will the postman find our house to deliver our letters? We'll be cut off from the rest of the world!"

Henry rolled his eyes but his slight hesitation before answering sent warning bells ringing in the older man's head.

"Our house is on a thoroughfare called Deadman's Rise."

Thomas exchanged a vaguely horrified look with Daniel as they processed that.

"Deadman's Rise," Thomas repeated, his tone dripping with what might have been contempt if his heart hadn't been racing so unpleasantly at how unnecessarily creepy the name sounded. "Lovely."

"They used to hang people up there I think," Henry added and Thomas shot him a withering look.

"Not helping, Henry."

Chapter 2: The House In The Forest

Thomas thought he understood why the house had been so suspiciously cheap now. His dad would have had a fit if he'd seen the state of it and Thomas honestly wouldn't have blamed him. A depressed silence saturated the car as they parked in the driveway and Thomas could feel it settling in his bones as he stared hopelessly out of the window at their new house… or *old* house, he supposed.

"So it still needs a bit of work," Henry said optimistically, just as the wind picked up outside and a slate fell off the roof with a startling crash. Henry buried his head in his hands against the steering wheel. "Oh god, this is a disaster."

"We'll be okay, Hal," Daniel murmured although his blue eyes were vaguely horrified. "We'll make this work." He rubbed the tanned man's shoulder gently and Henry relaxed a little, chewing his bottom lip worriedly as Daniel gave him a wan smile. "It didn't look like this the last time we came here, did it?" the blond man teased. Henry bit the inside of his mouth to keep from smiling.

"Maybe there was a storm," he said.

'*Or maybe it was so badly built that it's going to collapse on us in the night,*' the little voice in Thomas's head said spitefully as he stared out of the window in appalled silence. He couldn't even find it in himself to disagree and that was the worst part. The Victorian-era building looked just as ancient as Thomas had feared but, despite the estate agent insisting that it had undergone countless repairs and renovations, it still didn't look like somewhere he particularly wanted to live.

The estate agent had called it a *'charming family home in a pleasant location'* but, if this was the estate agent's definition of the word *'charming'* – with birds roosting in the rafters and a broken window on the side of the porch that needed to be boarded up – then she had clearly never looked in a dictionary before.

A low sigh escaped the older man as he slumped back in his seat, unwilling to get out of the car in case he got trapped here. Thomas really hated that this was his first impression of their new home: that it looked like it might fall down on them in a particularly strong gust of wind. Ivy and other creepers climbed the cracked stone walls, and the heavy scent of petrichor from recent rain hung in the air, like something tangible almost... like something Thomas could reach out and grab.

He didn't think he knew *anyone* who would be grateful to live in a place like this... except perhaps his mum. The house looked like the sort of a place a witch in a fairy tale might live, stirring potions in a great iron cauldron and turning people into toads... not that witchcraft was actually anything like that at all but Thomas wasn't feeling especially forgiving right now, mainly because he didn't want to get concussed by a falling roof slate.

The growing wind stirred through the branches of the surrounding trees and the clouds overhead were gathered, painted with a pinkish hue as the sun began its gradual descent behind the mountains. Thomas shivered.

"Were you planning on getting out of the car any time today, Tom, or are you going to make camp in here?"

Thomas gave Henry a dirty look when he turned to find the younger man standing beside the open car door. The red-haired man hadn't even noticed him or Daniel getting out of the car, and the removal van had arrived too which bothered Thomas a little because he wasn't *usually* so unobservant. Then again, he figured he had good reason to be distracted; they were moving into what looked like an incredibly tacky haunted house after all. Was this *really* what Thomas had spent so much of his grandpa's inheritance on?

Henry's brow creased at his best friend's face and he shuffled awkwardly on his feet, readjusting his grip on the box he'd got out of the back of the car. It was filled with items that Henry had deemed too precious to be transported in the removal van currently parked alongside them on the long driveway – privately, Thomas was pretty sure it just contained Henry's beloved comics – but the tanned man's head was tilted to one side curiously now and Thomas didn't want either of his best friends turning into mother hens again. They'd been doing that enough during the painfully long drive here and he was sick of being fussed over.

"Alright, alright. I'm getting out," the older man mumbled, bracing himself for the inevitable pain as he unwillingly released his seat belt. Shifting towards the open door was uncomfortable but actually putting weight on his leg took Thomas's breath away and the red-haired man leant hard against the car door, swallowing down the curse that wanted to escape him. His back was aching badly after so long sitting down and Daniel appeared nearby, his pale face concerned in the dimming light as Thomas stretched his spine out with an audible crack that made Henry wince.

"That's gas popping," Daniel said helpfully, smiling broadly when Thomas fixed him with what Henry lovingly referred to as his *'crocodile eyes'* – basically meaning that Thomas could pull off an unnerving blank stare *really* well when he wanted to – but Daniel's grin faded when he saw Thomas limping over to grab a box out of the car too.

"No way," the blond man said instantly, his voice so firm that Henry glanced back towards them in surprise from where he'd been heading towards the house. The front door was already wide open – the dark-haired man must have unlocked it without Thomas noticing *that* too – and Thomas's shoulders slumped when he saw the unhappy expression on Henry's face.

"You can't carry things with your back, Tom," Daniel said in a slightly softer voice. "I promised your mum I wouldn't let you do anything stupid to make it worse and I'm not planning on breaking that on the first day."

"It's just sciatica," Thomas argued weakly but even Henry was shaking his head now and Thomas lowered his gaze, his expression chagrined as the shame made his cheeks flush hot.

Daniel patted him awkwardly on the arm before he collected his own box, following Henry up the low slope towards the house as the dark-haired man balanced his box of beloved comics carefully on top of a crate of crockery.

Thomas kicked the tyre as hard as he could the moment their backs were turned before letting out a low curse, his cheeks flaming. His mindless viciousness hadn't made him feel any better; all he'd succeeded in doing was scuffing his Converse and jarring his back painfully. Now he was sort of starting to see why his mum had been so concerned at the prospect of him moving out, despite how much she'd tried to hide it.

Thomas was a liability.

"Where are you going, Tom?" Henry called from the front door, free of boxes now as he moved aside to let one of the workers carry in two kitchen chairs stacked together. "Come inside, yeah?" Thomas shook his head, forcing a smile onto his pale face despite how blotchy it had inevitably gone in his embarrassment.

"I'm gonna explore Deadman's Rise if you guys won't let me help you!" Thomas responded, trying to keep the sourness out of his voice although his words were probably too quiet to hear. Henry just gave him a long look before shrugging and going to grab another box which he carried swiftly into the house. When both of the younger men were out of sight, Thomas exhaled shakily as the smile slipped from his face.

He loved his best friends to the moon and back but they could be more than a little overprotective sometimes... and besides, Thomas wasn't a baby! It wasn't like he needed mollycoddling or... or having people tell him he wasn't healthy enough to pick a stupid box up and... yeah, okay, Thomas was kind of sulking now.

He shut the car door behind him hesitantly, lingering beside it with one small hand still pressed to the cool metal, feeling almost as though stepping away from it now would make him lose the last bit of where he had lived before. The wind was growing stronger as the sun sank behind the mountains and Thomas shivered, wrapping his arms around himself tightly as he gazed apprehensively towards their new home. The feeling of foreboding making his anxiety tighten in his chest was undeniable.

He wished uselessly that he'd been able to come here with Daniel and Henry when they'd visited. Even if his no-doubt acerbic commentary hadn't dissuaded them from choosing this house, at least he would've been prepared for it. The reality of it now – with nothing but a vaguely blurry photo that barely filled up Henry's phone screen to compare it to – was the reason Thomas wasn't exactly ecstatic at the prospect of the spooky-looking house crouched in front of him.

It was built into the side of the hill, its windows dark and vacant as the dying sunlight painted them a gristly blood-red. The broken porch window had a great splintering crack in it that resembled a spider-web and Thomas shuddered as he tore his eyes away. A gnarled old oak tree had erupted from the muddy, leaf-strewn ground beside the house and, even from this distance, Thomas could hear its twigs scraping eerily across the panes of glass.

Thomas hated it here so, *so* much.

He turned his back on the house sullenly, fixing the removal workers carefully carrying their sofa inside with a baleful look. Thomas didn't want to be here. He also didn't want to be home though and that was where the real problem lay. Thomas wasn't welcome within a mile radius of his father and he'd grown tired of his mum fussing over him too, even if it *did* come from a place of love. He'd been discussing with his counsellor the benefits of having a clean break for months now so, when Henry had finally been offered this job and Daniel had agreed to go with him (because of course he had), it had seemed like the perfect opportunity.

Now though, gazing around despairingly at the tangled snarl of forest edging the deserted road, Thomas wasn't so sure. It felt more like the beginning of a bad horror film instead.

The sunset stained the sky the colour of bruises overhead and the hairs on the back of Thomas's neck rose the longer he stood there. There was something instinctive in him demanding in increasingly shrill tones that he grab Henry and Daniel, and insist that they get back in the car and leave now but… but that was just Thomas's inner child probably. He'd spoken to his counsellor about this; about his tendency to 'catastrophise' what was most likely not a very big deal at all. He blew everything out of proportion and freaked himself out over it, and it usually tended to work out fine.

Usually.

Thomas should just stop watching terrible B-rated horror films probably. All they did was succeed in making him more than a little bit terrified of what could quite frankly turn into a fantastic piece of property investment (and god, Thomas was turning into his *dad* now).

Running a hand through his dyed red hair ruefully, Thomas fought down his guilt at leaving his friends to carry the boxes inside and looked back towards the dimly lit road again. Even despite the fact that the moon wasn't yet visible, the first stars were already blinking to life overhead and the fresh scent of pine carried towards the twenty one year old on the cool, damp air.

Slowly, as he stood there beneath the darkening sky, Thomas became aware of a low rumbling noise.

Frowning faintly, he limped down the long driveway towards the source of the sound, desperate for anything to distract him from how much he was regretting his decision to move here. He left the driveway behind completely, stepping from the dusty grey gravel onto the leaf-strewn pavement as he peered down the narrow thoroughfare curiously.

The mysterious sound was growing steadily louder now and Thomas shivered, looking around warily as he tried to place the noise. It was strange but the building roar seemed almost familiar now and –

Oh.

A large truck thundered around the corner and Thomas relaxed, feeling stupid for getting himself so worked up. The tension in his muscles made his back and leg ache painfully, and he grimaced, stretching carefully so that he wouldn't make his sciatica any worse than it already was after a long day of sitting huddled up in the car.

The truck was closer now, kicking up a mist of old rain-water and dust from whatever it was carrying, and Thomas was so grateful to be out of the car after so many hours of driving – and Daniel's awful 'I Spy' games – that he raised one pale hand in an awkward greeting. The driver honked the horn at him in response as he drove past and Thomas smiled wanly, his tired green eyes tracing the writing on the side as he realised it was coming from a place called Honister Slate Mine.

Thomas watched the truck drive away with something like longing. He hadn't seen any other traffic at all for a long time now – as soon as they'd left Wasdale Head behind actually – and Thomas almost wished he was in the cabin with the driver. The man was probably going home right now, heading back into one of the closest towns - almost twenty miles away from here. Maybe he had a family, a pet dog. Maybe he didn't feel so useless and *lost* all the time.

Thomas caught himself before his thoughts could really spiral out of control, struggling to take in a deep breath as he concentrated on one of the exercises Linda had given him. He was supposed to focus on his surroundings and distract himself with anything even mildly interesting which was sometimes a lot more difficult than it sounded.

Thomas's emerald eyes drifted a few hundred metres down the road towards the only other lived-in house on this side of Scafell Pike. Light glowed golden in the windows and he could hear the sound of a dog barking in the garden. Thomas smelt cooking on the air – roasted chicken or maybe turkey wafting from the open kitchen windows – and he drifted a little closer despite himself as he tried to get a better look in the dim light. The building was tucked back from the road which was why Thomas had only caught a brief glimpse of it on their drive up here and he wanted to see if it was the same style as their house was.

Their neighbours lived on the opposite side of the road, the tarmac between them littered with fallen debris from the forest, and beleaguered with so many potholes that Thomas was reminded of the wear and tear inevitably caused by heavy trucks thundering past who knew how often.

Thomas limped a little closer, taking in the sprawling double garage and the gleaming Land Rover parked in the driveway (and really, why did they need to show their car off if they had two garages? It wasn't like there was a great deal of foot traffic up here to be impressed by the frankly obnoxious shininess of the vehicle). There was a large conservatory just visible behind the house, and some fairy lights had been strung up in the pine trees closest to the porch which made Thomas think vaguely scathing things about the homeowners spending too much time trying to make their home Pinterest-worthy and not enough raking the leaves in front of their house.

Thomas was already more than halfway down the road towards the building when he happened to glance to his right and noticed, with no small amount of surprise, that there was a third house on Deadman's Rise. He hadn't seen it on the drive up but that didn't exactly surprise him now; the driveway was overgrown with ferns and what looked like thorny blackberry bushes, and a fallen pine tree lay across the cracked flagstones of the driveway.

Thomas shivered at the sight of the forest reclaiming its land. He knew that, within a hundred years, the house would probably be hidden from sight completely, buried beneath plants and wind and rain… all but gone from the world. The ivy eating into the house's brickwork would cause it to crumble and the pines would soar around it, and the weeds would break through the cracks in the flagstones and hide the evidence that anyone had ever lived there at all.

It made Thomas feel strangely mortal and he shuddered as he looked around him, taking in the ancient forest and the timeless mountains forcing their way out of the earth, and feeling smaller and more insignificant with every second. He felt as though no one should be here at all.

The House In The Forest – as Thomas had already fancifully nicknamed it, probably because he'd read too much Lord Of The Rings as a child (despite his taunt to Henry earlier that day) – didn't look like the other houses on Deadman's Rise. While their neighbouring house was nothing short of quaint and their own house was adequate, if slightly dilapidated, the building in front of Thomas now didn't look lived in at all although the red-haired man wasn't sure why this surprised him. There was basically nothing within walking distance – unless walking distance was two miles and the homeowners wanted to visit the bar or purchase outdoor supplies (which, admittedly, might be useful looking at the state of their driveway) –

and Thomas couldn't imagine how they'd get a car out of the driveway with the fallen tree in the way.

The building – partially obscured behind the thick branches of the overhanging trees but still visible if you knew it was there – was decrepit (and that was putting it kindly). Most of the windows were smashed and the paint on the front door was peeling away in flakes, a great scrape across the panelling like a wild animal had fought to get in.

Goosebumps rose on Thomas's arms as he stepped hesitantly into the driveway – and if he instantly regretted reminding himself of the book series with the same name the moment the thought crossed his mind, he didn't have to admit it to anyone – and he squinted through the darkness, taking in the broken fence panels edging the wildly overgrown garden and the way the rusting washing line was spinning in a slow circle all by itself on the breeze.

Thomas saw a sudden flicker of movement from one of the windows in his peripheral vision and he jerked his head up in fright, completely startled. There was no one in sight of course and the red-haired man immediately chastised himself for being such a baby; he'd probably just startled a bird or a squirrel in one of the pine trees close to the building. There was no way anyone still lived in that broken-down house.

Thomas forced a faint wry smile onto his face as he realised just how jumpy he was tonight. In truth though, he felt pathetic; his heart was still racing painfully in his chest and he'd broken out in a cold sweat. His sciatica was making his knee throb painfully and that tiny pessimistic little voice in Thomas's head cheerfully reminded him that, if the situation called for it, he wouldn't be able to run away. Shuddering again, the red-haired man dragged his gaze from the crumbling building and started the slow walk back to their new home instead, still struggling to calm his frantic heartbeat.

The air smelt fresher and cleaner out on the road again – he hadn't noticed it at the time but the dark house had had an almost stagnant air about it which only made itself apparent afterwards – and Thomas tried his counsellor's exercise again, this time with more success.

He could hear magpies calling to each other in the surrounding trees; he could taste petrichor on the breeze; he could see their new home built into the slopes leading up to Scafell Pike; he could see the surrounding, rolling hills hidden beneath pine trees; he could hear a small animal skittering in the undergrowth as the few streetlights nearby began to flicker on. The overhanging tree branches caught most of the light and Thomas walked through the dappled shade carefully, his pulse slowly calming in his veins.

The sky was already drifting towards a deep indigo and Thomas realised for the first time how dark it was likely to get out here; the mountains were going to block a lot of moonlight at certain times of the month and there were barely any other houses around so there would be little light pollution.

Absently, Thomas thought his grandpa would have loved living out here. Ken had always enjoyed stargazing through his telescope and he'd complained constantly that there was too much light in the retirement complex he had lived in.

Thomas hung his head as he walked slowly back towards his driveway, worrying his bottom lip between his teeth as the sadness unfurled inside him. It had been six months since his grandpa had passed away now and he'd left everything he had to his only grandson: all his money, his car (although Peter Barnes had taken this after the '*disappearance*' of his own vehicle)... even his telescope.

His telescope.

Thomas's face lit up and he quickened his pace as much as he was able, hurrying back down the shadowy road towards where Henry's car was parked in the driveway. Thomas had stowed the telescope safely under one of the back seats in its case and, although Henry and Daniel had told him he wasn't allowed to lift any boxes, Thomas decided this didn't count... and besides, it was *far* too precious for him to countenance someone else having the responsibility of bringing it into the house.

If one of them dropped it – Thomas's last tangible thing from his grandpa – he was likely never to speak to them again.

The twenty one year old unlocked the car and bent down carefully in the deserted driveway. The night had rushed in now like ink spreading in water and the removal van was long gone. Dimly, Thomas wondered how long he'd been alone.

He lifted the case with only a mild twinge of pain and, counting that as a win, the red-haired man followed his best friends inside. Light was streaming from the windows now – which, Thomas had to admit, made the place look a lot more appealing – and the warmth enveloped him as he let himself carefully into the house which at least meant the central heating was working.

Thomas locked the front door securely behind him and let out a low breath that he hadn't even realised he'd been holding in, setting the telescope carefully at the foot of the stairs in its case. He was just in time too because Daniel and Henry appeared in what seemed to be the living room doorway at that moment, worry and relief etched into their shadowy faces as they blocked the light from entering the hallway.

"Thomas, where were you?!" Daniel demanded, his voice several octaves too high which was never a good thing as it usually tended to imply that the blond man was ever so slightly stressed. "You were gone for over two hours!"

"I'm sorry if I... Wait, *what*? No, I wasn't!" Thomas argued but his green eyes widened as he glanced towards the dark sky outside. "I... I swear I only walked down the road." Henry pinched his nose between his thumb and forefinger like he had the beginnings of a headache, and Thomas's guilt crashed over him like a wave.

"I must have got distracted," he said and he felt small standing in front of them now, like he'd disappointed them somehow... like they were his *parents*. "I'm sorry if I worried you. I promise I'm fine."

"How's your back? Your leg?" Daniel pressed and Thomas managed a faint smile that hopefully disguised his tears lodging themselves in his throat. Thomas's eyes shone too brightly in the dim light and Henry hummed sadly when he saw the misery there, wrapping his arm warmly around the red-haired man's shoulders as he led Thomas into the living room.

"You're shivering, Tom. Do you want me to make a cup of tea?" Henry suggested gently. "Daniel did an excellent job of unpacking the mugs and stuff in the kitchen."

"I tidy faster when I'm worrying," Daniel said pointedly but he looked slightly mollified now and Thomas relaxed, aware and relieved that he had been forgiven.

Despite the living room obviously being a long way from complete, he liked it all the same. Daniel's old cracked leather sofa was pressed against the far side of the room and Henry's flat screen TV - literally his pride and joy (after his extensive comic collection at least) - was just waiting to be mounted on the wall opposite. The DVD rack was already set up in the corner and an old lamp Henry had found in a charity shop stood crookedly nearby, the tassels hanging from the lampshade swaying gently from where they'd stirred the air entering the room.

Thomas could see their dining table and chairs through a wide arch that separated the two rooms, and there was a serving hatch in one wall that showed a brightly lit kitchen. A rug Thomas's mum had donated was spread out on the grey panelled wood which made a lump rise in his throat and there was a low coffee table nearby too, currently home to Daniel's precious peace lily which was sitting proudly in the centre, its waxy white petals catching the yellow light filling the room. Two mismatched armchairs had been pulled up to the low table where a pair of half-drunk mugs of tea sat.

Clearly, this was the meeting point when they wanted to discuss Thomas's general well-being in anxious voices. Thomas had wondered where that would be in this house. Back in London, it had been the Costa down the street where the pair of them purchased overpriced frappes and tried to be serious while wearing whipped cream moustaches.

Fighting to suppress the agitation Thomas could feel at them babying him again, the red-haired man dragged a straight-backed chair over from the dining room - Daniel squawked in concern and Henry sighed heavily - and sank down onto it, letting out a low sigh as he took the weight off his aching leg. His sciatica made sitting on something comfortable like a *sofa* impossibly painful so Thomas always had to do this… always had to sit apart from everyone else while trying to keep the pain off his face.

"I'll boil the kettle again," Daniel said after a moment of awkward silence and the red-haired man sighed heavily, wondering what his poor friends had let themselves in for when they'd assured him they'd be ecstatic if he moved in with them. Henry was watching Thomas like he knew what the older man was thinking and, after a second of hesitation, the dark-haired man came to sit on the arm of the sofa beside Thomas, his dark curls just unruly enough that it became apparent he had been running his fingers through it repeatedly. (Maybe Daniel wasn't the *only* one who had been stressed at Thomas vanishing for so long.)

"You feeling okay, Tommy?" Henry asked softly, his chocolate brown eyes warm and familiar. They'd been close since they were just five years old, almost a decade before Daniel had come onto the scene, and Henry only used that nickname when he was feeling very fond. Clearly, he was more relieved than he'd let on at Thomas's sudden reappearance. "You're very quiet." Henry's full lips twitched into a smile as he nudged Thomas lightly with his elbow. "You're not homesick *already*, are you?"

"Not a chance, Bailey," Thomas retorted, managing a wry smile. His eyes flickered towards the large bay windows overlooking their dark driveway and the older man shivered fractionally, twisting his fingers together in his lap. He would have felt fine if he didn't suddenly feel like someone was watching him (and god, Thomas *really* needed to stop watching horror films). "I saw this other house earlier... when I was out walking."

"Yeah, I saw it on the drive up too," Henry said, reaching for Thomas's Stormtrooper mug on the coffee table and taking a sip of what remained of his drink. (Thomas didn't think he was allowed to be annoyed that Daniel had used his mug without asking; he had been presumed MIA at the time after all.) "It's the same size as ours with a big garage, right? They had a Land Rover outside I think."

Thomas shook his head instantly.

"No. Well... I mean yes - there *is* a house like that but... I meant a different one. On our side of the road. It's literally like a hundred metres in that direction right now," Thomas said, jerking his thumb to the right.

"What?" Henry's eyebrow rose and he fixed his best friend with a curious look, pursing his lips doubtfully. "That's funny. I didn't see another one when we drove in."

"But that's just it!" Thomas exclaimed with something that was almost excitement. "I didn't see it either at first! But it's there I promise; it's just further back from the road. A tree's fallen over its driveway so it's quite obscured. That's probably why we didn't see it…" Thomas's explanation trailed away as Daniel re-appeared with a mug of tea for the older man - he'd brewed this one in his favourite Joseph And The Technicolor Dreamcoat mug (and, really, Thomas was going to *have* to talk to him about his mug choices, even if this was clearly the blond man extending an olive branch). Daniel dropped down onto the sofa beside them with a weary sigh, letting his head fall to rest on Henry's knee.

"Aww," the dark-haired man said teasingly, patting Daniel on the cheek. "Is baby Danny tired already?"

"Shut up. I just unpacked *so* much of our stuff," Daniel grumbled but he looked pleased all the same, especially when Thomas reached over to stroke his blond hair too, running his fingers through it hesitantly the way he did to his family cat's fur back home. "You guys suck so bad."

Thomas hid his smug smile behind the rim of his mug as he took a sip and Daniel looked calmer when Henry rubbed the blond man's broad shoulder soothingly.

"So... what were you guys talking about while I was in the kitchen?" Daniel asked, the curiosity in his eyes mostly buried under weariness now. He looked like he was in sore need of sleep. "You sounded like you were arguing."

"Not arguing," Henry disagreed mildly. "We were just debating something." When Daniel raised an eyebrow curiously, Henry's lips twitched into a smile. "Tom says there's a house down the road that none of us noticed before. He found it when he was exploring."

"That's funny," Daniel said, sitting slowly upright. "I didn't see one when we drove in."

"That's exactly what I said!" Henry crowed triumphantly.

Rolling his eyes and trying to fight off the irrational urge to start sulking again, Thomas sipped more of his drink and refused to comment, at least until Henry asked him what the house looked like.

"Old," Thomas replied, after a slight hesitation. "Or just not taken care of since I imagine all the houses here were built at the same time." Daniel mouthed: *'Estate agent's son'* then and Thomas ignored him. "It doesn't look very safe though."

"Huh," Henry said, glancing in the direction Thomas had pointed earlier. "That's odd. How could you see that much from the road?"

Thomas's cheeks coloured and he braced himself for his best friends' inevitable squawking. "Well... I kind of went down the driveway a little... just to see what was down there, you know?"

"Thomas, that was dangerous!" Daniel said instantly, predictable as ever. "You just said it didn't look safe so why would you do that? What if some crazy person lives there or -" He faltered when Henry elbowed him hard in the ribs and Thomas looked away, cheeks colouring.

"Pretty sure no one lives there anymore... and I think you'll be safe, Daniel. The only crazy person around here is me." He spoke quietly, tried to make a joke of it but it fell painfully flat. His best friends knew he had issues with his mental health but that he didn't like to talk about it. Daniel flinched when he realised what he'd done. Thomas just stared down blankly into his tea.

"Sorry," Daniel whispered, reaching out to pat Thomas's knee although he withdrew his hand when the older man pulled away sharply. "Tom, I'm *sorry*," Daniel said imploringly.

Thomas just sniffed, shrugging jerkily and trying to pretend that the action *hadn't* sent pain shooting down his back.

"Doesn't matter," Thomas muttered but, abruptly, he was tired of the day. He didn't want to stay here with either of them for a moment longer; he didn't even want to have a shower or unpack. He just wanted to go to sleep.

"Did you guys choose which bedrooms you wanted already?" he asked and Henry nodded, lips pressed together silently. He looked deeply unhappy about the way the evening was going and Thomas wanted to tell them that he was sorry for making them feel uneasy but... he wasn't.

"We played rock-paper-scissors for the rooms but you weren't here," Henry lied, his tongue pressing into the side of his cheek which was a tell that he wasn't telling the truth. "You ended up with the room downstairs. Sorry, Tom." Daniel relaxed a little - probably because he wasn't the one who'd told Thomas - and the older man nodded silently, trying to pretend that he *didn't* feel like a cripple who wasn't capable of climbing the stairs on his own (and if this was the case during particularly bad days, Thomas wasn't feeling reasonable enough to appreciate that right now).

"I'm tired. I'm going to bed." Thomas wouldn't meet their eyes. "Is my stuff -"

"Already in there," Daniel said quickly, apparently keen to make amends. "I left your medicine out for you on your side table... and I've tried to put the bags with your clothes in by the wardrobe. There's... there's not a bathroom downstairs though unfortunately. You'll have to come upstairs for showers and stuff but..."

"No, I won't," Thomas said, making Daniel fall silent as his already-pale face grew ashen. "I'm never going to shower again. That'll teach you to give my mug to Hal, won't it?"

The blond man relaxed visibly as a bright smile lit up his face. Beside him, Henry let out a bark of surprised laughter.

"If you stop showering then I'm moving out," Daniel said instantly. "You'll smell like Stig of the Dump within a week."

"Well, you smell like him already," Thomas countered but he felt calmer now; happier almost because both of his best friends were smiling again and this was the clean break they needed.

"Both of you better stay away from me if you stink that bad then," Henry said cheerfully, looking deeply relieved that the red-haired man had cheered up now. His expression abruptly became excited as he remembered something. "Oh, Tom, I didn't get a chance to show you! While you were out, I was having a look through the cupboards down here and trying to see what storage space we have available -" '*Probably for his comics*,' Thomas thought wryly. "- and I found some old Polaroids of the people who I guess used to live here? I thought they were pretty cool so let me know when you want to have a look at them together. It's kind of awesome how much history this place has."

"It sounds it," Thomas said quietly but it didn't feel like sarcasm. It was nice to see Henry so enthusiastic about something that wasn't becoming a ranger and it meant a lot that the pair of them were both trying so hard to make him happy. "I'll have a look at them when I get up or something," he added, feeling a little worm of guilt as they both smiled at him with relief. Thomas sighed softly. "I love you guys," he murmured, biting his bottom lip awkwardly. "I'm sorry if I've been difficult today. I'm just…"

"A drama queen," Henry interjected, his eyes crinkling as he smiled. "But it just so happens that we love you too, Tom, okay? Even if you *are* crazy."

Daniel cringed and Thomas rolled his eyes but the fondness on his face was undeniable.

"You never know when to shut up, do you, Bailey?" the red-haired man asked softly.

Henry gave the pair of them his best smile.

"It's my only redeeming feature," he said cheerfully.

Chapter 3: The Book Of Shadows

Thomas woke with a low groan, the pained sound torn from him as he became aware of the familiar stabbing pain in his lower back and knee. He stared up at the ceiling unseeingly, his jaw tight with pain, his dull green eyes blank. He could already feel his depression unfurling like a fog and, gritting his teeth against the pain, Thomas pushed himself weakly into a sitting position and reached for the bottle of tablets Daniel had thoughtfully left on his bedside table beside the spell jar Diane had gifted him.

There were unpacked cardboard boxes of possessions piled all over the room and Thomas's eyes drifted over them distractedly as he tipped two of the painkillers into his shaking palm. He cursed softly when he realised he'd forgotten to bring a glass of water in with him the night before but he was too proud to call to his friends for help… and besides, he thought as he dry-swallowed the tablets with a grimace, they were probably still sleeping anyway. The pair of them had had a long day unpacking the house yesterday and there was still a ridiculous amount to do.

Thomas considered that as he glowered around at his new room, waiting for the painkillers to kick in. The usual feeling of guilt that accompanied him when he took them wasn't present today and the red-haired man relished in it as his eyes tracked his bedroom miserably.

Even after a long night's sleep, he didn't like the place any more in the daylight. It was messy and disorganised, and some of the labels had fallen off the cardboard boxes he'd packed so he knew it would be ages before he located all of his things.

A yawn escaped him and Thomas groaned again, worrying at his bottom lip with his teeth as the dull ache of pain finally began to ebb. He hadn't slept well the night before and that made him grouchy (or grouchier than usual, depending on who was being asked).

The smaller, more reasonable part of his brain didn't find it particularly surprising that he felt so unhappy in his current surroundings. Thomas never slept well in a new place, especially when he'd been that anxious in the evening before going to sleep. He felt weird sleeping downstairs, probably because he wasn't used to having a bedroom so far away from everyone else, and he missed his old room a lot more than he cared to admit.

For a moment, Thomas wanted to be back in his bedroom at his parents' house. He missed the too-narrow bed with its faded quilt and lumpy mattress, and the pin board on his wall covered with curling postcards of all the places he wanted to travel to, and all of the stuffed toys he totally *didn't* have stowed away in one of the boxes that the removal men had left in the hallway. (Thomas refused to let Henry and Daniel judge him for that; Daniel had a blue rabbit toy that he automatically sat on the lap of whoever was riding shotgun in their car and, to reiterate Thomas's previous point, Henry had a box of comics and action figures. He would *not* be made to feel guilty for transporting Madame Snuggles and her assortment of farmyard friends to the new house. No *way*.)

The wind picked up outside - it had been doing that all night long, howling eerily in the rafters like a bad sound effect from a werewolf film - and the branches of the oak tree growing beside the house scratched gratingly across the glass of the window. Thomas jumped but, despite tensing up immediately afterwards, the pain wasn't as bad as he'd expected. Luckily his tablets seemed to have kicked in pretty quickly today.

He let his duvet fall back onto the mattress and shivered at the cool air in his room. Already he was realising that the house was naturally very cold and draughty - not exactly a good thing for someone who suffered with sciatica although Thomas figured he'd just have to wrap up warm - and he didn't exactly love the fact that he'd been able to hear the fridge humming all night long from the next room either.

None of it was especially conducive to a good night's rest.

Thomas decided that, in order for him to continue living here without *really* losing his mind, he was going to have to do something about his sleeping conditions... like buying more quilts to spread over his duvet and purchasing some earplugs to drown out the noise of the fridge... or by drinking very strong cold medicine every night before he fell asleep.

Still dwelling vaguely on abusing over-the-counter pharmaceutical products with a slight smirk on his face, Thomas rose stiffly from the bed and struggled over to the closest of the boxes piled nearby. Since he was fairly certain the others were still asleep and he had no particular desire to sit alone in the kitchen, Thomas figured it might be worth starting to sort through some of his belongings so that they would be in some semblance of order when he felt awake enough to actually begin tidying them away.

The first box he looked in held old books he'd loved during his childhood and teenage years - Lord of the Rings and Harry Potter, and the Skulduggery Pleasant series which Thomas had adored - and the one beside it was full of his old art supplies which had seemed like a good idea back home but only seemed like a waste of space now.

Still frowning vaguely, Thomas limped around the pile and found a smaller box behind them, taped down carefully with no label in sight. Unable to recall what he'd packed in it, Thomas lifted it carefully - surprised by how heavy it was - and toyed with the tape, working what remained of a fingernail beneath it so that he could prise it open. His eyes widened in surprise when he finally managed it and a note fluttered out, written in his mum's delicate script.

Tommy, I hope aren't missing me too much… but if you are, I hope this will help. You know how healing I've always found witchcraft and that I don't often have the time to do it anymore. It seems a shame to let those spells go forgotten. I think perhaps it will help you too.

Inside this box, I have sealed my Book Of Shadows, and an assortment of ingredients and items to get you started. Don't feel obligated but

don't discount it immediately. I know what you're like, my stubborn
boy. But I think this will help you. I think it will make us closer.

Try setting up an altar. Try your hand at making a spell jar (and be
patient! They never look beautiful first time around. It's what's inside
that counts!) Try burning certain candles to calm yourself or give you
energy. Draw sigils to help you focus. Use witchcraft to help yourself
heal.

Until I see you next time. Love mum. xxx

Thomas sat on the edge of his bed heavily, his eyes prickling with
tears although a strange feeling was spreading through his chest. It
took the twenty one year old a moment to identify it as happiness.

His hands were shaking as he carefully spread the ingredients and
items out on his quilt. There was a small cast iron cauldron for
burning things in safely, a neatly labelled athame which seemed to be
some sort of fancy black-handled knife, a collection of different
crystals that he would sort through properly later, some incense cones
and a sage smudging stick, some wooden candle holders along with a
large box of multi-coloured spell candles, a kit of individually labelled
little bags of herbs, a bag of sea salt, and a surprising number of little
glass jars which were presumably for Thomas to use to create his own
spell jars with if he felt the need.

His heart felt too big for his chest as he gazed down at them but the
thing that finally made his tears boil over was when his trembling

hands settled on his mum's beloved Book of Shadows. She'd been adding to it for as long as he could remember, constantly jotting new spells and ideas down or doodling little diagrams in the margin; the sequence of the moon or the precise shape of a leaf, labelled and neatly coloured in. She hated to be parted from it but here it was, hundreds and hundreds of miles away because she trusted him to keep it safe for her.

He raised it to his face shakily, closing his eyes to keep his tears in as he inhaled deeply. It smelt like spices; like apples and rosemary and marjoram… like his mother.

Thomas packed everything away methodically, letting his fingertips brush the cool steel of the athame and the polished surface of the crystals; the gentle clinking of the glass jars and the smooth wax of the spell candles in their little cardboard bed. He put the book away last of all, his palm lingering on the cracked brown cover as he inhaled shakily.

It had made him feel stronger reading the note and discovering the box, and he was so grateful to Diane. Deciding to follow in his mum's footsteps now had made him feel so much stronger, just like remembering his grandpa's telescope had yesterday. It made Thomas feel like maybe not *everything* about living here was awful.

It gave him hope.

Thomas's limp was less pronounced than usual as he shuffled out into the hallway and that gave him cheer too, the thought that maybe he wouldn't even need to use his cane again. Maybe he was on an upward spiral now and his back would feel fine for weeks, like it had that one summer just over a year ago when he'd been able to walk into town unaided and free of pain. Maybe Thomas would be able to walk down into Wasdale Head and go exploring without the worry of him getting stranded somewhere, in too much agony to walk alone. Maybe moving here was just what he needed.

It wasn't to be though.

A burning twinge danced up Thomas's left leg and he gritted his teeth against it as he leant against the banister of the stairs for a moment, exhaling in a hiss of pained breath. He could hear Daniel singing softly to himself in the kitchen - probably something from whatever musical he was currently obsessed with which might have been *'Fame'* - and the low pounding of the shower against the tiles upstairs made Thomas sigh irritably. Henry must have got there first.

'Too slow. That's what you get for being a cripple.'

Shaking his head almost violently in an attempt to ignore the spiteful whisper in his head, Thomas struggled into the living room and looked around it dispassionately. The morning light was stark and pale against the dark wood of the room, and the lack of personal items in there just looked sad now. Even Daniel's precious peace lily was drooping a little at its change of scenery and Thomas glanced at it unhappily, making a mental note to remind the blond man to water it later before it died and he went into mourning.

The Polaroids Henry had mentioned last night were scattered across the coffee table too and Thomas looked at them briefly before his eyes settled on one in particular. Thomas picked it up and peered at it in the dim light, taking in the sight of a little family standing together in what must have been their new home at the time the picture was taken. The mother and father had their arms wrapped around each other lovingly, and the little boy at the front was giving a big dimpled smile beneath a mop of curls. Thomas let the picture fall back onto the table, his teeth sinking into his bottom lip again.

He was trying not to think vaguely bitter things about how happy that family looked but it was difficult in comparison to his own. He bet that little boy had grown up into a healthy, cheerful man with his whole life ahead of him. Thomas bet that little boy's dad had never once tried to hurt him.

Not like Peter.

A sad sigh escaped the red-haired man and Daniel's soft singing faltered from the kitchen.

"Tom? Is that you?" the blond man called suddenly and Thomas snorted as he followed the sound of the blond man's voice.

"*Thomas isn't here anymore,*" the older man said in the scariest voice he could manage, eager for any distraction at all as he hid in the dining room beneath the serving hatch that looked into the kitchen. (His voice came out sounding like he had a sore throat which wasn't quite what he'd been aiming for and this was only cemented when Daniel started giggling.) "*I am the ghost of... uh... some old white guy. Prepare to die.*"

"Please don't kill me!" Daniel wailed dramatically but the smile was audible in his voice. "I'll make you toast if you don't kill me. I'll even juice you an orange."

Thomas considered this from where he was lurking as a smile curved his lips.

"Throw in some scrambled eggs and you have yourself a deal," he said, forgetting to growl this time. Daniel giggled and Thomas straightened up, frowning when he saw the blond man staring suspiciously towards where the kitchen door was slightly ajar.

"You'll be so lucky, Tom," Daniel was saying, still facing the wrong direction. He was wearing a dressing gown over his pyjamas and his hair was damp like he'd already showered that morning. Apparently Daniel wasn't interested in having a lie-in when there was still so much to do. "I was actually going to ask you and Henry to go grocery shopping this morning while I finished unpacking the kitchen. We don't have any eggs yet... or milk... or coffee…"

"No coffee, huh?" Thomas asked sourly. "What a nightmare."

Daniel spun round in shock, hand flying to cover his heart as he stared at his best friend with wide eyes, the alarm plain on his ashen face.

"Oh my god," Daniel said faintly, leaning heavily back against the counter. "I thought you were in the doorway. Who the hell did I just see then?"

"Must be your eyes playing tricks on you," Thomas said, wiggling his eyebrows in a suggestive manner although the younger man's words had made something uneasy unfurl in his stomach as he remembered the unpleasant feeling of being watched the night before. "It was probably just a shadow, Danny. Now stop freaking us both out, okay?" The older man disappeared from the serving hatch momentarily as he walked round into the kitchen. "Now how about we make that orange juice instead, yeah?"

"Yeah," Daniel said but he still looked uncertain. "Yeah, have a look for the juicer in that box over there please." When Thomas went off to do as he was told, Daniel managed a weak smile. "I hope you and Henry don't mind drinking juice out of wine glasses. I haven't found the plastic cups yet and I didn't wash the mugs last night."

"You're letting the team down, Danny," Henry said as he padded into the kitchen, a towel slung low around his hips as he rifled through one of the boxes on the counter, emerging triumphantly a moment later with a pint glass. He filled it with water and Thomas rolled his eyes at his oldest friend as Henry leant there, muscular chest still glinting with drops of water as Daniel tried to pretend that he wasn't staring at him.

"Any particular reason you've come downstairs to show off your body?" Thomas asked sweetly. Henry gave him the finger but Thomas's smile grew when he saw the dark-haired man's eyes flickering hopefully towards Daniel. The pair were growing more smitten with every passing day and Thomas currently had a wager running with Henry's sister Jessica over who would confess their feelings first.

"Not really," the dark-haired man said with an amiable shrug. He downed the water in one go and answered Thomas's questioning look with an annoyingly cheerful smile. "So… what's the plan today, guys?"

"Well, I was just telling Tom," Daniel said after a long moment, his eyes still tracing the dark-haired man's chest although he dragged his gaze away with difficulty. "I… uh…" Daniel closed his eyes for a moment and Henry's smirk widened. "I was going to send you and Tom shopping while I sorted the kitchen. Then I figured I might cycle down to Wasdale Head, see if I can talk with the manager at the Inn. If they don't have any availability there, I'll probably head to Nether Wasdale tomorrow. The hotels there seem like they'll be more likely to need staff."

"That's a good idea," Henry said, looking ridiculously proud as a drop of water rolled down into the hollow of his throat. Daniel's wide blue eyes tracked it unashamedly and Henry blushed, coughing awkwardly. "What about you, Tom? When are you going to look for work?"

Thomas jerked his head up like a rabbit in the headlights, unused to being the centre of attention when Henry and Daniel were dancing around each other like this. His cheeks heated and he frowned at the floor as he tried to think of an answer that would placate them. Unfortunately, his words were woefully inadequate.

"Um… I mean I have grandpa's inheritance so I'm not really rushing right now," the red-haired man mumbled, shrugging awkwardly. Daniel pursed his lips unhappily when he heard that and Henry looked so disappointed in him that Thomas pressed his lips together hard in an effort not to lose his temper. After all, he knew it wasn't their fault that they wanted what they thought was '*best*' for him… and how were they to know that the expression they wore was the exact one that twisted his father's face whenever he looked at his only son? How were they to know that everything they did made Thomas feel like he wasn't good enough for them?

He could feel his eyes filling rapidly with angry tears and, apparently able to sense it, Daniel turned to Henry with something like alarm on his face.

"Forget work!" the blond man said quickly, tripping over his words in his haste to get them out. "Just talk about something else. *Anything* else!"

"Um…" Henry's dark eyes widened as he blatantly panicked and it might have been funny if Thomas's heart hadn't ached in his chest. "Uh… Well, I went for a run earlier - just on the slopes leading up to Scafell Pike, y'know? - and I had a look for that house you mentioned yesterday, Tom. Had a look on my way back."

"Did you see it?" Daniel asked but he looked a little calmer now that the red-haired man was watching them both curiously. Henry bit his bottom lip awkwardly, apparently silently berating himself for choosing this topic to distract his oldest friend.

"I couldn't see it," Henry said and it was almost apologetic. "I slowed down and everything. There's just forest."

"It was pretty far back from the road," Thomas muttered, finally daring to speak and cringing at how rough his voice sounded. No one answered though and, when he dragged his eyes up warily, he discovered that Henry's distraction had been caused by Daniel pressing a glass of freshly-squeezed orange juice into his hand.

"How are your calves after all that running uphill?" Daniel asked innocently and Henry's dimples creased his cheeks as he lifted the towel a little, glancing down at them with something that was *almost* self-effacing.

"I don't know," he said innocently. "How do they look?"

"Pretty good, Hal," Daniel said, nodding his head knowledgeably like he had a single clue what '*good*' calf muscles looked like. "You look *fit*," the blond man said before promptly blushing scarlet. "Like... you know... to be able to run up... up a mountain... um…"

"I didn't run up the *whole* mountain, Danny," Henry said modestly but his cheeks were reddening as he blushed too. "Just some of the way." Henry's face suddenly lit up. "Hey, you know what? You should come with me one day, Danny! It could be fun!"

Daniel snorted but his expression was undeniably fond. "Nah, you're alright, Hal. I don't like you enough to do that. I mean, have you ever seen me willingly do exercise?"

Henry raised an eyebrow, smirking slightly as he drank his juice. Daniel watched the movement of his throat as he swallowed and his cheeks heated pink when he realised Henry had seen him.

"I bet *I* can think of exercise you'd do willingly," the dark-haired man smirked but, before Daniel could melt into an embarrassed puddle on the floor, Thomas coughed to get their attention.

Watching the pair of them jump about ten feet in the air might have been amusing if he didn't feel so annoyed at being left out.

"Uh... guys? You know I'm still in the room, right?" Thomas muttered, his weak smile fading from his face when Henry took a guilty step away from Daniel. Thomas sighed softly. "Daniel wants me and you to go grocery shopping this morning, Hal, remember? We should get ready for the stupidly long trek there since the supermarket is basically on the other side of the planet."

"*Oh*, I - Yeah, I mean... Sure."

"Good." Thomas pushed away from the counter, biting his bottom lip hard when his back ached in protest. "I'm going to go shower and then I'll be ready, okay?"

"That's fine," Henry said slowly, his voice soft now, like he could tell that Thomas was upset again. "Will you be alright showering? You don't hurt too bad?"

Thomas closed his eyes for a moment, fighting down on the shame welling up inside him.

"I'll be fine, Henry."

The red-haired man was almost to the doorway by the time Daniel broke the awkward quiet that had fallen.

"What about your orange juice, Tom?" the blond man asked softly, his tone slightly wounded now. Thomas's shoulders slumped and he smiled humourlessly although neither of his best friends could see it.

"Give it to Henry," he said bitterly.

Chapter 4: The Man In The Mist

Thomas emerged blinking into the cool grey light of Saturday morning with a grumble. His wet hair was dripping into his eyes from under one of Daniel's beanies and, no matter how many layers he bundled up in, it was impossible to feel warm due to his lovely friends using up all of the hot water before he'd had a chance to shower.

Thomas was standing on the porch now, shoulders hunched and arms folded tightly across his chest as he huddled up in the thick grey hoodie he was wearing under last year's frayed denim jacket. He hadn't been able to find his winter coat in the boxes yet so this would have to do. The twenty one year old was wearing a pout too; he could *feel* it but it wasn't easy to stop when Henry had just disappeared into the house to say goodbye to Daniel again.

"Henry! Hurry up!" Thomas yelled, thumping on the open door with the flat of his palm. The dark-haired man appeared after a few moments, shaking his head and heaving a heavy sigh when he saw his best friend's face.

"Stop glowering at me, Tom, and shut the door, okay? You're letting all the heat out." Henry spoke so smartly that Thomas simply gaped at his best friend wordlessly. Smirking a tiny bit, the dark-haired man rolled his chocolate-coloured eyes and jumped lightly down the wooden steps so that he could open the garage. "I'm going to get the car out and move a couple of boxes around so they'll be easier to bring inside later but I'll be done in like ten minutes, grumpy. Just don't run off this time, okay?"

"Yeah, yeah. Whatever," Thomas muttered, trying his hardest not to outwardly sulk as he carefully descended the steps with one hand gripping the railing tightly, his knee sorely protesting the movement. "Try not to run me over when you reverse out of the garage at the speed of light, Bailey."

"I'll see what I can do," Henry said, flashing a teasing smile at the older man before he swung the garage door open with a metallic clang. "No promises though." Thomas turned away with a faint wry smile, heading carefully down the driveway through the thick mist as he breathed in the fresh smell of the pine trees.

He wasn't exactly relishing the idea of going grocery shopping but at least the pair of them could listen to Green Day on the thirty minute drive there. They'd probably need to get petrol too and, as Thomas thought about trundling around the supermarket with a list as he told Henry in no uncertain terms that they didn't *need* eight packs of different-flavoured gummy snakes (and usually being persuaded to buy them anyway), Thomas had to admit that the familiar task would at least help him to feel more settled. (That was the sort of thing both his mum and his counsellor had been saying anyway, and Thomas was inclined to believe them.)

The road at the end of their driveway was deserted, the only sounds for miles around the gentle cooing of wood pigeons and the rustle of woodland animals in the undergrowth. Thomas sighed softly and his breath ghosted in the air in front of him, hanging there like a little cloud of steam as he shivered at the sudden frightening feeling of being watched.

His old life didn't feel real out here. The narrow streets of north London with its twists and turns, its bus stops and nightclubs, its bars and restaurants… they felt like another world entirely.

Thomas felt a million miles removed from all of it.

He could hear Henry rootling around in the garage behind him; heard the distinctive sound of a cardboard box falling onto the ground and spilling its contents everywhere, shortly followed by soft swearing, and Thomas rolled his eyes as he tapped his foot impatiently on the damp pavement.

Sourly, he figured that Henry had probably got distracted looking at old comics again and the red-haired man was so caught up in his one-hundred-per-cent-righteous-anger that he almost didn't notice that he was no longer alone until he looked up and saw the stranger standing motionless on the opposite side of the road.

Thomas frowned at the strange man which seemed to be his automatic expression to anything that took him by surprise and, hurrying to school his expression into something that looked slightly more friendly, Thomas gave the grim-faced stranger an awkward nod. The man must be one of the people who lived in the big house with the fairy lights at the end but, even as Thomas processed this fact, he contradicted himself.

The stranger was little more than a *boy* really, probably two or three years younger even than Thomas was as he held a baseball loosely in his hand. He had soft honey-coloured curls and wide hazel eyes hidden behind glasses sitting crookedly on his tanned face. He was dressed in peeling trainers, loose blue jeans, and a red-checked flannel over a 1991 Metallica t-shirt that looked vintage.

Also, he seemed to be frozen.

The stranger had been staring at Thomas steadily for almost thirty seconds now, and it had gone past the stage of unnerving and was well on the way to becoming '*I'm a cannibal who wants to eat your internal organs*' instead. Thomas smiled wanly at the stranger before silently cursing himself for doing that when he was nervous. Smiling was probably only going to *encourage* his possibly-insane-new-neighbour to talk to him and Thomas was kind of hoping that wouldn't happen.

"Morning," he called out anyway, because he was awkward and stupid, and too polite for his own good. (Damn his mother for raising him to have manners!) The silence was stretching between them again and Thomas was getting vaguely antsy because apparently the man didn't need to blink and Thomas had never exactly enjoyed prolonged periods of quiet which might have explained why he continued with: "My name's Thomas. I just moved in with my friends. Who are -"

He broke off when he heard the sudden intake of breath; wondered why he was giving this stranger his life story when the younger man was simply gazing at the older man with such terrifying longing.

Thomas's eyebrow rose as his fingers curled into fists and he couldn't help starting to wonder if maybe the stranger might not be a little unhinged. The twenty one year old wasn't sure he was ready for this sort of conversation so early in the morning… except it didn't really count as a conversation, did it? He was the only one bloody talking!

Thomas could see the whites of the peculiar man's eyes now as his tanned hands fell to hang limply by his sides and, even from the distance between them, Thomas could tell that the stranger was trembling badly as he stared across at the older man in absolute shock.

"You mean… you can *see* me?" the stranger blurted out in disbelief, his voice weak with fear and wonder as his legs seemed to weaken beneath him.

Thomas's heart gave a little lurch of fear in his chest but he raised his eyebrow anyway, aiming for disdain and probably just ending up with confusion instead.

"Uh... yes?" he said awkwardly, watching the strange man with wide green eyes. "You're standing right in front of me and we're having a vaguely disturbing conversation. I probably won't want to talk to any potential new neighbour ever again. You've scarred me for life."

"Oh my god," the man said but he was smiling faintly now, his hazel eyes sparkling with light. It took years from him - made him look like little more than a *child* almost - and, as he glowed with what could only be described as relief, Thomas realised that perhaps the stranger wasn't so bad after all. "You said your name was Thomas, right?

Well, I'm Nicholas May! But you can call me Nick... or Nicky... or May… or anything really - I don't mind at all!"

The younger man was babbling now, the excitement on his face so contagious as dimples sprang into his cheeks that Thomas couldn't resist smiling back at him despite the confusion he could feel. The man - Nicholas - had an infectious smile. Thomas could feel it curving his own lips even as the younger man beamed back at him, his eyes gleaming with tears.

"I can't believe you can really see me!" Nicholas continued happily, covering his smile with his hands although Thomas could tell it was still there by the crinkling of the younger man's tear-wet hazel eyes. "I really can't believe -"

The garage door shut behind them with a resounding clang and Thomas jumped badly, turning away from Nicholas to glance back towards the house.

"Hey, Henry!" Thomas called, waving his hand in the air vaguely to get the taller man's attention. "Put those comics away and come down here to meet -"

Something made Thomas fall quiet; some instinct that sent his heart galloping with nervousness in his chest as the dark-haired man reversed the car carefully down the driveway. Henry opened the door and stepped out lightly onto the gravel, tilting his head to one side.

"What are you yelling about, Tom?" he asked and the red-haired man shook his head wordlessly, staring at the empty space on the other side of the road where the younger man must have slipped away into the trees.

"Never mind," Thomas said softly. He limped back to the car slowly, his confusion beginning to eat away at him as the comfort his painkillers had initially provided finally began to fade. Henry manoeuvred the car carefully out onto the tarmac, chancing a worried glance at his best friend as he did so. Thomas remained silent, still staring blankly out of the window as he tried to process what had happened.

Henry's old car sped along beneath the towering pine trees with Green Day playing loudly to drown out the silence that had fallen but it didn't make Thomas feel any less bewildered.

Despite how impossible it was to disappear that quickly, the outcome was indisputable.

Nicholas was nowhere to be seen.

Chapter 5: The Noose

"How's the house, Tommy?" Diane Barnes asked kindly. "How are you finding it?"

Her voice sounded crackly over the phone line and Thomas scowled at how typical that was; of course even the mobile signal was horrendous over here. The internet speed was nothing to smile about either and the twenty one year old felt a sinking feeling as he drummed his fingers agitatedly on the desktop. All he had to amuse him now were old novels and the Book of Shadows his mum had gifted him, the latter of which was, admittedly, incredibly interesting. (Thomas almost wished it *wasn't* though because, the more time he spent pouring over the spells, the less he spent actually doing something useful like looking for a job.)

"It's not too bad here," he replied, a beat too late. Guilt rippled through him when he realised that it felt like he was lying to her but he fought against it. In the house's defence, it wasn't *all* terrible. He'd spent most of Sunday improving his bedroom which had helped him feel a lot more comfortable there. He'd even dragged a space heater in from the garage while Daniel and Henry were busy flirting in the kitchen - his leg was aching badly enough that he couldn't quite manage the stairs alone now - but he'd unpacked some more boxes too, uncovering more of his clothes and some spare blankets (and possibly all of his cuddly toys although this couldn't be proved of course). It had helped him feel more settled.

"Is the heating working? Are the stairs okay for you?" Diane asked anxiously. "You know I worry about you. Your father said –"

Thomas zoned out. He might not want to force his mother to choose between them but that didn't mean he had to listen to anecdotes about the man who had almost undoubtedly tried to kill him. Thomas couldn't delude himself in the same way Diane could, mostly because it wasn't only *his* life Peter had ruined. Thomas had never much cared about himself but the way Peter had treated Thomas's grandpa – his own *father* – in his final years? That was something the red-haired man would never be able to forgive. Clearly, Thomas had inherited his father's stubbornness.

"Tom? You've gone quiet," Diane said gently and Thomas sighed, leaning back in his desk chair in a useless attempt to get comfortable. It spun him round slowly before he caught himself on the edge of the desk, stopping the chair's movement with a soft gasp. He could see out of his bedroom window from this angle and he shivered as he took in the view before him; the ramshackle fence several metres away and, behind it, forest stretching up towards the rocky slopes of the mountains. The pine trees grew right up to the fence, their spiky branches breaching the property as they littered the long, gently swaying grass with pine needles. The wooden panels right below Thomas's window were broken and splintering where the large oak tree had forced its way through, and the old tree creaked as the wind picked up outside. The moon was full tonight and the window was peppered with raindrops that caught the silvery light, illuminated like so many shards of crystal.

Thomas didn't know if the night looked beautiful or terrifying, and he found himself growing increasingly disturbed at the uneasy realisation that perhaps it could be both.

"Tom?"

"Sorry, mum," he said quickly, chagrined. "I just got distracted for a minute there. I was looking at the mountains. It's really beautiful tonight."

"You'll have to send me a picture," she said and Thomas struggled to inject some cheer into his voice. He loved his mum more than anything and he didn't want her to be sitting at home worrying about him.

"You'll have to come over and visit, show me how to do some spells," Thomas countered and he could almost hear her beaming over the phone. He relaxed a little but the small smile on his face faded at her next words.

"I'd love that, Tommy. I'm curious though – are there many other houses where you live?" she asked. "Many people up there? Families?" *People you could make friends with so that you're not so dependent on Henry and Daniel.*' The little voice in Thomas's head whispered that last bit and he shuddered as the truth of it sank into his skin. It made him feel small and lost, and the vulnerability only worsened when he thought of his mum's question.

His memories of the previous morning rippled like water before his eyes as a knot of anxiety tightened in his chest. He'd met Nicholas after all but... but the man had disappeared into the trees – almost like he'd never been there at all – and Thomas wasn't certain he hadn't imagined it now. Honestly, the entire encounter hadn't made any sense, from the man's palpable shock right down to his stunned: '*You can see me?*' that had sent the red-haired man's blood running cold in his veins.

Dimly, Thomas wondered if he was going crazy… or crazier, he supposed.

"There aren't many people around here," he said at last, distinctly uncomfortable although he couldn't have explained why he was suddenly so on edge. "We haven't met the neighbours properly yet."

"Oh, well I'm sure you'll get to know them soon enough," she said and Thomas mumbled his assent, suppressing a yawn as a cloud passed over the moon outside, casting the hillside in shadow. Diane made a soft clucking sound and Thomas thought he knew what was coming.

"So how have you been holding up?" she asked gently. "Are you still taking two of those painkillers every morning?" She sounded unhappy at the mention of the medication and Thomas glanced towards the bottle grimly, deciding at the last second not to tell her that he was also taking them in the middle of the day and before bed too. She'd only worry.

"Sometimes I need them if I'm expected to get out of bed," Thomas muttered and he didn't mean to sound sullen but there wasn't much he could do about it when the bitterness was welling inside him like acid.

"Tom, I hope you're not taking too many of them again. You know the doctor said they could become addictive and –"

"Mum, I'm not five," Thomas said sharply. "I think I'm sensible enough to know not to take too many of them, don't you?" Diane made a small hurt sound but she didn't respond because they both knew Thomas wasn't telling the truth. Something withered in the red-haired man's chest and he sighed, dropping his head into his hand for a moment as he cradled the phone more loosely to his ear. "And besides," Thomas continued, working hard to make his voice sound gentler. "I've got Daniel and Henry to look after me too, yeah? So you don't have to worry."

"I suppose so," Diane said grudgingly but she sounded a little more relaxed now before her tone suddenly brightened. "Oh, Tom, did I tell you what the cat did this morning? It was so funny! He –"

Thomas's eyes drifted towards the window once more and he reeled back in shock, his heart soaring into his throat, his stomach tying itself into painful knots. There, swaying gently from the branch of the oak tree growing outside Thomas's window, was a noose.

"Oh god," Thomas choked out, his blood icy in his veins as he stared at the loop of rope in abject horror. It was securely tied, the rope fraying and old as it swayed in the breeze. Goosebumps crawled over Thomas's skin and he shuddered violently, unable to put into words quite how horrified he felt at this discovery.

"Thomas?" Diane sounded deeply concerned now and he would have cursed himself for worrying her again if he hadn't been desperately fighting to stave off a panic attack. "Tom, what's happened? Do you need me to hang up and call Henry or Daniel? Are you hurting?"

"What?" Thomas asked blankly, his heart pounding so hard in his chest that he couldn't focus on anything else. "I - No, mum, no... I... I'm fine." He couldn't tear his gaze away from the rope, his stomach knotting sickeningly as the worst thing of all occurred to him: that hadn't been there this morning. Thomas was certain of that.

"I have to go now, mum," Thomas said softly and the silence over the phone was strained before Diane hesitantly broke it.

"Oh... of course, Tom," she said, her voice purposefully gentle although Thomas thought he could detect unhappiness in it. "You take care of yourself, okay? I'll ring you in a few days. I love you."

"Love you, mum," Thomas murmured, ending the call. He set his mobile down on the desk with trembling hands, still unable to look away from the sinister coil of rope. He just couldn't understand how it was there, right outside his window for no discernible reason at all. Maybe one of the new neighbours was playing a horrible practical joke on the newcomers, Thomas thought wildly, or *maybe* –

His jaw set and he pushed himself up from the chair sharply. Pain rocketed down to his knee at the sudden movement and, swallowing a curse as fury at his own weakness welled inside him, Thomas snatched his cane up from where it was resting against the wall. He tried to avoid using it if he could – it made him feel even more self-hatred than usual which was never exactly a good thing – but right now Thomas was too upset to care.

He just couldn't believe they would *do* this to him. The three of them were supposed to be as good as brothers and… and here they were, treating him like this… like someone they could humiliate just for fun.

Thomas limped out of his bedroom and slammed the door shut behind him, so hard it was still rattling in the frame as he lurched forwards to burst into the living room.

Daniel and Henry sprang apart in shock, staring up at Thomas with guilt staining their flushed faces as they tried to pretend that they *hadn't* just been kissing on the sofa. Henry's dark curls were in disarray and Daniel's cheeks were scarlet, and Thomas's sudden loneliness in that moment would have overwhelmed him if he hadn't felt like bursting into livid tears. "Shit," Daniel breathed which was the moment Thomas realised how awful he must look right now, sweating and ashen with shock as tremors rocked through him. Only the cane and his tenuous grip on the doorframe were keeping him standing, and Thomas half wanted to crumple down onto the floor, if only to distract himself from how terrible he felt right now.

"Which of you did it?!" he demanded, his voice several octaves too high. His green eyes were faintly wild because he was panicking and frightened and... and screw this house honestly. Fucking *screw* it. He hated it. "Who tied the rope outside my window? Which of you thought that would be funny?!"

Henry scrambled to his feet instantly, darting over to where Thomas was leaning heavily on his cane and thumbing the smaller man's tears away gently. Thomas hadn't even realised they were falling and he felt more vulnerable than ever now... completely out of control.

"Tom, just slow down," Henry said soothingly, helping Thomas to sit down on the sofa between him and Daniel although it made the red-haired man's back ache with a pain searing enough that it tore a ragged gasp from him. "What's happened? Why are you so upset?"

"I'm not upset! I'm *angry*!" Thomas argued but his voice came out broken with the sobs he was fighting against. "Who tied that rope to the branch outside my window?" he repeated tearfully. "Who thought it was funny to hang a fucking *noose* on the tree?!"

Daniel looked aghast but he pulled Thomas into a tight hug, apparently uncaring that the red-haired man was now sweaty and tearful, and not particularly in the mood to be cuddled. Both of them were staring at the older man in concern because it was no secret that Thomas had been suicidal a few years before. They knew what their best friend had tried to do and it was because of this that they understood why he was so freaked out now. It must have been like having his very worst memories replayed right before his eyes… like a nightmare turned reality.

"I'll go check it out, Tom," Henry said softly but he looked frightened as he watched his best friend fall apart in front of him. Thomas's eyelashes were spiky with tears when he looked up at the dark-haired man but something died in his chest when he saw his best friend's kiss-bruised lips.

Thomas felt more alone than ever.

"Be careful, Hal," Daniel said softly. Thomas let his forehead fall to rest on the blond man's broad shoulder and Daniel rubbed his arm soothingly, trying to keep him calm. "If someone *did* tie that up there for a joke then they might still be around here somewhere."

Henry shivered at that but he set his jaw as he disappeared out into the hallway. The wind howled when Henry disappeared out into the night and Thomas flinched when the door swung shut. Daniel shushed him gently, his fingers carding lightly through the smaller man's dyed red hair as Thomas struggled to regain control of his breathing.

"Tom?" Daniel's tone was one of forced calm but, even in his current state, Thomas could hear the hurt in it. "You don't *really* think Hal or I would do that to you, do you?" Daniel sniffed beside him and Thomas refused to let himself look up because, god, if he made Daniel cry now then he might as well just move back home. He'd feel like the worst human ever.

"No," Thomas whispered after a moment of hesitation. "I'm just... scared." He glanced sideways suddenly, unable to help himself, and took in how red Daniel's cheeks still were; remembered how messy Henry's curls had been in the moments before he marched out of the door. Thomas's expression became sullen. "Are you two together now then?" he asked bluntly and he hadn't intended to make his voice cold but Daniel's arm slipped away from around his shoulders anyway, taking his comforting warmth with it.

"I don't know," Daniel said quietly but, as Thomas drew breath to say something that would probably be unforgivable, the front door opened and closed, signalling Henry's return.

Abruptly, Thomas's heart began to beat a mile a minute again as he remembered the noose swaying gently from the branch outside his window, the rope old and fraying as it brushed tenderly against the glass. Thomas sank back into the sofa with a little whimper when Henry appeared in the doorway, obviously shivering as he held up the object of Thomas's fears in front of him.

"It was just vines, Tom," Henry said as one of the wilted leaves he was holding fell down onto the floor. Thomas closed his eyes tightly, hating the tears burning there. "Just ivy."

Beside him, Daniel bit his lip as he shot a wide-eyed glance at the red-haired man. Thomas's cheeks were flaming and his fear was rapidly being replaced with humiliation as his shame seared him.

"Okay," Thomas said mechanically as he remembered Nicholas disappearing into the trees; pictured the rope hanging there in the moonlight. "I'm sorry I made you check. I'm... I'm sorry."

His earlier accusation lingered in the dusty air between them.

Daniel swallowed audibly and Thomas wondered what he'd been about to say.

"It's okay, Tom," Henry whispered, even though the older man knew it wasn't. He was scared he was getting bad again but... god, he'd never been like *this* before. He didn't know what was wrong with him.

"I'm gonna go to bed," Thomas said softly. Daniel wordlessly helped him stand up and passed him the cane from where it had fallen on the floor. Thomas couldn't look him in the eye when he muttered his thanks.

The living room remained deadly silent behind him as the older man left. He thought again of Henry and Daniel lying tangled together on the sofa and, with a heavy heart, he limped into his bedroom and shut the door firmly behind him, leaning against it until the catch clicked.

Thomas crossed the room as quickly as he was able, wrenching the curtains shut without looking up and throwing his cane carelessly onto the floor. His room was lit only by the lamp on his bedside table and the shadows crept up the walls like ink as he slumped down painfully onto his bed, staring up despairingly at the ceiling.

Thomas's mobile was still lying on the desk where he'd left it after ending the phone call and there was some vicious satisfaction in him when he reached out blindly for the bottle of painkillers, emptying two into his palm. Thomas swallowed them dry and settled back on the mattress with a pained groan, too tired and achy to even consider taking his clothes off first.

Outside his door, he heard Daniel and Henry ascending the creaking stairs as they talked quietly together in low, worried voices. Thomas closed his eyes and pulled the pillow tighter around his ears, not wanting to hear what they were inevitably saying about him. He wondered if they regretted asking him to move in with them now. He wondered if this had been a mistake.

The red numbers on his clock flicked closer to midnight and Thomas closed his eyes against the tears boiling down his cheeks in the darkness as he pictured the noose illuminated sinisterly in the moonlight.

First he saw someone who wasn't there and now this had happened.

Thomas was scared he was going insane.

Chapter 6: The Chest In The Attic

Daniel had left a bucket in the middle of the bathroom floor.

Thomas frowned at it as he cleaned his teeth, scowling vaguely at his reflection in the smeared mirror as he moved the toothbrush lazily around. It took a while but finally his curiosity got the better of him and, gripping the sink with one hand, he leant closer and peered down into the bucket, eyebrow rising in surprise when he saw almost an inch of water in there. He looked up and his frown deepened at the wet mark on the ceiling.

"Looks like we have a leak," Thomas said to no one in particular. Neither Daniel nor Henry were within hearing distance but he was almost glad of it. At least if they weren't around, he didn't have to watch the pair of them trying in vain to hide their feelings. That was somehow even more frustrating than when they'd been silently pining for each other before.

Thomas forced his bitterness away with difficulty as he shuffled back to the sink to rinse his mouth out. He didn't like thinking about his friends anymore. It just made him feel more alone than ever, stranded out here… loveless. He'd possibly never felt lonelier than he did right then, with his mouth tasting of mint and his red hair tumbling into his eyes.

Daniel had been gone for well over two hours by now. He'd been almost painfully optimistic as he left the house that morning on his bike, apparently uncaring that the closest job he'd managed to secure was seven miles away. The closest place hiring was the Inn in Santon Bridge but he had refused to let it sway him, instead insisting that '*everything happened for a reason*' as he set out on the forty-something minute bike ride that morning. Thomas had watched him go from the living room window with a sceptical expression on his face. Henry had practically been waving a handkerchief from the driveway.

The dark-haired man was gone too, off to meet his new team leader at whatever Headquarters the rangers operating in the western side of the Lake District used as a base. Henry had been as excited as a child on Christmas day that morning, running around the house in his boxers with his shirt half-done up and a piece of toast wedged in his mouth as he searched frantically for his other shoe.

Thomas had politely suggested that perhaps Henry get ready the night before next time. Henry had politely told Thomas just how far he could stick his completely innocent suggestion.

A wry smile tugged at the red-haired man's lips although a frown creased his brow as he looked up at the watermark on the ceiling. He knew he should probably just call someone to come out and fix it but Thomas had never been what you'd call sensible and, with a half-hearted shrug, he figured he'd just have a look himself.

Dropping his toothbrush back into the mug on the shelf, Thomas shuffled out onto the landing. He hadn't been in the attic himself yet but he'd seen Henry testing the ladder out the day before so Thomas knew the basic mechanics of it; he needed to open the hatch, reach up, and pull the handle which would make the ladder descend. It was probably easier said than done but, for once in his life, Thomas was glad he had the cane. At least it would finally come in handy now.

He peered up at the hatch doubtfully, shaking away his unease with irritation when he realised he was stalling. *'No time like the present,'* the little voice whispered and Thomas agreed with it, something that was beginning to happen increasingly often lately. It was starting to talk sense.

Reaching up towards the hatch was painful but Thomas managed it, gritting his teeth against the dull pain as he used his cane to push the hatch open. It was unexpectedly simple to hook the end over the handle and tug it down, and Thomas felt triumphant as the ladder descended surprisingly smoothly towards him. Unfortunately, his smugness faded when he began the difficult climb up the ladder. His knee protested the movement and his back promised him that he would regret this later but he managed to amuse himself by picturing how horrified his best friends would look if they could see him right now.

When Thomas finally heaved himself up onto the dusty floor with immense difficulty, he simply lay there for a few minutes, his flushed cheek pressed to the cool wooden panels as he struggled to get his breath back. His back twinged when he pushed himself slowly into a standing position but Thomas forced himself to straighten up, stretching his arms out and hearing the familiar cracks as his spine protested the movement.

"Now where's that leak?" Thomas muttered to himself, emerald eyes drifting around the dark attic. He moved forward carefully, avoiding various sheet-covered boxes that seemed to have been up there for a long time if the spider webs were any indication. Henry would have hated it up there and Thomas smirked at that; spiders were one of the only things he *wasn't* scared of.

He found the source of the leak by accident in the end. His foot caught on one of the covered boxes and, in an attempt not to fall, he flung his arms out and his hand collided with the sloping roof overhead. His palm came away wet and, once he'd steadied himself with a wince, Thomas stepped closer to investigate. He had to squint in the semi-darkness but he thought he could see where the problem had come from now: some of the roof tiles were loose and the rainwater from outside had been running down the rafters to drip into a big puddle on the floor, directly above the bathroom downstairs.

They definitely needed to call someone out to fix that before it got any worse.

Thomas worried his bottom lip between his teeth idly, glancing around to make sure there was nothing of any value in the attic that might get damaged by the water. His gaze settled on the covered boxes after a moment and he frowned, limping closer and ducking his head warily under one of the water-marked rafters before he reached the closest box. The sheet sent out a cloud of dust when Thomas pulled it free and he coughed wheezily as he realised with slight surprise that it wasn't a box at all; it was a wooden chest instead.

The red-haired man sank down onto the floor beside it with a pained groan, turning his face away into his shoulder in case there was more dust as he pushed the lid open. It swung back with a low creak and, as the hairs on the back of Thomas's neck rose, he was reminded again of those ridiculous so-bad-they're-good B-rated horror films that Henry loved to make him watch so much.

It took Thomas's eyes a little while to adjust to the shadowy depths of the chest tucked away in the corner but he stayed crouched there in the dark, even despite the growing pain he could feel. He was starting to worry that his sciatica might flare up and leave him trapped up here but this was a mystery, and Thomas wanted to get to the bottom of it.

He emptied the chest slowly, his curiosity burning dully as he lay the contents out on the floor beside him. There were a strange mixture of things in there and, as Thomas sorted through them, he got the distinct impression that they belonged to a child or teenager; maybe someone who had lived in the house before them?

There were a pile of books on photography, a hockey stick, a bundle of crumpled old clothes, a pair of drumsticks, some once-colourful bandanas that had long since faded, a collection of records that Thomas really needed to sort through properly later, and a leather baseball glove with no ball.

There was another Polaroid too, faded and slightly crumpled but still clear. It had been taken of a family relaxing in a sunlit garden together - maybe even their overgrown garden behind this very house. The parents looked happy, dimples creasing the mother's cheeks as the father pressed a kiss to her flowing caramel-coloured hair. She was cradling a bright-eyed baby to her chest and Thomas swallowed thickly past the lump in his throat as he saw the infant's hand curling around the edge of the yellow blanket it was wrapped in.

A date had been scrawled across the bottom in faded blue ink and Thomas held it closer, squinting to make out the numbers in the darkness. Most of them were illegible now but he could just about make out the year: 1975. That was almost two decades before he'd been born.

Thomas felt a peculiar ache in his chest as he looked down at the mysterious possessions in front of him. Someone's whole life was contained in this chest and he couldn't put into words why it made him feel so shaken up. It wasn't even that long ago; the family might well be living their lives happily somewhere else right now but, looking down at the picture cradled in his shaking hands, Thomas had a horrible feeling that wasn't the case at all.

He carefully stowed the possessions back in the chest but there was something that stopped him from putting the Polaroid back too. Thomas tried to convince himself that it was because he was worried the rainwater might damage it – not that he could explain why it mattered to him so much – but he thought it might be more to do with the curiosity he could feel burning the anxiety away in his chest.

Thomas tucked the Polaroid away into his pocket and covered the chest with the sheet exactly as he'd found it. It took him a little while to climb safely down the ladder and even longer to get the hatch shut with his cane and, by the time he finally made it downstairs, Thomas was desperate for more painkillers because his sciatica was killing him now.

There was a deep frown on the red-haired man's face when he finally settled down at the dining room table with his laptop, waiting for the painkillers to take effect as he switched the computer on. He was going to search for a nearby job and, although the idea of it filled his stomach with butterflies, he hoped he'd be successful because going out to work would hit two birds with one stone - it would stop his friends and mum from worrying about him quite so much, and it would get him out of this horrible house so that he didn't end up going completely insane in there. The rain was sliding down the glass of the windows outside in rivulets and, although he had stowed the Polaroid safely in his desk drawer, it remained very present in his thoughts.

Thomas hadn't solved any of the mysteries at all.

Now he was more confused than ever.

Chapter 7: The Word Please

Thomas ended the call with a sour expression on his face.

He'd just been speaking to Alison - the owner of the Barn Door Shop down in Wasdale Head - about the potential of any possible work that might be arising in the near future. He'd only been asking out of a sense of duty; he wanted to help his friends pay rent and hopefully stop them from worrying about him sitting alone here all day long. He hadn't really believed Alison would say yes.

Then again, he also hadn't factored in quite how desperate she'd be for a new employee after the old one had apparently left without notice.

A heavy sigh escaped Thomas as he glared down at his dark phone screen. He wished he could feel more enthusiastic about the opportunity but it didn't seem possible with the mood he was currently in. Thomas couldn't shake off his negativity no matter how hard he tried.

He wasn't sure he liked having all this spare time to kill either, especially given the fact that he was in the house all alone. Daniel had settled into his new job incredibly well and Henry was ecstatic. It felt almost as though Thomas was just rattling around the house all by himself, forgotten.

His bad mood definitely wasn't helped by the fact that his sciatica kept him essentially trapped at the dining room table too. He sat hunched painfully in the wooden chair as he messed around on his laptop, cringing when the wind howled outside and the hairs on the back of his neck rose.

More than twice now, Thomas had twisted around painfully as the unpleasant sensation of someone watching him sent his blood running cold. Once he thought he saw the flicker of a shadow just out of sight of the doorway but, when he finally limped over to investigate - cane held tightly in his hands like a weapon - there was nothing there.

He thought again of the hazel-eyed man out on the road and the frayed noose swaying gently from the tree branch, and his self-loathing doubled.

Thomas hated it here; hated everything about being trapped in the middle of nowhere with two best friends so focused on falling for each other that they couldn't even see him crumbling apart right in front of them.

By noon, Thomas had given up the pretence of even *pretending* he was happy to sit in the house.

He knew Daniel had left some food in the fridge for him but Thomas didn't feel like foraging for a snack now. His stomach was twisting with nervousness and he'd lost his appetite around the time the howling wind had started to sound like a wolf.

In fact, Thomas had got himself so jumpy that his muscles were tense and the dull aching pain shooting down to his knee had only worsened. He felt stupid for getting so worked up and he buried his head in his hands for a moment, fighting not to remember the moonlight shining through the loop of rope or the horror unfurling inside him as his phone clattered onto the desk.

Feeling abruptly sick, Thomas pushed his chair away from the table and rose on stiff legs. The house was silent without his friends and he knew they wouldn't be back until later that evening so he didn't see the point of sitting here any longer. It was only one o'clock now and Thomas couldn't stand this. He could feel the craving beginning to settle under his skin again, an itch that was impossible to scratch but oh-so-easy to soothe for a little while.

Abandoning his cane by the dining room table, Thomas limped into his bedroom on the way towards the front door and grabbed the bottle of painkillers on his bedside table. The pain burning in his back and leg was slowly worsening, and Thomas felt that same surge of vicious satisfaction as he swallowed two dry.

He didn't care that taking a short walk might be enough to alleviate the pain. Thomas had never been very patient and that made itself apparent now as he choked the tablets down. He would always take an immediate quick fix over a slower long-term solution; it was one of his biggest failings and he knew that was why his mum grew so worried about him sometimes. Thomas often acted without thinking of the consequences.

Shrugging those worries away for now, the red-haired man shouldered the front door open and limped out into the rain. It was just beginning to fall; more a light mist than a downpour. The air smelt fresh and clean, and the wooden banister felt slippery under his pale hand when Thomas carefully descended the steps of the porch, his breath escaping him in a pained hiss.

Henry and Daniel would probably have something to say about him doing this but, just as Thomas's anxiety began to flutter unpleasantly in his chest, his emerald green eyes settled on a painfully familiar figure standing on the other side of the road again.

Thomas's heart raced ridiculously in his chest at the sight of Nicholas watching him, his expression critical as he stood in the same place as before. He was dressed in the same outfit but the red-checked flannel was done up this time, the baseball gripped tightly in his trembling hands as he shivered like he felt cold. His hazel eyes never wavered from where Thomas's bad leg was dragging painfully beneath him.

"You again," the red-haired man said breathlessly and Nicholas's expression flickered with something that was almost relief when the older man's heavy gaze locked on him.

"Should you be outside?" the younger man asked dryly and Thomas couldn't suppress his slight smile as he shrugged, brushing Nicholas's worries away absently.

"I thought I was going crazy," Thomas said weakly. His eyes were locked on Nicholas's face as he drank everything in: the way his honey-coloured curls fell artfully across his forehead; the glimmer of his hazel eyes behind his crooked glasses; his heart-shaped lips and the tiny hint of a smirk curving the corner of his mouth.

"I thought I'd imagined you," Thomas confessed and the light in Nicholas's eyes went out.

"Maybe you did," he said flatly.

Nicholas stepped closer to the kerb, stumbling slightly as his scuffed trainers carried him into the dusty road. For just a moment, Thomas remembered the large trucks travelling to and from the slate mine, and his pulse quickened with concern when Nicholas seemed content to simply stand there. Thomas took a faltering step backwards and the younger man's eyes locked on the movement.

"*Please*," Nicholas spat out, his voice thick with something like desperation, his expression twisted as though begging pained him. "Please don't leave."

Thomas watched him with wide green eyes, glancing anxiously up and down the deserted road as Nicholas simply stood there in the middle. He seemed rooted to the spot almost and Thomas worried for a moment that Daniel or Henry might drive home earlier than expected, not watching where they were going properly in the mist of rain; worried that one of the monstrously huge trucks would come thundering past on their long trek across the country.

The thought had barely crossed his mind when he heard the tell-tale rumble of one of the colossal vehicles approaching, the low roar of its engine growing steadily louder as it approached through the mist.

Thomas's breath punched out of him like he'd been kicked in the stomach, his insides knotting together unpleasantly as he began to panic that he was about to see Nicholas get smeared in the road.

"Get back on the pavement," Thomas said, and he tried to sound firm like Daniel and Henry did but his voice sounded small and scared instead. The younger man simply planted his feet more carefully in the road, like he was balancing on the balls of his feet almost, and Thomas realised with a thrill of horror that the younger man had no intention of moving. "C'mon, Nicholas, *please*."

The red-haired man glanced around helplessly but there was no one around to help. The truck was roaring closer than ever now and Thomas's heart pounded painfully in his chest.

"I hate the word please," Nicholas muttered, his voice twisting around it like it was something unpleasant, but he didn't step back. Thomas's sciatica was hurting worse than ever now and his bad leg felt wobbly under him but the red-haired man fought to ignore it, taking a staggering step into the road and gasping out a pained groan.

"*Stop*," the younger man ordered and Thomas froze in place as he took in the shocking calm on Nicholas's tanned face with something like disbelief. "You don't have to worry," the younger man added and Thomas's green eyes widened at the strange, almost empty determination colouring Nicholas's expression. "I won't get hurt."

The truck had rounded the corner now and Thomas's heart was trying to beat right out of his ribcage as the mist of rain slowly began to soak him. His red hair was plastered to his forehead but Nicholas seemed strangely untouched by it, like maybe he wasn't even here anymore.

The driver was blasting his horn now, leaning on it as he stamped on his screeching brakes. Thomas hesitated, staring at Nicholas in complete panic as the younger man folded his arms calmly, apparently content to stand there and get flattened. The horn sounded again and it finally broke through the terrified daze Thomas had fallen into. He stumbled clumsily backwards, staggering onto the rain-wet pavement as nausea rose inside him.

The younger man was still standing there. Motionless.

Thomas flinched when the truck roared past them, its heavy tyres throwing up muddy rainwater and splattering Thomas's jumper. Nicholas's baseball rolled slowly through the mist towards him and Thomas choked on a sob, completely overwhelmed. He squeezed his eyes tightly shut when the ball lightly hit the kerb, his pulse quickening in panic as he pictured what was surely a scene of absolute carnage except -

"You can open your eyes now, Thomas."

Nicholas's voice was light and amused, his curls tousled lightly in the breeze as the truck thundered out of sight. Thomas's breath tore out of him in a choked gasp, his relief so consuming that his knees gave out beneath him. He fell down heavily onto the damp pavement and buried his head in his hands, much to the apparent amusement of Nicholas as he sat down beside him, swiping his baseball from the puddles.

"I hate you," Thomas said weakly, making Nicholas's smile grow wider. "How did you do that?!" Thomas's demand was faint at best, his voice slightly choked as he glared at Nicholas accusingly through his shaking fingers. "How did you move out of the way in time?"

"Oh, that's easy. My lightning fast reflexes are almost as quick as my wit," the younger man said instantly, smiling thinly at Thomas as his hazel eyes flashed with some quickly-suppressed emotion behind the smeary lenses of his glasses. Thomas's lips twitched faintly despite himself and he rolled his eyes when Nicholas rose fluidly to his feet.

"I was just messing around," the younger man said suddenly and Thomas gave him a long look, his heart just beginning to calm as he tried - and failed - to straighten his left leg without wincing.

"Did you hurt yourself worse when you fell down?" the younger man asked guiltily and Thomas groaned at the bite of pain he could feel flaring up almost in response. His sciatic nerve was searing painfully now and he let out a shaky sigh, hanging his head for a moment as he swallowed down the defensive retort he'd been about to snap.

"Yeah," the red-haired man said at last. "You scared me kind of a lot just then."

"My bad," Nicholas said. He extended a hand to help the older man up and, after considering it for a moment, Thomas reached out to lace their fingers together. The younger man's eyes widened fractionally when Thomas allowed himself to be pulled to his feet but Nicholas was smiling softly all the same.

He gave Thomas his hand back slowly and the red-haired man swallowed audibly when he felt his cheeks blushing a soft pink. His green-eyed gaze drifted towards where the truck had driven out of sight and he exhaled deeply, hoping his voice would be a little steadier now.

"Tell me, do you have a death wish, Nicholas?" the red-haired man asked curiously.

The younger man rolled his eyes, flashing Thomas a crooked grin.

"It has been said," Nicholas admitted.

Chapter 8: The Colour Of Gemstones

Thomas's spell jar wasn't working.

He'd used black pepper, cloves, and basil for banishing negativity but it hadn't fixed anything (possibly because he didn't really want it to). Thomas still didn't want to be here, leaning heavily against the counter as he fiddled with the little glass jar in his pocket and glowered around at the Barn Door Shop. Alison had told him his part-time job would be ringing up purchases and tidying the store, when in actual fact it was just an exercise in trying his hardest not to swear at the customers.

"Only ten minutes left of your shift, Tom," Alison said as she emerged from the back of the shop, cradling a pile of neatly-folded anoraks in her arms. "How did you find your first week here?"

"It was good," Thomas said after a slight hesitation, unsure if he was lying or not. He was tired and achy from standing up for so long but he supposed it was nice to talk to people again… especially if those people weren't Henry and Daniel, so wrapped up in each other that it felt like they didn't even notice Thomas anymore.

He was being unfair probably but it didn't change anything. The red-haired man still felt like his heart had been hollowed right out of his chest.

"Tom?" Alison asked softly, drifting a little bit closer. "Are you okay, sweetheart? You look a little..." Her voice trailed away delicately and Thomas grimaced at her, cheeks flaming as he picked awkwardly at the uniform shirt he'd been provided. It was a dull forest green that was rapidly becoming blurry and Thomas's heart shuddered in his chest when he realised he was on the brink of tears.

"Oh, honey," Alison murmured, drawing him into a hug that Thomas melted into without meaning to. He wasn't usually a tactile person but moving up here had made him feel so pathetically lonely that it was all he could do not to sob into her shoulder as his shaking hands fisted in the back of her jumper.

"Sorry," he gasped out, his cheeks stained with blood as he realised how ridiculous he was being. "Sorry, I'm just... I'm not good with change and things are really hard right now, and I miss my mum and - "

"Tom, it's okay," Alison said softly, shooting the empty shop a grateful look as she gave his shoulder a gentle squeeze, nudging him back so that she could see him properly. "You're allowed to be homesick and you're allowed to cry. Growing up and moving out doesn't change that." Thomas's eyelashes were spiky with tears but he managed a watery smile as he rubbed the back of his neck awkwardly.

"Thanks," he muttered, voice breaking enough that he had to clear his throat before trying to speak again. "Well, that was embarrassing."

"Not embarrassing," she chided gently, giving him a warm smile when he rolled his eyes. "You just need something to cheer you up. You need to get out there, pet. Do something to make you smile."

"I'm meant to be going out tonight," the twenty one year old said hesitantly, brushing his hair back from his forehead with a chagrined expression. "Daniel, my… my friend, he… he works at the Santon Bridge Inn and apparently there's this thing going on tonight."

"Ah yes," Alison said with a smile. "The World's Biggest Liar competition. It happens every November here and it's something most of us try to go to. It's a good time to get together… to catch up with people you haven't seen in a while."

Thomas's thoughts drifted unconsciously to Nicholas and he blushed a little as he stretched the hem of his polo shirt. He wondered if the curly-haired man would be there tonight and Thomas didn't know what it meant that he so badly hoped this was the case.

"Everything will be fine, pet," Alison said gently, apparently noticing the way his expression had brightened. Thomas dried his tired eyes with his sleeve, his teeth worrying at his bottom lip as Alison sent him a knowing look, clearly able to see that he badly needed reassurance.

"I'll see you at work tomorrow, okay?" she said with just enough finality that she sounded like a school teacher. "Bright and early."

"Be there or be square, right?" Thomas asked jokingly. Alison rolled her eyes at him.

"Better make sure you're *a-round*," she said with a wink. Thomas laughed so hard he snorted.

"I like this job," he decided as his green eyes twinkled in the dust motes illuminated in the watery sunlight. "Working here is going to be fun."

Thomas made the walk home in just under half an hour that day, barely limping which was a relief. The late afternoon was bright and crisp, and autumn had come quickly that year, unfurling through Deadman's Rise with barely a rustle as the leaves turned the colour of gemstones.

Thomas thought his spell jar might even be working by the time he finally made it back to the house because the negativity he'd been feeling all day long had almost gone now. He greeted Henry with a wave when he saw the younger man nursing a coffee on the decking outside, sat on the bench with a comic spread out in front of him. Daniel appeared just as Thomas approached and Henry's attention was instantly ensnared as he rose to draw the taller man into a tight hug.

Daniel's blond hair was damp from the shower he had just taken and he was already changed out of his new work uniform, and into the outfit he would be wearing to the inn later. Henry's palm was rubbing soothingly over Daniel's back and Thomas felt a stabbing pain ripple down his leg as he watched the pair of them.

"Oh, hey, Tom," Henry said distractedly when the pair of them finally separated. "You gonna go and get ready now, yeah? We have to head out soon if we're going to get there in time."

Thomas swallowed down the bitterness he could feel rising inside him as the spell jar weighed like lead in his pocket.

"Whatever," Thomas muttered, shouldering past them as he limped into the house. "I'll try not to hold you up too much."

The thirty minute drive to Santon Bridge Inn seemed to take a lifetime as the sun sank behind the mountains. Thomas felt like he was drowning in the awkward silence, Daniel looked lost at the uneasiness rolling off of the red-haired man in waves, and even Henry's shoulders were tense with stress, his face set in an unhappy frown that the evening wasn't going the way he'd planned.

"Tom?" Daniel tried softly but the red-haired man simply squared his jaw, glaring stubbornly out of the window as Henry finally parked the car outside the inn. His dark curls had grown unruly where he'd been dragging his fingers through them and the atmosphere in the car had clearly affected him too.

"I need a cigarette before we go in," Henry said abruptly which was enough to make his passengers stare at him in shock because the dark-haired man only smoked when he was very, *very* stressed. Henry muttered something withering under his breath when he saw their faces, opening the car door and stomping out onto the gravel once he'd dragged the crumpled packet of cigarettes from the glove compartment. Daniel watched Henry with ill-disguised concern and Thomas made a scornful noise in his throat, almost bristling with indignation as he folded his arms tightly across his chest.

"You're not going to make sure your boyfriend's alright?" the older man asked coldly and Daniel flinched when he heard the acid in Thomas's voice. He didn't correct the red-haired man though - didn't tell him that Henry *wasn't* his boyfriend; that the pair of them weren't really serious. He just looked at Thomas with this naked sort of panic in his eyes that made the older man feel like he was heading for a fall.

"Why didn't you guys tell me you two were official?" Thomas croaked, suddenly feeling small as he hunched there on the backseat like an unwanted child. "Why didn't you *tell* me?"

"Well…" Daniel bit his bottom lip awkwardly. "Tom, I'm not being horrible but you kind of haven't had a good word to say about us recently... and we didn't really want to shove '*us*' in your face, you know what I mean? You seemed to be struggling enough as it was."

Thomas swallowed past the lump that had rapidly risen in his throat as Daniel stared at him with worried blue eyes.

"Fuck you, Daniel," Thomas choked out as his eyes boiled with tears. "*Fuck. You.*"

The blond man reached out a shaking hand towards him but Thomas batted it away weakly as he half-fell from the car.

"Just… just leave me alone," Thomas gasped out when Daniel stumbled desperately after him. The car park was beginning to fill up around them now and Thomas's head spun with how badly he was trying to hold in his tears. "Just get away from me, Daniel! I feel like I can't breathe when you crowd me like this!"

Daniel took a jerky step backwards like Thomas had punched him in the stomach, his face growing red and blotchy like it only did when he was freaking out.

"I'm sorry," Daniel whispered, his blue eyes more red now as he twisted his fingers tightly in his neat blond hair. "We should have told you. We should have... God, I'm so *sorry*, Tom."

Thomas's guilt tore through him like wildfire but he beat it down like his father had always done him. He wished he hadn't made Daniel apologise because, really, this wasn't even the younger man's fault. He was just the sort of person to say sorry for the sake of a quiet life and Thomas wanted to feel terrible for it - for reducing Daniel to the snivelling teary-eyed mess currently wringing his hands in front of him now - but he didn't... not when this was exactly how Daniel and Henry made him feel on a daily basis.

"Just forget it," Thomas muttered, wiping his eyes fiercely with his sleeve before his green eyes flickered over to the inn. "Hal's waiting by the door now. Let's just... let's go inside." He thought of Alison's words earlier that day and a fresh wave of tears threatened to boil up behind his eyes. "Let's try to enjoy this evening."

Daniel stayed standing meekly behind him, his arms hanging limply by his sides like Thomas had leeched all of his enthusiasm away.

"Tom, how can I make this okay?" Daniel whispered as a big tear rolled down his flushed cheek. Thomas paused, his face downcast as he glared down at the dusty gravel beneath their feet.

"You can't," he said softly, swallowing past the tears clogging his throat. "Nothing about this is okay, Daniel."

The atmosphere inside Santon Bridge Inn couldn't have been further from Thomas's mood as he slumped down at one of the sticky tables with a pint cradled between his shaking hands. Music was playing from a jukebox somewhere as the landlord waited for everyone to arrive and Thomas's expression was furtive as he reached into his pocket for the painkillers he'd stashed in there earlier. He chased them down with the alcohol and, by the time Henry and Daniel finally reappeared with their own drinks, his poisonous mood had abated somewhat.

"I feel like I should say something to break this awkward tension but…" Thomas watched the pair of them owlishly over the rim of his glass as he paused to take a sip. "I got nothing."

The two younger men watched him wordlessly for a moment before Henry's dark eyes crinkled with relief as he laughed weakly at his oldest friend.

"I'm just glad you've finally stopped glowering," Henry teased as he reached out to punch Thomas lightly on the shoulder. "You're going to get wrinkles if you keep that up."

"He already has wrinkles," Daniel said spitefully but his lips twitched a little all the same. Thomas looked up at the blond man hopefully but something withered in his chest when he saw that Daniel's smile hadn't touched his eyes. The blond man's gaze remained cold and the look he shot Thomas was searching, like he couldn't quite understand why the older man had to be so horrible sometimes. Thomas gazed back at Daniel with an unspoken apology in his eyes because, quite honestly, he didn't understand it either.

He'd been nice once, hadn't he? Or maybe he *hadn't*. Maybe that was why his father hated him so much. Thomas wouldn't have blamed him.

He must have been a terrible person to be around.

His increasingly grim thoughts were interrupted when the landlord stepped up to the makeshift stage and got everyone's attention with the microphone he was holding in one meaty hand.

"Welcome, everybody, to this year's World's Biggest Liar competition!" the old man said enthusiastically, beaming beneath his bushy white beard as several of the patrons called back greetings to him. "We have a lot of people signed up to go tonight so, without further ado, let the competition begin!"

The evening passed in a blur after that, the pub filled with either uncomfortable silences when someone told a weak lie or uproarious laughter when one of the competitors told a wild tale that was just realistic enough to be acceptable.

By the time Henry finally took his turn onstage, Daniel had relaxed enough to give Thomas wan smiles and the red-haired man's painkillers had long since been pumping through his system, allowing him to relax back in the high-backed chair with a tired smile on his face.

Henry's lie was one of the most elaborate yet as he gesticulated wildly, clutching his half-empty pint in one hand as he spun a tale about how the new house they'd just moved into was haunted. Henry talked about the ghosts of a family; of nightmares starting to come true and knives disappearing from the block in the kitchen which would reappear in shadowy places in the house. Henry spoke of the howling sounds in the night and the unsettling feeling of being watched everywhere he went but, when he mentioned a noose hanging from the tree outside, Thomas had had enough. He pushed his chair back with a loud creak, his cheeks flaming with embarrassment because, even if no one else here knew what Henry had done, Thomas and Daniel did.

Henry was betraying his trust, spilling his most frightening secrets out for everyone else to hear… to pick apart and laugh over because this was only a competition after all. It was only a *joke*. It was only Thomas's terror he was picking at like a vulture over bones.

Daniel followed Thomas outside when the red-haired man stumbled for the doorway, his head reeling when the cold night air rushed to greet him. Daniel's hand settled on Thomas's shoulder and the red-haired man bit back a sob as he forced himself to calm down.

"I'm going to walk home," Thomas said through gritted teeth, raking a hand through his wild hair and swaying as the alcohol in his system made itself apparent. "I don't want to listen to this anymore."

"You can't, Tom," Daniel blurted out, his eyes wide with worry but also disapproval as he frowned back uneasily towards where Henry was still talking inside, much to the delight of the punters. "It's too far for your sciatica and it's dark, and besides -"

"I can drive you home, Tom," a familiar voice said from the darkness nearby. Daniel jumped and Thomas jerked round to see Alison standing there, arm in arm with her husband who seemed a little worse for wear. "I'd have to drop you off by the Barn Door Shop but it's not a long walk from there, is it?"

"That would be brilliant," Thomas said breathlessly, shooting a hopeful look towards Daniel whose iron resolve seemed to be weakening by the second. "You don't mind staying, do you, Danny? Hal will need you to drive him home after the amount he's drank."

Thomas felt a bit spiteful saying it but Daniel's shoulders slumped in defeat and Thomas's smugness died quickly when the blond man sloped back into the pub with nothing but a grunted goodbye. Thomas could feel Alison watching him worriedly but, before she had a chance to say anything, her husband suddenly muttered something about feeling sick and staggered off drunkenly towards the hedge growing around the car park.

"Delightful," she said dryly and Thomas shot her a crooked smile as he loped along behind her towards her car. His head felt worse than ever now - possibly due to the mixture of alcohol and painkillers he had ill-advisedly imbibed - but he relaxed a little when he slumped down into the backseat of the car. By the time she'd dropped him off outside the Barn Door Shop after making him promise to take care of himself, Thomas almost felt sober again.

The night sky was pitch dark above him, silent save for the strangled cry of a crow somewhere in the trees growing nearby. Wasdale Head was quiet this late, the windows dark with their curtains drawn as Thomas limped down the narrow street.

His shuffling footsteps sounded loud as he tried to retrace his steps from earlier that day but he was finding it increasingly difficult to remember where he was going. Everything looked so different at night-time. Thomas couldn't pinpoint his location by that one tree with the ruby-coloured leaves or the little cottage with its sunshine yellow door smiling out from beneath dappled leaves.

Thomas's head whipped about uselessly as he stumbled along but it was no good and, soon enough, he was hopelessly lost.

The clouds were drifting to cover the moon overhead now and the inky black shadows seemed to stretch like puddles across the ground that Thomas kept threatening to trip over. He didn't have a clue how to get to Deadman's Rise from here - unless he was already there? - and, as his heart started to pound unevenly in his chest, a cold hand closed around his wrist.

Thomas ripped his arm free with what might have passed as a wail but, before he could really start panicking that he was going to get dragged away, never to be seen again, he came face to face with Nicholas.

The younger man was watching him with poorly-disguised concern, his honey-coloured hair delightfully tousled as he scrutinised Thomas worriedly.

"You're drunk?" he asked softly. "Why are you all the way out here by yourself if you're drunk?"

"Thank god you're here, Nick," Thomas mumbled mindlessly, ignoring the question in favour of draping himself over Nicholas in a clumsy hug instead, a broad sunny smile stretching across his pale face when the younger man patted his back feebly. Thomas was possibly drunker than he had initially realised. "Man, am I glad to see you!"

"Likewise," Nicholas said but he was smiling wryly all the same. "Honestly, why are you out here though, Tom? It's not safe all alone. Do you know the way back?"

"Of course I do," Thomas said loftily, despite blushing a little at the way the younger man had shortened his name. "I'm just out for a night-time walk so, if you'll *excuse* me, I'd like to continue it in peace. Off you go. Disappear like you always do."

Nicholas's eyes flashed with something Thomas hadn't seen before and the red-haired man processed it slowly, his movements sluggish as he followed at a trot when the younger man abruptly strode off in the opposite direction.

"I think you're lying," Nicholas said, rolling his eyes at Thomas as he shook his head fondly. "You have the look of a man who stormed off and managed to get himself lost in the process. Bet you're too proud to call one of your friends to help you, right?"

"Right," Thomas muttered, cheeks flushing. "No way you could have just guessed that though. Are you, like, psychic or something?"

Nicholas gave him that look again - the one that told him he was deliberately missing something that was right in front of him - before his face softened as he drew Thomas to a stop.

"This is the way we need to go," he said softly. "But you look tired and also like your leg is hurting you." The moment he said it, Thomas became aware of the ache in his knee and his face crumpled a little. Nicholas made a soft clucking sound as he stepped closer. "Just rest it for a second and then we'll carry on, yeah? I'll help you get home. Why don't you tell me about your evening first though? I'd like to hear what you've been doing."

His tone was nothing short of wistful which was possibly the only reason Thomas recounted the events he had just experienced. Nicholas's expression became melancholy when he heard about the World's Biggest Liar competition but a startled choking sound escaped him when Thomas bitterly recounted the details of Henry's lie.

"- and then he started talking about knives and the noose I saw, and I just… I couldn't stay there. I *couldn't*. Not when he was telling everyone things like that. He should've known how that would make me feel… and I get why Daniel didn't say anything because his family make him feel shitty for who he is and he just wants Henry to love him but… but doesn't he love me too? Don't they *care*? The noose was… it was a secret," Thomas mumbled, his words starting to grow jumbled as the alcohol slurred his words. "Hal should never have said."

Nicholas watched Thomas with an unreadable expression on his tanned face, his beautiful eyes damp with tears as he let his palm settle hesitantly on the older man's arm.

"Oh, Tom," he breathed softly. "Of course you see those too. Of *course* you do."

A lump rose in Thomas's throat at the pain on Nicholas's face but he was too drunk to process it anymore. His head was spinning and even standing up felt like too much effort now, and he had no idea how to get back to the house at all because, knowing him, he'd probably been going in completely the wrong direction.

"I'll help you get home, Tom," Nicholas said softly, seemingly able to read the older man's mind as he reached out hesitantly for Thomas's hand. The road Nicholas was leading them down was dark and empty, and Thomas shivered violently as he saw the inky shadows stretching out towards him like clawed hands.

"Do you trust me?" Nicholas asked and Thomas looked up at him helplessly, taking in the younger man's empty hazel eyes and the worry prematurely lining his tanned face.

Something calmed in the older man's chest as he entwined their fingers together carefully.

"Yes," Thomas whispered and he tightened his grip as he followed Nicholas into the darkness. "I trust you."

Chapter 9: The Rain

Daniel was crying.

Thomas heard it as soon as he turned his music off and tossed his headphones aside. He could hear the blond man's soft sobs as he choked out barely-legible words into his phone and Thomas's heart broke in his chest as he pushed himself painfully into a sitting position. The raindrops were sliding gently down the window and Thomas's hand was shaking when it came to rest gently on the wood of his door.

He knew who Daniel was talking to on the other side.

He didn't need to hear the venom that would no doubt be being spat over the line to know that it was Daniel's family trying to tear his self-confidence to pieces. They did this sometimes, whenever they thought enough time might have passed that perhaps the youngest Evans sibling was *finally* happy. They called him and took it in turns to rip him apart.

Thomas hated the Evans family even more than he did his own father.

When he opened his bedroom door with trembling hands, Daniel stiffened, his back to Thomas as he leant over the narrow table they kept their door keys on. His shoulders were tight with stress and shaking with sobs, and Thomas limped over to take the blond man's hand gently.

"You don't deserve this, Danny," Thomas breathed, tightening his grip on the younger man's hand when another sob tore its way violently out of him. Thomas had barely talked to Daniel since that night at the pub, too embarrassed that the blond man had had to reveal his relationship in such an uncomfortable way… too ashamed that he'd brought Daniel to tears himself when that was exactly what he hated so much about the blond man's homophobic family.

"Daniel," Thomas said imploringly when another terrible sob escaped him. Daniel looked like he was going to fall but the phone was still clasped so tightly against his ear that it was all Thomas could do to gently pry the younger man's fingers away. Daniel let the phone fall limply and Thomas brought it to his ear, barely concentrating on the crackly voice because he was more focused on pulling the blond man into a one-armed hug in an effort to stop his crying.

"Stop," Thomas said when he caught the tail-end of an insult vicious enough that it sent the hairs on the back of his neck rising. No wonder Daniel had been such a wreck when he'd finally ran away from home to sleep on his best friends' sofas. No wonder it had taken Thomas and Henry six months to make Daniel feel like he was even worthy of their loving attention.

"*Excuse* me?!" a vaguely familiar voice snapped and it took Thomas a moment to realise it was Adam, one of Daniel's older brothers. "Who the fuck is this?" Thomas almost heard the unpleasant smile slowly spreading across Adam's face. "Wait. Is this *Barnes*?"

Thomas bristled at the unpleasant laugh that greeted him and Daniel whimpered beside him, burying his face in the red-haired man's shoulder and fisting the back of his hoodie in one shaking fist.

"God, Barnes, it's really you, isn't it? You need to mind your own business. Give the phone back to Daniel and piss off. *Now*."

"Oh, go fuck yourself, Adam," Thomas said heavily and he was about to hang up when he heard Daniel's brother spit: "You should have killed yourself when you had the chance."

Thomas closed his eyes for a moment, forcing down how badly he wanted to tell Adam to take a leaf out of his book because the red-haired man refused to sink that low.

"Don't call this number again," Thomas said instead. "*Ever*."

He stabbed the '*end call*' button with his thumb and took a deep, calming breath. Daniel was shaking when Thomas folded him up into a tight hug and the kiss he pressed to the blond man's forehead only seemed to make him cry harder.

"I love you, Danny," Thomas whispered. "I'm sorry. I love you." Daniel's usually-pale face was blotchy with how upset he had become and the red-haired man was starting to panic himself now, hating that he couldn't take the pain from Daniel's tear-filled eyes. "Let me get Henry for you, Danny," Thomas whispered, already hating himself for the fact that he couldn't help his youngest best friend alone. "Let me find him."

Daniel crumpled down onto the bottom step when Thomas drew back, burying his head in his hands and tangling his fingers through his messy blond hair. The kitchen door was shut at the end of the dark hallway but Thomas could see a thin strip of gold beneath it and he headed towards it, his face setting into a grim expression as he pushed the door open with a creak.

Henry was sitting at the table with the radio playing crackly rock music as he leant back in his chair. There was a mostly-full bottle of beer set beside some paperwork he seemed to be filling out for work but what was more a call for concern were the bruise-like circles smeared under the dark-haired man's eyes and the stale smell of cigarettes lingering on the clothes he'd been wearing the day before.

Clearly, Henry wasn't having the best time right now and Thomas wanted to feel a vicious surge of satisfaction for that but hating Henry didn't come easily to him. It didn't matter that Thomas had been doing his best to avoid him since the night of the competition; that Thomas had preferred to lock himself away in his room with Diane's Book Of Shadows and his dog-eared novels instead of actually discussing all of the ways he felt Henry had broken his trust.

"Tom?" The dark-haired man set his pen down and pushed the form he'd been working on aside with something like disgust. "You haven't actively sought me out in almost a week now."

Thomas pressed his lips together hard to keep from telling the younger man exactly what he thought of that statement. Henry looked so world-weary as he looked up at the red-haired man and Thomas swallowed down the guilt he could feel welling inside him.

Henry seemed to be having a horrible time of it lately, probably made worse in no small part by Thomas spitting at him to fuck off whenever Henry accidentally crossed paths with him. That was why the red-haired man caught himself from cursing again now. He didn't want to tear Henry down the way Adam did Daniel.

Thomas wasn't like that… was he?

"*No*," the red-haired man blurted out loud and Henry gave him a curious look, taking a sip of his beer although he didn't seem to be in the mood for it.

"Are you ready to forgive me now?" the dark-haired man asked and his tone was bland. "It was just a joke." His chocolate brown eyes drifted unwillingly back to his paperwork and Thomas gritted his teeth, spreading his palms on the desk so that the paper was blocked from the younger man's view.

"What the fuck, Thomas?" Henry asked, glaring petulantly, but Thomas had never been less affected by it.

"Quit it, Henry," Thomas snapped and there must have been something serious in his eyes because Henry fell silent instantly. "No, I haven't come here to assuage your guilt. This is actually a little bit more important than that." There was concern growing in the dark-haired man's face now and Thomas was glad of it.

"What I came to tell you was that your fucking boyfriend - and thanks for telling me, by the way - is sobbing his heart out in the hallway." Thomas's knee was twinging with pain but he gritted his teeth against it, battling on regardless. "Maybe take him out tonight and actually treat him well unlike his shitty family, and don't come back home until you're ready to think about someone other than yourself for once, okay?"

"Tom, that's out of line!" Henry argued but his dark eyes had become slightly panicked and Thomas knew he was afraid of the things Daniel might have heard from his relatives.

"It's not out of line," Thomas said. "It's really, *really* not… but I'm too tired to fight with you. I don't care anymore. Just… just fucking help Danny, okay? I can't do it. He needs you."

Henry rose on weak legs, his mouth falling open for a moment although no sound came out. Abruptly, he turned away and left the room as the shadows enfolded him. Thomas could hear him softly murmuring to Daniel, along with a muffled sob and the zip of a coat, and then the front door opening and shutting.

Thomas let out a shaky sigh in the sudden silence, pinching the bridge of his nose between his thumb and forefinger as he tried to breathe through the stress headache that was beginning to develop behind his eyes. He hated confrontation so much; hated the tightness in his chest and the way the anxiety made his hands shake.

"Tom?" a soft voice asked and Thomas swore his heart stopped in his chest for a moment. He spun round to find Henry lingering in the doorway, his eyelashes spiky with tears as he fiddled with the hem of the coat he'd just pulled on over his clothes. He was biting his bottom lip so hard Thomas was scared he'd draw blood, fidgeting and sad as he glanced up at the older man. He looked so shockingly small for a moment that it reminded Thomas of the day they'd met and a lump rose in his throat that he almost couldn't swallow past.

"I thought you'd gone," he said when he could breathe again. Henry just shook his head sadly, one hand rubbing awkwardly at the back of his neck.

"Just told Daniel I'd take him out for a drink at the Inn down in Wasdale Head. You probably heard him getting in the car," the dark-haired man said but the fight seemed to have left him and he looked hopeless without it. "I just realised… well, you're right. *I'm* the one who's been out of line. I shouldn't take out my bad mood on you. That's not right."

"Is… is something wrong?" Thomas breathed, momentarily forgetting about Daniel probably crying in the car right now in the face of Henry's pain lurking just below the surface. "Something I don't know about?"

Henry smiled but it didn't touch his eyes.

"Do you remember how much I loved learning about the Lake District at school?" he asked and the randomness of the topic took Thomas so by surprise that all he could do was silently nod. "I always wanted to become a ranger. I wanted to work in this beautiful place but…" For just a moment, Henry's calm expression flickered and Thomas saw the shocking agony hidden underneath.

"What is it?" the red-haired man asked and Henry smiled despite the tears welling in his eyes.

"Tom, I fucking *hate* it," he said softly, his voice thick with the sob he didn't want to release. "It's not what I expected at all. I've never hated anything more."

Henry faltered for a moment, one arm coming to wrap around himself as he glanced guiltily towards where Daniel was waiting for him outside. Thomas had half-reached to give the younger man's shoulder a gentle squeeze but his hand fell to hang limply by his side instead.

It didn't feel right anymore, just like it didn't feel right to help Henry find the positives in this situation, at least not tonight. Thomas didn't feel comfortable being around the dark-haired man anymore. He knew Henry was sorry - genuinely believed the younger man meant it - but he also knew that Henry would do exactly the same thing again if he thought it would help him achieve his ends.

It wasn't cruelty for the sake of being cruel. Henry was just selfish; he always had been, no matter how kind he tried to be. It probably came from the way he'd been raised, constantly babied and given everything he wanted.

God, Henry had used Thomas's terror for his own gain and, thinking about that, the red-haired man abruptly found it difficult to even look his oldest best friend in the face.

"Come on," Thomas muttered, gesturing for Henry to head outside and following at a slow limp. "Daniel's waiting for you. Just… just go, Hal."

"No," the dark-haired man argued weakly. "Not yet. Not until you forgive me."

"Don't do this," Thomas pleaded and he was so tired now. *So* fucking tired of all of this.

"But I need to," Henry said sadly and the apology was shining in his eyes, mingling with the tears there. "I really *am* sorry. I shouldn't have said those things just to win the competition and… and I shouldn't have kept my relationship a secret and put Daniel in the awkward position of having to tell you alone, just because I didn't think you could handle it…" Henry's bottom lip wobbled at the pain on Thomas's face and his voice dropped to a murmur. "But… most of all… Shit, most of all, Tom, I should be treating you like my best friend… because that's what you are… if you'll have me back at least. My *best* friend."

The rain was starting to come down in sheets, the sky threatening a storm overhead, and Thomas felt his resolve weaken a little.

"Get in the car, Hal," he sighed but his eyes were softer now. "The rain's soaking you."

Chapter 10: The Northern Lights

Thomas didn't mind the house so much nowadays.

He didn't mind the wind howling through the forest edging their driveway anymore because the breeze carried the fresh scent of pine with it. The mountains looked pretty at dusk too - painted pink in the reddish light of the setting sun - and, if Thomas was *really* desperate to feel positive about the damp place they'd ended up living in, at least the seemingly endless rain meant that they never had to wash their car by hand.

Admittedly, he still didn't like how cold and wet it was - hated the steepness of the stairs that aggravated his sciatica and the broken-down fence creaking eerily outside his window - but he quite liked the rest of their new home.

His friends didn't seem to share his grudging fondness though. Daniel was constantly complaining about the terrible water pressure in the shower and Henry was still annoyed about the leak in the bathroom ceiling upstairs.

Thomas was almost glad of the dark-haired man's discomfort, largely because he hadn't yet forgiven Henry for the way he'd treated him. Sure, the apology had *helped* but… it just didn't feel that easy anymore. Ever since the phone call, Daniel had been incredibly clingy to Henry and Thomas felt more alone than ever.

Maybe that was where his fondness for the house had come from… because if he didn't feel welcome in the house, there was nothing keeping him here. Not Henry and Daniel, so wrapped up in each other that they barely noticed him anymore. Not his job at the Barn Door Shop and Alison's pity.

Nothing… except perhaps Nicholas.

Not wanting to think too much about that though, Thomas forced his attention back to the house. He'd decided that it had *character*, even if the peculiar sensation of not being alone in an empty room *did* unnerve him sometimes. At least nothing else strange had happened like that night with the vines hanging like a noose outside his window. The house almost felt safer when he wasn't looking for reasons to hate it.

It was a good thing Thomas didn't mind staying in the house alone too because he was spending a lot more time by himself these days.

Perhaps worryingly, Thomas was starting to enjoy the solitude in a way he never had done before. He was sure his counsellor would have had something to say about him isolating himself from the rest of the world like this - his mother *definitely* would have - but the red-haired man couldn't find it in himself to care anymore. Staying home alone made it easier to take his painkillers in privacy and he didn't even have to get dressed if he didn't want to.

However, in a strange turn of events, Thomas was actually wearing clothes today. He'd taken his morning coffee and his laptop outside onto the porch with only minor struggling, and he was settled unusually comfortably on the bench now, his mug sitting on the table in front of him as his cane rested against the wall nearby. A light mist was still curling lazily around the tree trunks, and for once the air was fresh and crisp as the darkening clouds hinted at the chance of rain.

Gazing around at the damp green world that had somehow become his home, Thomas knew nothing had changed. There was no *reason* for his heart to feel lighter in his chest at the prospect of being essentially trapped here in the middle of nowhere -

And then Nicholas appeared at the foot of the driveway with his ever-present baseball in his hand and Thomas realised that maybe things *were* different after all.

"Hey, Nicholas," the red-haired man called, his pale face lighting up as he raised his hand in greeting and almost knocked his coffee over in the process. His cheeks heated with embarrassment at his utter lack of cool and Nicholas smiled wryly as he drifted closer, tossing the ball up into the air and catching it as he meandered through the mist, shooting the old house a joyless look.

"That was smooth. I don't think laptops are designed to withstand being soaked with coffee," Nicholas pointed out as he reached the bottom of the steps. The wooden planks looked slippery with last night's rain and Nicholas hesitated for a moment before he stepped up them lightly, mirroring Thomas's weak grin when he realised that the red-haired man was blushing.

"You weren't supposed to notice that," Thomas said after a long moment, shooting his coffee a chagrined look. His back was beginning to ache dully and his knee was throbbing but there were dimples creasing Nicholas's soft cheeks now, and the baseball flying from one hand to the other was mesmerising. "I was trying to come off as suave."

"Well, the cane probably adds to that," Nicholas said fairly, shooting Thomas a crooked smile as he stowed the baseball neatly in his shirt pocket. "I'm sure you look very refined."

"I look *elegant*," Thomas corrected, obviously lying as he mirrored the younger man's smile. "Like Lucius Malfoy with *his* cane."

Nicholas - who had been in the process of clambering up to sit on the banister - paused for a moment and shot Thomas a blank look before winding his arm securely around one of the wooden supports, anchoring himself in place.

"Lucius *who*?" he asked and Thomas clutched his chest, pretending to reel back in shock. A light smile touched Nicholas's lips despite his apparent uncertainty.

"Your knowledge of pop culture and shitty movie references is severely lacking," Thomas declared, forcing a sneer although he mainly just wanted to smile at Nicholas until his cheeks hurt. "We definitely need to fix that. Are you *seriously* telling me you've never heard of Harry Potter?"

Nicholas shrugged, looking a little embarrassed but mostly just confused, and Thomas tore his gaze away with difficulty when he felt the smile softening on his face. He scowled down into his drink instead as, briefly, he remembered the first time Nicholas had dropped by to visit him while the red-haired man sat outside with his laptop. It had been a week or two ago now and, since then, their morning chats had become almost routine.

It made dragging himself out of bed easier anyway.

Waiting for his painkillers to kick in wasn't so agonising when he knew he'd be seeing the younger man soon and butterflies began to flutter in his stomach when he sat down alone to eat breakfast in the silent house. His favourite part of the morning before he went to work was when he headed out onto the porch with his laptop to drink his coffee in the fresh air and found Nicholas waiting for him (and if that sent his heart racing too fast in his chest, no one else had to know).

"Can I get you a drink or something?" Thomas asked suddenly as he remembered his manners, squirming on the bench a little when Nicholas's solemn hazel eyes settled on his face. He didn't think Nicholas would take him up on the offer but it still felt polite to ask; after all, Diane really *had* raised him to be polite. The younger man watched Thomas carefully for a long moment, taking in his cane and the way his pale fingers curled hesitantly around the china handle, and Nicholas smiled faintly as he shook his head.

"No, thank you," the younger man said politely. "I'm not very thirsty. Plus, your mugs are more likely to survive if I stay away from them." Thomas had to smile at that, aware that Nicholas was obviously still embarrassed about the first time he'd come to visit the older man while he was working.

Thomas had made Nicholas a cup of coffee but the drink had seemed to slip right through the younger man's fingers when he reached for it instinctively, spilling the hot liquid all over the floor as the mug smashed on the porch. Nicholas had flinched away in shock, apparently completely mortified; Thomas had just felt bad for not making sure the younger man had a proper grip on the mug.

Thomas had made Nicholas another drink the next time he'd come to visit but, despite looking touched, the younger man hadn't drank it so Thomas had decided not to bother without asking again, not wanting to make him feel uncomfortable.

Maybe Nicholas didn't like drinking or eating in front of people. Maybe he'd just been too polite to refuse.

The younger man looked a little uneasy now - still obviously embarrassed - and Thomas hurried to distract him. He wasn't sure why it mattered to him so much that the younger man felt comfortable with him but there was something vulnerable in Nicholas's eyes that made Thomas's heart beat just a little too fast in his chest.

"We just got *so* waylaid," Thomas announced, a faint smile touching his lips as he clearly tried to cheer the younger man up. "The topic of discussion was that I, Thomas Owen Barnes, am suave."

Nicholas's eyebrows took a jaunt up to his hairline but he looked grateful all the same and Thomas tried not to stare when the younger man carded his fingers through his soft hair, letting the honey-coloured curls tumble back across his forehead with a casual sort of grace.

"You're not suave. You don't take any notice of where you put your coffee," Nicholas pointed out as he leant his cheek against the cool wood, exhaling heavily. "It's hard to look charming when you've just poured boiling liquid all over yourself." Nicholas's smile became faintly apologetic. "That just makes you look *clumsy* probably. Not a particularly desired trait."

Thomas snorted, finding the jibe more amusing than he would have done if Daniel or Henry had said it. Then again, everything they did at the moment seemed to be getting his back up so maybe Thomas was just biased. He knew he was probably being unfair but it was difficult to be mature when he remembered the way they'd been kissing on the sofa a few weeks previously... when he realised they'd never trusted him with the truth even once.

"You look sad," Nicholas said suddenly, his eyebrows pulling together in a worried frown. "Do you want to talk about it?" His words were soft and they took Thomas by surprise as the older man looked up jerkily, biting his bottom lip hard when the movement made his back flare with pain. The weak smile he forced on his face didn't touch his eyes.

"I'm not really," Thomas lied but his teeth worrying uncertainly at his bottom lip contradicted him. "I was just thinking about my friends," he said after a long moment, jerking his thumb towards the empty house as though Daniel and Henry were still hiding inside somewhere. When Nicholas seemed content to simply watch Thomas curiously, the red-haired man felt a little tension leak out of his shoulders. "I walked in on them kissing a few weeks ago." He didn't elaborate but the betrayal he felt saturated his words and something withered in his chest that might have been shame.

Nicholas's hazel eyes widened in surprise and his little intake of breath was just quiet enough that Thomas thought he might have imagined it.

"They're… gay?" Nicholas asked blankly, a look of utter confusion on his face. "Whenever I imagined them, I always thought of them as straight." The younger man instantly seemed to regret those words and, although Thomas gave him a funny look, he decided it wasn't really worth pursuing now. In a quiet place like this, any change at all must have been interesting so he figured it made sense that Nicholas had given them so much consideration. Maybe he just had an overactive imagination.

"Well, Daniel is gay; Henry is bisexual." Thomas shrugged like it didn't matter and Nicholas watched him carefully, hazel eyes narrowing as he slipped down off the banister so that he could lean on the edge of the table instead, a serious expression on his tanned face.

"What about you?" he asked eventually and Thomas took a long time to drag his gaze up, the shame and confusion he was battling evident in his eyes as his palms fell flat on the tabletop.

"I don't know," Thomas said honestly, a humourless smile twisting his cherry-red lips as the pain in his leg seared through the nerves. "And I don't really care either. I can't even walk properly without swearing and being in pain… I'm not exactly beating devoted people away with a stick, Nick." Thomas snorted suddenly, his smile fading. "Huh. A *stick*. Guess I should've said '*cane*' instead."

Nicholas's face fell as he looked at Thomas carefully, taking in the older man's emerald green eyes and the way his crimson hair fell messily across his pale forehead. The younger man moved slowly around the table, sinking down fluidly onto the bench and twisting so that he was facing the older man.

"Do you really think that?" Nicholas asked softly, his hazel eyes so sad that Thomas couldn't let himself look at him anymore. "Do you really think no one's ever going to love you, Tom?"

"I didn't say that," Thomas muttered but his cheeks were heating and he looked off towards the forest, biting the inside of his cheek as his expression twisted with something like pain. When Nicholas's palm settled hesitantly on his wrist, both of them let out little gasps of surprise.

"No… but you were thinking it though," the younger man said softly, his voice slightly breathless as he gazed down at where his hand was resting gently on the older man's arm. "And you couldn't be more wrong, Tom, honestly." Nicholas's voice was earnest although his cheeks heated a little. "If someone doesn't want to be with you because you're in pain then… then they're the wrong person!" Nicholas looked momentarily embarrassed at his outburst but there was still something soft in his hazel eyes. "I think you're *great*," he said softly.

"You don't even know me," Thomas said, his voice heavy as he tried to ignore how warm the younger man's words had made him feel. "Not *really* anyway."

"We're getting there though," Nicholas teased, bumping Thomas lightly in the ribs with his elbow and looking jubilant when the older man let out an exasperated laugh, nudging him back. "We have jokes and things."

"And *things*?" Thomas asked doubtfully, smirking a little now despite himself as he settled more comfortably in the chair. His back wasn't aching so much now and Nicholas seemed happier today; more talkative. "If you say so, Nick."

"I do," Nicholas said proudly. "The other day you - Hold up, do you *seriously* drink your coffee through a straw, Thomas?" The younger man's eyes were glittering with mirth now and Thomas adopted a purposefully innocent expression as he ducked his head to take another sip of his drink. It was hard to pretend that Nicholas's disbelieving laughter *hadn't* made something raw soften in his chest but Thomas was trying valiantly all the same.

"Sometimes when I can be bothered to *find* a straw," Thomas replied after a long moment, still grinning weakly although he sobered a little as he spoke again. "My grandpa used to insist that it was the best idea ever. He had these dentures when he got old and he told me his dentist said it was better to drink everything through a straw because, that way, they were less likely to get stained. He wanted to save money I guess... and I do it now because... it reminds me of him I suppose." Thomas shrugged and Nicholas considered this, taking in the slight tightening of Thomas's expression and presumably correctly guessing that the older man's grandpa was no longer around.

"Maybe your grandpa had the right idea," Nicholas said in a grave voice, biting his lip as he seemingly tried to think of a way to cheer the older man up. "After all, we wouldn't want you staining *your* dentures, Thomas."

"Screw you! I don't have dentures!" Thomas yelled, the righteous indignation clear in his voice as his words echoed through the damp emptiness surrounding them. The breeze whistled through the trees and Nicholas looked so proud of his silly comment that Thomas laughed without meaning to, his green eyes warm and so fond that the younger man became flustered. Nicholas tucked his face away shyly into Thomas's shoulder, still giggling weakly, and the older man's heart raced unevenly in his chest as his cheeks flushed with blood.

"Being all cute isn't going to distract me from how mean you were about my coffee drinking habits," Thomas said pointedly, almost forgetting he even *hurt* at the broad smile curving across the younger man's face. Nicholas's dimples were creasing his cheeks again but, by the mischievous light in his eyes, Thomas had a feeling he was about to say something stupid.

"That's beside the point. You're still old enough to have dentures probably," Nicholas muttered, hiding his pleased smile behind his hands. The wind was picking up, the boughs of the pine trees swaying as the breeze tousled Nicholas's curls playfully. Thomas shook his head slowly, still smiling faintly even as he calmed a little.

"Enough about how supposedly ancient I am," he said but his voice was much softer now. "How old are *you* anyway? Because I'm only twenty one and you can't be *that* much younger than me, surely?"

A strange look came over Nicholas's face when Thomas asked him his age, a hollow sort of smile that only succeeded in making him look sadder.

"I'm… nineteen. Nineteen I guess," the younger man said, proving that Thomas's previous guess about his age had been correct. Nicholas sighed as the words escaped, his eyes darting once more towards the old house before his gaze settled on Thomas's face. There was something almost pleading in the younger man's eyes but Thomas didn't know what he was hoping for. He didn't know why Nicholas looked so *lost*.

"You don't sound sure," Thomas teased and Nicholas rolled his eyes, looking away and hunching his shoulders a little. Thomas bit his lip cautiously, glancing irritably towards his laptop when a low power warning popped up before his green eyes flickered back to the sad slump of the younger man's shoulders.

"So… no school or college or whatever?" Thomas asked when it became clear that Nicholas wasn't going to break the silence. "You don't have a job or anything?"

"No. Nothing at the moment," Nicholas said slowly, considering his words carefully before voicing them. "I'd love a job though. Something to do with sports or music or… or meeting *people*." Nicholas's eyes shone for a moment before the light in them seemed to flicker out. "I love to meet people but… it never happens anymore." He looked up hesitantly, giving Thomas a shy smile that didn't really touch his eyes. "You're the first person I've met in a very long time."

"Maybe you should get out of the house a bit more then," Thomas said but the statement was so obviously hypocritical that Nicholas had to laugh. Thomas knew there was something dishonest in the younger man's answer and, despite not being certain of *why* Nicholas was keeping something from him, Thomas didn't push it. He understood that everyone had their secrets and he accepted it. It was a part of life.

"What job do *you* do, Tom?" Nicholas asked curiously, resting his elbow on the table and propping his chin up in his palm. He was wearing the same red-checked flannel shirt as before but it was mostly fastened this time with only the buttons at his throat open to reveal the tanned skin. Thomas swallowed, dragging his eyes back up to the younger man's face and flushing when he realised he'd been caught.

"I work part-time in the Barn Door Shop down in Wasdale Head," Thomas said with a shrug. "I sell climbing gear, walking boots, camping stuff…" He listed them off on his fingers with an awkward smile before leaning forward to finish his coffee. The painkillers were in full effect now and he stretched his leg out fully with a quiet groan of satisfaction, relieved that he wasn't aching at all. "I've done it pretty much since we came here. It's kind of all I fill my days with."

"It sounds… fun?" Nicholas's voice was doubtful and Thomas laughed easily, brushing the younger man's shoulder lightly with his knuckles.

"It's not… but I can do most of it without leaving the hamlet which I enjoy," Thomas said. "Makes it easier when my sciatica is, like, trying to kill me so stretching my legs helps a bit." Nicholas's expression flickered but his eyes became concerned as Thomas's tone became self-deprecating. "Plus we only have one car, and Danny and Hal need that to go be actual functioning adults so…"

"Tom, please…" Nicholas's teeth sank into his bottom lip as his palm settled lightly over the older man's hand. "Don't keep putting yourself down like that. You… you don't see how *good* you are but… I do. I can see it."

"I can't even walk properly," Thomas whispered, his throat thickening with the sudden tears he desperately fought against. "My dad couldn't give two shits about me - thinks I'm a waste of space - and… and I tried to kill myself a few years ago and - and fuck, I don't even know why I'm *telling* you all this shit because I only met you two weeks ago and I don't know a single thing about you but… but I feel like you're the only person I can even talk to now and… and sometimes, when I'm talking to you, you make me feel less crazy than I am." A tear slipped down Thomas's cheek as he inhaled shakily. "You make me feel like maybe I'm still going to be okay."

Nicholas pulled Thomas into a gentle hug, his arms loose enough that the older man could pull away if he wanted to. Thomas tucked his face away into Nicholas's neck as his arms slipped gently around the younger man's waist and they both held each other for a moment. Nicholas's skin smelt… *cold*. It only made Thomas hold him tighter, a soft sigh escaping him when he felt the pads of Nicholas's fingertips rubbing his back in comforting circles.

"Thank you," Thomas whispered when they finally had to break apart, his sciatica protesting the stretch as it throbbed dully. Nicholas's hazel eyes were soft and wet, his eyelashes spiky with tears. Thomas hated that he'd made him cry but he hated that he'd put Nicholas in this position even more.

"It was nothing," the younger man said softly, shrugging awkwardly as he put a little space between them again. A part of Thomas wished he wouldn't. "You're... you're my *friend*, Thomas." He stuttered over the word and Thomas's eyes softened, growing warmer as he nodded confirmation. Seemingly heartened, Nicholas grinned at him. "I want to be there for you. That's what you do for your friends."

Thomas couldn't stop himself from smiling at that, his heart damn near melting as he mussed Nicholas's hair up. Despite the younger man making a big show of ducking out of the way, he still leant into the warmth of Thomas's palm for a moment, apparently craving the comfort. Neither of them mentioned it.

"I'm glad you live next door," Thomas said quietly and Nicholas's mouth dropped open in shock, the younger man looking almost surprised before he forced a weak smile onto his face and nodded agreement. Worried that the younger man was still upset about something, Thomas hurried to hopefully alleviate his concerns. "You know, besides Danny and Hal... well, I don't know." Thomas smiled awkwardly, rubbing the back of his neck in embarrassment. "I think you three are my only friends in the world... and I'm kind of oddly okay with that."

The last of the worry in Nicholas's eyes bled away and he smiled happily, his expression becoming relieved as he lifted his feet onto the bench, drawing his knees up to his chest and wrapping his arms tightly around his legs to keep him there. It made him look small and almost *soft*, and Thomas was glad Nicholas trusted him enough to show him this side of him. He seemed nothing like the sharp-tongued man who had almost given Thomas a heart attack by standing in front of the quarry truck a few weeks previously. He seemed uncertain and desperate for friendship now, and Thomas was more than happy to give it to him.

"Tell me why you moved here," Nicholas said and it didn't sound like a question. Thomas allowed a small smirk to curve his lips but he couldn't deny that the words made his heart feel a little heavier in his chest because they reminded him of home... reminded him of the phone conversation with his mum a few weeks before... the noose in the moonlight and the horror knotting itself like thorny vines around Thomas's heart.

"Well... I don't really know where to start. There were a number of things that contributed to it I guess..." Thomas's voice trailed away uncomfortably but, when Nicholas seemed content to simply watch him, the red-haired man felt braver. "Um... so I guess I've never been that happy at home really? Like, I love my mum to pieces and my grandpa was, like, my role model when I was a kid. He used to take me outside on clear nights and let me look through his telescope sometimes. I'd see planets and stars and... and whole *constellations*, Nicholas." Thomas's eyes were almost shining now and Nicholas smiled at him encouragingly, gesturing for the older man to continue. "When my grandpa died half a year ago, I just couldn't stand being at home anymore. My mum was sad I guess but... he was my dad's *father*... and my dad never even cared. It just made me hate him… and dad *loathed* everything about me. He's the reason I'm in almost constant pain now and… I just couldn't stand it anymore. I couldn't stay there for even a moment longer."

Thomas seemed to be struggling with his words and Nicholas took his hand gently, giving it a brief squeeze before he withdrew to take the baseball from his pocket. He looked down at it with sad eyes for a moment before he pressed it gently into Thomas's palms, curling the older man's fingers around it. Somehow, it seemed to help.

"My... uh... my counsellor thought it would be a good idea too," Thomas continued, unable to meet the younger man's gaze as he rolled the ball carefully across the table, letting it bump lightly against his laptop. "A clean break... that's what she said." Thomas shrugged, glancing up warily and visibly relaxing when he saw Nicholas watching him softly, without a trace of judgement on his upturned face. It felt strangely good to say the words out loud; made him feel *lighter* almost. Thomas had never confessed to feeling these things to anyone except his counsellor before. It felt surprisingly cathartic.

"When I found out Daniel and Henry were planning to leave London, it seemed like the perfect opportunity," Thomas continued. "I don't know why they chose this place though. I wasn't with them when they looked around it - I was in way too much pain to even get out of bed at the time - but... I don't know. They don't love the house so much anymore. I don't mind it though." He glanced once more towards the the old building but his eyebrows rose in surprise when he saw Nicholas levelling a dark look at the house. "There's definitely *something* weird about it here but... it's sort of starting to grow on me now. At least I'm not back home with my dad anyway."

Nicholas's face darkened but he still managed a weak smile when Thomas tossed the baseball back towards him lightly.

"My dad's awful too… nowadays anyway," Nicholas admitted, glancing around fearfully before he shifted a little closer. "I love my mum though. She was the kindest person in the world."

Thomas felt his heart break in his chest when he saw the sheen of tears in the younger man's eyes. He knew without a doubt that she was dead and the fact that Nicholas was stuck alone in a house with a man he hated made Thomas want to break down. He fought against it though, determined to make Nicholas smile again.

"Tell me about her," Thomas said softly. "Please. I want to hear about the woman who raised someone as lovely as you."

Nicholas ducked his head, his hazel eyes gleaming with gratitude in his tired face. His curls were messy when he dragged his fingers through them nervously and Thomas's hand was trembling a little when he reached to help flatten them. The younger man closed his eyes for a moment, leaning his cheek subtly into the older man's palm.

"My mum was… She was *everything* to me. Still is," Nicholas admitted softly, still refusing to open his eyes. Thomas's thumb stroked the soft skin beneath the younger man's eye and Nicholas's eyelashes fluttered when he looked up at him with something like longing on his face. "She was so patient and kind. Beautiful too. *So* beautiful."

"I can well believe that," Thomas mumbled without meaning to, his emerald eyes tracing the younger man's face and liking what he saw there. Nicholas's cheeks heated and, despite the grin that he seemed to be trying to smother, he shoved the older man weakly in the shoulder.

"Do you want to hear about her or not?" he demanded but he was trying not to smile and Thomas didn't regret his throwaway comment for even a moment. Instead, he simply nodded silently and pressed his lips together, fighting not to show just how ridiculously *fond* he felt. "She loved Abba and dancing and… and *me*. She used to be able to make me laugh when no one else could. Like, no matter how shitty school was or how stupid I felt when I couldn't do my homework, she always used to cheer me up." Nicholas hesitated, taking in the soft look on Thomas's face and seeming to steel himself for a moment. "She believed in, like, witchcraft too. *Spells* and stuff."

Thomas's expression quickly became delighted and the prickly defensiveness that Nicholas had apparently been prepared to wrap himself in fell away like water.

"My mum is the same!" Thomas said excitedly. "She's even given me her Book Of Shadows to work from while I'm stuck up here without her. I… haven't told Daniel and Henry she gave it to me. I don't think they'd understand."

"It's probably not quite what they imagine," Nicholas said wryly. "I mean… burning candles and herbs… energy and intent… It's not waving a magic wand and bringing a beloved rabbit back from the dead, is it? Like, you can't change something that isn't already going to happen but maybe you can alter how you'll feel about it, right?"

Nicholas's face suddenly softened and he continued in a softer voice as his eyes grew misty with old memories: "Mum used to do that for me a lot. She used to draw sigils for me whenever I was having a bad time. They used to make me feel less anxious or depressed or whatever. She had some good pain remedies too." Nicholas's eyes were focused again now and he was giving Thomas a knowing look. "I don't know if any of her books survived but maybe there's something in them that could help you."

Thomas looked even more excited now and Nicholas relaxed visibly as a broad smile spread across the older man's pale face.

"Your mum was a witch too," Thomas blurted out and he definitely looked impressed. "That's so fucking cool." Nicholas giggled a little despite himself.

"She dabbled," he said with a shrug and Thomas shook his head, his eyes glittering.

"Our mums are cooler than us," he said and Nicholas's laughter sounded bright in the misty morning.

"Infinitely," the younger man agreed. "Now that's enough about me. Tell me about your friends please. I want to understand them better."

"You're odd," Thomas said, reaching out unthinkingly to poke the younger man on the nose. Nicholas ducked his head, snorting weakly with laughter although his hazel eyes were glittering. He seemed to mean what he'd said though and Thomas shrugged, considering carefully before he began to speak.

"My friends are… a little obnoxious," the older man began wryly. Nicholas shoved him gently in the shoulder.

"Do it properly," he said in a reproachful voice and Thomas held his hands up defensively, green eyes warmer than they'd been for a long time.

"I *am*," he said lightly, settling back more comfortably in the chair as he continued. "My friends are a little obnoxious… *but*... they're also two of the nicest guys I've ever met… or they were, at least until we came here." The wall Thomas had built to keep his two best friends shut out started to weaken beneath the weight of his emotions. "They insisted on being there for me when I wouldn't even let anyone else get close."

He felt older as the truth of his words sank in but it also made the icy pit in his heart begin to melt and he found he was surprisingly glad of it.

"They used to spend a lot of time clubbing when we were back in the city. They liked bars and dating weirdos because they were trying to

pretend they weren't head-over-heels in love with each other."
Nicholas was listening intently as Thomas gave a fond shake of his
head, unable to completely keep the tiny smile from twisting his lips.
"I had a wager going with Hal's sister actually. We were betting on
how long they'd take to finally confess." Thomas pulled a face,
looking vaguely disgruntled. "Jessica won. I misguidedly thought they
were less stubborn than this… then again, they're official now, aren't
they? Maybe I should get the exact dates from them and see if Jess
owes me some money."

Nicholas snorted with amusement but gestured for Thomas to
continue, his hazel eyes hopeful in his tanned face as he gazed up at
the older man.

"Um… what else can I tell you?" Thomas mumbled, frowning faintly
before his lips suddenly tugged up into a faint crooked smile. "I met
them when we were just kids. I've known Hal since I was five years
old and we met Danny in drama class when we were about fourteen.
We got put in a group with him and he turned out to be so good that
we actually took the lesson seriously for once, and the teacher kept
putting us together after that. I guess I'm glad she did. We'd probably
never have spoken without her, let alone become best friends…" His
voice trailed away for a moment as he recalled how bitter he'd been
feeling recently and something that was almost guilt coloured his face
when he met Nicholas's eyes. "They're like the brothers I never had. I
love them both to pieces."

"They love you too," the younger man said and it wasn't a question.
His face fell when he saw Thomas wince slightly at the growing pain

in his leg but the curiosity in his eyes didn't dull. "Tell me more," Nicholas pressed softly. "Please. I... I really like hearing about them."

Since Thomas was beginning to get the feeling that maybe Nicholas didn't have many friends of his own - and *god*, he hoped he wasn't the only one - he couldn't blame the younger man for being curious. Daniel and Henry shone so brightly that it seemed almost expected to the older man that they would guide people in. It had worked for Thomas after all.

"Uh... let me think..." The red-haired man scratched the back of his neck, chewing his lip as he mulled over what to say. "Huh. I guess we've all been on some good holidays together too? Like, back before my sciatica got bad at least." Despite the downcast expression on his face, Thomas kept his tone as cheerful as possible, not wanting to make Nicholas sad. "We went to Sydney and Los Angeles and... and Finland once too. I liked Finland most. We saw the Northern Lights there and it was... it was absolutely breathtaking. I remember wishing I'd brought grandpa with me so that we could look up through the telescope together."

Nicholas's face softened and his hand was trembling a little when he reached to settle it gently over Thomas's.

"We don't get to see the Northern Lights here unfortunately but the snows can be impressive," he said quietly. "Sometimes it slides down off the mountain and covers the road, and none of the trucks from the slate mine can get through. You don't realise how much noise they make until it stops. It's just... silent." His expression flickered and he smiled humourlessly. "*Deadly* silent."

There was something strangely melancholy in the younger man's face and Thomas hated that he could see it festering there… wanted nothing more than to wipe it away and leave him smiling underneath.

"So," Thomas said impulsively, keen to distract Nicholas from whatever was making the growing sadness unfurl on his face. "What do you think of Hal and Danny then? Are they everything you imagined? Are you impressed?" His tone was distinctly sarcastic but the younger man simply nodded earnestly.

"Yes," Nicholas said softly. "They sound very… alive."

"Well, they are," Thomas joked, green eyes glittering. "They were the last time I checked anyway."

Nicholas forced a giggle but he looked faintly sad again and Thomas watched him uneasily, aware that that had been a strange thing to say.

(With hindsight, Thomas realised Nicholas said a *lot* of odd things. He figured that maybe Nicholas had wanted him to know his secret from the very beginning.)

Chapter 11: The Nightmare

Thomas knew he was dreaming because he was running through the house without pain.

The wooden floorboards were rotting and splintering beneath his feet, and Thomas lurched unsteadily as he staggered through the shadowy house. Daniel and Henry were nowhere to be seen, and Thomas's heart was pounding fit to burst in the fragile cage of his ribs.

He could feel someone following him - something dark and dangerous and *close* - and the panic inside ignited like a flame to gasoline.

Thomas was crushing the Polaroid of the family from the attic in his sweaty, shaking hand as he burst into the living room, desperate to be free of the sinister figure chasing him.

A choked gasp escaped him when the windows shattered, the shards of glass tumbling like blades as the scratching branches of the gnarled old oak tree forced their way in to claw at his face and the noose swung ominously towards him.

Thomas shouted out in pain and fear, covering his eyes protectively with his hands, and when he lowered them he realised with a jolt of shock that everything had changed.

A carpet of thick moss covered the floor and the ferns outside had forced their way in, twisting up in tangled snarls through the broken floorboards to knot like shackles around his ankles, binding him in place.

Dimly, Thomas wondered if their living room now resembled The House In The Forest and felt his stomach lurch sickeningly as the thought crossed his mind.

Thorny vines joined the ferns around his ankles and Thomas cried when he tried to tear them away because it was utterly useless; all that happened were the thorns piercing the sensitive skin of his palm.

He could hear his grandpa's voice in his head, the words too soft to make out although the pain in them was obvious, and Daniel and Henry's concerned voices were joining the din now as thunder rumbled directly overhead.

A bolt of lightning seared down through the ceiling and the Polaroid was torn from Thomas's hand.

He glimpsed it for a fraction of a second before it was lost in the shadows, momentarily illuminated in a way that made his blood run cold as he saw the ominous spatters of red liquid running down the glossy surface before it plummeted to land on the rotting floor beside a rusty knife that had appeared from the shadows.

A strangled cry ripped out of his throat as the lightning struck his leg and Thomas lurched violently awake, tangling his gangly limbs in the duvet and crashing down onto his bedroom floor hard enough to drive all the air from his lungs.

He was sobbing as he lay curled there in the dark, his cheeks stinging with what had to be boiling tears, his sciatica agony as a shudder tore through him. His pyjama shirt was sticking to his back with sweat and

Thomas was almost sick when he forced his eyes open to see blood welling on his palm in just the same place as the thorns in his dream. His throat felt sore from how hard he'd been crying but all Thomas could feel was gratitude that Henry and Daniel hadn't been woken by his nightmare.

They already thought he was broken. They didn't need to see him like this too.

Thomas clawed his way to his feet with more pain than he could ever remember feeling, the hot tears leaking sluggishly down his blotchy cheeks as he dragged his cane towards him. He could hear rain pounding against the glass outside and, when thunder rumbled ominously overhead, his heart lurched in his chest as the finer details of his dream came rushing back.

His bedroom door creaked achingly loudly when he pushed it open but the hallway was bathed in bright light as the storm lit the sky outside, and it was different enough to his dream that Thomas found the courage to drag himself upstairs towards the bathroom.

It took a very long time for him to climb the stairs, his bad leg weak beneath him as his back ached with pain. He made it without falling though, his cherry-red lips twisted into a grimly satisfied smile that never once touched his eyes, and Thomas relaxed visibly when he limped into the pitch black bathroom.

He heard a muffled sound coming from Henry's room - a word spoken in the younger man's sleep maybe - but all thoughts of potentially having woken his oldest friend went straight out of Thomas's head when he made the mistake of turning the bathroom light on.

The sight that greeted him in the mirror was horrifying. Thomas's face was littered with scrapes and scratches, and the splinters puncturing his pale skin were unmistakable. There were even dried leaves tangled in his blood-red hair and Thomas's jaw fell open in shock as he stumbled backwards, jarring himself painfully against the edge of the bath. His blackened, bruised eyes fluttered shut for a moment as he struggled to regain control of his breathing but, when he opened them, he swore he almost passed out.

His face was clean and unblemished, no dirt or blood in sight. His eyelashes remained spiky with tears but the bruises staining his skin from the cruel tree branches were gone, along with the splinters and the leaves. Even the thorns tearing the skin of his palm had vanished although a graze remained - maybe from where he'd fallen out of bed? - and Thomas sat down on the edge of the bath weakly, tangling his fingers in his scarlet hair as he pushed his fringe back from his sweaty forehead. He still felt shaky but the relief was starting to seep through him now as the reality that everything was back to normal sank in.

God, Thomas needed to stop consuming dairy products before bed probably.

He rose stiffly, smiling wryly at himself in the mirror as he filled his palms with cool water in the sink and splashed his sweaty face with it in an attempt to cool down. He could almost laugh at himself for having such a ridiculously vivid imagination… at least until he finally began to pay attention to his surroundings and identified the sounds he could still hear coming from Henry's room.

He'd been right earlier when he thought it was a voice but the significance of *who* was speaking made Thomas flush scarlet when he realised it was Daniel. The blond man's voice was rougher than usual, the words soft and pleading as he gasped out "*please, please, please*" before Henry presumably kissed him silent.

Thomas could hear the gentle slap of skin on skin now that he knew to listen for it, and his heart lurched painfully in his chest when he heard the sounds they were making, their voices perfectly harmonised even now as Thomas stood lifelessly on the cracked tiles of the bathroom, his shoulders slumped like he was carrying a great weight as the unforgiving light flickered before he reached out blindly to switch it off. Above him, the wet mark on the ceiling grew larger.

"You're so fucking perfect. Love you so much. Always will, Danny. *Always*," Henry gasped out desperately, the words so sincere and saturated with adoration that Thomas almost plunged down the stairs in his haste to escape. His eyes were blurring with tears again although he wasn't certain why; maybe it was the loneliness coursing like poison through his veins... maybe it was because he'd never felt so unwanted before -

And then Thomas remembered the earnest look in Nicholas's eyes that day on the porch; the softness of his voice as he told the red-haired man how great he thought he was; how *good* Thomas was, even if he couldn't see it himself. Thomas remembered sparkling hazel eyes hidden behind crooked glasses and heart-shaped lips with just the smallest hint of a smirk, and suddenly there was a confusing mixture of guilt and *lust* rippling through him like wildfire.

Thomas made it down the stairs in one piece somehow, his cane falling onto the floorboards with a muffled clatter as he got his bedroom door shut. His skin felt like it was stretched too tight over his bones but his thoughts were a mess of Nicholas now; the tanned skin of his throat and the subtle strength of his grip when his long fingers had wrapped around Thomas's that day, helping the older man up out of the road.

Thomas wanted to cry a little bit but he also kind of wanted to jerk off, and it was with a sticky hand and a heavy heart that he finally sank back down onto his rumpled sheets. Confusion was bleeding sluggishly through him as he breathed in the undeniable scent of the forest outside - maybe he'd left his window cracked open before he'd gone to bed - but his disturbing nightmare was all but gone from his mind now, buried under wave after rolling wave of Nicholas; his face lit up with hesitant smiles... his hazel eyes glimmering... his baseball shooting up through the mist, only to land deftly in his waiting palm far below.

The red-haired man swallowed two pills dry and squeezed his eyes tightly shut in an effort to ignore the guilt he could feel but it was no good. All Thomas could think of was Nicholas.

It took him a long time to fall asleep again that night.

Chapter 12: The Morning After

Daniel was frying bacon and eggs when Thomas limped into the kitchen the next morning. The windows were misty with condensation, painting the forest as little more than a jade green blur through the glass. Thomas leant against the doorway to take the weight off his bad leg, his tired eyes drifting over his best friend as Daniel whistled softly.

The younger man's blond hair was still a rumpled mess from the night before and, despite the weariness saturating his expression, his blue eyes were bright. Thomas could see a bruise sucked into the pale skin of the younger man's shoulder where Henry's too-large t-shirt was slipping. Thomas felt something that was almost jealousy unfurling inside him before Nicholas's soft hazel eyes flashed into his mind.

"I think your bacon's burning," the red-haired man called from his place in the doorway. Daniel reeled around in shock, one hand flying to his heart as he slammed back against the counter. Thomas snickered quietly at how jumpy his best friend was and Daniel rolled his eyes, exhaling shakily as he gave the older man a disapproving look.

"You *really* need to stop scaring me like that," Daniel sighed, his tone just a little bit sharp as he waited for his frantic pulse to slow. Thomas's lips twisted into a weak grin as he limped over to the kitchen table, sinking down into one of the wooden chairs with a quiet groan of relief.

"At least I wasn't hiding through the serving hatch this time," he pointed out, thinking back to that first morning when Daniel had mistakenly thought he was hiding behind the door and had almost jumped out of his skin when Thomas had revealed himself. "Daniel, I wasn't kidding. Your bacon really is burning."

"Damnit!" Daniel rushed to save it and Thomas couldn't quite resist it when he said: "Worried it's ruined? I reckon you gave Henry enough last night so I'm pretty sure he'll forgive you for this."

His words didn't even really make sense but the meaning was clear and Daniel stiffened, muscles tense although he pointedly didn't look back at the smaller man.

"That's disgusting, Tom," he said stiffly. "What the hell are you talking about?"

"Didn't think it was disgusting last night, did you?" Thomas muttered sullenly but Daniel had turned to face him now, his lips pressed together tightly as he regarded Thomas with something like disappointment. "Where is Hal anyway?" the older man continued, keen to stop Daniel from frowning at him like that. "Another morning run?"

"Yep." Daniel was still watching him with grave blue eyes as he took the eggs and bacon off the heat. His cheeks flamed suddenly and he bit his lip, worrying the metal ring with his teeth. "We didn't know you were awake last night or we wouldn't have… y'know..." His voice trailed away awkwardly and he rubbed the back of his neck just a little too hard; one of his more obvious nervous habits in Thomas's opinion. "We wouldn't have done anything to make you uncomfortable on purpose. I'm sorry if we did."

Thomas groaned, folding his arms on the table and burying his face in them for a moment before he turned to look up at Daniel, his cheek resting in the crook of his elbow.

"Why're you still being nice to me?" the red-haired man asked in a pained voice, his words coming out muffled when he buried his face in his arm again. "I literally *just* said something shitty to make you feel bad and now you're being nice to me. I really don't think I deserve that."

"Well… no offence, Tom, but I'm kind of used to you being a dick," Daniel said with a shrug. "Doesn't change anything though. I know you only act like this when you feel vulnerable or whatever, as shitty as that admittedly is. I can't speak for Hal but I know you don't mean it… not *really* anyway. I try not to let it get to me." Thomas didn't like that Daniel had said '*try*'; did that mean sometimes he actually *did* get hurt over Thomas's shitty coping mechanisms? That wasn't fair at all.

"Fuck, that makes me want to crawl off and bury myself somewhere," the older man said blandly, straightening up in his seat and resisting the urge to maybe punch himself in the face or something. "I'm sorry I'm such an arsehole, Danny," he said quietly, his cheeks flaming although hopefully that might at least convince Daniel of his sincerity. "But… I'm happy for you guys." When Daniel looked doubtful, Thomas's face crumpled as the guilt burnt inside him. "I mean… I'm really trying to be," he corrected, still looking uneasy. "Was… was last night your first time together or…?"

"Yeah," Daniel murmured, blushing too although this was undoubtedly for a different reason. He looked sort of pretty with his pink cheeks and shining eyes as his lips curved up happily, and Thomas thought he might be able to see what Henry saw in him. Daniel's smile could light a room. "Yeah, it was."

Thomas's face softened and for once he didn't try to hide how he was feeling. His counsellor had always told him that he didn't need to hide his emotions, especially from those closest to him so... maybe he *didn't* have to hide anymore, at least from his best friends. Maybe Daniel deserved to know how he felt.

"Let's see how much of this bacon we can salvage, yeah?" The blond man grinned as he turned to fix their food, dishing the fried eggs onto two plates before he grabbed the toast from the toaster. Henry would apparently be fending for himself once he got back from his morning run and Thomas felt touched as Daniel set his food down in front of him with a warm hand lightly squeezing his shoulder.

"Thanks," Thomas said softly as he grabbed his cutlery but Daniel frowned suddenly, reaching out to take Thomas's wrist. His blue eyes were focused on the older man's hand and Thomas frowned as he followed Daniel's gaze, taking in the graze marring the pale skin of his palm.

"What happened there?" the blond man asked and Thomas shrugged uncomfortably, tugging his hand free gently so that he could start cutting up his food. He shoved a piece of crispy bacon into his mouth and chewed it slowly, buying time although he wasn't sure why. He just knew he didn't want to think about how petrified he'd been the night before.

"I just… fell out of bed last night. Must've caught it on something," Thomas said with a weak shrug, fighting not to remember the thorns puncturing his skin or the terror in the bathroom when, for just a few seconds, his injuries had been *real*. "I had a bit of a nightmare and woke up thrashing around, and I must've over-balanced or something… I don't know. It's not bad though. Doesn't really hurt."

"You had a nightmare?" Daniel asked quietly, his blue eyes sad. "Another one?" Thomas shifted uncomfortably under the blond man's gaze, not liking the sympathy in Daniel's eyes. Thomas knew they were both remembering those sleepovers the three of them had had during secondary school. Thomas always used to have nightmares which resulted in him waking up in tears and apparently the knowledge that this was something he still struggled with cut Daniel deep.

"Oh, Tom, I had no idea," the blond man said gently, his blue eyes wide and sad. "I'm so sorry. Do you want to talk about it?"

"I - I don't know." Thomas had opened his mouth to say no but those weren't the words that came out. He felt *small* sitting hunched there at the kitchen table and Daniel busied himself with his food, apparently aware that the longer he looked at Thomas, the more uncomfortable the red-haired man became. "I guess it just… shook me up a bit?"

Thomas stared fixedly down at his plate, rapidly losing his appetite now, but he could feel Daniel's eyes flickering towards him briefly and he felt the urge to tell him… to just spill everything that had been upsetting him. He didn't want to tell Henry - the dark-haired man knew him better than anyone and he'd probably tell Thomas's mum if he heard how messed up his oldest friend was - but Daniel was easier to placate. All Thomas had to do was promise to take care of himself and the blond man would probably be appeased by that… and Thomas got to vent a little too. That way everybody won.

"It was just really horrible," the older man said softly. "Like… there was someone chasing me in the house, right? Some shadowy figure I couldn't see." Daniel stiffened as he processed that but Thomas continued on regardless. "The building was breaking apart around me. It was like the forest was trying to get inside and all the branches were cutting me, and I was -" Thomas broke off before he accidentally revealed to Daniel the Polaroid he'd found while he'd been up in the attic. "I was… I was scared," he said lamely. "I was *terrified*. You and Hal were there… and I could hear my grandpa too but I couldn't get to any of you and… and our house was turning into that overgrown house down the road and I felt like we were all going to be *trapped* and… and it was just... not a very nice dream."

Daniel's eyes were wide but he didn't look alarmed; just sympathetic and mildly unhappy. He patted Thomas's wrist gently, giving it a comforting squeeze.

"Shit, Tom," Daniel said heavily. "No wonder you're being irritable if you're having nightmares like that." The blond man seemed to hesitate before he looked up once more, fixing the older man with a long look. "You're still bothered by that mysterious house you saw, aren't you?"

he realised and Thomas shrugged uneasily. Daniel shook his head, his teeth worrying at his bottom lip as he glanced in the direction his best friend had insisted it was.

"You still don't believe it's there, do you?" Thomas murmured, chagrined. Daniel looked uncomfortable but he set his jaw, watching the red-haired man with the same blazing determination that he had displayed back when they'd first met in drama class, when he'd asked Thomas and Henry if they wanted to be friends with him.

"We've lived here for a couple of months now and I still haven't seen it… not that I've really been looking for it," Daniel amended after a long moment. "But I don't think you're lying. I think you really do believe something's out there… but I don't know if it's like that night with the ivy in the tree, Tom. I don't know if you're torturing yourself over something that was never there at all."

Thomas's cheeks flamed scarlet and he dropped his head into his trembling hands for a moment, hating the ripple of fear that spread through him as he remembered his absolute terror that night; remembered the appalled look on Daniel's face and the poorly hidden fear in Henry's eyes when they'd both started to wonder if Thomas was losing his mind.

"I've never seen the house," Daniel repeated gently. "But I don't want you to keep having nightmares about it so… so if you *want* to then… then how about we take a walk over there after breakfast before Hal gets home? We can stretch our legs and maybe it'll help your sciatica a bit, and we can put your mind at rest once and for all."

Thomas regarded Daniel with wide green eyes, his exhaustion burnt away by the force of his surprise. "You'd really do that for me?" he asked quietly, barely able to believe it. "Even though the house might not be safe? Even though you thought a crazy person could live there?" Even though Nicholas and his horrible father somehow *survived* in it, Thomas worried silently, going cold all over at the prospect of seeing the person who made the younger man look so unhappy and frightened.

"I don't think the house is real, Tom," Daniel said softly. "So I have nothing to lose by coming with you, do I?" There was a note of finality in his voice and Thomas didn't like how mature it made the blond man sound. It matched the purposefully calming tone of voice Henry sometimes adopted when the red-haired man was panicking and it almost felt like they were leaving Thomas behind.

"Does that mean you still think I'm crazy then?" the older man whispered, a note of fear creeping into his voice before he could beat it down. "You think I'm getting bad again? That I've been bad all along?"

Daniel closed his eyes for a moment, shaking his head.

"You know that's not what I meant," the blond man said gently, still keeping his eyes squeezed tightly shut like that would make this conversation easier.

Thomas retracted his hand slowly, his heart squeezing painfully in his chest.

"You were thinking it though," he whispered and the blond man didn't seem to have an answer for that. He just opened his glassy, tear-wet eyes and pressed his lips together like he was trying not to cry.

Daniel was looking at Thomas like the red-haired man was breaking apart right in front of him and he had no idea how to save him.

Thomas couldn't blame Daniel for that though.

Thomas had never known how to save himself either.

Chapter 13: The Way Things Were

"Watch the step there, Tom. It's slippery."

Thomas's arm was looped unwillingly through Daniel's, his pale fingers biting into the taller man's bicep as his face tightened with pain. He was struggling to keep his weight off his bad leg, and he wished he'd swallowed his pride and brought his cane with him.

A large truck thundered along at the end of their drive, sending a cascade of dirty rain water flying into the air through the mist. The tendrils of fog coiled lovingly around the branches of the trees and Thomas shivered, felt the hairs on the back of his neck rising as the unpleasant sensation of someone watching them began to settle in his bones. They were out on the pavement now, stumbling through the dappled grey light of the morning as the breeze whistled through the branches. A violent shudder tore through Daniel and Thomas stiffened as he realised the blond man felt it too.

"I think there's something following us," the red-haired man breathed and his fingers tightened on Daniel's arm.

"I know," the blond man breathed, his face ashen. The wind was howling now and goosebumps crept across Thomas's pale skin. The trees rustled behind them and his blood felt like ice in his veins.

"I think it's behind us," Thomas choked out, hating the growing fear making his voice strangled. His green eyes were wide now and his heart was pounding so loudly that he was surprised Daniel couldn't hear the roar of it.

"Fuck," the blond man whispered, closing his eyes for a moment and biting his bottom lip so hard he almost drew blood. "Fuck, fuck, *fuck*, Thomas! What do we do?!" He was still speaking in a hiss, trying to keep quiet enough so that whatever was following them didn't realise they were onto it. Their steps were cautious now, their breathing shallow and panicky. Thomas swallowed against the bile rising in his throat, tightening his grip on Daniel's arm and silently wishing once more that he hadn't been too stubborn to bring his cane with him. That would have been a handy weapon now and Thomas definitely wasn't above using it to hit someone if the need arose.

He absolutely refused to let something hurt Daniel when he always tried so hard to keep his best friends safe. Only over Thomas's dead body would anyone lay a finger on him.

"We've gotta look behind us," the red-haired man breathed, shivering despite himself as something a lot like dread unfurled in his chest. The rustling in the undergrowth grew louder and Thomas could hear Daniel murmuring to himself, soft words that sounded like: "Stop being a baby. It's just an animal. Nothing's going to hurt you."

Thomas didn't agree with him. His heart was restless in his chest and he wished –

Fuck, he wished that *Nicholas* was here. He was calm and steady and comforting; he always made Thomas feel like everything was alright… but everything *wasn't* alright.

His mind was yelling at him that something was badly *wrong* and Daniel trembling beside him as he reached for his best friend's hand only cemented it. The low roar of another truck was growing steadily louder through the mist and Thomas's instincts were screaming because he felt like it was *close* now; like it was looming up behind them, prepared to strike.

He spun round with his heart in his throat, choking the air from his lungs as the truck thundered closer and Daniel's fingers cut off the blood supply to his hand. Confusion roared through Thomas as his tear-wet vision steadied because... there was nothing there.

They were completely alone.

"Oh my god," Daniel said and he was laughing now but it sounded completely hysterical. "Fuck, Tom, we're such *babies*!" Thomas's green eyes crinkled with relief and he gave a low chuckle, running a hand through his crimson hair as the truck rumbled past them, the driver honking the horn in greeting.

"Phew," Thomas breathed. The blond man grinned at him as the pair of them turned around again and Daniel reeled back in shock, a cry tearing from him as Thomas found himself face to face with a figure standing there, dressed all in black. They wore a hood and they were less than a metre away, and when Thomas remembered the awful cloaked apparition in his nightmare, it felt like second nature to drag Daniel off the pavement into the forest, a scream ripping from his lungs.

Daniel let out a terrified sob beside him and all Thomas could focus on was keeping his feet moving as his eyes stung at the pain rocketing down his leg. He felt half-blind with tears and that was the last thought that crossed his mind before he caught his foot on a twisted root which sent him hurtling face-first onto the forest floor, his elbow and ankle exploding with pain.

"Run, Daniel! *Run!*" Thomas cried but the blond man refused to leave him, simply throwing himself back and hauling Thomas to his feet before a familiar sound greeted them.

Laughter. *Cackling* almost. That crazy fucking laughter that they only ever heard when Henry pulled one of his infamous pranks and managed to *destroy* them.

"Your faces!" the dark-haired man gasped out as he shoved his hood back from his sweaty face, still dressed in the black tracksuit he'd gone running in. "You should have seen your fucking faces! Oh my *god*, you guys!"

"That wasn't fucking funny, Henry!" Daniel screamed, still breathing like he'd ran a marathon as he lurched forwards to smack the older man weakly on the chest. Henry barked out a laugh although he rapidly sobered when he saw the tears prickling in Daniel's eyes. The dark-haired man's face fell rapidly.

"Shit, I'm so sorry," Henry said guiltily, his cheeks staining red now as he took in the blotchiness of Daniel's face and Thomas's anguished expression. "I was only joking around. I thought you'd guessed I was there. I... Shit, I didn't mean to scare you like *that*."

"You're a fucking arsehole, Hal," Daniel spat tearfully but he looked mollified when Henry drew him into a hesitant hug, at least until he wrinkled his nose and said: "Don't touch me until you've had a shower. You smell like our locker room back at school."

"Harsh," Henry said with a wince as he stepped backwards, glancing around at the shadowy trees that towered over them warily. "But I guess I deserved that though, yeah?"

"Too fucking right you did," Daniel snapped but there was the faintest hint of a smile on his lips now, like even when he was this furious, he still couldn't stay mad at Henry. Maybe that was the price of falling in love with someone. All of your principles flew straight out of the window as soon as they so much as looked at you.

Thomas turned away from them, a curious mixture of disgust and longing warping inside him as he reached out for a nearby tree branch, limping unsteadily as his knee loudly protested his impromptu run and the tumble he'd taken afterwards. He'd never been this far from the road before but he thought he recognised the trees anyway and it took him a long moment to realise why: Henry had chased the pair of them almost all the way to The House In The Forest.

Thomas's sudden fear felt like a fist gripping his heart as he spun around clumsily, suddenly frantic with the need to see their house too. It felt almost like an anchor now, like something he needed to see before he stumbled any deeper into these trees. The forest felt ancient rising up around them now and Thomas was panicking a little as he twisted in a circle, his green eyes searching frantically.

He felt half-crazy when he finally spotted their house through the smallest gap between the pine trees. It was like looking at something through so many spider webs that the shape was distorted but he could make out the old building all the same; the Victorian-era architecture and the ivy climbing the stone walls. For just a moment, the house looked ruined and Thomas's breath tore out of him in a shocked gasp.

What if that wasn't their house at all? What if that *was* The House In The Forest and the three of them were just hopelessly lost? What if Thomas's nightmare had come true and the trees had broken in to reclaim what had once been their own? It was like the first time Thomas had staggered down the driveway of the mysterious house, realising that within a century there would be no evidence that the house had ever existed there at all… unless Daniel was right.

Unless the house really didn't exist and Thomas was just losing his mind. He felt like crying as he stood there hopelessly among the trees, remembering the bruises and cuts marring his face the night before, the thorns breaking into his skin because the evidence was here right now in the sensitive skin on his palm. Thomas curled his hands into fists, fighting back a sob.

"Tom?" Daniel whispered and their sudden silence told him that they'd noticed how preoccupied he was. Thomas spun round to look at them, his green eyes wild, his cheeks still crimson with panic and exertion. The pain on his face was unmistakable.

"Tom, what's wrong?" Henry asked gently. Thomas raked a hand roughly through his blood-red hair, tearing at it as he felt a sinking feeling in his chest. This was like when Nicholas had disappeared into the forest like he'd never been there at all; like the noose that was really just ivy… just one more incident that proved how badly Thomas was deteriorating.

"It should be here," he whispered and, while Henry simply looked at him in confusion, Daniel's expression became grim.

"What should be here?" the dark-haired man asked gently, apparently detecting just how close to snapping Thomas was. The red-haired man heaved in a desperate gasp, his eyes darting about frantically as he tried to gather his bearings.

"The House In The Forest," he breathed before, suddenly, he was shouting. "That *fucking* house! The one that you both insist doesn't exist! The one that I *saw*! I can't fucking find it and now you're both gonna think I'm crazy and – and, fuck, you're probably gonna call my mum and make her come bring me home and – and I'll actually go mad if that happens, okay?! I'm gonna go fucking crazy if I have to go live in that shithole with my fucking father, and all because I can't find that *fucking* house!"

Thomas's eyes were stinging with tears and Daniel was wearing that same appalled look from that night when Henry had ventured out into the cold to investigate the noose. Thomas's knees weakened beneath him and it felt like the sudden explosion had stolen all of the air from his lungs as he forced himself to turn away, to keep searching as he stumbled blindly through the trees.

"Tom," Henry whispered, his voice shaking with tears. "Tom, where are you going?"

It had to be here. It *had* to be. Thomas could feel how close it was; could almost *feel* the comforting aura that Nicholas exuded whenever he was with Thomas, tossing that damn baseball up and down as he talked in his soft voice.

They had to be close now. There was no other option worth considering.

There was a break in the trees overhead and Thomas rushed towards it with renewed vigour, fighting against the pain in his leg, the twinge in his ankle after he'd fallen or what would surely be a magnificent bruise on his elbow from where it had struck a rotten tree trunk on his way down. He thought he could see a cracked flagstone up ahead and Thomas's breathing sped up as he limped hopefully towards it.

"Tom, come back!" Daniel yelled, voice cracking with strain. The pair of them were following him now but Thomas could feel the hairs on the back of his neck rising again; could feel the adrenaline burning in his system as the feeling of '*this is it*' began to settle in his bones.

The strange, suffocating atmosphere enveloped Thomas as he burst through the trees onto the far side of the driveway. His vision was obscured by the colossal fallen tree that had tumbled down in front of the house but he could just about make out the slates on the roof; the slowly crumbling brickwork as the ivy bit into the walls. Thomas's relief made him feel dizzy and he almost lost his footing when Daniel crashed into him from behind, leaving Henry far behind since the blond man's legs were longer and he hadn't been the one to go for a run.

Thomas pitched forwards into the dirt and Daniel looked frantic as he knelt to help him up, his eyes darting around with fear although the fallen tree trunk was the only thing at eye level now. There were hundreds of rings marking the wood and Thomas hated to see something that must once have been so magnificent simply rotting now. There would be nothing left of it at all soon.

"Daniel, did you see the house?!" Thomas asked desperately but the blond man's face was scared now, his expression rapidly becoming closed off as he refused to raise his head, apparently unwilling to peer through the branches towards the building that had been haunting Thomas's nightmares for so long.

"For… for just a moment I…" Daniel was trembling violently now and it looked like the strange atmosphere was getting to him too. His voice became strangled. "Tom, I thought I saw –"

"What?!" Thomas gasped out frantically, gripping Daniel's broad shoulders tightly in both hands as he gave him a tiny shake. "*What* did you think you saw, Daniel? A house? Did you see the house?!"

"What?" Daniel choked out, shaking his head jerkily as he stared at Thomas in complete shock. "I thought I saw a *kid*, Tom! Just standing there in the trees! But… but I can't have done, can I? There's nothing around here for miles."

Henry burst out of the trees behind them, dropping onto his knees as a wheezy breath escaped him. He looked exhausted now and, for the first time, Thomas felt guilty at having dragged the pair of them so deep into the forest with him.

"Will you fucking *stop* running off, Tom?!" Henry snapped and it was so uncharacteristic that Thomas realised his best friend really *must* have been stressed. "Jeez, you gave us a fucking heart attack almost and – Shit, Tom, you're bleeding!" Henry groaned. Daniel's face paled.

"Did you hurt yourself when you fell?" the blond man gasped. "God, why didn't you say something, Tom? Why did you keep running?"

Thomas could feel the situation sliding rapidly out of his control and it sent the panic burning in his veins again; the sheer fucking *unfairness* because, even now, neither of them were taking him seriously.

"Please just forget the damn blood!" he cried. "What were you saying, Daniel? What kid did you see?!"

"Tom, drop it! You're hurt!" Henry yelled, startling a crow from a nearby tree. It cawed its displeasure as it flapped up into the grey morning like an overgrown bat and Thomas shuddered to watch it. His eyes were welling with tears again and he peered frantically through the branches as his two best friends hauled him to his feet, slipping their arms around his waist and shoulders as they led him back the way they'd come.

"Danny, I can *see* it!" Thomas said desperately before they stepped back into the trees, the old building hidden from sight once more. "The house was there! It was *right* there! I swear it was!"

Neither of them said anything but they tightened their grips, almost like they were afraid he was going to escape again. He was acting crazy and they all knew it. Thomas deflated like someone had stabbed him with a pin.

He was frightened for Nicholas.

The fear came suddenly and unbidden but it felt like he should have been dwelling on it all along as the worry unfurled inside him. He didn't understand how the younger man could live in a place like that. The windows seemed broken and the driveway was impossible to navigate with a car, and there was no way someone could live here without transport. No way on earth.

Thomas didn't have a clue but he wanted to ask Nicholas about it; needed to understand because otherwise he wouldn't be able to sleep at night with all of the damn questions spinning around like a hurricane in his head.

"We're not going into those damn trees again," Daniel said suddenly, the heavy tone of his voice distracting Thomas from his troubling thoughts as the blond man wiped his forehead shakily with the back of his hand. "This morning walk idea kind of sucked, didn't it? What a fucking disaster."

Thomas badly wanted to make some stupid joke to lessen the guilt on Daniel's face but in the end it wasn't necessary. Henry's arm remained around the red-haired man's shoulders but he reached to card his fingers gently through the soft blond hairs that grew at the base of Daniel's skull, simultaneously calming and reassuring. Thomas's shoulders slumped between them.

The three of them fell silent when they finally made it back onto the pavement, all of them breathing heavily and covered in scratches from the cruel overhanging branches that had whipped against them as they ran. Daniel's blond hair was in disarray and there was a dried leaf caught in Henry's dark curls. When Thomas glanced down at himself as his eyes continued to blur with stubborn tears, he saw that he was covered in mud and debris from the forest floor, and his jeans were torn open at the knee to reveal a shallow gouge in his pale skin. That was where the blood was coming from.

Any words he might have spoken to break the silence dried up in his throat and Thomas felt like he was sinking into himself almost; felt like he was being locked away as Henry and Daniel continued to tow him along beneath the empty grey sky.

A Land Rover drove past them slowly, kicking up a fountain of rainwater and mud, and Thomas's heart sank in his chest when Henry and Daniel returned the driver's wave. It was their neighbours from the house with the fairy lights and the conservatory, and Thomas hated that the couple could see him like this now, when he was white-faced and bleeding, and fighting not to fall apart.

The car trundled out of sight and none of them spoke as they finally made it back to their own driveway, Thomas limping heavily between them as his sciatica throbbed painfully. The blood on his knee was drying sticky and strange now, and his ankle still twinged from where he'd tripped in the forest. His breath was coming in pants and he could barely see straight past the shameful tears boiling over in his emerald eyes as he hung his head, wishing he was anywhere else. His elbow ached badly from where he'd fallen down.

He couldn't even run when he thought his life depended on it.

He really *was* as big of a failure as his father had always insisted.

"Did you see the house?" Daniel breathed suddenly, his voice soft enough that it was clearly only intended for Henry to hear it. He wasn't quiet enough though; Thomas could feel the words cutting through him like knives. "Back in the trees when I was helping Tom up. Did you see it?"

Henry hesitated but Thomas felt the muscles tense where he was still leaning heavily against him.

"No," Henry murmured at last and Thomas's heart sank like a stone in his chest. "I don't think there's anything there at all."

Thomas's pent-up breath heaved out of him in a quiet sob but they all heard it and he loathed the angry tears burning down his face. He hated himself for dragging his two best friends into this stupid mess; hated that he could feel everything welling up chokingly inside him: the anger, the frustration, the agony, the fucking *terror*.

He hated the depression and the anxiety, and the bone-deep loneliness that not even Nicholas or his two best friends could burn away.

God, Thomas almost wished he *had* been successful when he'd tried to kill himself a few years before. At least then he wouldn't be dragging everyone else down into the fire with him. At least then they'd have a fucking *chance* at being happy here.

That seemed like an impossibility with the way things were now.

Thomas was sure he was losing his mind.

Chapter 14: Before Now

The atmosphere in the car was akin to the drive home from a funeral, Thomas was fairly certain. He'd just gone to the supermarket with Henry to pick up some groceries while Daniel cleaned the bathroom and kitchen and, if Thomas had hoped that it might prove a good opportunity to clear the tension, he had been sorely mistaken. His sciatica had pained him so much that he'd had to hold himself up on the trolley and Henry had just looked lost, wandering around with the shopping list clutched tightly in one shaking hand as he shot Thomas helpless looks whenever he thought the older man was distracted.

Thomas hated it so damn much. He wasn't used to things feeling so strained between himself and Henry, and it was cutting him up inside. Henry was as good as a brother to him and the fact that things were so uncomfortable between them now was agony. Thomas knew it was just because Henry was frightened; knew it was only because the younger man was upset that he didn't know how to help his oldest friend. Thomas couldn't blame him for that. He couldn't be very easy to live with and the guilt was eating Thomas up inside. Henry and Daniel would always deserve so much better than the mess that was Thomas, and he hated that they'd been put in this position almost as much as he loathed himself.

The tears came to his eyes unbidden and they made Thomas *so* fucking angry. He turned away from Henry as subtly as he could, squaring his jaw against the pain shooting down his leg. He gritted his teeth against the sob that wanted to escape him as he glared out of the window at the bleak landscape flying by outside. The sky was a washed-out grey and the drizzle was splattering against the windows as the wind ripped through the pine trees.

"Do you think Danny will be pissed off that we couldn't find those yoghurts he asked for?" Henry joked weakly from the driving seat, his knuckles white with how tightly he was gripping the steering wheel in his discomfort. Thomas wanted to appreciate that the dark-haired man was trying so hard to lighten the atmosphere in the car but Thomas was fighting too hard not to break down in tears. He'd never felt more pathetic. Nothing had even happened to upset him today - nothing *new* anyway - and here he was struggling not to cry while his best friend cracked shitty jokes, exhausted and unhappy thanks to him.

"Tom?" Henry said uneasily. "Did you -" Henry faltered and presumably glanced over because his voice rapidly became saturated with concern. "*God*, Tom, what's wrong? Why're you crying?" The only answer the dark-haired man received was a ragged sob tearing out of his best friend's chest and Henry grew frantic as he hurriedly stopped the car, letting it roll to a halt on a patch of muddy grass by the side of the road. He unclipped his seat belt and leant across to get Thomas's undone too, leaving his hand settled gently on his best friend's knee afterwards.

"Tom?" Henry murmured, his chocolate brown eyes wide and soft when Thomas finally dragged his gaze up to him unwillingly. His dark hair curled around his ears just the same as it had done back when they were only little and Thomas's tears boiled over. "Is it your sciatica?" Henry asked helplessly. "Are you hurting? Fuck, Tom, didn't you take your pills today? You should have said something!"

"It doesn't matter," Thomas choked out, his cheeks flaming with humiliation as he dried his tears hard with the sleeve of Daniel's soft grey jumper the blond man had wrestled him into before the pair of them had left the house. He'd been worried about the red-haired man getting too cold and, with that thought in mind, Thomas completely broke down in tears.

His shoulders heaved with sobs and Henry looked alarmed as he struggled closer, wrapping his arms warmly around the older man's waist as Thomas sobbed into his neck. Henry seemed to realise that this was something more than just pain and he stayed silent as he rocked Thomas gently, making soft calming noises under his breath as he kissed the older man's messy red hair.

"What's going on in there, Tommy?" Henry murmured, tapping Thomas's forehead gently with his fingertip. "Tell me what you're thinking. I want to help."

Thomas tried to smile at him reassuringly but his pale face was blotchy from crying and the tears refused to stop falling.

"It doesn't matter," Thomas promised with absolute certainty, hunching up as small as he possibly could in the car seat. His back ached painfully and his injuries from falling in the forest the day before didn't feel much better, the gouge on his knee especially. "*I* don't matter. I'm not worth... anything." Thomas shrugged, a tiny humourless laugh escaping him in a huff as he let his overheated cheek press against the cool glass of the window. "I don't know why you keep me around. I really don't."

Henry began vehemently to dispute this but Thomas let the words wash over him like the rain outside, going limp in his best friend's grip as the dark-haired man pulled him back in for another careful hug. All Thomas could think was how much Nicholas would hate to hear him talk about himself like that.

"Tom, are you listening to me?" Henry asked and his voice was softer now as he rubbed the red-haired man's tears away with the pad of his thumb. He waited until Thomas was watching him before continuing. "We keep you around because we love you, Tom. We always will."

Still shooting his best friend timid looks whenever there was a straight stretch of road, Henry hesitantly put the car back into gear and continued the drive home through the damp. He took the bends slowly and his hand remained gently squeezing Thomas's good knee whenever it was safe to steer with only one hand.

As they turned onto Deadman's Rise and Thomas's exhaustion threatened to leech all of the oxygen out of the car, Henry let out a small noise of surprise as they saw one of their neighbours properly for the first time.

He was an older man with a neatly trimmed beard, dressed in a navy flannel shirt with the sleeves rolled up as he cleaned his Land Rover with soapy water. He raised his hand to them in greeting and Henry slowed the car, unwinding the window so that he could greet the stranger. Thomas watched him nervously, his reddened eyes tracking the bubbles making their slow way down the older man's wrist as he wiped his hands on his jeans.

"Good afternoon, boys," their neighbour said, smiling at them warmly as Henry reached out to shake his hand. The dark-haired man's foot slipped off the clutch and the car stalled spectacularly, making the man let out a bark of surprised laughter. Henry groaned in embarrassment before grudgingly chuckling and even Thomas managed to dredge up a smile.

"My wife Amanda and I have been meaning to welcome you to the neighbourhood ever since you arrived," the man said once their laughter had faded a little. "We've been renovating our house so I've been so busy that I kept forgetting to come over to introduce myself. I'm sorry it wasn't earlier. We wanted to invite you boys over for dinner - and your friend. There *are* three of you, aren't there?"

"There are. Don't worry about not coming over before now though - that's okay," Henry said sincerely. "We've been busy unpacking and getting set up with new jobs anyway so we probably wouldn't have been great company." They laughed easily together and Thomas watched them as though through glass, his eyelashes still spiky with tears.

"My name's Martin by the way," their neighbour continued. "You know, Amanda wanted me to invite you yesterday but it looked like you three were a little busy…" His voice trailed off delicately and he shot Thomas a questioning look, his smile fading at the unhappiness on the red-haired man's face. "What were you three up to, if you don't mind me asking?"

"Oh, we…" Henry hesitated, rubbing the back of his neck awkwardly. "We were just looking to see if there were any other houses up on Deadman's Rise. We had a…. well, a bit of a disagreement about it."

Martin's eyes softened when he saw Thomas visibly wither at his best friend's words and he quickly spoke over Henry.

"Well these woods can be pretty spooky at times. Why, it's easy to lose your way and think you're looking at something strange or new. Just the other day I was out with Baxter and I got completely lost, and I've lived here nearly forty years!"

"Is Baxter your dog?" Henry asked excitedly. "Because I'm sure I've seen you walking a dog around here before and I just wondered -"

Martin looked equally excited as they began to discuss dog breeds and Thomas slumped back in his seat, vaguely considering death.

His leg flared with pain but Thomas knew it didn't matter.

The hurt was no more than he deserved.

Chapter 15: As The Sun Disappeared

"He's *definitely* a serial killer," Thomas joked weakly. "I mean, who else invites people they've never met before round their house for *dinner*? That's kind of weird."

"Maybe he's just friendly," Daniel suggested, looking slightly awkward that he'd missed the introductions earlier that day. His arms were wrapped tightly around himself against the evening's chill and his blond hair was soft under his beanie. "Maybe he and his wife are lonely up here. Maybe they just needed some company."

"Or maybe they're both serial killers," Thomas repeated sulkily as Henry locked their front door behind him. The dark-haired man gave Thomas a wry smile as he bounded easily down the wooden stairs, apparently relieved that the older man was finally cracking jokes again.

The trees were changing colour as the slow procession started down the long driveway. Whereas the leaves had been bright rubies and ambers before, they were faded yellows and browns now. Autumn was already almost over and Thomas wondered how he felt about it as he leant heavily on his cane.

Their time in the Lake District was flying past at an alarming rate. The events of the last few days already felt about a million years ago and Thomas felt strangely *old* as he followed his two best friends down the driveway, watching their fingers hesitantly entwine as they wandered along beneath the falling leaves.

"Oh crap," Daniel exclaimed when they reached the pavement, his teeth sinking into his lower lip as worry rippled on his face. "We have nothing to bring them as a present."

Henry looked slightly concerned too and Thomas's heart softened in his chest.

His best friends had had enough worry to last them a lifetime.

"Well I don't know about you two," Thomas piped up, completely deadpan. "But *I'm* bringing my sparkling personality."

Daniel snorted with surprised laughter, his posture becoming more relaxed as he turned to give Thomas a beaming smile. The light in his eyes took Thomas's breath away for a moment and he felt like he was staring into the sun as he dragged his gaze away towards Henry's happy, dimpled face.

Thomas's own relief melted away as his knee ached with pain but he fought to keep pretending that he felt happier than he was. He didn't need them to worry about him again; didn't need humiliating offers of them driving him twenty metres down the road or barely veiled concern at the state he had made of himself in the forest as he searched in vain for the house that may or may not have been there.

Martin was waiting for them as they approached the house, Daniel pointing out the fairy lights dreamily while Henry admired the gleaming Land Rover. It was polished to a shine and Thomas hastily avoided his reflection in the bright silver paint, not keen to take in his haggard face and the deep bruise-like circles staining the pale skin under his eyes.

"There you are!" Martin greeted them as Henry stepped up to shake his hand. "We were wondering what time you'd be round." He glanced at Thomas limping the last few paces with his cane and seemed to regret his words. "And you must be Daniel!" Martin said to cover his blunder, giving the blond man a cheerful smile. "Pleasure to meet you, young man. Henry was telling me all about you earlier today -"

Thomas zoned out as the introductions led them into the hallway. A grizzled old Yorkshire terrier lay curled up on a rug in the living room and Thomas held its gaze for a moment, realising that this must be the famous Baxter who Henry had been so excited to meet.

"- and this is my wife Amanda," Martin was saying as Thomas refocused on the conversation, shooting Daniel what was hopefully a calming smile when he noticed the blond man watching him uneasily for a moment. "She's been so looking forward to meeting you boys."

"*Serial killer*," Thomas mouthed, because he was hilarious and a comedy genius, and felt rewarded when Daniel hastily disguised his laughter with a cough.

"Hello, boys. I thought it would be nice for us to eat in the conservatory," Amanda said with a warm smile, wiping her hands on the apron she was wearing over faded blue jeans and a hand-knitted jumper made from pearly pink wool. She reached out to shake their hands in turn, Thomas's last.

"The sunset should be beautiful tonight with how clear the day's been. We'll be able to see Scafell Pike while we have supper."

"That sounds lovely, Mrs...?" Daniel trailed off delicately and the older woman's smile grew even kinder if possible. She looked like she wanted to pull all of them into hugs and Thomas wondered vaguely if the couple had children of their own and, if so, whether they had moved out by now.

"Mrs Hobbs," she answered. "But please, love, I *insist* you call me Amanda. Now, how do you boys fancy a nice roast dinner? We have beef, some lovely potatoes, some homegrown vegetables, and a Yorkshire Pudding too. Should be enough to fill you all up, eh?" She suddenly looked worried. "None of you are vegetarians are you?"

"Not us. That sounds perfect, Mrs - *Amanda*," Daniel corrected himself and the older woman didn't seem able to resist reaching out to pat him on the shoulder.

"You boys go and sit down in the conservatory while I finish up the cooking," she said fondly. "Martin, love, be kind enough to sort them some drinks please, yes? Dinner will be ready in about twenty minutes."

Thomas settled into a hard-backed chair in the conservatory easily enough, appreciating the natural light flooding the room as Henry and Daniel made themselves comfortable on the sofa covered in a homemade patchwork blanket nearby. Martin settled himself in a chair beside Thomas's once the drinks had been poured.

"I must say," he began in a conspiratorial tone. "It's a relief to Amanda and I that you boys have moved in across the road." That caught Thomas's attention and he looked up with a frown on his face as Henry watched Martin intently, momentarily distracted from where he'd been fussing over Baxter who had finally deigned to reward them with his presence.

"How do you mean?" Henry asked, his dark eyes strangely wary as the sun began to set in the sky outside. The world was slowly being painted in various shades of pinkish-red and Martin gazed out at the thin wisps of cloud for a moment before answering.

"Very occasionally some of the local kids down from Wasdale Head proper would break in to your new house," he said carefully, giving a half-hearted shrug of one shoulder. "They used to mess around in there, playing with Ouija boards and the like. Used to say it was *haunted*. There were sightings too, supposedly - kids said they saw a figure in the trees, rope tied in the branches. *Apparently* they heard someone screaming and other such nonsense. Ridiculous, isn't it? The things kids will make up for attention these days."

Henry scoffed at that and, although Daniel looked a little frightened, he managed a weak chuckle too. Thomas felt cold wash over him as the hairs on the back of his neck rose.

"Did that go on for a long time then?" Daniel asked weakly, his face paler than it had been before this conversation had started. "The trespassing and stuff," he amended when Martin looked at him silently. "How long has it been since someone lived there before us?"

Martin's wrinkled face crumpled for a moment and he reached to stroke his beard thoughtfully, his eyes faraway for a moment as he remembered, counting the years on slightly trembling fingers.

"We've lived here since the late seventies," he said slowly, seemingly out of nowhere. "Amanda and I moved in after our wedding in Gretna Green. We had a boy, Kevin. He's almost forty now," Martin said and he shook his head slowly in disbelief, reaching down to scratch gently beneath Baxter's collar. "A family lived in the house then. They're the only family I've ever known to live there."

"What were they like?" Thomas asked without thinking. He didn't know what had prompted him to say it and his voice was hoarse with misuse. Martin peered over at Thomas through his glasses for a moment, his eyes fathoms deep as he took a steadying sip of his beer.

"They were very kind people," the older man said softly. "Generous and friendly. It was just the three of them living there; a husband and wife, and their little boy. He was friends with our Kevin, see? They used to play together in the street, football and the like. I'm sure those two explored all of Deadman's Rise. No one knew the thoroughfare as well as they did."

Martin settled back in his seat with a low sigh, his gaze drifting towards the mountain as the sun disappeared behind it. The conservatory was getting dark now but nobody moved to switch on one of the many lamps neatly placed around the room. The shadows stretched across the ground like ink.

"The boys escaped from our back garden once, a *long* time ago now," Martin said in a softer voice, his eyes shiny with tears as he took a big gulp of his beer. "They could only have been about four or five. They tried to ride their bikes up Scafell Pike, stabilisers and all. It was *hours* before we could find them again. Amanda and I were worried sick."

He laughed quietly but the sound was distinctly watery and his eyes were damp, steeped in history. Quite suddenly, his chuckles died and he sniffed softly, his shaking hands settling on his knees through the worn brown corduroy of his trousers.

"Kevin's friend died," Martin said quietly and, abruptly, Thomas couldn't stand to hear another word. He rose painfully, his jaw set and teeth gritted as the other three looked up at him in surprise.

"Sorry, I have to use the bathroom," he explained awkwardly, cheeks flaming as he reached unwillingly for his cane. The gouge under his jeans was stinging from when he had fallen and Thomas listened to Martin's murmured directions inattentively before he limped out into the hallway towards the stairs.

It seemed to take him an age to climb them although, judging by Amanda's continued humming as she worked in the kitchen, neither his ascent nor their unnerving conversation could have taken very long at all.

Thomas paused to catch his breath at the top of the stairs but it escaped him in a pained whine as his knee flared with pain and the red-haired man simply closed his eyes, waiting for it to pass. When he opened them again, he saw Amanda hovering anxiously at the foot of the stairs.

"Are you alright up there, love?" she asked. "I thought I heard -"

"I'm fine," Thomas interrupted before softening slightly at the fleeting wounded look on her face. "Sorry, I just… forgot my painkillers tonight… but it's nothing I'm not used to. It'll be okay when I sit down again in a minute."

Her eyes became gentler as she climbed the stairs hesitantly, settling a cool hand lightly on his elbow through the sweatshirt he was wearing.

"You're very strong," she said quietly but, when he ducked his head in embarrassment to avoid her kind gaze, his eyes settled on something on the shelf behind her.

"That's you," he said quietly, taking in a faded photograph of a much younger Amanda accompanied with a pretty woman who looked a little like the lady Thomas had found a picture of in their attic. Both women were holding babies and Amanda sighed softly as she reached to take the frame off the shelf, tilting it into the pool of amber cast from the streetlight outside so that they could both see it better.

"This is my son Kevin," Amanda said, tapping the bundle she was holding in her arms. The baby had a pleasant sort of face, dark eyes twinkling with something that would one day become mischief as he reached up to grab a handful of his mother's wavy blonde hair.

"He's very sweet," Thomas replied and it surprised him a little to discover that he meant the words. "Is that him in this picture then? He looks so much like you… but he has Martin's hair, doesn't he? It's very dark."

Thomas was pointing to another photo, this one slightly more recent. It showed three primary school aged children with their arms wrapped around each other - a dark-haired boy, a blonde girl, and a smaller boy with a wild head of curls.

Thomas sighed wearily as he gazed down at their carefree faces. He could scarcely remember what those days spent with Henry had felt like.

"You're right. That's Kevin," Amanda said with a smile which softened as she took in the children's cheeky grins. "The little blonde girl is Emma. They're married now," she added with a gentle tinkling laugh. "Would you believe that? Two kids of their own and another one on the way. It still doesn't feel real."

"Congratulations," Thomas said softly and Amanda gave him a warm smile, her eyes growing damp with tears. She patted Thomas's hand where it had come to rest gently on her arm and something about the action reminded him of his mother. He swallowed past the lump rising in his throat with difficulty.

"Who's the other boy in the picture?" Thomas asked after a moment, one fingertip lightly tapping the curly-haired boy through the glass. Amanda just shook her head sadly, a shaky sigh escaping her as she settled the frame carefully back on the shelf without looking at it.

"Maybe now isn't the time," she said before silently walking downstairs back into the brightly-lit kitchen.

Thomas watched her go, standing there silently in the dark as his confusion reared up like the great mountain behind him.

Feeling as though he was being watched, Thomas turned away from the window fearfully, his eyes settling once more on the faded photograph as he looked at the children's faces staring blindly back at him.

The picture of those three friends - so much like Thomas, Daniel, and Henry - remained fixed firmly in his vision even when the red-haired man turned away. He felt uneasy as he began the slow limp back downstairs but, no matter how much he tried to bury himself in conversation, it did him no good.

He couldn't shake the worry from his mind and the picture refused to leave his thoughts.

The boy looked just like Nicholas.

Chapter 16: Mad All Along

The spell jar was full of lavender flowers, chamomile, and elderberries - anything Thomas could think of to promote peaceful sleep.

He'd been having nightmares again, dreaming of blood curdling screams and a swaying noose, and the screech of brakes piercing the stillness of the night.

Even swallowing a few painkillers when he lay in bed at night wasn't enough to knock him out anymore. Thomas was at his wits' end, hence him finally turning to his mum's Book of Shadows for an answer which was what had led him to this moment: sitting painfully at his desk after waking from yet another nightmare at little after four in the morning.

The tears he had woken up to were drying sticky on his cheeks and his expression was doubtful as he limped over to set the jar on his bedside table. Thomas gazed at it dispassionately, taking in the messiness of the sealing wax and how uneven the layers of ingredients were inside the jar. He chewed on his bottom lip unhappily; it looked nothing like the ones his mum made.

He'd talked to her on the phone the night before actually, somehow managing to reassure her that he was doing well up here, enjoying life and befriending the neighbours. She had sounded happier than Thomas had heard her in months. It was all he could do to keep his voice from shaking as he lied to her.

When the clock reached five and he still didn't feel tired, the red-haired man pushed himself laboriously to his feet and - after swallowing a few painkillers dry and shrugging into his dressing gown - Thomas struggled into the kitchen.

Intending to make himself a coffee, he filled the kettle and stood there for a moment in the empty room, arms wrapped around himself as the humming of the fridge filled the silence.

Quite abruptly, Thomas felt so unbearably lonely that he couldn't stand to spend another moment longer in the house.

He flicked the kettle off before it was ready and poured the lukewarm water over the coffee granules, his pale hands trembling a little as they steadied the mug.

Thomas felt tired and *old*, and his movements were painfully slow as he made his way outside onto the porch.

It was still dark out there, the sky a dull charcoal grey as Scafell Pike soared into the emptiness. The wind howled through the pine trees and the low rumble of a truck sounded in the distance.

Thomas shivered, quite taken aback when one single hopeless tear rolled down his cheek. He hadn't been expecting it but more followed and he simply let them fall as he settled down on the bench.

His coffee burnt his lips despite him not letting the water come to a boil. His mind was *racing*.

Thomas had gone back up into the attic yesterday while his friends were out shopping. He'd knelt there in the dust for well over an hour, trembling hands spreading out the Polaroids from the trunk as his tear-filled eyes drifted over them desperately.

He'd found pictures of the previous family who had lived here back in the seventies. Their home hadn't yet been renovated and to see it looking so much like The House In The Forest did now had shocked Thomas to the core. He had never realised that he and Nicholas lived in such a similar space.

There was still something he was missing though; Thomas was *sure* of that but he couldn't put his finger on what it was.

All he knew was that he'd sat there in the shadowy room for so long, his instincts screaming at him to *notice* for once, his posture tense as that ever-present sensation of being watched followed him even into the attic.

Sometimes Thomas wondered if there was anything there at all.

Sometimes Thomas wondered if he'd been going mad all along.

He'd been so shaken up that, even when Daniel and Henry finally made it back (an hour later than planned with love bites sucked into their throats), Thomas hadn't been able to hide it.

He'd been in a strange mood because of it all weekend and the unpleasant fog of confusion followed him into his Monday morning shift at the Barn Door Shop.

The only time he had felt anything like his old self during that week had been on Monday evening when he came back from work.

Daniel and Henry had been lingering in the kitchen, heads close together as they discussed what their neighbour had said about kids breaking in to use Ouija boards.

The pair of them had jumped so violently when Thomas had limped into the kitchen with his cane - Daniel wincing sympathetically at the sight of it - that the oldest man had actually managed a weak laugh at their shocked faces.

Henry's hand slipped from where it had been resting on his boyfriend's back and Daniel's face fell a little, like a cloud passing over the sun.

"How was your day of being a Super Ranger?" Thomas asked Henry a little sarcastically as he went to rummage in the fridge for something to eat. Daniel snorted but Henry only looked disgruntled.

"Same as always," the dark-haired man said sulkily. "And then I came home and found out that leak in the bathroom is worse than ever which is just fucking *brilliant*."

"We really should call out a plumber," Daniel said glumly but Henry simply scowled.

"I just wish we knew what was causing it!" he muttered.

"I bet I can guess what it is," Thomas said as he turned his face away, aiming for nonchalant but probably failing badly. "Some of the roof tiles have probably come loose. I bet there'll be water marks on the surrounding rafters."

He smiled innocently at them as they gawped at him in surprise but Henry was the first to recover.

"You really are the son of an estate agent," he said but, for once, being reminded of his father didn't hurt Thomas anymore.

His old world felt too far away from this strange green planet he had found himself on now.

Those London ghosts couldn't touch him anymore.

Thomas shivered again as the wind picked up once more, stirring the branches of the oak tree that grew beside their house as the trunk creaked, jarring him from his memories. His coffee was cold between his palms now. The sky was bleak overhead.

Thomas thought again of the family's pictures he had found in the attic; the young parents with their baby wrapped in its soft blanket.

He thought of Martin and Amanda's son Kevin who would be in his forties now, married with kids and maybe even a pet.

Thomas thought of an empty baseball glove and the strange boy in the picture at the Hobbs' house who had looked just like Nicholas.

Thomas wondered what had happened to him.

He wondered where the boy was now.

When the red-haired man looked up next, Nicholas was standing just beyond the porch, even despite the early hour. His glasses were still crooked. The baseball still filled his large palm.

Thomas's heart fluttered in his chest.

"Hey, Nick," he murmured. "I missed you."

"I missed you too, Tom," the younger man said gently. "You look exhausted. Why don't you sleep?"

"If you come and sit with me," Thomas said hopefully, gesturing to the bench as obligingly as he could. Nicholas considered the request before smiling softly.

"Just for a little while," he agreed as he climbed the steps.

The curly-haired man slipped his arm gently around Thomas's shoulders and, thinking of the spell jar on his bedside table, the older man felt something calm inside him.

The sun rose slowly over the mountains and the golden light spread across the driveway like the inexorable push of the tide.

Lying cushioned against Nicholas's chest, Thomas slept peacefully for the first time in weeks.

Chapter 17: With All His Heart

The light was soft in Thomas's bedroom, the quilt a little threadbare beneath him as he lay on his bed, staring up at the ceiling and relishing feeling little pain for once. Nicholas was huddled up beside him, his cheek on the older man's chest, his waist narrow under Thomas's limp arm. The red-haired man sighed contentedly.

The atmosphere was warm and comfortable, even as winter sank its teeth into the landscape outside. The oak tree was losing its leaves and an icy wind howled down the mountain.

"This is nice," Thomas murmured sleepily, cuddling closer. "Damn, why have you never been in this house before?"

Nicholas raised his head from where he had been lying in the circle of the older man's arms, still cold even despite the heater. He smiled but it didn't reach his tired hazel eyes and that was the only answer Thomas received.

The younger man had never accepted one of Thomas's invitations before - the red-haired man assumed he was shy of meeting Daniel and Henry - but they were alone tonight after the other two had gone to the Santon Bridge Inn for a date and Thomas had been determined to spend the evening with Nicholas.

"You have quite a few spell jars in here, Tom," the curly-haired man said out of nowhere as he glanced around the bedroom appraisingly. "I didn't realise you'd followed in your mum's footsteps like this."

Thomas's cheeks heated as he glanced around the room, seeing what Nicholas was seeing for the first time: the sheer number of spell jars littering the surfaces; the dried herbs hanging from the ceiling; a grid of crystals charging on one corner of the desk; even the start of an altar on a rickety little table by the wardrobe, cluttered with candles and fading tarot cards.

Thomas rarely let Daniel or Henry come in here anymore. His room was private, just like so much else of his life these days.

Somehow over the last few months, Thomas had become a closed book.

"You don't think it's weird, do you?" the red-haired man asked uncomfortably. "I'm not sure my friends would get it - Hal especially - so I've been keeping it quiet."

Nicholas rolled over to look at him fondly, socked feet tucked under his knees, shoes discarded on the floor nearby. His eyes glittered dully as he lay his hand briefly on the older man's cheek.

"I think it's brilliant, Tom," Nicholas said softly, his expression blazing sincerity. "It reminds me of my mum."

"I'm so glad mum gave me her Book of Shadows," Thomas confessed reverently and Nicholas's face crumpled with something too fond to be pain.

"Mine left hers to me too," he said after a moment of consideration. "But my dad… Well, when he went… when he turned *bad*... it got destroyed I think. I never saw it again."

The frown on Nicholas's face was far too mild in comparison to the pain in his eyes and Thomas had to swallow hard past the lump rising in his throat as he drew the smaller man into a hug.

"That's terrible," Thomas said weakly, wishing in vain that he knew how to help and deciding that perhaps he should try to remain positive. "But… do you remember any of the spells? Maybe you could start your own."

Nicholas's sad eyes became thoughtful and he gave Thomas a wan smile that did little to brighten his features.

"I remember a couple of things," he hedged, still looking uncertain. When Thomas encouraged him to give an example, Nicholas looked a little more confident. "Okay… here's one: if you write a wish on a bay leaf and then burn it, it can help the wish come true."

"I love that!" Thomas said excitedly. "I think my mum knew that one." His eyes sparkled suddenly. "I want to do it right now! We have bay leaves in the kitchen too I think. Nick, can you pass me my cane please? I'm going to go find us some."

Nicholas hesitated for a moment before taking a deep breath and reaching for the walking stick. Thomas watched the concentration on the younger man's face and found it so sweet that he almost forgot his excitement for a moment.

"I'll be right back," he said softly, one hand absently brushing Nicholas's curls out of his eyes before Thomas blushed in realisation of what he had done and hurried away as quickly as he could manage.

Out of the corner of his eye as he disappeared through the door, Thomas was sure he caught Nicholas smiling to himself.

The red-haired man located the bay leaves easily enough and returned to his bedroom with two carried carefully in his palm. He sighed with relief when he discovered that the curly-haired man was still waiting for him on his bed and a smile lit up Thomas's face when Nicholas patted the spot next to him in invitation.

Thomas rushed lighting the candle and finding them each a pen so that he could return to the bed, and his eagerness was so obvious that Nicholas let out a peal of laughter, his dimples creasing his cheeks and melting Thomas's heart in his chest.

"Here you go," the older man said softly, keeping his voice low so that it wouldn't have a chance to crack like it wanted to. "Now we can both make a wish."

Thomas turned away from Nicholas for privacy, balancing the leaf on his good knee before he leant forwards to write on it.

'*I wish Nicholas will end up somewhere he can finally be happy.*'

The letters were cramped and messy, the words barely legible, but Thomas desperately wished they would come true with all his heart.

"Done," Thomas said needlessly as he held the leaf carefully over the flame, keeping his scrawl facing away from the other man. "What did you wish for, Nick?"

The curly-haired man simply smiled at him as he let his own leaf catch alight.

"It's a secret," Nicholas said quietly, the fire reflecting in his dark eyes. "You'll have to wait and see."

Thomas grinned, accepting it easily enough. He didn't want to share his wish either. It was sappy and probably a little bit *too* sweet, and he wasn't even sure Nicholas would appreciate it.

"I like doing stuff like this," the younger man offered suddenly, one arm tucked behind his head as he lay there on Thomas's bed, looking almost like he belonged there. "It reminds me of when I used to help mum with spells. Makes me feel like she's still here, kind of… like she's still alive."

His voice trailed away sadly and Thomas felt his eyes sting with unexpected tears.

"Oh, Nick," he said helplessly, his eyelashes growing damp as he reached out to draw the younger man into a hug. Nicholas accepted it readily enough, tucking his face away into the older man's neck as they lay together.

"It's okay, Tom," Nicholas said weakly before a note of curiosity entered his voice. "Random question but… do you believe in other universes? Like, other timelines or versions of reality or… I don't know. Just parallel universes? Other versions of us?"

"You've been watching too much Fringe," Thomas teased but his eyes remained damp and a sadness swelled within him at Nicholas's uncomprehending expression.

"I've never seen Fringe."

"Oh, Nick, *I* don't know," Thomas said heavily. "What are you getting at?"

"I just… I wondered if maybe there was a universe out there where my mum was still alive… where my dad was still good and my mum was still here, and everyone still loved each other."

The words seemed to have escaped Nicholas unbidden and he clamped his lips tightly shut against the sob rising inside him. His eyes were haunted as Thomas gazed at him silently, tears rolling down his cheeks.

"Maybe there's a world where you and her got to meet," Nicholas continued after a moment, his voice weaker and more fragile now. *Delicate* almost. "Maybe she could come up with something to make you stop hurting and - and we'd be *better* and you wouldn't be in pain and… and I wouldn't be like *this*."

Nicholas's voice was wretched and he didn't seem to realise he was crying until Thomas held him closer, one hand soothingly rubbing the younger man's back through his familiar shirt.

"Please don't cry, Nick," Thomas pleaded, frightened because he had never seen the younger man like this before. "I'm sorry if I made you sad. Just… *please…*"

"It's such a human thing, isn't it?" Nicholas said coldly, like it was something he wasn't, even as the tears ran relentlessly down his face. "Apologising for someone else's grief."

"Nick, please, I'm *sorry* -"

"I hate the word please," Nicholas said sharply but he still closed the distance between them, covering the older man's lips with his own and stealing the breath from Thomas's lungs.

Nicholas kissed him like he was never going to stop.

Thomas hoped he never did.

Chapter 18: No Room For Love

The oak tree was inside their house and a shadowy figure circled it.

Thomas stared in appalled silence as the tree grew, the wooden panels covering the floor splintering around its trunk. The building creaked as the oak tree forced its way up to the second floor and, dimly, the red-haired man heard the distant dismayed cries of Henry and Daniel.

Its branches filled his bedroom and tore at Thomas's skin, and he let out a cry of horror as a noose of ivy dropped down from the ceiling. It snagged around Thomas's neck and, as he started to choke for breath, the shadowy figure overwhelmed him, as suffocating as smoke flooding into his lungs… his veins… his whole *being*.

Thomas tried to fight it away but there was nothing he could do when it was already inside him. His terror reached new heights at this realisation and, as he reached to claw clumsily at the ivy knotted around his throat, he discovered a knife clenched tightly in his hand.

The blade was rusting and old but it did the job and, as the ivy fluttered down onto the ground, cold purpose swam through Thomas like ice.

There were green tendrils wrapping themselves lovingly around his ankles but Thomas kicked them away brutally, uncaring. There was no room for love in him now. The shadowy figure filled him up to the brim and everything seemed darker with it festering in him, feeling nothing but anguish and rage.

Thomas walked across the broken floorboards without a thought, hindered neither by the undergrowth forcing its way into the house or the lack of his cane. Thomas's body was painless and his cheeks were streaked with teardrops of blood from the cruel scratch of the branches.

A great section of wall was missing from the front of the house and, as Thomas ascended the creaking stairs - as silent as a wraith - he caught a glimpse of his reflection in the mirror Daniel had hung up in the hallway. The moonlight made his blood-splattered face look demonic and, as he looked down haltingly at the knife in his hand and realised what the shadowy figure had intended, he felt it dissipate, leaving a wretched hollowness in its place that couldn't quite hide the images of Daniel and Henry bleeding to death because of... god, because of *him*.

Thomas staggered backwards in shock, losing his footing and plunging down the last few steps with a dull thud as his body crashed onto the hallway floor. The knife clattered out of his hand and disappeared through one of the cracks in the floor as a vine wrapped around the handle, coaxing it down into the darkness.

A terrible sob rose and clawed its way out of his throat like an animal as the vines rose to wrap around him. Thomas writhed away from them, thrashing in panic as one tightened around his chest, making his breath catch painfully as he struggled. Black spots danced in front of his tear-filled eyes and, as the terror he felt finally began to overwhelm him, something broke inside his head, jagged and torn.

Pain was lancing through him now, radiating from the small of his back and spreading down his bad leg like a disease. Thomas was keening and, as he became aware of the great sobs ripping out of him, he became aware of other things too.

The darkness of the house was gone now, replaced by the dim hallway light as it flickered to life. The shadowy figure was gone and the moonlight could no longer shine into the house because the wall was intact once more. There were no vines preventing Thomas from catching his breath; only startling pain and his own anxiety wrapping itself red-hot around his lungs.

Thomas was not alone.

Daniel was crouched down beside him, his blue eyes damp with tears and nothing less than horrified as he stroked Thomas's hair back gently from his sweaty forehead. Daniel's hands were shaking badly and his blond curls were rumpled from sleep. Over Daniel's broad shoulder, Thomas saw Henry hurrying down the stairs too, his face paling rapidly.

"Oh my god," the dark-haired man breathed, crumpling down beside them as his hand settled soothingly on Thomas's chest, reminding him to control his breathing before his panic attack truly overwhelmed him.

"Tom, what *happened*?" Daniel asked brokenly but Thomas couldn't look at the kindness on his best friends' faces. He didn't *deserve* it after the nightmare that had just plagued him because... god, what if it came true? What if Thomas *hurt* them without realising it?

"Did you fall the whole way down?" Henry asked weakly, reaching for his mobile like he was going to call for an ambulance or something. Thomas thought tearfully that maybe his oldest friend should have been calling the *police* instead. "Do you need to go to the hospital, Tom?"

"Do you, Tom?" Daniel asked in a much softer voice, his soft hands still gently cradling the older man's cheeks as he tried to get Thomas to calm down. "Are you hurt badly?"

Thomas tried to focus on the words through the fog of panic and, gazing up desperately into the blond man's kind tear-wet blue eyes, Thomas found the perspective he had been searching for that helped him to realise that, while he *was* in terrible pain, it was no worse than he'd felt in those first months following the car accident.

He had jarred his back painfully by falling the last few steps down the stairs and his sciatica had flared up because of it. The agony might have been breathtaking in its awfulness but it was familiar and nothing for his friends to be worried about.

Thomas drew in a ragged breath, holding the oxygen in for as long as he could in the hope that it would help his head stop spinning quite so sickeningly.

"I'm okay," he croaked, unsure whether he was lying or not. His chest still felt tight and his words came out broken, like he had to wring each syllable out with immense effort. "It's just... sciatica. Bad but... used to it. I'm okay."

Neither Daniel nor Henry seemed to believe him but Thomas couldn't let himself look at them anymore so there would be no beseeching expressions in the hopes of calming them down. Thomas felt ill every time he remembered the knife, dripping blood onto the ruined wooden floor.

Thomas's palm trembled against the panels as he reached to feel one nearby. It was still intact, not slippery with blood or warped with vines. The unthinkable had not happened.

It had only been a nightmare.

"I want… to get up," he gasped out, eyes still stubbornly shut. "Need… shower…"

"Tom, I… I don't think you'll be able to stand when you're like this," Henry said softly, his tone deeply unhappy. He'd seen his oldest best friend like this before and Thomas knew it must be hurting Henry to see it again now. "But… we can help you have a bath, yeah? Hot water always helps you when your muscles are bad… and maybe it'll calm you down so you can get some more sleep before we have to go to work tomorrow, yeah? Sounds like a plan?"

Thomas let out a broken whimper at that and Daniel's face creased with pain as he helped the red-haired man slowly up into a sitting position, keeping one arm wrapped firmly around Thomas's waist.

"Don't worry," Daniel murmured as Henry joined them too, both of them counting to three before lifting Thomas slowly between them.

"I'll call the shop tomorrow morning to let them know you won't be in."

"Thank you," Thomas breathed but he barely knew what he was expressing gratitude for now. The fog of exhaustion and shame was flooding through him again, and he hung heavily between his two friends, trusting them completely as they slowly helped him climb the stairs.

"Almost there, Tommy," Henry murmured, his voice thick even despite the tone of forced joviality he had adopted. He was trying to smile like his bottom lip *wasn't* wobbling dangerously under the threat of tears but it was no good. They broke free and Henry turned his face away almost frantically, stubbornly looking in the opposite direction as his composure crumpled. His body shook violently with the strength of the sobs he was trying to keep at bay but no one commented; not even Daniel although a tear slipped wordlessly down the blond man's cheek.

It seemed to take an age to reach the top of the stairs but, when they finally made it, Daniel did his best to take back control of the situation.

"Right, Tom, let's get you sorted," the blond man said gently. "Hal, you get him sat on the toilet or something so he doesn't have to keep standing up, okay?" Daniel marched to turn on the taps without checking to see if Henry would follow his instructions but he seemed to trust that things would go the way he wanted and Daniel wasn't disappointed.

Once the water was just on the right side of too hot, he turned the taps off and turned to look at his two friends. Thomas was sitting slumped where he had been left, his muscles spasming with pain as he gritted his teeth against the twisting burn of it. He felt like his knee was being stabbed repeatedly and the idea of putting any weight on his leg at all terrified him.

"Are you going to be okay in there on your own, Tom?" Daniel asked gently and, when Thomas looked up at him with frightened eyes, the blond man took that as all the answer he needed. "Right, okay, guess we're sharing then. Don't want you drowning on my watch."

Daniel glanced down at the boxers and t-shirt he had been wearing to sleep in before he shrugged, climbing into the steaming water with his clothes still on. His pale skin seemed to shine bone-white in the harsh light of the bathroom and, as Henry helped Thomas painfully into the bath, the red-haired man gazed up at the damp patch stretching across the ceiling.

The leak was worse than it had ever been now.

"There you go," Henry whispered, his voice still choked with tears as he helped Thomas settle down painfully against the blond man's chest. Daniel's arms came to wind around his friend's midriff automatically and Thomas let out a small broken whimper as the enormity of the situation slowly began to sink in.

He could feel the throbbing of his knee lessening a little as the bite of the hot water distracted him from his sciatica. Instead, he slowly became aware of how many bruises there were slowly blooming all over his skin from his fall down the stairs.

"We'll get you a hot water bottle and maybe your electric blanket after this, Tom, yeah?" Daniel suggested softly. "I know heat always works better for you when you feel like this."

"He can bunk with us tonight too, yeah?" Henry croaked, drying his eyes subtly with his sleeve as he watched the pair of them unhappily. "No point in him having to struggle with the stairs again."

"Good plan," Daniel said, giving Henry a warm smile although the frown on his forehead didn't lessen. "Can you go get Tom his painkillers and some water please too, Hal? He'll need them before he tries getting out of the bath and -"

"I know, Daniel," Henry said quietly, his words gentle but brooking no room for argument. Finally, he seemed to have regained his usual calm composure that often made itself apparent during emergencies. "I've looked after Tom just as long as you have."

Daniel fell silent abruptly and Henry shot him a fearful look before he tore his gaze away, drifting unwillingly towards the doorway leading back out onto the landing.

"Will you two be okay up here on your own for a few minutes?" the dark-haired man asked softly, hesitating there as Daniel continued to support Thomas in the hot water.

"I've got him, Hal," the blond man said quietly, his words a little stiff. Henry nodded mutely.

"I thought I could make us some tea," the dark-haired man said after a moment, looking a little lost there under the starkness of the bathroom light. "That might help us unwind a little."

The tap dripped loudly in the quiet and Thomas turned his face away into Daniel's neck as the shame welled inside him like acid.

"That sounds nice, Hal," Daniel said heavily, his words exhausted as he leant against the side of the bath, keeping Thomas resting limply against him. When Henry continued to linger, Daniel rolled his eyes but the unhappy set of his jaw did nothing to make the action look fond.

"I said I've got him, Hal," Daniel snapped, barely able to mask the bitterness in his voice. "He's safe with me."

Thomas closed his eyes against the tears boiling over behind his lids. He hated it when Daniel and Henry argued because of him. It made him wish the ground would open up beneath him and swallow him whole.

Thomas just wanted this suffering to be over.

"I'm sorry," the red-haired man breathed when the bathroom door clicked gently closed behind Henry. Daniel made a small noise of surprise, one damp hand returning to stroke Thomas's hair gently.

"For what?" Daniel honestly sounded like he couldn't imagine why Thomas was apologising and it struck the older man just how lucky he was to have a friend like him.

"For making you and Hal …" Thomas's voice trailed away for a moment as he struggled to find the right word. "… *unhappy*," he settled for at last, the word far too weak to sum up the weight of the guilt Thomas was buckling under.

"Try not to think like that," Daniel said quietly but he sounded a lot older suddenly, like the events of the night had aged him. "Hal and I… we have some things we need to work through, Tom. It's nothing you need to worry about. You haven't caused this… whatever *this* is."

Daniel sounded so bitter that they fell silent for a moment, just breathing as the steam dissipated like the shadowy figure had done in Thomas's nightmare. The red-haired man shuddered and Daniel only held him closer.

"That night outside Santon Bridge Inn," Thomas said suddenly, his voice breaking from the grief he could still feel even now. "You were angry with him then, weren't you? And *that* was because of me."

Daniel was so quiet that Thomas wished he'd never spoken.

"That… that wasn't your fault, Tom," the blond man said at last, his voice small and sad. "Look, I… I love Hal but… sometimes it isn't as effortless as it should be."

Thomas stayed quiet, sensing that this was something Daniel obviously needed to get off his chest.

"That night just showed me that… maybe Henry and I have different priorities," the blond man said uneasily, one hand smoothing up and down Thomas's arm automatically as it always did when Daniel felt inner turmoil. "I didn't think that Hal and I dating would… would fucking *ruin* the dynamic the three of us had like this. I thought we were going to be best friends forever - the three of us against the world - but it doesn't feel like that anymore. I love him. I *love* him. I just… hope it's enough."

Thomas didn't know what to say.

He could hear the low buzz of the light bulb overhead now; the gentle lapping of the water and the steady beat of Daniel's heart where his ear was resting on the blond man's chest.

"I love Henry," Daniel said again, like he was trying to force the words to make everything okay again. "And I love you too, Thomas," Daniel added in a softer voice, pressing a chaste kiss to the red-haired man's head. "You two are the only people I have left in the world."

"Henry loves us too," Thomas said when the sticky guilt he could feel became too much. "He loves us the only way he knows how. It might not be healthy sometimes but it's all he knows. He's trying his hardest to fix things."

"He needs to try harder then," the blond man said flatly but his hands were shaking again. "Because it isn't working."

Daniel set his jaw as he stared up at the dampness on the ceiling. He didn't make a sound but Thomas knew he was crying. He reached for the younger man's hands gently, squeezing them comfortingly between his own as Daniel tucked his tear-wet face into Thomas's shoulder.

"I'm sorry," the blond man breathed. "I shouldn't lay all our crap on you. That's not right."

"It's okay," Thomas said dully, his green eyes glassy as he lay there, taking in the watermark spreading above their heads… remembering the wonder of Nicholas's kiss filling his ribcage with flame.

That felt about a million years ago now, despite it only having been a few days.

"What were you even doing climbing the stairs like that in the dark tonight, Tom?" Daniel asked quite suddenly, his voice soft despite how jarring the older man found the unexpected words. "You don't usually get up at night like that and…" Daniel hesitated, biting his lip worriedly as he smoothed his hand comfortingly down his friend's arm again. "You didn't even look awake when we found you."

Thomas remained lying slumped against Daniel's chest, his damp clothes billowing out in the cooling bathwater, his eyes sticky and swollen with tears. He swallowed down the lump rising in his throat so that he could breathe again.

"I don't know," Thomas whispered, his voice hoarse and scratchy from crying for so long. His heart rate sped up as he remembered the fear he had felt… the slickness of the knife in his grip. "I can't remember."

Chapter 19: Just A Little Too Late

As the days skulked by, Thomas's exhaustion threatened to overwhelm him. It had settled in his *bones* now and nothing would shake it free; not his spell jars or his candles or his tarot card spreads. Only Nicholas could even come close to making Thomas feel the way he used to back in London before he had sustained the injury that was ruining his life.

The clock on his bedside table was ticking towards midnight but he couldn't sleep, even despite knowing he finally had to return to work the next morning. Daniel and Henry were watching a film in the other room, presumably just as stilted and uncomfortable as they had seemed before Thomas stormed out to escape the pair of them. The illuminated red of the numbers hurt Thomas's eyes as he silently counted how many minutes of sleep he would have if he fell asleep before twelve o'clock.

Thomas let out a frustrated sigh and kicked the duvet away recklessly, holding his breath in anticipation of pain although his knee did little more than twinge dully. He'd already taken two painkillers about half an hour ago but they weren't doing anything to make him feel tired now – they never did anymore; he felt like he barely *slept* – and there was an itchiness under his skin that was impossible to scratch.

Thomas's realisation hit him like a sledgehammer and he immediately felt stupid for it. He was addicted again. Of *course* he was.

His irritability… his mood swings and deliberate isolation… his worsened depression and anxiety… even the confusion he felt sometimes at relatively simple instructions he was given at work. He was clumsier than ever now as his coordination worsened – how else had he managed to fall down the stairs so easily? – and the light-headedness and chest pains he sometimes experienced could easily be caused by an irregular heartbeat.

Thomas lay on his bed in appalled silence for a moment, staring up at the ceiling blankly. He couldn't believe he'd let this happen again, after everything he'd put his loved ones through last time. He'd done this to *himself*.

A lump rose in his throat as he reached out for the large dark brown pill bottle, shaking it and fighting down his dread as he realised just how few tablets remained. He wondered why this revelation had taken him so by surprise.

He wasn't *stupid*, even if he did feel like he was sometimes. Thomas had known the risks of using painkillers after the pain for which they had been prescribed had subsided. He should have stopped taking them after his final check-up at the hospital, when they'd declared him fit enough to get by with nothing more than physical therapy and over-the-counter medication.

Maybe buried somewhere deep down in Thomas's brain, a little part of him had been hoping that the prescription painkillers would cure him of sciatica. Maybe he'd been hoping that one day he'd wake up pain-free and never have to feel that fiery burn stretching down his sciatic nerve ever again… but the reality should have been no shock to him.

His sciatica was chronic and Thomas knew that. He'd *always* known that. He'd just wilfully ignored it in a childish attempt to hide from himself.

He needed to call his counsellor again.

No, scratch that. Maybe he needed to go *home* instead.

The house creaked around him as it settled for the night, almost like it agreed with him. The eerie scratching sound of the oak tree's branches scraping across the glass sounded and Thomas squeezed his emerald eyes tightly shut, hating the tears he could feel there. His fingers twisted in his duvet cover as he fought down a sob.

He didn't want things to get the way they had done before. He'd overdosed by mistake, the first time. His heart had fluttered painfully in his chest and his head had swam sickeningly, and then he'd had a seizure and woken up in the hospital days later, only to discharge himself and attempt to take his own life after the absolute shame he felt.

That had been the darkest period of Thomas's life without a doubt and he was more frightened than he could put into words that he might be heading down that path again.

The wind howled as the rain pounded against the window but it made his sobs sound quiet by comparison so Thomas found he didn't really mind. He raked his fingers through his blood-red hair, struggling to get himself back under control. He didn't want to lose it now and spend the night in tears. He felt bad enough as it was and, if he was expecting himself to be able to walk to and from work tomorrow – *and* somehow manage to be civil to customers – Thomas needed to keep calm so that he could fall asleep.

He tried to steady his breathing but the tree branch was still clawing at the glass and the jarring sound was making the hairs on the back of his neck rise. Thomas shivered, drawing the duvet up to his chin. The discomfort and wariness he could feel mirrored his first night spent in the new house and, as though remembering was enough to bring the sensation back, Thomas abruptly felt as though he was being watched.

A shadow flickered through the curtains and Thomas froze in terror as he remembered his nightmare; as he recalled the *horrific* feeling of being filled from the inside out by an invisible force hell-bent on hurting those he cared about. It had twisted him into a demon; into a terrible creature prepared to destroy everything he loved in the blink of an eye.

It was outside his window *right now*, prepared to strike. It was –

"Nicholas?" Thomas asked blankly, sitting bolt upright when he caught a glimpse of the younger man's face through a crack in the curtains. "What are you doing here?"

He flicked the lamp on and stumbled across his bedroom in the dim light, wrenching the curtains back. Nicholas was standing on the other side, rain running down his face like tears as he sheltered under the sparse foliage of the oak tree. His palm was resting flat against the glass and his eyes were dark in the moonlight as he gazed back at Thomas.

The red-haired man swallowed, feeling a fluttering of something that might have been fear as he threw caution to the wind, reaching to unlock the window. It creaked open sickeningly loudly but Thomas barely noticed as Nicholas crawled inside, his flannel shirt tied casually around his waist, his curls a flyaway mess from the damp weather outside. His skin smelt like rain when he drew Thomas into a hug, tucking his cold nose away into the warmth of the older man's neck. Thomas knew his own face was pale with shock.

"Nick?" he murmured, his fingers carding lightly through the damp curls. "Are you okay? You never come round this late."

"I'm fine," Nicholas said but there was a tightness to the set of his mouth that hinted at a lie when he drew away. "I just… didn't want to be alone with dad. Not on a night like tonight."

"You're not okay at all, are you?" Thomas whispered, one hand cupping the younger man's cheek gently. Nicholas looked away, hazel eyes flashing as he distractedly nudged his shoes off. Apparently he was planning on staying for a while but Thomas found he didn't mind very much. "Why won't you tell me what's wrong? Your dad…"

The red-haired man's voice faded away as his eyes finally adjusted properly to the light and Nicholas flinched, like he'd realised his mistake just a little too late.

The younger man's arms were covered in bruises, deep purples and blacks, and Thomas felt sick as he caught Nicholas's gaze. He'd never noticed them before but that didn't surprise him; he didn't think he'd ever seen the younger man without his flannel shirt on before.

Quite abruptly, Thomas realised he couldn't see Nicholas at all but that was because of the tears boiling up in his eyes. The younger man looked ashamed of himself and Thomas couldn't help it when he drew Nicholas carefully into his arms, keeping every movement gentle as he pressed a soft kiss to the curly-haired man's shoulder.

"I'm sorry he hurt you," Thomas whispered but Nicholas didn't say anything at all.

The older man sighed softly, tangling their fingers carefully as he went to sit down on his bed. Nicholas hovered in front of him for a moment, standing so close that Thomas had to crane his head up to look at him in the shadowy room. Nicholas's eyes were darker than ever now, his eyelashes spiky with tears as he reached to stroke Thomas's hair back from his forehead slowly.

"How can I help you?" Thomas asked and Nicholas's dimpled face creased into a watery smile.

"I just want to forget," he whispered and it was the closest to a plea that Thomas had ever heard him utter.

"Then let's forget."

The rest of Thomas's words were stolen when Nicholas pushed him gently back down onto the bed, both of them giggling breathlessly into each other's mouths as they struggled to find the pillows so that they could lie down comfortably. The kiss remained light and sweet for a moment, their hands fumbling as their noses brushed together. Nicholas's long-fingered hands tangled in Thomas's hair and he nipped lightly at the older man's bottom lip, his tongue flicking out afterwards to soothe the sting.

Thomas's soft huff of laughter became a moan as Nicholas straddled him and the younger man deepened the kiss, his intentions clear now as Thomas associated Nicholas with heat and *not* cold for the first time since meeting him.

"Nick -" Thomas gasped out but he broke off when Nicholas rolled his hips down pointedly, two spots of colour appearing faintly in his cheeks as he ducked his head to kiss Thomas's neck. He was trembling and the older man reached to stroke his back soothingly through his Metallica t-shirt. Nicholas's glasses sat crookedly on his face.

"Can we?" the younger man asked desperately and Thomas groaned when he felt the faintest trace of teeth on his skin.

"Yes," he whispered.

Nicholas closed the gap between them with something bordering on hunger, kissing Thomas so desperately that the older man swore he caught the faintest taste of blood as the younger man licked into his mouth. When Thomas arched up against him with a moan, Nicholas let out a soft whimper and Thomas realised that maybe he wasn't the only one who felt out of his depth here.

Nicholas was only nineteen and, if Thomas was judging him by his own standards, he hadn't exactly been well-versed in sex at that age. Even thinking about it had made him stammer and trip over his own feet.

Now that he knew to look for that uncertainty, he could see it in every move Nicholas made and something softened in Thomas's chest. It didn't matter to him that Nicholas had asked for this and seemed content to rush it. He wanted it to be special for him, so that he could look back on it when he was older and know that he didn't regret it.

"You're so beautiful, Nicky," Thomas murmured as he stroked up Nicholas's arms gently, being mindful of the bruises. His fingers tangled lightly in the honey-coloured curls, keeping the younger man close to him as he sucked on Nicholas's bottom lip to make him whine. Thomas kissed him hotter, desperate for the sounds Nicholas was making.

God, it had been so long since Thomas had kissed someone and that had been *Daniel*, years ago now after a drunken party that Henry hadn't wanted to go to. Thomas shook the memories away like rainwater, burying his guilt in Nicholas's skin.

The younger man's pupils were blown now, his hazel eyes scrunched shut as his hips rocked against Thomas's, the friction close to unbearable. When Thomas gently gripped the younger man's hips to calm his frantic movements, Nicholas threw his head back with a groan. The dim light cast pretty shadows across his features but something tightened in Thomas's chest when he saw the hint of a bruise on Nicholas's neck, the muscles bunched tight under the skin like they were hurting him.

"Nick," Thomas croaked but - before he could speak further - the sound of approaching footsteps resonated in the hallway outside. Nicholas panicked, rolling off of the older man and slipping fluidly beneath the duvet. His hair tickled Thomas's stomach as his hands settled coolly on the older man's thighs and Thomas's breath escaped him in a whimper as Henry opened the door to peer in.

"You okay in here, Tommy?" the dark-haired man asked softly. "Danny and I thought we heard something but -"

"I'm fine," Thomas said but his voice cracked and his cheeks flushed scarlet. Nicholas shifted a little beneath the duvet and Thomas groaned softly before he covered his face with embarrassment. Abruptly, a mischievous grin spread across Henry's face and he let out a cackle.

"We heard you jerking off!" he realised with a gasp, doubling over and clutching at his sides like it was the funniest thing he could imagine. "Oh *shit*, Tom, that's so fucking funny! We thought you were hurt again or something. Danny was worried we'd have to call an *ambulance*!"

Henry was actually wiping tears from his eyes now and Thomas briefly considered throwing a pillow at his friend before worrying that he might dislodge Nicholas where he was still hiding under the duvet. Desperately, he prayed that Henry wouldn't look down and notice the peeling trainers lying on the rug.

"I *wasn't* jerking off!" Thomas insisted defensively but Henry was already turning away, covering his eyes up in a ridiculous pantomime fashion and snickering profusely.

"I didn't see anything, Tom, I promise," Henry teased.

"But... there was nothing to see!" Thomas said imploringly but it was no good. Henry had already shut the door again and ran away giggling.

'*Well*', Thomas thought wryly. '*At least he's happy.*'

Nicholas pushed the duvet back slowly but he didn't move from where he had settled down between Thomas's legs. A strange look had come into his hazel eyes that had the amusement on Thomas's face quickly turning to lust. Nicholas ran his fingertip hesitantly over the pale skin of Thomas's thigh, clearly dwelling on the older man's words when he softly asked: "Would you *like* there to be something to see?"

Thomas whimpered, nodding desperately.

"*Please*," he whispered and, for once, the younger man didn't reprimand Thomas for using the word he hated most. He just eased Thomas's boxers down instead, fingers wrapped firmly around the older man as he leant forwards to taste him.

Nicholas stayed buried between the red-haired man's trembling thighs for what seemed like hours, coaxing out whimpers and broken moans until Thomas forgot how to talk... forgot his pain... forgot his own *name*.

Until he forgot anything but Nicholas.

Chapter 20: Chase Away The Shadows

The first thing Thomas became aware of the next morning was the creak as his bedroom door swung open. A figure stood illuminated in the brightness of the hallway outside and the red-haired man's heart pounded frantically in his chest as he sat bolt upright. He was panting as he struggled to get his breath back, his chest heaving from how much his nightmare had frightened him.

Thomas couldn't even remember what had happened now. He just had a vague sense of unease; remembered creaking rope and broken flashes of a forest blurring around him like he was running through it. Thomas had seen footsteps in dust and a pool of blood spreading beneath his feet but nothing more concrete than that... nothing that made any *sense*.

"Tom?" the figure asked softly and, as Thomas's eyes slowly adjusted to the light, he saw that it was Daniel. The younger man looked tired and stressed in the hallway, bundled up in slippers and a navy blue dressing gown as he wrapped his arms tightly around himself. "I thought I heard you in here. Did you have a bad dream?" Daniel asked sympathetically.

Thomas gave a morose nod, slumping back down onto his pillows with an unhappy sigh. It felt like his night with Nicholas had been a hundred years ago now but the memory of it resurfaced slowly in his rumpled sheets and the love bite sucked into his hip beneath the faded pyjama trousers he was wearing.

"I swear you never used to have this many nightmares back in London," Daniel said sadly, hesitating for a moment before venturing into the darkness of the older man's messy bedroom. "You feel okay though?"

Thomas considered this for a moment before shaking his head, his pale face unhappy as he dwelled on the anxiety brought on by the dream. The house always felt unsafe in the darkness and Thomas let out a relieved sigh when Daniel opened the curtains, allowing the early morning light to flood in and chase away the shadows.

Thomas was still worried and his anxiety must have shown on his face because Daniel went to him wordlessly, settling down under the duvet behind his best friend and wrapping an arm around the older man's soft stomach. He didn't comment on the tarot cards or the dried herbs hanging from the ceiling, and Thomas relaxed without meaning to, one hand coming to cover Daniel's as the pair of them lay there while the world slowly woke up outside.

He missed morning cuddles with Daniel. Ever since the blond man had started falling for Henry, they had fallen by the wayside and Thomas hadn't realised how special these times were for him until they were gone. He felt as though he missed Daniel even when they were lying next to each other.

"I can practically *hear* you thinking," the blond man murmured, his forehead resting on Thomas's shoulder as their legs tangled together lazily under the blankets. "Penny for your thoughts."

"Not on your life," Thomas murmured, smiling weakly.

He didn't know how to put into words the conflicting emotions he was wading through. He was thinking about last night with Nicholas; about the younger man's soft curls and haunted eyes, and the evening they'd cast a spell together and shared their first kiss… but he was *also* thinking about the party when he'd kissed Daniel; about two clumsy sixteen year olds drunkenly making out in someone else's garden for what felt like *hours* as their hands slipped beneath clothes, touching and tasting. The pair of them had ended up in the flower bed and Thomas remembered it like it was happening right then for a moment; remembered the taste of cider on Daniel's tongue and the way his kind face was framed with flowers in the darkness.

Confusion welled up inside him and Thomas sank into the bitterness without resistance. He was twenty two years old as of November and that night in the flower bed felt a very long time ago. He didn't know what to do.

He knew Daniel loved Henry now and Thomas loved *both* of his best friends… but he thought he might be starting to love Nicholas too. A heavy sigh left him as he considered his options and not even Daniel pressing a chaste kiss to his shoulder did anything to make the ache lessen.

God, Thomas had made such a mess of things.

"You shouldn't be beating yourself up for having a nightmare," Daniel said softly from behind him, getting completely the wrong end of the stick but being so sweet about it that Thomas only felt *more* guilty. "I had a bad dream last night too. It just happens sometimes, Tom. It's normal."

"You had a nightmare as well?" Thomas asked curiously, craning his head to take in Daniel's unhappy expression. Now the stress he had donned like a cloak this morning made sense. "You want to talk about it?"

Daniel just shrugged wearily, his expression oddly protective as his head came to rest on Thomas's shoulder again.

"It was just…" The blond man's voice trailed away for a moment and he sighed, long and low. "I dreamt about this woman," he said softly. "She was really pretty – like, *strikingly* – but her eyes were the saddest I've ever seen. Even sadder than *yours*, Tom." Daniel pressed another kiss to his shoulder and, out of nowhere, Thomas realised a lump had risen in his throat which he forced himself to fight back down.

"What was the woman doing?" he asked roughly to distract them both from his reaction to Daniel's words.

The blond man bit his lip, looking more unhappy now.

"Crying," the younger man replied quietly. "Just crying. She was walking around our house and sobbing. It sounded so real though, Tom. Like if I'd opened our bedroom door, she would've been right outside."

Daniel exhaled shakily when Thomas rolled over painfully to meet his gaze, green peering into blue. Daniel drew his wrist over his eyes and Thomas was surprised to see tears streaking the younger man's face.

"I heard footsteps too," Daniel said suddenly, his voice a lot softer now. "And I think that's when I realised I wasn't sleeping anymore."

A dull shock of horror seared through Thomas but Daniel seemed not to notice it.

"I could still hear the crying so I… I jumped out of bed and ran to open the door and… and the crying stopped. The footsteps stopped. All I could hear was…"

Daniel fell suddenly quiet, shaking his head wordlessly. The hairs on the back of Thomas's neck rose as though the pair of them were being watched.

"What did you hear, Danny?" he whispered. The blond man worried at his bottom lip with his teeth.

"Rope creaking," Daniel breathed, his eyes wetter now, as though he was about to cry. Cold fear flooded through Thomas, consuming him. "I think she *hanged* herself, Tom… but… but why would I dream that? Why the *fuck* would I dream that?"

Daniel was gazing at him beseechingly, intense blue eyes shining with tears as he gripped his friend's shoulders.

Dimly, Thomas became aware that Daniel was trembling violently. He knew the blond man rarely swore either – only when he was very, *very* upset – and Thomas would have done anything in that moment to distract him.

Anything at all.

Without thinking, Thomas leant forwards and kissed him.

Daniel gasped into his mouth, fingers tangling in the older man's soft red hair for a moment as he kissed him back. A tightness that Thomas had never noticed before eased in his chest, running over his heart like warm water, and – as he sighed into the blond man's mouth – Daniel finally came to his senses.

"No," he whispered, pushing Thomas back gently although his palm lingered on the red-haired man's shoulder. "*No*, Tom. We can't. You *know* we can't."

Thomas's face crumpled as he rolled away, moving to sit on the edge of the bed. Daniel remained lying behind him, lips a little swollen, hair rumpled as he stared up at the ceiling in silence. Thomas felt something wither in his chest.

"I'm sorry," he whispered. '*Sorry for making you uncomfortable. Not sorry I kissed you.*'

Daniel reached out wordlessly to take Thomas's hand, giving it a gentle squeeze. Neither of them spoke for a while, simply existing in the same space as they avoided each other's gaze. As though from very far away, the sound of Henry unlocking the front door and toeing off his running trainers sounded.

Daniel's hand slipped from Thomas's and disappeared back under the duvet. Thomas gritted his teeth, wishing he had enough painkillers to drown his guilt out. The room was brighter now as the sun cleared the top of the trees but it seemed to dim when Henry appeared in the doorway, his dark eyes instantly zeroing in on Daniel lying beneath the covers and what could almost be described as grief colouring Thomas's face.

"You two okay?" Henry asked weakly, still breathless from his run. Neither Thomas nor Daniel seemed able to look Henry in the face but the red-haired man saw his oldest best friend wilting out of the corner of his eye and knew they needed to pull themselves together.

"We're alright," Thomas said, unsure if he was lying or not. "We both had nightmares last night so we were having a support group for it." He tried to smile and Henry's lips twitched faintly in answer. Abruptly, Thomas's guilt overwhelmed him. "We were just having a chat really."

Thomas searched desperately for a change of conversation, and settled on the mottled skin of Henry's arms and legs where he was shivering, even despite the sweat.

"Should you really go out running when it's this cold?" Thomas asked, aiming for disapproving but probably just sounding desperate instead. "It's not good to go out if it's freezing. Also you could slip over or something and I don't think you'd want me taking your precious car out in a bid to search for you, do you?"

"Nah, maybe not," Henry grinned. "Do you two want a coffee or anything before work this morning? I thought I could do us some breakfast before I shower. Peace offering, y'know? I know things have been a bit strained the last few weeks."

"That sounds really nice, Hal –" Thomas began but Daniel cut across him.

"It's fine. I can make my own coffee." The blond man finally sat up, easing himself past Thomas awkwardly beneath Henry's gaze. "I'm going to put the washing in the tumble dryer."

Henry watched Daniel leave, crestfallen. His dark curls were getting longer now, almost tumbling into his eyes as he stood there with his shoulders slumped. Thomas went to him hesitantly, leaning on his cane and ruffling the shaggy hair with a weak smile on his face that didn't touch his eyes.

"You can still make me a coffee if you're offering," the older man joked weakly. "Although if you're fixing breakfast first, I'm going to have a shower before you."

"Even after my run?!" Henry complained but his eyes twinkled faintly all the same, even despite the anger and hurt lingering on his tanned face. "Fine. But I'll leave Daniel alone for now. Seems like he needs some space." Henry glanced again at Thomas with a faint frown creasing his brow before he seemed to shake his worries away. "I'll go get my work clothes sorted while I wait for you, I guess. Think I'm going to need an undershirt today. It's bloody *freezing* out there."

Henry followed as Thomas limped slowly up the stairs, his heart racing too fast as he caught Daniel's gaze for a moment where the blond man was unloading the washing machine. Henry's hand settled on the small of the older man's back when he hesitated and Thomas thought he was going to cry for a moment as he continued up the stairs.

"Try not to freeze to death today, Hal, yeah?" Thomas suggested to cover the awkward silence. "It really is cold out there." The world was covered in frost through the bathroom window and Thomas shivered just looking at it.

"I'm sure the excitement of my job will keep me toasty warm," Henry said scathingly from his and Daniel's bedroom. The dark-haired man was somehow managing not to freeze in just a vest and shorts as he laid out some thermals to wear under his ranger uniform. Thomas bit his bottom lip, watching his oldest friend worriedly as he leant on his cane.

"Are you not liking the job any better now?" he asked, remembering that day when he'd found Henry drinking himself to distraction in the kitchen because he hated his job so much… because he'd never hated anything *more*.

Thomas wondered if Henry would hate *him* more if he found out he'd kissed Daniel.

"It's just… a job." Henry seemed upset as the truth of that sank in. "It isn't amazing like I imagined growing up. It's like when I worked in the supermarket round the corner from you, Tom. It's like work experience or… or *school*. It just *is* and wishing that would change isn't going to make it any better. I've accepted it."

Thomas's heart ached in his chest as he looked at his friend, taking in Henry's slumped shoulders and the downhearted look on his face as they heard Daniel stamping around below them.

"I didn't think living here was going to be like this," Henry said softly. "I thought we'd all be *happy*."

"I don't think anyone ever is," Thomas said, leaning against the doorframe for a moment as the words sank in. "Not in the end. Not if they really thought about it."

"How cheery," Henry muttered, sighing as he shook his head and disappeared to get something out of the wardrobe. Thomas just shut the bathroom door quietly behind him, trying to lose himself in the burn of the hot water and the steam fogging up all the mirrors but, even when he squeezed his eyes tightly shut, all he could picture was Daniel's face and Nicholas's mouth on his skin.

Thomas sagged against the cold tiles of the shower, his arms wrapping tightly around himself. He wondered what his mother would say if she could see what a mess of things he'd made. He wondered if his grandpa was ashamed of him, looking down at his only grandson now, addicted to painkillers and apparently doing his level best to ruin the relationship of his two best friends.

Thomas looked down at himself, taking in the bruises fading to yellow from where he had fallen down the stairs. He took in how his left leg was bent a little to avoid putting all of his weight on it and self-loathing unfurled inside him. Thomas wished he was small enough to disappear down the plug with the water.

He wished none of this had ever happened to him.

A heaviness settled over him as he shut the water off and stepped unwillingly onto the cold floor of the bathroom, and it reminded Thomas dimly of the nightmare when the shadowy figure had forced its way inside him, suffocating like smoke. As soon as the thought occurred to him, he regretted it because it stirred up memories of his conversation with Daniel that morning; reminded him of creaking rope and ominous forests, and the metallic stench of spilt blood.

Thomas felt distinctly jumpy as he unwillingly covered his face to towel his hair dry and he was just painfully pulling his pyjamas back on so that he could go downstairs to get dressed when a startled yell broke the quiet. There was silence for just long enough that Thomas began to think he had imagined it before he heard a cry again, closer this time, muffled only by the old wooden door of the bathroom.

Flinging his wet towel in the vague direction of the radiator, Thomas slipped across the damp floor to grab his cane and wrench the door open. Henry was hurtling out of the bedroom with a look of horror on his face, reaching for Thomas desperately before he tripped over the rug stretched across the landing floor and smacked down onto his stomach, winding himself.

"Shit, Hal, are you okay?!" Thomas asked urgently, his voice rather higher than he would have liked as he bent awkwardly with his cane to help the dark-haired man up. "What happened? What did you see?"

Henry was staring at him in helpless terror as he staggered to his feet, his finger shaking as he turned to point back in the direction he had just fled from.

"There's a…" He shuddered, giving Thomas's shoulders a little shake. "There's a huge *spider* in there!"

"Oh for fuck's sake." A relieved snort of laughter escaped Thomas even despite the dryness of his tone but he couldn't quite get his heart to stop pounding. "I thought there was something really wrong, you dick!"

"Uh… *excuse* me?" Henry asked, regaining some of his sass now even as he shot a fearful look towards the harmless arachnid. "There is a giant fucking spider in my bedroom and if you think for even a *second* that I'm going to let it live there, you have another thing coming, mate."

"Maybe you should try and get rid of it on your own," Thomas suggested sweetly, his damp red hair sticking to his forehead like blood as he raised an eyebrow at Henry. "You're meant to be a fearless ranger. You wouldn't have made it past the first chapter in the Ranger's Apprentice books with *this* attitude."

"You know I never read those silly books," Henry muttered, apparently sulking because Thomas didn't want to help him. The red-haired man gasped, giving his shoulder a light shove.

"You take that sacrilege back!" he insisted but Henry was smirking smugly now, arms folded across his broad chest.

"Maybe if you get rid of the spider for me," he said and, with a long-suffering sigh, Thomas went to let it out of the window into the freezing morning where it promptly disappeared into the ivy.

"*Baby*," Thomas said, poking his tongue out when he saw Henry peering cautiously around the edge of the doorframe. "I can't believe you screamed like that. I literally thought there was an axe murderer here to kill you. Maybe even a demon." Thomas grinned to show he was joking but Henry seemed to be considering that.

"Maybe it was a ghost," the dark-haired man teased and, when Thomas looked at him warily, Henry grinned. "What?" he asked defensively. "This is a creepy house!"

"Fair point," Thomas admitted although he was still watching Henry suspiciously, like he didn't quite trust him. "But you better not yell like that again without good reason. I mean, you scared the crap out of me! Next time I'm hitting you with my cane."

Henry snorted with laughter as he loped down the stairs easily beside Thomas who rolled his eyes in high dudgeon. Henry looked like he was fighting giggles as they reached the hallway and Thomas's own amusement was just beginning to alleviate some of the guilt he could feel when something made his heart threaten to stop beating.

Daniel was lying unconscious on the kitchen floor, one arm outstretched like he was reaching for something, his nose dripping blood down his bone-white face.

Both of them froze in horror for a moment before, as one, they rushed towards their friend. Daniel woke up almost as soon as Henry gently shook him, his blue eyes instantly filling with tears as he jerked his head towards the kitchen doorway, reminding Thomas of that morning when Daniel had wrongly thought he was hiding there. The blond man jerked his head round so quickly his neck cracked and Henry looked like he was trying not to cry as he drew his boyfriend into his arms.

"Danny?" Henry asked weakly, his sweet brown eyes damp. "Danny, what *happened*?"

Daniel's blue eyes spun wildly for a moment and, for the first time, Thomas worried that Daniel had hit his head.

"Maybe we shouldn't have moved him," he worried in a low mumble, exchanging a frightened look with Henry as the wind howled like a beast outside the windows, fighting to get in.

Upon hearing Thomas's voice, Daniel's panicked eyes became sharper and more saturated with fear.

"Someone was here," the blond man said fearfully, his voice dropping to a whisper as he looked around at the brightly lit kitchen, his words almost lost beneath the sound of the tumble dryer. "There was someone in the kitchen with me. I couldn't see their face."

"*What*?!" Henry gasped, horrified. Thomas shuddered, reaching out to take the blond man's hand and feeling a tear slip down his cheek when Daniel entwined their fingers tightly. "But who would break in like that?" Henry continued in a tight voice, his face ashen as he held the youngest man closer.

"I told you, I didn't see them properly!" Daniel snapped but his harshness was only because he was frightened. "One minute I was on my own and the next someone was taking a swing at me and – Look, I know how it sounds but I'm not lying! I *swear* I'm not. It was just this dark figure, okay? Like... like a shadow. I have no idea who it was or how they got in. *None*."

Daniel broke off in tears, his panic tearing at him like an animal as Henry wrapped his arms tightly around the blond man, trying to hold him together.

Thomas felt sick as Daniel's words sank in and he sat down heavily on the floor.

The attack sounded like one of his nightmares come to life and, as Daniel wiped the blood from his nose and buried his face in the dark-haired man's neck, Thomas felt more frightened than he ever had.

None of them went to work and Henry called the police who conducted a thorough investigation over the next few days but it was no good.

Thomas didn't think it was possible to catch a ghost.

Chapter 21: The Only Saving Grace

The weeks passed slowly as winter dug her claws into the landscape outside.

The Lake District in early December was a sight to behold, the snow clinging to Scafell Pike and weighing down the boughs of the pine trees like the picture on a Christmas card. The house grew colder with every passing day, until not even the space heaters they had dragged in from the garage were enough to keep them warm anymore.

Thomas spent his days bundled up in thick jumpers and wrapped in blankets, carrying a mug of tea close to his chest as his breath ghosted in the air in front of him. Daniel and Henry weren't much better, neither ever far from the other as they drifted from room to room, burning wood in the long-forgotten fireplaces and huddling up under thick quilts to keep warm.

Their household came to a standstill in this weather. It was impossible to get their car out of the garage and onto the thoroughfare with how heavily the snow had drifted against the house, and the only way Henry could even make it to work was by their neighbour Martin very kindly picking the dark-haired man up every morning in his Land Rover which he had intelligently equipped with snow chains for just such weather as this.

Even the trucks headed for Honister Slate Mine could barely make it along the slippery tarmac outside now. No one had expected the storm to hit so hard and, with every day that passed without a break in the snow, Thomas slowly came to the realisation that they were trapped up here.

The only saving grace was that the red-haired man no longer felt like he was going crazy.

Ever since Daniel had been ambushed by the shadowy figure in the kitchen, Thomas had realised that he had been right all along. There *was* something strange about their house. Maybe there always had been.

If Daniel agreed with him, he never said. The blond man rarely spoke anymore, his pale face set grimly instead as his exhausted blue eyes flickered warily to every shadowy corner in the house. They never mentioned the kiss they had shared but, whenever Henry went out for work, Daniel went to Thomas.

They sat together on the sofa, Daniel huddled there in Thomas's arms as they watched old films on Henry's precious flat screen TV. Daniel's breath shuddered out of him in tears sometimes but that was something else he never mentioned.

There were a lot of things they weren't allowed to talk about anymore: the guilt saturating Thomas's every moment or the want he sometimes saw burning in Daniel's eyes whenever their gazes met. These were just two more secrets left to steep in the bitter silence of the house.

Thomas could feel it pressing on his chest sometimes, a steady pounding ache of loneliness and fear, and no spell jar he made even came close to banishing the crushing sensation of *wrongness* that filled every room of their house like icy water.

The only time Thomas felt soothed was with Nicholas now and even *his* visits had become more infrequent in the wake of the shadowy figure's attack. Nicholas looked paler these days, his curls flatter and his hazel eyes taking on a strangely hollow quality that made him look ill. The bruises on his grey skin were almost black now and Thomas wished he could put a stop to the abuse but he couldn't even make it down their front steps in this ice.

He'd never make it to Nicholas's home… if The House In The Forest *was* Nicholas's home. Thomas didn't believe it but he also didn't see what other options there were. How else would the younger man appear even when the weather was so horrendously bad? Why else would Nicholas always be lingering nearby whenever Thomas was of a mind to look for him?

A knowing expression was twisting Nicholas's face as he watched the red-haired man now, almost as though he knew what Thomas was thinking. They were on the upstairs landing together, standing face to face a short distance apart in the otherwise-empty house.

Henry had persuaded Daniel to come for a walk with him, probably hoping that the change of scenery might snap him out of the fearful lethargy he had sunk into. Nicholas had arrived almost as soon as the door had shut behind them, illuminated in the weak sunlight of another late winter afternoon.

"So… remind me again why we're going into the attic?" Nicholas asked scathingly. "Because I swear you just complained about how freezing you are and I'm pretty sure it's common knowledge that broken roof tiles *definitely* don't equate to a cozy afternoon make-out den."

"Jeez, alright, Nick," Thomas muttered, rolling his eyes. "Don't pull your punches, will you? I didn't say it was going to be warm up there and I *definitely* didn't plan on us staying up there for too long. I just… I wanted to show you some stuff I found up here once. Old stuff. I think it's from the people who lived here before." When Nicholas simply scoffed a little bit, looking weirdly *afraid*, Thomas just sighed softly. "You don't *have* to come up here. There's no need to be so snarky."

The younger man wilted a little, the fear in his hazel eyes becoming more pronounced for a moment before he fought it down, his gaze flickering around them wearily as the day raced towards its end outside.

"Sorry," he muttered, clearly hating the word if the bitterness on his face was any indication. "Sometimes I guess I… I just try to hide my feelings by being like that…"

"What? A sarcastic, jumped-up, little arsehole?" Thomas asked innocently and Nicholas's lips twitched into a smile that *almost* warmed his eyes although his shoulders remained stiff with stress.

"Yeah," Nicholas replied honestly and the older man snorted, brushing his knuckles lightly over Nicholas's shoulder through the damp material of his shirt. He hadn't been wearing a coat when he'd arrived today but his skin had been just as cool as normal. Thomas didn't understand how he wasn't shivering.

"And how's that shitty coping mechanism working out for you?" the older man asked, sticking his tongue out when Nicholas elbowed him lightly in the stomach, apparently uncaring that he had a painful-looking bruise on his skinny arm.

"You talk too much," the younger man said softly. "And you *don't* ask the right questions."

Thomas looked at him in surprise, snapping his mouth shut when he realised he must look stupid for gawking but desperately wishing he knew what the younger man meant.

"There's something odd going on here, Nick," Thomas said at last, his green eyes flickering to the younger man's peeling trainers and the bruising on his neck. "I just can't put my finger on what."

Nicholas regarded him in silence for a few moments.

"Are you going to show me the old stuff you found in the attic or not, Tom?" he asked at last and the red-haired man shrugged, a little uneasy as he finally gave the younger man a hesitant nod.

"After you then," Nicholas said, his eyes inscrutable. Thomas shivered, the hairs on the back of his neck rising as he turned away, climbing up into the darkness.

Nicholas hadn't been kidding about the attic. It was *freezing* up there and Thomas's teeth started chattering almost at once, at least until Nicholas sidled towards one of the boxes nearby and conveniently returned with a musty-smelling blanket. He wrapped it around Thomas's shoulders with a strange melancholy in his eyes and the red-haired man felt a jolt when he realised it was the same yellow blanket that had been wrapped around the baby in the Polaroid he'd found.

Nicholas stroked the material gently with his thumb, his eyes glistening with something so tender that Thomas found he had to look away for a moment.

"Is it always like this up here?" Nicholas asked at last, his voice a little choked although Thomas put it down to the dust. "So *sad*?"

"I think that's just the house," Thomas said softly. "Bad things happened here. That's what our neighbour said. I don't think this is a good place anymore - maybe it never was."

"Then you shouldn't stay," Nicholas said, his voice little louder than the whisper of the wind outside. "You don't belong here."

But *Nicholas* looked like he belonged here.

He was kneeling fluidly by one of the chests Thomas had already uncovered, picking through the contents so longingly that it stole the breath from Thomas's lungs. Nicholas's fingers trembled as he sorted through the drumsticks and the bandanas.

When the younger man came across the empty glove, a funny look came over his lovely face and a shudder ran through him as he slipped his baseball from the pocket of his jeans. Nicholas nestled it carefully in the glove and he seemed to flicker for a moment in the half-light of the attic, and the sudden terror of losing him filled Thomas's lungs with panic.

He could feel the puzzle pieces falling into place but he blocked it out, refusing to accept the earth-shattering realisation that was twisting shapeless on the fringes of his consciousness.

'*Not now*,' Thomas thought desperately, even though his subconscious already knew the truth. '*Not yet.*'

When Nicholas uncovered an armchair in the corner from under a sheet with a fondly expectant look on his face, Thomas felt it in his chest: the moment The House In The Forest bled away into nothing but ivy and dirt.

This was where Nicholas belonged; not in some twisted shadow of a place that no one but Thomas could see.

"I like having you here with me," the red-haired man said quietly, his voice thick with tears he refused to shed. "We should bring my grandad's telescope up here one day. We could look at the stars together."

Nicholas looked across at Thomas through the darkness, at their two sets of footprints in the dust, as the tears sparkled on his face like rainwater.

"We've lived under the same stars all our lives," he said in lieu of answering. "We've already seen them."

Thomas looked down at his feet, his expression downcast. He wanted to beg but he wasn't sure what he'd say and besides, he knew how much Nicholas hated pleading.

"You know I have to leave, don't you?" the younger man said quietly. "I should never have come here at all. First you got hurt, then Daniel." Quite suddenly, Nicholas's eyes became urgent and he looked much younger. "It's my fault he's so angry. I brought him here. I put you all at risk just because I wanted someone to finally - *finally* - see me again."

"I see you, Nick," Thomas whispered, so frightened but unsure why. "I always have done."

"I know," Nicholas whispered, his hands soft on Thomas's face although the older man couldn't remember him crossing the space between them. He was simply there. "Thank you for seeing me, Thomas. Thank you for taking the time to look."

Thomas closed his eyes when Nicholas's lips briefly touched his, his breath cold and smelling of the forest outside - of wind and rain, and things too old to count. His fingertips brushed Thomas's face like snowflakes.

"I'm sorry you're hurting," Thomas whispered but he knew it was no good when his only answer was another whisper of wind. His emerald eyes fluttered open and the sinking feeling in his chest tore into a gaping chasm.

Nicholas was already gone.

Thomas wasn't sure how long he stood there for, the faded baby's blanket wrapped tightly around his shoulders as the tremors ran through him. Judging by the stickiness on his cheeks, Thomas thought he might be crying but he wasn't sure if that was really the case.

He wasn't sure of a lot of things.

There were footsteps and raised voices coming from somewhere far below him and, as he processed this, the pain in Thomas's knee returned with full force and he sat down heavily on the floor. His eyes had adjusted to the shadows now and a broken cry escaped him when he looked down at the wooden panels beneath him.

There was only one set of footprints in the dust. That was all there had ever been.

Thomas stared around at the emptiness with tears rolling down his face, drowning in memories and the dreams of the dead. He felt like he was in a morgue and the silence was only broken when Henry's face suddenly appeared through the hatch, tight with worry and righteous anger.

"Tom, what the hell are you doing up here?!" the dark-haired man demanded, apparently choosing to disguise his panic with frustration. "It's dangerous for you to be climbing up here with your sciatica! What if you'd got stuck up here? What if you'd *fallen*?"

"It's okay," Thomas breathed, his eyelashes still sticky with tears as his dusty fingertips brushed his lips numbly where Nicholas had kissed him. "I won't come up here again."

Henry looked a little calmer now, his chest still heaving from where he'd sprinted up the stairs, even as his dark eyes softened.

"Hey, are... are you okay, Tommy?" he asked in a gentler voice. "You seem upset."

"I... I just don't think I can live like this for much longer," Thomas croaked, drying his eyes with his sleeve. "Everything is *dead* up here except us. This place isn't beautiful anymore; it's scaring me."

Henry swallowed audibly, his eyes flickering around the shadowy space as he beckoned for Thomas to follow him carefully back down the ladder. Maybe Henry agreed... or maybe he just didn't want to put up with the red-haired man's shit anymore.

"Tom? *Tom*! I need you!" Daniel's feeble voice broke the uncomfortable quiet between them and Thomas tensed up when he took in how weak the blond man sounded... how *frightened*.

"I'm here, Danny!" Thomas called, avoiding Henry's gaze. "I'll be right down, okay?"

Daniel muttered his assent and Thomas's cheeks heated as he looked up warily into Henry's face, hating himself for how much *hurt* there was saturating his oldest friend's soft features.

"Why doesn't he ask for me anymore?" Henry whispered but Thomas didn't have any answer he was willing to share and, from the pain spreading across the younger man's tanned face, Thomas thought Henry already had his suspicions.

He left the dark-haired man alone on the landing instead, with no one for company but the spiders. His arms were wrapped tightly around himself - almost like he was trying to stop himself from falling apart - as the dust motes spun around him like planets.

From the foot of the stairs, Thomas glanced back and felt his heart tear cleanly in two at the sight of the tears rolling silently down the dark-haired man's face.

Thomas turned his back, only hating himself more as he limped away.

Henry was left alone.

Chapter 22: Surface Wounds

The stars were going out overhead, one by one. Thomas was clinging to the roof of their house, his legs firmly entangled in ivy as he clutched his grandpa's precious telescope to his chest. The wind was whipping around him like a tornado, tearing away the slate roof tiles as their house was methodically dismantled, brick by brick.

The twister was like a beast as it pressed in closer, familiar faces swimming amongst the grey smoke of it as it howled around him. He saw Henry for a moment, his dark eyes betrayed as his lips asked *'Why?'*. Daniel spun past too, limp and pale, his eyes spilling tears down his beautiful face as he turned away from the red-haired man in disgust. Nicholas floated past next, lifeless and cold, his head lolling as his broken body was battered in the wind.

A sob lodged itself in Thomas's throat when Diane reached for him, so close that their fingertips almost brushed before she was wrenched away, suffocated by the smoke. Thomas tried to stand - to reach her - but the telescope tumbled away and the wind snatched it, tearing it to pieces.

"Grandpa Ken," he croaked, choking on tears as he reached out in vain, even as the ivy tightened around his legs. "I'm sorry. I'm so *sorry*. I -"

Thomas jerked awake in shock as the front door slammed open in the hallway. It crashed into the wall with a thunderous bang and his heart raced in his chest as he tried to work out his surroundings. The wind was still doing its best to mangle the house but there was no tornado in sight now and old Ken Barnes's telescope still sat safely in its case on his bedside table.

"What the fuck?" the red-haired man breathed, feeling faintly sick at how fast his pulse was. He reached clumsily for his cane - more out of habit than need - and limped out into the hallway, freezing when he heard the creak of their front door as it swung on its hinges all by itself.

The night sky was inky black outside, the stars hidden behind thick storm clouds as the pine trees bent under the force of the wind. Snow still stretched glittering across the ground, pure and unsullied. There were no footsteps in sight… so how was the door open?

Thomas was trembling as he reached for the handle but it was no good. The wind was so strong that he had to exert a real effort to drag the door closed and the hairs on the back of his neck rose instantly, his palms growing sweaty as he had the sudden sickening feeling that something was running towards him... *chasing* him.

Thomas was panicking, shaking so badly he could barely stay upright as he forced the door shut behind him, leaning against the wood as the wind renewed its attack on the house with a threatening rattle of brick and mortar.

"Just the wind," Thomas breathed, knees still wobbly beneath him as he turned to double check that the front door was locked. "Just the wind, Barnes. Pull yourself together."

As Thomas made his slow way back down the hallway to his bedroom, a sense of dread crawled over him, impeding his every movement like spiderwebs as he slowed to a shuffle. His heartbeat sounded like gunfire in his ears and, when Thomas finally came to an uncertain halt in his bedroom doorway, he stiffened as though icy water was trickling down his spine.

There was a Polaroid lying on his bedroom floor, face-up as the smiling family stared unseeingly at the ceiling. It hadn't been there a moment before - Thomas was *certain* of that - and he felt like he was drowning in his terror as he staggered towards it, falling painfully to his knees as he scrabbled to pick it up.

He felt cold all over as he stared at it, his eyes slipping past the mother and father for a moment as he focused on the baby, taking in the honey-coloured curls and the hint of dimples creasing soft cheeks, still rounded with baby fat. Thomas took in those familiar hazel eyes and his own welled with tears, at least until the moment his bedroom window shattered over him and the shards of glass rained down onto the floor around him.

Thomas fell backwards with a cry, his hands raised to protect himself from the razor-sharp fragments as the shadowy figure barrelled into the room, its edges obscure as black mist as it twisted in the empty air, outline blurring again and again until it didn't seem to have a form at all.

"*Get out,*" a livid voice rasped, cold and numbing as it settled over Thomas's skin, flattening him to the ground as the broken glass sparkled around him like crystals. "*Get out.*" The voice became sharper, more desperate: "*Get out of me.*"

Thomas stared up at it in shock, more confused than frightened now. The moment he stopped fighting, the smoke twisted away into emptiness, leaving nothing but the uncomfortable sensation that he was *not alone*, lying there limply on his bedroom floor.

Thomas blinked, wincing a little as he became aware of a small cut on his forehead caused by the broken glass. It stung and, when he pushed himself up weakly into a sitting position, he had to blink blood out of his eyes. Leaves were blowing into his room through the shattered windowpane now and the snowflakes were already being buffeted in on the breeze, melting all over his desk.

The Polaroid was nowhere to be seen but Thomas knew he hadn't imagined it, just like he knew the disembodied voice he had heard hadn't been a horrifying demon from inside his own head. This time, it was **real**.

He was sure of it.

Thomas left his cane lying on the floor as he picked his way carefully through the broken glass, making his way to the bottom of the stairs. He had been so frightened for so long that it almost felt normal now. He wasn't sure who he would be without this fear wrapped around him like jaws.

The stairs creaked under his weight as Thomas limped upstairs, every bone in his body feeling achingly heavy as he gripped the bannister.

His palm was bleeding too and all of the bruises he had sustained from falling down the stairs throbbed in time with his exhausted heart.

Thomas couldn't be expected to go on like this. *No one* could.

He felt far older than his years when he finally came to a stop on the upstairs landing, reaching out to rap lightly on Henry and Daniel's bedroom door. His shaky exhales rose in the air in front of him like dragon's breath and Thomas shivered as he wrapped his arms around himself, smearing blood on his pyjama top.

The door creaked open after a moment and Henry peered through the gap, his expression surprisingly fearful for someone who refused to admit that there was anything strange about the house.

"Tom?" Henry whispered, glancing back over his shoulder at the sleeping lump in his double bed before he looked back at his oldest friend. "It's three in the morning. What's going on?"

Thomas's shoulders slumped a little as he reached up to rub at his head, smearing the blood across his forehead in a stark crimson line as the scrape ached.

"Something opened the front door," Thomas replied quietly, fighting the urge to glance back over his shoulder because he could *feel* that the shadowy figure was lurking there somewhere, watching, *waiting.* "I went to go shut it, then when I got back into my bedroom, the window smashed. I'm bleeding but not a lot. There was glass and snow everywhere though. I can't sleep there tonight."

"*Shit*," Henry breathed, his tired brown eyes wide with fear. Thomas shuddered, his relief blooming in his chest when the dark-haired reached for his shoulder, pulling him hurriedly inside.

It was so dark in the room with the curtains drawn that Thomas could barely make out anything; just the vague outline of the large bed and the ancient wardrobe in the corner, looming ominously out of the inky blackness like a tombstone.

"Did you say you were bleeding, Tom?" Henry asked suddenly, his voice tightening with concern and a bone-deep exhaustion that should *not* have been so easy to identify with.

"Only a tiny bit," the red-haired man said heavily. "From the glass, y'know?" He faltered, unwilling to mention his encounter with the shadowy figure although he was uncertain why. "It'll be okay. They're only surface wounds."

"Okay," Henry said tiredly, his shoulders slumping as he hung his head dejectedly. "Okay, Tom. If you're sure. Just get into bed, okay? I want this night to be over. We'll clean up the mess in the morning."

The tension felt suddenly brittle between them and Thomas's heart ached when he heard the lump rising in Henry's throat. All at once, he realised that the younger man had opened the door far too quickly for someone who had been sleeping before Thomas knocked. He must have been lying up here in the darkness, thinking… maybe even *crying*.

When Thomas clambered painfully up onto the mattress and settled down beneath the covers, he realised too late that he had taken the spot between Henry and Daniel.

He sensed the dark-haired man lingering by the edge of the bed for a moment, his arms wrapped around himself as he stood on the fringes of his own relationship.

"Come to bed, Hal," Thomas murmured, holding the duvet back and shivering a little when Henry did as he was asked, his cold feet brushing Thomas's between the sheets. Daniel murmured sleepily behind them, one arm finding its way languidly around the red-haired man's waist as the blond man settled down to sleep again. Henry's breath escaped him in a tearful sigh.

"You know I'm not stupid, right?" the dark-haired man whispered suddenly, his tears boiling into Thomas's shoulder when Henry tucked his face into the pillow. "I have *eyes*, Tom. I see how you two look at each other. I know he doesn't want me anymore."

"Hal, you don't understand -"

"No, *you* don't understand, Thomas!" Henry whispered hotly, the tears falling faster now, his sobs catching in his chest. He'd moved as close to the edge of the bed as he possibly could and Thomas couldn't go after him; he was pinned down by the blond man's arm draped over his waist.

"What don't I understand, Henry?" Thomas asked softly, too tired to fight now. "Why don't you enlighten me?"

The younger man prodded Thomas in the chest hard with a shaking fingertip, his tear-wet eyes smouldering like burning coals in the darkness of the room.

"He was *mine* first," Henry said in a hard little voice, his fingers twisting in the duvet like it was all that he had left to hold onto anymore.

"Actually he wasn't," Thomas replied a little more sharply than he'd intended to. He remembered the party; the flowers framing Daniel's pale face and the effortless rhythm of their bodies together beneath the stars. His heart seemed to swell in his chest when the blond man's forehead came to rest lightly on his shoulder, reminding him of their stolen kiss. "Daniel doesn't belong to anybody. Not me and definitely not you either."

Henry froze, gazing through the blinding darkness at Thomas with a horror that saturated the air around them. They were sharing the same pillow, so close the tips of their noses were almost touching, but they had never felt further apart.

"You… you mean that…" Henry's voice trailed away dully. There was a note of uncertainty in his voice that had rarely been present before they'd moved to the Lake District and had their lives turned upside down. Henry was shaking with anger as he lay there but the tears were still falling and Thomas's guilt was warring with *strength* now as the conflicting emotions tore him up inside… not that the dark-haired man seemed to be feeling much better than Thomas did.

Henry was used to getting his own way.

This was unfamiliar territory for both of them now.

"I'm sorry, Hal," Thomas said softly, the words sticking in his throat although he forced them out painfully anyway. "I can't speak for Daniel but... I don't think either of us wanted to hurt you. Sometimes life just... kicks you in the teeth. You have to learn to roll with the punches. You have to keep the things that are good close to your chest... otherwise, what's the point of it? What's the point of *any* of it? If you don't keep what matters close, you'll just lose it."

"Spare me the fucking lecture, you backstabbing prick!" Henry spat, rolling over and hunching up into a tight little ball under the duvet, radiating betrayal and fury. His shoulders were shaking with humiliated sobs and it was a mark of just how scared Henry really was that he *still* didn't leave the room, even now.

"I'm sorry," Thomas repeated, softer this time. He was at a complete loss to know what to do. "I really am sorry for hurting you."

"That's not enough, *Tommy*," Henry whispered, his tone venomous, his eyes scrunched tightly shut as the tears boiled down his cheeks in the darkness. "That will never, *ever* be enough."

A soft sound broke the quiet behind Thomas and his heart broke in his chest when he felt Daniel's tears soaking into his bloodstained pyjama shirt. He must have been awake for long enough to hear the fight and something inside Thomas felt like it was shattering as he lay there between them, drained of any tears he might have had left as the blood welled on his forehead and they broke down on either side of him.

The pain roared through him like a bonfire and Thomas closed his eyes tightly as he waited for the night to be over.

It felt like it was never going to end.

Chapter 23: Funeral Bell

In the cold light of day, Thomas regretted his casually cruel words from the night before.

Henry had lay crying silently beside him for what seemed like hours before finally slipping into a fitful sleep and Daniel hadn't been much better, still soaking Thomas's pyjama top with his tears. The guilt had settled over them like a shroud and Thomas knew then that this had all been a terrible mistake.

He should never have been so blunt to Henry and he *definitely* shouldn't have made such an impulsive decision without speaking to Daniel first. Thomas had torn everything to pieces and he couldn't see any way of putting things back together again.

Henry would never forgive him and the older man couldn't find it in himself to resent his oldest friend for that. Thomas had tried to carve Henry's heart right out of his chest and he couldn't think of a single excuse as to why his behaviour had been acceptable.

Maybe it was the house, messing with his head and making him latch on to anything that made him feel safe… or maybe this was just who Thomas was now – just who Thomas had *always* been – twisted and broken, and lashing out at everyone around him because, if *he* couldn't be happy, why did anyone else deserve to be?

That was the one that rang truthfully as a funeral bell in his chest. It was the reason that Thomas had never had any friends except Henry and Daniel. It was the reason that none of his cousins had ever wanted to play with him when he was a child.

It was the reason that Thomas was slowly turning into his father the older he got.

Thomas saw Peter Barnes's face when he looked in the mirror sometimes, eyes burning with this desperate fear that nothing he did would ever be enough. It felt like everything was sliding out of Thomas's grip like the melting snow outside. Thomas was following in his father's footsteps and there seemed to be no way off the path that had been set out for him. It felt like fate that Thomas was destined to cause so much unhappiness to the people he cared about.

He dwelled on this for hours before finally drifting into unconsciousness sometime around five in the morning but, when he finally gave up on the pretence of sleep when the sun was just beginning to clear the horizon, Henry was already gone.

Daniel was still lying beside Thomas but he wasn't sleeping. His arms were wrapped tightly around his folded legs and his eyes were sore from crying so much the night before. Daniel was watching Thomas with this appalled kind of resignation, shying away when the older man reached for him hesitantly.

"Don't," Daniel whispered, his bright eyes welling with tears again. "We can't, Tom. Surely even *you* can see that."

The blond man struggled out from under the covers and Thomas didn't stop him. He simply watched through exhausted gritty-feeling eyes as Daniel walked away from him into the brighter light of the hallway.

"I didn't mean to hurt anyone," Thomas said softly and the younger man stiffened, his shoulders tense as he shot a reproachful glance over his shoulder.

"Do you think that makes a single bit of difference?" Daniel asked sharply. Thomas's cheeks heated and he resisted the urge to drag the duvet over his head in a sulk.

"I don't need *you* talking to me like that too," he snapped. "You're not innocent in this, Daniel. You kissed me back, remember?"

Henry – who had just reappeared in the doorway – made a sound like someone had kicked him in the stomach.

"Great job, Tom," Daniel said tightly, his eyes spilling furious tears again as he stormed out of the room, refusing to look at either of them. "This is just *perfect*."

Henry was sagging against the doorframe, his face paler than Thomas had ever seen it and – quite suddenly – all of the pain and fear the house had caused Thomas was *nothing* compared to the agony saturating Henry's face.

He looked broken inside and Thomas didn't think he could fix things this time.

"I've boarded up the window in your room," Henry muttered without looking the older man in the eye. "I'm going to work now. Handing my resignation in after so I won't be back 'til late."

Thomas sat up stiffly, worrying at his bottom lip between his teeth as he regarded the dark-haired man unhappily.

"You're quitting?" he whispered. "After everything that's happened?"

"No other option for me now," Henry said heavily, still directing his gaze at the floor. "Quite frankly, I can't stand to look at either of you for a second longer than I have to." A hint of last night's venom had returned to his voice but he just sounded tired now, like he was almost too weak to stand up. "You make me *sick*, Thomas."

"But... but, Hal..." Thomas didn't know how to put into words the emotions that were roaring through him. He just wanted the dark-haired man to see *sense*. "But this was your dream," he said imploringly, his green eyes downcast. "All you ever wanted was to be a ranger."

Henry actually laughed and the sound was like nails grating over a blackboard, making Thomas wince.

"My dream? My *dream*?!" Another bubble of helpless laughter escaped him but his eyes were so cold. "No, this is a fucking nightmare, Thomas. You and this godforsaken house made sure of that."

Henry took a deep, steadying breath before he finally pushed away from the doorframe, strong enough to stand alone.

"As soon as this snow melts," he said quietly. "I'm leaving."

Thomas watched him go – his best friend of almost two decades – and realised far too late that there was a hole in his heart now that would never be filled. Henry had spent so many years dedicating himself to building Thomas's confidence and happiness, and Thomas had repaid him by destroying Henry's relationships both with the first man he had ever loved and his first true friend, all in one fell swoop.

"Hal?" Thomas asked in a small voice, speaking before he could overthink it. "Do you think I'm a bit like my dad now?"

The younger man froze, his shoulders hunched as he clearly weighed his response carefully before speaking.

"No," Henry said after a moment, his voice even harder now, his hands curled into fists by his sides. "No, I think you're *exactly* like him."

Henry went downstairs, leaving Thomas to slump back down onto the rumpled sheets again as he stared up listlessly at the ceiling, unable to find it in himself to deny the words… and maybe that was the worst part. What Henry had said was *true*.

There was no one who felt more like the world was holding out on him than Peter Barnes… except perhaps his son.

Thomas always went for the quickest fix to his problems instead of addressing them properly. That was why he tried to lose himself in Daniel when the mystery of Nicholas caused him too much fear… and that was why Peter had ran his own son over in the car.

He had always hated Thomas; had thought him a waste of space because he never listened to his father, always intentionally defying him and refusing to let them get close to each other. The hatred had burnt deeper than that though; had stemmed from Peter's own unhealthy relationship with his father and the abandonment he had experienced after losing his mother at a young age.

After exploring it in counselling with Linda, Thomas had come to the conclusion that Peter felt the way he did about his son because he was scared of losing Diane too. He was afraid that if she loved her son, there wouldn't be enough left for him and – being more than a little unhinged anyway after years of alcohol and drug dependency (which required a mind-set that seemed to be hereditary, Thomas thought bitterly) – Peter had done everything he could to make his son leave, first shouting and threatening him before trying more permanent methods.

Peter had seen his son crossing the road on his way home from college and his foot hadn't shifted from the accelerator. The car had hurtled on and Thomas had noticed far too late that he was directly in its path.

It was coincidence… chance... *fate*.

'*No, I think you're **exactly** like him.*'

The light in Thomas's eyes waned.

Was that how Henry felt now? Like Thomas had betrayed him *that* badly?

He stayed lying on the bed until he heard the front door close behind Henry an hour later, cowardly to the end.

Daniel was waiting for him downstairs, pale-faced and exhausted as he drank coffee at the dining table. The colour scheme in that room was largely grey and it seemed to match their moods when Thomas finally sat down across from him, cradling a glass of orange juice between his shaking hands.

"Did he talk to you after I left?" Daniel asked quietly, grimacing a little when he broke the silence. Thomas nodded mournfully and the blond man sighed, his broad shoulders slumping as though under a great weight. "What did he say?"

Thomas hesitated, mulling the words over in silence for a moment as he allowed them to sink in.

"That I'm just like my dad… and that I make him sick." A frown creased Daniel's brow as he heard those words but Thomas ploughed on regardless. "Oh, he's quitting his job too. Says he's moving out once the snow melts." An awkward silence grew between them as Thomas spoke one last time. "He said living here was a nightmare."

Daniel shivered, glaring around at the living room's shadowy corners and squaring his shoulders against the chill.

"It is," he agreed before taking a sip of his coffee, his nose red with the cold. "Hal was wrong last night though… about me not wanting him anymore. I just… I guess I was just never ready to admit that I wanted you too, Tom."

Daniel's face seemed to collapse in on itself as a tear slipped down his cheek. "You were right earlier when you said that I wasn't innocent," he said quietly, his voice weak and ashamed. "I've always loved you both too much. Ever since I came out and my family didn't want to know, I loved you both."

Another tear rolled down Daniel's cheek and his bottom lip wobbled as he peered into the depths of his mug like, if he only searched hard enough, it might give him the answers he needed.

"I've loved you both for so long now," the blond man murmured, looking up at Thomas with something like loss. "I don't know who I am without you both. I don't know how I'll cope."

"You'll have to cope," Thomas said softly. "There's no other option left."

Daniel pushed his coffee away shakily, burying his face in his hands as he took a deep breath.

"Henry hates me now," he whispered and, although Thomas's hand twitched towards Daniel in an effort to offer comfort, he didn't touch him. He wasn't sure he was allowed anymore.

"Did he tell you that?" Thomas asked but Daniel shook his head, the tear tracks silvery on his cheeks as the winter sun drifted higher in the sky outside. The icicles hanging on the branches of the oak tree were beginning to melt and the steady dripping sound was like a ticking clock, bringing them closer and closer to the moment when Henry would leave them for good.

"No," Daniel replied after so long that Thomas almost forgot he'd even asked a question. "But I know he does. He… he told me this morning that he's moving back in with his family. He said I can go with him, if I want to… like a second chance." Daniel's voice twisted around the words and he reached out to grip Thomas's hand tightly, their knuckles white as pearls in the muted light. "He told me that… if I stay here with you, we're over."

"What did you tell him?" Thomas breathed, his heart rising in his throat. Daniel raised their entwined hands, pressing a tear-wet kiss to the older man's knuckles.

"I told him I guessed I was staying here then."

Despite how nonchalantly Daniel had spoken, Thomas knew it was forced. The younger man was shaking, his eyelashes spiky with tears, the pain on his face clear for anyone who cared enough to look.

"I couldn't go back to London," Daniel whispered, sounding almost like he was trying to convince himself now. "My family are… they're never going to forgive me for being the way I am… and you wouldn't exactly rush back either, would you? I won't lose *both* of you. I can't."

"This is all my fault," Thomas muttered and Daniel gave him a watery smile that didn't touch his eyes.

"That's awfully self-centred of you," the blond man said, his weak grin fading away as he gazed out of the window, at the fateful dripping of the melting snow. "I'm big enough to make my own mistakes."

Thomas recoiled, stung.

"*Mistake*?" he asked, his hand slipping free even though he'd thought the same thing himself the night before. Daniel gazed at him steadily, unapologetic.

"I love you both, Tom, but what the hell would you call this mess we've got ourselves in?" he asked, tone dry. "This is a fuck-up of epic proportions."

"It's not a joke, Daniel," Thomas pointed out and the blond man sighed heavily.

"Don't you think I know that, Tom?" Daniel shook his head, his expression nothing short of shattered. "If I don't laugh, I'll cry… and I think I've cried enough for a lifetime since moving here, don't you?"

"True enough," Thomas admitted.

They lapsed into silence again, watching as the world woke up outside. Daniel had to work later that day – his first shift since he'd been attacked – and Thomas wasn't relishing spending the afternoon on his own.

"I do love Henry," Daniel said into the silence, his gaze fixed stubbornly on the table. "I won't just be able to turn that off."

"And I love Nicholas," Thomas muttered unthinkingly. "But if something isn't meant to be, that's all there is to it." He didn't realise he'd made a mistake until he saw Daniel staring at him in confusion, a frown creasing his brow at Thomas's dangerously stupid slip-up.

"Nicholas?" Daniel repeated. "Who's Nicholas? Someone from work? I've never heard you mention him before." Daniel tried to smile but it didn't warm his eyes. "You didn't make him up, did you?"

"I'm not crazy!" Thomas snapped and Daniel drew back a little, his face paling. Clearly he'd been joking to relieve the tension and the red-haired man instantly regretted his outburst. He bit his lip hard as they sat there in silence, his teeth pressing deep enough to draw blood as he weighed up whether to answer or not. He knew there was no real choice though. After all of the anguish he'd caused, Thomas owed Daniel the truth.

"Nicholas May used to live in this house, Danny. I saw him right after we moved in. He was sweet and funny and… and sad. His mum is dead. His dad is awful to him. He just… he *needed* me… and I needed him. I guess maybe we found each other at the right time."

"But… that doesn't make any sense," Daniel said, his frown deepening to wariness now. "There's nowhere up here he could live… and… and didn't John say how long it had been since another family had lived here?" Daniel's expression quickly became uncomfortable. "Wait, he's… he's not like forty or something, is he?"

"No!" Thomas exclaimed, far too loudly for so early in the morning. "No, he's… he's nineteen."

"So… what? He's homeless or something? He lives in the attic? How come Hal and I have never seen him?!"

"Because…" Thomas faltered, his cheeks flaming. He could feel himself losing control of the situation but there was nothing he could do now. He was in freefall and the ground was rushing rapidly towards him. "Because it's like that night with the noose… or when we searched for the other house… he's –"

"Not real," Daniel supplied, his eyes widening with alarm. It wasn't a question and Thomas bristled at the insinuation.

"I'm not crazy!" he repeated but Daniel was standing up now, pressed just a little too close to the wall for comfort.

"No, of course you're not, Tom," the blond man said mechanically but his face was blotchy with stress and he looked afraid. "I… I need to get ready for work."

"But you don't work 'til the evening," Thomas whispered, sitting alone at the table with his arms wrapped tightly around himself. Daniel was backing away now.

"I have the afternoon shift," the blond man said faintly. "And… and I think it'll take a while to wheel my bike down to Wasdale Head with all this snow."

"Be careful then," Thomas murmured. Daniel sniffed behind him, tearful yet again.

"I'll be okay, Tom," he promised. "It'll be easier to cycle from there. The roads should be clearer."

"Okay," Thomas whispered, shaking badly now. "Okay, I'll see you later."

Daniel disappeared upstairs to get dressed but he left a few minutes later, disappearing out into the crisp morning light without a word.

Daniel thought he'd cracked. Thomas could see it in his eyes when he'd finally told someone the truth about Nicholas… except, how could it be the truth? What could the things Thomas had discovered possibly add up to?

Nothing made *sense* anymore.

"Stupid," Thomas said harshly to himself as he rose shakily, limping back towards his bedroom. "Stupid, *stupid*, **stupid**!"

No wonder his father had hated him. No wonder his mum had probably wanted him gone. No wonder his grandpa had died and left him behind. No wonder Thomas was losing everyone he loved.

It was darker than he was used to in his bedroom now that the window had been boarded up. The glass had been swept up from the floor and the snowmelt dried with paper towels. Thomas wanted to fall down when he saw how hard Henry had worked that morning, even despite everything he had been put through.

Thomas had thought of his best friend as selfish once but suddenly that didn't seem fair at all.

Henry was the kindest of all of them.

A sob tore out of Thomas as he realised the truth of this and he buckled under the weight of the realisation, his knee giving way with a vicious stab of pain. He crawled to his bedside table, bad leg dragging behind him as he reached up blindly for the pill bottle. There were only a few left now – maybe three or four – and he swallowed them uncaringly, not thinking of the consequences as he sank down onto the rug.

If he'd been concerned for his own wellbeing, it might have worried him that he hadn't taken any of his medication at all for around a week now and that a double dose would hit him *very* hard but Thomas just couldn't bring himself to care. Everything felt too hopeless.

The pills stuck in his throat and he fought the urge to gag as he rummaged clumsily through the boxes under his bed in his search for something to wash them down with. Thomas's fingertips encountered glass and he withdrew the bottle swiftly, cracking open the lid and downing the fiery liquid with a grimace.

He'd bought the bottle of vodka to celebrate Henry starting his job as a ranger but, since the dark-haired man had hated it so much, the alcohol had never been consumed until now.

Thomas gulped it down steadily, his otherwise-empty stomach churning at the abuse it was receiving as he slumped face-down onto the floor. The bottle rolled away and the last dregs of the vodka seeped down into the cracks between the wooden panels.

Thomas's head was spinning and his stomach was heaving now. The tears were boiling as they trickled down his cheeks and he honestly felt like he was going to die.

His eyes fluttered shut and the next time they opened – rolling wildly as he failed to work out where he was – the light under his door was shining which meant that it was evening and someone was home. He could hear movement in the kitchen, the soft sound of music playing gently. It must have been Daniel then.

He hadn't even checked to make sure Thomas was okay.

His insides churned again and the red-haired man choked, his back arching as his stomach emptied itself on the floor. He had been copiously sick but he was so exhausted that he couldn't even bring himself to move. His bones felt too big for his skin, aching whenever he so much as shifted.

When his bedroom door seemed to swing open of its own accord, there was no way Thomas had the strength to turn around.

"I'm dying," he whispered, unsure whether it was true or not. The shadows in the room shifted and a familiar face made itself apparent as his bedroom door clicked shut again.

"No, you're not," Henry promised, kneeling down beside him and brushing Thomas's hair away from his sweaty forehead. Henry's jaw was still squared with anger but there was a pity in his eyes all the same. "Sit up now, Tom, okay? Drink this water."

"But I hurt you," Thomas croaked, his eyes stinging with tears as he slumped against Henry. "Hurt you so bad."

"Yeah, you did," Henry said bluntly, still combing Thomas's hair back soothingly. "But that doesn't matter right now, Tom. I'm not letting you choke to death on your own vomit."

Henry dragged Thomas over so that they were both leaning against his bed, the red-haired man's head resting heavily on his shoulder as Henry sighed softly in the quiet. For just a moment, it felt like nothing had changed… like they'd never left London… never even met *Daniel*.

It was just them – Thomas and Henry – maybe for the last time.

It was bittersweet.

"I don't deserve you," Thomas whispered and Henry sighed again, like all of the fight was leaking out of him.

"No, you don't," he replied softly but he didn't leave.

Henry stayed with Thomas all night.

Chapter 24: Strange And Unusual

Thomas woke up to an empty house.

He lay there just breathing for a moment, drowning in the silence. There was no sound of footsteps upstairs; no clatter of crockery as Daniel sorted breakfast or Henry poured himself some water after a morning run. There didn't seem to be anyone else there at all.

Thomas rose stiffly, his sciatica aching as he padded across the wooden floor into the hallway outside. The morning light was gloomy as it saturated the room, painting everything muted greys and silvers. Henry and Daniel's shoes were gone from their place beside the doormat. Only Thomas's scuffed combat boots remained.

"Oh," he said softly as his heart broke quietly in his chest. "Right."

The pain he could feel lessened a little when he entered the living room. Despite there being no evidence of morning coffees or plates of mostly-eaten toast, the crumpled quilt Henry had been sleeping under on the sofa was lying abandoned on the floor, almost like he'd left in a rush. The shadow in Thomas's head was certain that they had been planning to desert him for weeks but the rational part of him still remaining didn't believe this for a second.

Through the living room window, the trees were stark and bare as winter came to an end. Most of the ice had melted into muddy puddles and the snow was almost gone entirely but Henry hadn't left, even despite his threat of returning to London as soon as it was safe. Privately, Thomas didn't think Henry had ever meant to leave at all; only to scare them and make them feel just a tiny part of the pain he felt himself.

Thomas couldn't say he blamed him for that.

What he and Daniel had done to Henry was *horrendous*.

Thomas just wished he could feel conviction as to why he had believed it necessary to act so rashly in the first place. With no one else in the house aside from him, it was suddenly easy to separate his thoughts from the senseless animosity rattling around in his head.

As Thomas came to a stop in the centre of the living room, a pang went through him. Daniel's previously beloved peace lily was sitting dead in its pot on the coffee table and, beside it, there was a note.

Tom,

Sorry to leave without warning. Daniel's family called last night to tell him that his mum is sick. It sounds really bad.

I'm driving Daniel to London so he can say goodbye. He didn't want to wake you - I don't know why but I figured you could do with the rest too, after what you did the other night.

Please don't do anything stupid.

We'll come back as soon as we can.

- Henry

"Oh god. Poor Danny," Thomas muttered, his teeth worrying at his bottom lip as he let the note flutter back down again. He didn't know what to do now. He was off work for the week after Henry had kindly made up a lie about *why* Thomas had been unwell and there was nothing to fill his day with but thinking. The empty hours stretched out in front of him endlessly for a moment and a shiver ran through him as his knee throbbed with pain.

He wished he'd brought his cane in from the bedroom but he hadn't thought to this morning, too tired and confused by the unusual quiet of their house. He knew that had been a mistake now though; ever since he had riskily taken the last of his painkillers a few days previously, a sick sort of fragility had descended upon him until even walking to the next room unaided felt impossible.

He didn't want to be alone here. The realisation came to him out of nowhere and Thomas shuddered as he limped out of the living room, getting ready as quickly as he could. The watermark in the bathroom had covered almost all of the ceiling now and he stared up at it warily as he cleaned his teeth, trying to avoid his exhausted reflection in the mirror. It was easier to focus on the spider web in the corner; the chipped porcelain of the sink and the way the whorls of frost on the window looked like a handprint on the icy glass.

Thomas almost fell in his haste to rush downstairs and, by the time he had finally dressed in warm clothes and located his cane from where it had rolled under the bed, his heart was pounding too fast in his chest. He had already wrenched the front door open and was making his way as quickly as he could down the long driveway when he realised that he was no longer alone.

Nicholas was keeping pace beside him, his hands buried in his pockets, seeming smaller without the ever-present baseball flying between his palms. His curls were limper than usual and his glasses were as crooked as ever. Nicholas wavered like a spark that was about to flicker out.

Thomas was not surprised to see him standing there. He realised that on some level he had been waiting for the younger man, without quite understanding why. Nicholas always appeared when Thomas felt lost or alone. Why should this time be any different?

"Hey, Tom," the younger man said softly as they stepped out onto Deadman's Rise together. "I saw your friends leaving this morning without you. You wanna tell me what's wrong?"

"Okay," Thomas said uncertainly, finding it difficult to concentrate. He was trying to avoid eye contact with Nicholas; ever since his realisation in the attic on the day he was trying so hard to forget, the older man found it difficult to even look at him. He thought of the words he would need to say – thought of Daniel and Henry, and the dismay that followed every move Thomas made – and sadness welled inside him like rainwater. "It's kind of a long story though."

"That's alright," Nicholas said kindly as they walked through the puddles together. "We still have time."

The further from the house they walked, the clearer Thomas's head felt.

There was an unsettling feeling gnawing in the back of his mind as his battered boots carried him onwards and Thomas identified it easily as guilt. It burnt inside him like a candle flame, steady and destructive as the fire licked down to the wick.

Thomas couldn't understand why he'd done it; why he'd deliberately torn Henry and Daniel apart, chipping away at their love for *months* until they fell to pieces in his grasping hands – but that wasn't Thomas, was it?

It certainly *hadn't* been, back before they'd left London.

Thomas might have been unhappy then but he'd also loved his best friends more than anything on the planet. He would've given anything for them to finally get their act together and admit their love. Hell, he'd set up a wager with Jessica over when they'd confess their feelings to each other. Would he have done *that* if he hadn't wanted to accept their relationship?

Thomas couldn't understand how everything had blown so out of control.

He hadn't looked at Daniel in a remotely romantic light since they were sixteen and both of them had been happy with that. It had been one drunken mistake that, fortunately, they had been able to move past without ruining their friendship. There had been no reason at all to pick at that scar until it bled now and *especially* not when their dear friend Henry would inevitably be caught in the crossfire… so *fuck*, what had possessed them to do it? To throw all caution and common sense to the wind for the briefest taste of long-forgotten lust?

Thomas felt like all of the choices he had made since moving here had been decided by somebody else entirely.

He looked in the mirror sometimes and didn't even recognise the face staring back at him.

"So… that's it," the red-haired man finished quietly as they left Deadman's Rise behind. "It feels like we're not the same people who moved up here all those months ago. Daniel and I have ruined *everything*. Henry hates the job he's always wanted to do. Everything is *destroyed*, Nick, and I don't know how to fix it. I don't even know how it all got so broken in the first place."

Thomas led Nicholas down the long forest-lined road that would eventually take them towards the centre of the hamlet. It usually took around half an hour to reach the most thriving part of Wasdale Head but, on a slippery day like today, Thomas knew it would be closer to an hour.

He was cold already but the air was fresh and the freezing temperature could be used to explain away the tears in his eyes if Nicholas was cruel enough to point them out. The younger man didn't seem to be in a judgemental mood however; he simply wandered along beside Thomas in silence, his hands still buried in the pockets of his jeans as he glanced over at the older man unhappily.

"I don't even know why we did it," Thomas said suddenly, his voice little more than a breath as he stared down at the damp floor morosely. "We've been so… so *horrible* to Henry but… I don't know why. Whenever I try to remember, it just slips away."

Nicholas was looking at him so intently that Thomas could feel the younger man's gaze on his cheek but he still avoided eye contact, too frightened of the secrets he might find if he looked for too long.

"It doesn't sound like you knew what you were doing," Nicholas said carefully, his tone measured as he finally looked away from Thomas with a disappointed sigh. "If you really didn't feel anything for each other before, maybe… maybe I know what happened."

"What are you talking about?" Thomas asked weakly, leaning on his cane as a heavy sigh escaped him.

Instead of answering him, Nicholas simply stood there with his hands shaking as he reached for Thomas, drawing the older man to a stop. Nicholas's hazel eyes were damp with tears as his fingers wrapped gently around Thomas's pale wrist and there was something in his tormented expression that kept the red-haired man from looking away.

"You already know, don't you?" Nicholas asked, a half-smile touching his lips as a tear rolled down his cheek. "Deep down at least. I never could pull the wool over your eyes, Tom. Not for a minute."

"Well, you really weren't very subtle," Thomas murmured, unsure whether to laugh or cry when Nicholas leant against the low stone wall nearby, patting the space next to him in invitation. They sat down together in silence for a long moment before Nicholas's head came to rest hesitantly on the older man's shoulder and Thomas shuddered a little, dropping a soft kiss onto the honey-coloured curls.

"It's time for answers, Nicky," he said gently. "Don't you trust me with the truth?"

Nicholas's eyes fluttered shut and his shoulders tensed as he steeled himself to speak.

"Do you remember when I told you I was nineteen?" he asked softly. Thomas's teeth sank into his bottom lip as he gave a wordless nod and Nicholas's smile didn't touch his eyes. "Well... I didn't tell you the whole truth, Tom. I... I've been nineteen for a very long time."

"What do you mean?" Thomas asked weakly, shivering from the cold as the stone wall made his sciatica ache dully. Nicholas's eyes were glassy with tears as he turned to look at the older man, their faces so close that Thomas could have counted each individual eyelash if he wanted to. Nicholas closed his eyes again, pressing a kiss to the older man's shoulder through his thick winter coat, the touch so light that it was barely there at all.

"I *died* when I was nineteen," Nicholas confessed as the tears rolled down his cheeks. "I'm *dead*, Thomas, and I've been trapped here all alone for twenty two years in that *awful* house... until you and your friends moved in. You all shone so brightly that I didn't hurt anymore... but then it started to ruin you three as well. I watched it happen but I was too scared to tell you... because then you might have left... because then I would have been *alone* again."

Nicholas couldn't look at him as he sat there, his hands gripping the wall hard as the tears dripped down his nose. Thomas watched the droplets falling but they never seemed to reach the ground. It was almost as though Nicholas wasn't quite there anymore, now that he had told the truth… or maybe it was just that Thomas knew to look for it now.

"I'm sorry you've been hurting for so long," the older man said quietly, unsure of what else to say. He couldn't wrap his head around everything Nicholas had said because, god, how could what Nicholas was telling him even be possible? And yet… there was no alternative. Nicholas was the living proof - no pun intended - that it was possible to have a conversation with a dead man.

God, Nicholas was *dead*… and he had been for as long as Thomas had known him.

"Not even my best friend could see me," the younger man whispered, his whole posture slumping as any fight that remained left him.

"Kevin?" Thomas guessed, making the connection quickly. Nicholas shot him a curious look, wiping the tears away clumsily with his sleeve.

"Wait, *you* know him too?"

"Know *of* him," Thomas corrected, his voice soft and sad as he took in the longing on Nicholas's face. "We had dinner with Mr and Mrs Hobbs a while ago, and John was telling us about his son. He said

Kevin's almost forty now. He married… I think her name was Emma? Their third baby's on the way."

Nicholas's watery smile only served to make him look forlorn.

"Saw that one coming," he mumbled, trying to look happy and failing dismally as the tears began to fall faster. "It's not fair," he croaked and Thomas's heart broke for a second time that morning. "It's not *fair* that he... that…"

The icy facade that Nicholas had been hiding behind since the day they met finally thawed and, as the younger man broke down in great heaving sobs, Thomas held him close.

"It's not fair that he had the chance to grow old when that was taken from you," the older man supplied softly. "I understand. You're allowed to be angry about that. Who wouldn't be?" What Thomas was hearing still didn't make complete sense to him but he was trying to be understanding; trying to be kind and patient because that was who he *was*, damnit. He didn't want to lose himself again.

"I don't want to be angry anymore," Nicholas said, his voice as quiet as the distant winds raking across the surrounding mountains. "There's been something dark in that house for a very long time. It's like a shadow. It's insidious… so quiet that you hardly notice it's there until you're already on the brink of being lost. Don't deny it, Thomas. I know you've seen it too. It's why you've been having nightmares and seeing things that aren't there."

"But…" Thomas's voice was shaking as he wrapped his arms around himself tightly. "But how do you *know*?"

"Because it happened to my family too," Nicholas whispered. "The shadow took my dad. It tore all of the happiness in our lives to pieces."

Thomas didn't want to listen anymore. Hearing someone *else* talking about the shadowy figure made bile rise in his throat because… god, it was *real*; not just some toxic figment of Thomas's own madness.

"I want to believe you," the red-haired man began slowly, his voice growing increasingly desperate. "But… but you must know how this sounds, Nick. I mean… how can the things you're saying be true? Can you *prove* that they happened? Because… because I've been going crazy for a really long time and sometimes…" Thomas's voice trailed away as he remembered the fear in Daniel's eyes when he'd started talking about Nicholas; the worried looks his friends had exchanged when he'd had desperately searched for a house that didn't exist. "Sometimes I doubt my reality exists the way I see it at the best of times."

Nicholas looked at him solemnly, one hand rising to cradle Thomas's cheek gently.

"Tell me how you felt about Henry and Daniel before you moved here," he suggested and the red-haired man blinked at him in surprise, unsure where Nicholas was going with this line of questioning.

"Well… I loved them," he said hesitantly, worrying at his bottom lip again as he remembered that day on the porch when he'd described them as his brothers. "They could always make me happy, no matter how sad I was. They were funny and they shone so *brightly*, and I would've done anything to keep them glowing like that. I just wanted them to love each other. I never wanted them to stop smiling."

"And after that?" Nicholas asked tentatively. "Once you'd moved to the house, how did you feel about them then?"

Thomas wrapped his arms around himself more tightly, hating the ugly sticky feeling clogging his veins like poison. "I hated them sometimes," he whispered, wishing the words weren't true but unable to deny them. "I hated them for being happier than I was. I resented them every single time I saw them together. I didn't want to be anywhere near them – *either* of them. I just…" His words faded and he hung his head in shame. "I wanted them to hurt the way I do," he admitted, hating himself for it.

Nicholas was nodding, his lips pressed flatly together in an unhappy line as he reached out to squeeze Thomas's hand tightly in his own, tethering him there.

"That's what happened to my family too," he whispered, blinking back tears as his despairing eyes bore into Thomas's. "We were so *happy* before we moved to Wasdale Head in the seventies. We came here when I was only a little kid but… I still remember what happened. Things changed so slowly at first. My mum stopped kissing me goodnight. My dad didn't want us leaving the house. No one sang along to the radio anymore. Dad started hurting us. I had bad dreams every night for *years*."

Thomas tried to hold Nicholas's hands but his fingers slipped right through and the younger man flinched at Thomas's gasp, apologising distractedly and concentrating so that he became solid once more. It seemed to be becoming more and more difficult for him to remain.

"You said it yourself, didn't you?" Nicholas laughed weakly as the tears began to fall faster. "Bad things happened in that house. You said it was a bad place... and you were right. It always has been. There were stories before we moved there - kids saying it was haunted; that it wasn't safe to go there alone - but my parents didn't believe them. Why would they? It was only scaremongering."

"Except... it was true, wasn't it?" Thomas whispered, shuddering. "There's something dark in that house. Like... like a shadow... but there's more to it than that, isn't there?" He remembered the disembodied voice that night as he lay on his bedroom floor; remembered the door slamming and the windows smashing, and Daniel getting knocked unconscious by seemingly nothing at all. "There's something inside that wants everyone gone."

Nicholas nodded, his wobbling lips pressed together to keep his frightened tears locked away.

"I tried to tell my parents that we should leave... that we weren't alone there," Nicholas continued in a softer voice, his eyes far away now. "I'd always known the shadow was nearby, poisoning everything. I grew up with it. It was always there; always watching me. My parents didn't believe me at first but, by the time they started to notice it too, it was already too late. Dad was lost. There was no reasoning with him after that."

The fear in Nicholas's eyes was withered now, faded; like it had been eating away at him for a very long time. Thomas wondered how he'd never noticed it before and a pang of guilt shook him to the core as they sat there hunched on the wall together. Thomas rubbed Nicholas's cold, trembling hands gently with the pads of his thumbs but there would be no warming the younger man now. He was already too far gone.

"What… what *is* the shadow?" Thomas breathed. "Because… it hit Daniel once… attacked him in our kitchen. Was that… was that your *dad*, Nick? Is he still trapped here too?"

"Not… not quite," Nicholas said slowly. "I've had a lot of time to think about it and the best explanation I can come to is that someone very angry, very scared, and very unhappy must have lived and died in that house. I think those emotions were so powerful that they lingered even after the person was gone and that they infect anyone who enters. Why else would my dad have dragged my mum across the room by her hair or shoved me down the stairs? He wouldn't have hurt a *fly* before we moved there, Tom. He *loved* us."

Nicholas was shaking, the movement so violent that his edges seemed to blur as he clutched the stone wall tightly.

"That wasn't my dad, Tom," the younger man said fiercely, his eyelashes spiky with tears. "I remember looking at him after he'd pushed me and realising that I'd never seen that man before in my life. He was so *cold* and… dad had always been the gentlest man I knew. The house twisted something inside him. It chewed him up and spat someone else out again, and nothing in the world would bring him back. I don't know what else to tell you, Tom," Nicholas continued and his words were catching with sobs now. "I'm being honest. I *swear* I am."

"I believe you," Thomas promised and, somehow, it was the truth.

He knew Nicholas was right because he had sensed the malevolence in the house himself back in those early days before he had become accustomed to it. Living there had turned Thomas into a shell of the man he'd been before, and it had been doing its best to hollow Daniel and Henry out too. There would be nothing left behind of *any* of them if they didn't leave for good.

Goosebumps crawled across Thomas's skin as he remembered his nightmare where the shadow had filled him for a moment; remembered the knife dripping blood as his best friends died by his hand. Thomas's shiver had nothing to do with the cold air.

Maybe the house had been infecting them all along.

Maybe that was where their hatred and terror had come from.

Nicholas was watching the emotions play out across the older man's face with a tired sort of sympathy, like he had experienced all of them himself which – Thomas realised with a dull jolt of horror – he *had*.

"Mum killed herself because of that house," Nicholas said in a weaker voice, flickering completely from view for a moment before he was solid again, nestled under Thomas's arm. The red-haired man held him closer in alarm. "She… she didn't think dad loved her anymore, even though they'd adored each other all their life… and she thought I'd be better off without her." Nicholas seemed strangely numb now. "She hanged herself in the oak tree outside our house."

The younger man spoke so matter-of-factly that hot tears rolled down Thomas's cheeks as a thrill of horror shot through him. He had been hearing the creaking of rope every night in his dreams for weeks now and, as the memory of the noose rose unbidden to the forefront of his mind, Thomas drew Nicholas into his arms protectively. The younger man was trembling so badly now that he could hardly talk and Thomas tucked Nicholas's head beneath his chin, rocking him gently. The curly-haired man clung to him like a child, his fingers knotted in Thomas's coat as he held on for dear life.

Nicholas didn't sob, as Thomas had perhaps been expecting. The younger man didn't seem to have any tears left to cry now and, after twenty two years of isolation after his family had been so cruelly snatched from him, Thomas was starting to understand why.

"You don't have to say anymore if it's too hard," the red-haired man murmured, stroking Nicholas's curls back gently. "I believe you. I *promise* I do. You don't have to prove anything to me."

"But you deserve the truth." Nicholas spoke so quietly that Thomas had to strain to hear him now and the loss he could already feel resonating through him was painful as the younger man flickered again, momentarily disappearing from sight. "I haven't got long left and I… I want you to know… to *understand*... to believe that what happened with your friends isn't your fault, Tom. It's the *house*. It's been the house all along."

"Oh, Nick," Thomas breathed, pressing a sweet kiss to the younger man's forehead. "Thank you for caring so much." Nicholas pressed his cold nose to Thomas's neck, inhaling the comforting smell deeply, and a tear slipped down the red-haired man's cheek as he held him closer. "If you think it will help you to tell me what happened then… I'm here for you. For as long as you need me to be. I swear it."

"I know you are," Nicholas murmured, his hazel eyes sparkling with tears as he gave the older man another beautiful, damp smile. "Thank you."

Thomas squeezed Nicholas's hand encouragingly, waiting in silence as the sun rose behind the wisps of cloud and the rays painted the world like gold for the briefest of moments.

The younger man looked so beautiful in the sunlight that Thomas knew he'd never forget this moment for as long as he lived.

"I killed my own father," Nicholas confessed and the stunning beauty of the morning was broken, fracturing like shards of glass. The forced emotionlessness of his voice made Thomas shudder but he listened in silence as the younger man finally came clean after two lonely decades.

Nicholas's fingers brushed the bruising on his neck before his hand fell back down to cover Thomas's, cold and familiar.

"The day after mum killed herself, dad came for me," Nicholas said quietly, staring down at his peeling trainers as he described what must have been the worst day of his life without question. The younger man stared into the distance as he remembered and even Thomas's arm wrapping warmly around the younger man's shoulders wasn't enough to break through the reverie he was sinking into.

"Dad was so *angry* that mum had left him and… and he took that out on me. He wasn't going to work and he hadn't been letting me leave for school for *weeks*. I was going to sneak out but… he caught me coming out of my bedroom. He was waiting on the landing with a *knife* and… and we wrestled for it and…"

"He *stabbed* you?" Thomas asked, his hollow eyes sickened and afraid as an appalled expression saturated his ashen face. Nicholas shook his head grimly, his tanned face unusually pale.

"No," the younger man whispered, his eyes growing damp again as a wave of guilt crashed over him, heavy enough to destroy a city. "He was going to hurt me… maybe even try to *kill* me… so I… I pushed him down the stairs."

"But… *Nicky*," Thomas said imploringly, his green eyes damp as he took in the self-loathing on the younger man's face. "That was self-defence. There was nothing else you could have done. If you hadn't done that, he would have killed you…" But Thomas's words trailed away as he looked at the younger man, the hairs on the back of his neck rising when he realised he could see very faintly *through* Nicholas; the outlines of the trees - stark against the morning sky - showed like spiderwebs through the younger man's skin.

"But I died anyway," Nicholas said quietly, his fingers once more drifting to touch the bruising on his neck. "I watched him lying at the bottom of the stairs. He'd smashed his head and… and as he was bleeding, his eyes went soft again. It was like all the darkness was seeping out with the blood and… and I didn't know what to do… so I ran."

Nicholas didn't seem to realise that the tears were still falling but he was holding Thomas's hands like the older man was the only thing keeping him here at all.

"I made it all the way down the driveway before the shadowy figure appeared. Dad was dead inside and… and mum was still hanging in the tree… and I just wasn't looking where I was going, Tom," Nicholas breathed, his hazel eyes brimming with grief as he held the older man's gaze. "I ran out into the road and… and there was a truck… and I didn't even try to move out of the way. I just… I just felt it hit me and… and then my body was on the ground but I was still *running*."

"Where did you go?" Thomas asked, his voice catching in his throat as his own tears caught up with him. Suddenly the bruising and the horrible twist of muscle around Nicholas's throat made sense; he must have broken his neck in the collision.

"I couldn't get anywhere at all," Nicholas croaked, rubbing at his eyes absently as the tears soaked the sleeve of his red-checked flannel. "No matter how hard I ran, I always ended up right back where I'd started. The shadow had me trapped. I couldn't leave. I can *never* leave."

Thomas held him closer, cradling Nicholas's jaw gently between his palms as he pressed the briefest kiss to the younger man's lips.

"But... you *are* leaving," he said softly, terrified of losing him but also desperately praying that maybe Nicholas could finally have *peace*. "You're flickering out of sight right now... and each time it's getting longer, Nick. I think it's almost time for you to go. Maybe you're just holding on too tightly."

"I've *tried* to let go before but it never works," the younger man whispered, so dejected and lost that even Thomas couldn't call him back now. "I... I tried to kill myself so many times after my parents were gone, Tom, but it never worked. No one could ever see me or touch me or... or hear me, even when I was screaming for them to just look... just glance *once*."

"No one?" Thomas repeated brokenly, trembling as the chill of the stone wall began to settle in his bones. "Not *one* person in twenty two years?"

Nicholas's eyes were distant as he looked at the snowmelt beneath their feet, watching the reflection of the bare branches drifting in the breeze.

"One man saw me for a few seconds," he admitted softly. "He was driving another truck. I stepped in front of it - wondered if maybe going back to how it had ended would be enough to finish things - but… but he *saw* me. He swerved out of the way and ended up being so injured that he had to go to hospital, and I stopped after that. I couldn't stand having someone *else*'s death on my conscience. One was bad enough."

"Oh, Nick," Thomas whispered when his hand passed through the younger man's cheek as he became incorporeal again. "But… I don't understand. Why can *I* see you? That doesn't make any sense."

Nicholas gave him a long look, staring just as hard as he had on that very first day when they'd noticed each other. He remembered the younger man's wide-eyed gaze and his gasp of breath as stared at Thomas with such terrifying longing.

"I don't know," Nicholas said at length, his words dropping softer than ever now, like a radio that was losing its signal. "Maybe you just paid more attention than everyone else. Maybe you notice things that other people don't want to see."

"Like in Beetlejuice," Thomas whispered, the wonder in his heart combining with the grief to create something painfully melancholy. "'*Live people ignore the strange and unusual*'."

Nicholas's lips twitched into the saddest smile that Thomas had ever seen.

"Are you calling *me* strange and unusual, Tom?"

"You're no worse than I am," Thomas said with a teasing smile as the tears continued to tumble down his cheeks.

"No, I guess not," Nicholas murmured, his voice appraising. "I think… I think that's why I dropped the mug that day but… but I could still pull you to your feet. You… you gave me energy somehow. Made me feel *alive* again, even if it *was* only for a short while. It's strange."

"Hey, I just thought of something," Thomas said suddenly, cracking a stupid joke to break the tense atmosphere that had rolled over them like fog. "This all explains why you're never heard of Harry Potter, right? It was published in 1997."

Nicholas rolled his eyes fondly but the endearment of the action was ruined when a droplet of snowmelt tumbled from the branches overhead, splashing *through* Nicholas's face and sending the facade rippling like the surface of a lake.

The pair sat in silence for a few moments, content to simply entwine their fingers and hold on for the short time they had left together. The sun was burning higher in the sky now but the heat of it wasn't touching them. Nicholas's fingers were cold around Thomas's.

Thomas never wanted him to let go.

"Don't hate yourself for what happened with your dad, Nick," the red-haired man pleaded softly. "You were just a kid. You're… you're *still* a kid really. None of this was ever your fault. Just… please. Believe me."

Nicholas watched him, his lower lip jutting out unconsciously as his wet eyes sparkled in the light.

"I hate the word please," he murmured, as he had said so many times before, but the sentence sounded habitual now. There was no heat in Nicholas's words.

"Why?" Thomas asked, his head tilted to the side curiously. He had to stretch his leg out as the ache burnt in his knee and Nicholas reached to soothe it gently, his fingertips resting lightly over the sore joint.

"Because, when the shadow took my dad, I begged for a really long time... but it never helped." Nicholas looked down at the fraying blue denim of Thomas's jeans, unable to meet the older man's gaze. "It didn't matter how many times I said '*please*'. No one ever came to save me."

There was nothing Thomas could say to that.

He simply held the younger man's hand and tried to wrap his head around everything he'd heard. Sadness seared through him when he realised that Nicholas had been killed the year he was born but there was no doubt lingering in Thomas now. The claims were so ridiculous that they could only have been the truth.

"It's been so long now," Nicholas said tearfully, burying his head in his hands as he leant against the red-haired man's shoulder. "Two whole *decades*. I want to... I just..."

"You're tired," Thomas supplied, swallowing with difficulty past the lump rising in his throat. "I understand. You… you need to be at peace."

"But I don't know *how*," Nicholas said, groaning softly. "It seems impossible. I think… I think I'll just keep fading slowly away anyway."

"Maybe… maybe we need to get rid of everything tying you here. What if we… maybe we could burn the stuff in the attic? What about the whole damn house? Because I'll do anything, Nick. You know I will. I don't want to lose you - I don't want to feel alone anymore - but my god, I want you to stop hurting a million times more." A softer look soothed the anguish in Thomas's eyes as he reached for Nicholas once more, letting his fingers hover where the younger man's cheekbone had been before. "I'll never forget you, Nicholas May. Not for as long as I live. You're the best thing that's ever happened to me."

"You're the best thing that's ever happened to me too," Nicholas admitted, his hazel eyes overflowing with tears that Thomas couldn't feel. The red-haired man didn't know how to put his tumultuous emotions into words.

"I wish I could kiss you again," Thomas whispered.

He wished he could hold Nicholas too but he settled for wrapping his arms around himself, dwelling on everything they'd shared together; their bay leaf wish and first kiss, and the morning Thomas slept in Nicholas's arms as the sunlight painted the world golden.

He was so glad he had had the chance to live in the same world as this beautiful creature, even if it *was* only for a short time.

Thomas could never resent that.

Some people went their whole *lives* without ever feeling this way about another person and Thomas had been lucky enough to cherish it for *months*.

The silence stretched between them but there was no reason to break it.

There was nothing left to say.

The day shifted towards afternoon and, although Thomas recognised dimly that he was hungry and cold, he didn't feel any inclination to leave. He wanted to stay with Nicholas until he was gone. After all of the comfort the younger man had offered him during his time in the Lake District, Thomas thought he at least owed Nicholas that.

"Shall we walk a bit to keep you warm?" the younger man asked softly, his fingers fluttering over Thomas's hand although of course he couldn't feel it. "You've gone blue, Tom. Don't want you freezing to death on my account."

Thomas resisted making quite a few jokes in very poor taste then but, by the wistful amusement on the younger man's face, he seemed to be thinking the same thing.

"Not a *chance*, Tom," Nicholas chided gently. "You're going to live to be a tiny, wizened, old man with a ridiculous beard who spends all his time looking through your grandpa's telescope." The amusement in Nicholas's fading eyes was quickly replaced with sincerity. "You're going to be *happy*, Thomas. I know you are. I can feel it."

They walked side by side back the way they had come, close enough that their arms would have been brushing if they'd truly been next to one another. Birds sang in the trees as spring hovered just out of sight but the warmth it offered seemed a long way off.

"I'm so glad I met you," Thomas said quietly. "I just wish the circumstances could have been better."

"Y'know, I'm not sure I'd change them," Nicholas admitted, looking stunned with himself but quite certain. "You've made me happier than I was before I died. I'll never be able to thank you enough for that."

Everything was still and peaceful, until it wasn't anymore.

There was a dull roaring sound that set the hairs on the back of Thomas's neck prickling. He stepped in front of Nicholas unthinkingly, his cane still lying beside the stone wall far behind them as he searched for the source of the noise. It was menacing and constant, growing louder and louder until -

"Look out!" Nicholas cried, rushing *through* Thomas to shield him as the shadowy figure crashed through the trees in front of them. It was still faceless but it vaguely resembled a human now, its chest heaving as it stalked purposefully towards them.

Thomas had never seen it manifest itself like this before and, by the crackling fiery sound it made, it seemed to be burning itself up fast.

Nicholas froze as it neared them and Thomas saw why when he recognised the face of the man in the Polaroid. This was Nicholas's father, twisted beyond all recognition.

Flickers of shadow were drifting into the air now, curling up like ash and disappearing into nothing. The figure seemed furious to realise that its time on this earth was limited and it snatched a hand back, curling its long clawed fingers into a fist before it swung at Thomas's skull.

The force of it hit him like his father's car all over again, sending him flying into the road like a ragdoll. The tarmac slammed into his already-bleeding head and Thomas's eyes rolled with the sudden unexpected agony of it as he glimpsed the blurriness of the shadow finally burning itself to nothing, leaving behind a mousy-haired man in an olive green jumper that smiled gently before fading away forever.

Nicholas was almost translucent now, his long fingers little more than cold wafts of air as he tried to stroke Thomas's cheeks. The younger man looked terrified, *appalled*, but the softness in his frightened eyes remained when the older man managed to focus on his face.

"I love you," Thomas croaked, his eyes fluttering for a moment before he felt Nicholas's hand in the pocket of his jeans, easing his mobile out. The younger man was concentrating *hard* as he focused on being substantial enough to dial for the emergency services.

Thomas listened to Nicholas asking for an ambulance and directing them to Deadman's Rise through what felt like a fog, barely able to feel the pain now as the blood beneath his head spread out in the melting snow like a grisly halo.

"You're gonna be okay, Tom," Nicholas whispered, his lips brushing butterfly-soft over Thomas's blood-spattered cheekbone before he was fading once more. "I can be with mum and dad now. I'll be fine. Just… hold on. Survive for me, okay? *Please*," Nicholas begged and there was nothing but love in his eyes. "Please, don't give up. I love you too."

"You're… leaving?" Thomas could barely keep his eyes open and he had no recollection of how long he had been lying in the road but Nicholas was crying again, and the sound of sirens could be heard growing louder in the distance.

"It's time," Nicholas breathed. "Holding him back and saving dad… it was too much… but I can feel my parents now. They're waiting. I have to say goodbye to you."

The regret in his voice was breathtakingly painful as he leant forwards to press a soft kiss to Thomas's forehead. It was the last kiss they would ever share.

"Do you remember the wish we made with the bay leaves, Tom?" Nicholas whispered, the tears falling down like raindrops as he gazed into Thomas's cloudy green eyes. "I wished for *you*, Thomas. I just wished that you could finally be happy."

He disappeared from sight then, like a cloud passing over the sun, and Thomas knew that it was over. The younger man was gone.

Thomas lay there limply in the puddles as the ambulance finally pulled to a stop a few minutes later and, when the paramedics asked him if he was alone, the tears Thomas had been fighting back swelled out of him like a tidal wave.

"*Yes*," he sobbed, unable to bear the look of sympathy on their faces.

Thomas had never been more alone in his life.

Chapter 25: Ghost Stories

Thomas rose from sleep slowly, the light golden behind his eyelids as he returned to wakefulness. There was an intermittent beeping noise that buzzed on the fringes of his consciousness like a clumsy bumblebee and it was this confusing sound that finally forced Thomas to open his gritty eyes.

He was lying in an unfamiliar bed, the blankets tucked in neatly around his prone form as he looked blearily at the ceiling. There were strange whorls in the plaster and Thomas gazed at the shapes they made for a moment, tracing leaves and constellations.

"I think he's waking up!" a familiar voice exclaimed excitedly, far too loud for the silence. Thomas winced, closing his eyes against the beginnings of a headache as he uselessly willed himself to continue floating on the strange clouds he'd found himself on. They were dissipating like dust though and Thomas was returning to reality with a bang as the events leading up to this moment quickly made themselves apparent: the almost-overdose, the desertion of his friends, the emptiness he had felt when Nicholas... god, *Nicholas* -

"Awake, are you?" a woman asked as she bustled into the room and Thomas blinked at her owlishly, his confusion and exhaustion swelling inside to make his eyes prickle with tears. "You're in West Cumberland Hospital, Mr. Barnes. Do you remember how you got here?"

Thomas remembered events backwards almost; remembered lying in the road with Nicholas kneeling over him, the violence of the blow that had thrown him across the street, the tears rolling down the dead man's cheeks as he confessed the truth after two decades.

Thomas knew he'd gone pale but he forced himself to loosen his fingers on the blankets; tried to breathe calmly and adopt an expression of puzzlement that probably fooled no one at all.

"I don't remember anything," he said hoarsely, his voice cracking from misuse. Dimly, he wondered how long he'd been sleeping. "I remember waking up alone in the house and... nothing."

"Well, you did hit your head very hard," the doctor said in a softer tone, her dark eyes kind. "It's fairly normal for someone with an injury like you suffered to feel disoriented or forgetful." She glanced at a clipboard as she stood there and Thomas's eyes darted away for a moment, his heart squeezing painfully in his chest when he saw Henry and Daniel sitting by the window, their faces exhausted and worried as they gazed back.

"You've been unconscious for around four hours now, Mr. Barnes," the doctor said, bringing his attention back to her with practiced ease. He felt a jolt of shock that it had been such a short time. He felt like Nicholas had left him years ago already, and he couldn't understand how Henry and Daniel were still here, when they should have been halfway to London by now. "You'll still feel drowsy and unwell for a little while yet which is normal but you'll be pleased to know that your CT scan results were very promising. There was no bleeding or swelling on the brain, and it looks as though you're only suffering with a concussion although we'll keep you in for observation. You were very lucky."

Thomas nodded gratefully but his pale face crumpled when his headache throbbed threateningly and he quickly stopped. The doctor gave him another reassuring smile as she tucked the clipboard back under her arm.

"You'll feel right as rain in no time at all," she said cheerfully before her expression clouded over a little. "I'm obligated to tell you that there are some police officers waiting for a chance to speak to you once you're feeling a little more awake. I'll pass on the fact that you've told me you don't remember anything but they have to question you. The circumstances of your injury seem to indicate that you were attacked so you'll understand why it's necessary that they pay you a visit. They're only doing their job."

"Of course," Thomas mumbled, letting his eyes slide shut again. He'd learnt his lesson this time and would not be nodding for the foreseeable future. "Thank you."

"That's quite alright," the doctor said, giving him a kinder smile once more. "Your next of kin are travelling up from London to visit you, so I've been told. You should expect them tomorrow morning at some point, as I imagine visiting hours will long be over by the time they arrive tonight." She wrongly assumed that his face had suddenly paled due to exhaustion. "Get some rest, Mr. Barnes. If you need any pain relief, ring the bell and a nurse will be in to see you."

There was silence in the room for almost a minute before he heard the scraping of chairs as Daniel and Henry moved closer to him. Thomas opened his eyes but he didn't speak, content to simply watch them as they sat together quietly. Henry was holding Daniel's hand and Thomas felt something flutter in his chest at the sight of it.

"Sorry about this," he said quietly, gesturing to his bandaged head with a grazed, trembling flutter of his fingers. Daniel's blue eyes filled rapidly with tears and Henry sighed slowly, like all of the air was seeping out of him.

"I thought I told you *not* to do anything stupid, Tom," the dark-haired man said at last, his eyelashes spiky with his own tears as he tried (and failed) to glare at his oldest best friend. "Now you've done some stupid shit over the last few months but -" He faltered, glancing towards the open doorway before he moved closer to angrily hiss: "-but lying to the *doctor*? That's stupid, even for you!" Henry's eyes flashed when Thomas opened his mouth to protest. "Don't you dare deny it, Tom! I've known you since we were five! You've always been a shit liar."

Thomas's lips twitched a little despite himself and, almost as though he couldn't help himself, Henry's dimples creased his cheeks.

"You're such a dick, Tom," the younger man said and, abruptly, the tears were rolling down his cheeks again. "You scared me so fucking bad. Don't *ever* do that again, okay?! Not ever."

Thomas looked between the two of them, utterly lost.

"I don't know why you two even came," he muttered, rubbing his temples in an effort to relieve the headache before a hiss escaped him when he realised he had a black eye. "All I've done is… is *hurt* you both… ever since we moved here. Why are you here now? What did I do to deserve this?"

Daniel swallowed audibly, leaning forwards to settle his warm fingers gently on Thomas's bruised wrist.

"We hurt you too, Tom," the blond man said tearfully. "We've all hurt each other… so, *so* badly… and I can't understand why. That's why I came to see you before I went back to London. I have to make this right again! We were always so close before -"

"*Best friends,*" Henry interjected earnestly, his chocolate brown eyes so caring and sad that - for just a moment - it reminded Thomas of the drive up to the Lake District in the first place, when he'd looked at Thomas so kindly in the rear view mirror that the red-haired man had almost broken down in tears.

"I… I want to tell you what happened but…" Suddenly, it was all Thomas could do to keep the secret; it roiled inside him like a storm and he pushed himself achingly into a sitting position, gripping the rails on either side of his bed as he leant towards his friends. "You'll think I'm crazy," he breathed, his heart pounding too fast in his chest. He wanted to look away but this was too important. "You'll think I'm mad and I *can't* lose you both again. I can't."

Daniel and Henry were watching him with knowing eyes, no trace of scorn or disapproval distorting their expressions. Thomas couldn't understand why they weren't doubting him. He knew it must look like he'd finally lost it. His injuries made no sense and he'd *clearly* been attacked but there was an old fear in him gnawing away, setting his nerves alight with anxiety.

Henry reached to grip his hand and Daniel's teeth sank nervously into his lower lip as he eased his phone out of his pocket.

"How about I give you some security?" the blond man asked hesitantly. "I'll show you something *I* know now… and then you can tell us what you found out after, yeah?"

Thomas's trembling fingers settled on the blankets and he sought out Henry's gaze for a moment, relishing in the fact that there was no hatred or despair in those dark eyes anymore; only curiosity and a fond sort of sadness that seemed like it would never fade.

"We *believe* you," Henry whispered, before Thomas could even speak, and it lit a fire in his chest that could only be hope.

"While… while you were sleeping," Daniel began hesitantly, his voice trailing away for a few moments as he typed something into his phone. "Well… we found him, Tom. We found Nicholas."

Thomas's heart clenched painfully in his chest when Daniel turned his phone towards the hospital bed, displaying a webpage aptly named 'Find A Grave'. The words blurred before his eyes as tears prickled and Henry clambered carefully onto the bed beside him, easing his arm around Thomas's aching shoulders.

"There's only been one Nicholas May in Wasdale Head for as long as the citizens have been recorded and… and I think this is him." Daniel's voice was almost apologetic as he began to read from the screen again, his pale face determined, even as his bottom lip wobbled a little at the emotion radiating from Thomas. "His full name was Nicholas Andrew May. He was born in -"

"1975," the red-haired man breathed, his eyes fluttering shut as a tear rolled down his cheek. "And he died in -"

"1995," Daniel finished, his expression sombre as he reached to squeeze Thomas's ankle comfortingly. "He's buried in Saint Olaf's Churchyard in Wasdale Head. I… I'm so sorry I didn't believe you, Tom. It just… it sounded too impossible… too frightening... but it was all true, wasn't it? I can see that now."

Henry nodded in agreement.

"We were talking about it earlier," the dark-haired man added gently. "Like that time Daniel got attacked in the kitchen, remember? The police couldn't find anything but… but *someone* had to have hurt him." Henry looked suddenly wary as he shot Thomas a sideways glance. "Was *that* Nicholas?"

Thomas bristled, his cheeks heating with something that might have become anger if he could summon enough energy to feed the flame of it.

"No," the oldest man said with a heaviness that hadn't existed before that morning. "No, it was what became of his his father."

"Oh," Daniel murmured. There was silence for a long moment before: "That's why I didn't want to believe in Nicholas, you know. Because if I believed in him, it made the shadowy figure I saw real… and I wasn't sure I could live with the reality of that." Daniel's expression was downcast as he picked idly at a loose thread on the blanket. "I'm sorry, Tom."

Thomas swallowed past the lump rising in his throat, feeling so unbearably old that it was almost too much effort to put his thoughts into words anymore.

"You two deserve to know what happened but… I still don't know how to explain it. I don't even know where to *start*."

Henry gave him a watery smile, his dimples creasing his cheeks.

"How about the beginning?" Daniel asked with a teasing lilt to his voice. Thomas snorted, rolling his eyes fondly.

"You cheek," he muttered but something had calmed in him as he inhaled shakily. "Fine… but just remember, you asked for it."

Thomas told them about meeting Nicholas on that very first morning; described the way the truck had gone right through the boy and the reality of The House In The Forest. He told them the origin of the noose and the shadowy figure that lived in the house, slowly corrupting everything inside it; he told them how it had torn Nicholas's family apart and done its best to destroy them too.

He confessed his nightmares and those stolen moments with Nicholas when no one else was around, and the way the May family had reached its horrible end. He told them about the strange sickness inside him that grew as his addiction did; the hatred and the fear, and the reason he had instinctively tried to tear everyone else apart to distract himself from his own self-destruction.

As Thomas shakily volunteered this information, Henry and Daniel began to chip in too, murmuring quiet fears and realisations with wide eyes as the puzzle pieces fell into place. Daniel recalled the ill-omened day when the three of them had gone searching for the house that didn't exist when he had caught a glimpse of someone standing in the trees and Henry's eyes widened when he remembered the conversation with Martin Hobbs when he had described the 'haunted house' they had moved into.

The sky outside was darkening by the time the revelations came to an end but, despite the bone-deep ache and the too-fast beating of his heart, Thomas felt relief coursing through him at the trust he could see reflected back at him in his best friends' eyes.

"There's one more thing," the red-haired man said softly in the half-light. His hair wasn't really crimson anymore; instead it was mostly a faded brown that made his green eyes glow again, even just a little.

"What is it, Tommy?" Henry murmured as Daniel leaned closer to pat the older man's hand. Daniel was sitting cross-legged on the end of the bed now, all three of them cramped together like they used to be during sleepovers when they'd told ghost stories... but the ghosts were real now and all they had left was each other.

"I… I was - I *am* - in love with Nicholas… and I never felt that way about either of you two, no matter what it might have looked like." Thomas felt stronger as the words left him, even despite the bruise-like circles under his sore eyes and the continued trembling of his grazed knuckles. "You two are my brothers. You will *always* be my brothers. That's never going to change again."

"We're not leaving you," Henry said softly and Daniel smiled, his blue eyes crinkling.

"If some weird murderous ghost couldn't tear us apart then nothing will," the blond man grinned but, below his forced joviality, there was something more sincere in his face. "We're with you to the end, Tom. Nothing can change that."

It felt like nothing had changed at all for a moment; felt like those long visiting hours in the hospital after the car accident that had almost ruined Thomas's life. He was so glad Henry and Daniel were here with him, finally believing him after everything they'd suffered through together.

It meant more than he could ever put into words to feel the three of them slotting back comfortably together again… but their blind faith wouldn't be enough forever. Eventually their doubts might return, creeping in as insidious as the shadowy figure, and Thomas knew that there was only one way to solve that: he needed concrete proof of what had happened up in the house, both for them and for himself.

He wouldn't rest until this was finally over.

Chapter 26: Love And Light

When Thomas woke up the next morning, he was alone again.

Despite the fact that spring was fast approaching, the warmer climes felt a long way off today. The world outside was grey and damp, the raindrops sliding down the window like tears. That same wildness that had first threatened Thomas on the long drive up to Cumbria was still present in the desolation of the landscape outside but it didn't frighten him anymore. He took solace in it instead, because the cyclical nature of his emotions now meant that this chapter of his life was almost over.

Soon, he would not have to endure it any longer.

"Hey, Tom," Henry said as he appeared behind the curtain. Thomas had been moved onto the ward now that he was healing so well, and the quiet hubbub of the patients and staff through the thin layer of material reminded him that the rest of the world was still waiting beyond the frightening green world he had found himself in so many months before.

The planet would continue to turn no matter what and life would carry on. Thomas understood that now.

"I brought you coffee," Henry said as he raised a takeout cup proudly before hesitating. "Wait... are you *allowed* coffee?"

"Not sure," Thomas said, making grabby hands for it. "But I don't care. Thank you for bringing me caffeine. I owe you."

Henry's chocolate brown eyes were soft as he passed his oldest best friend the drink carefully.

"No, you don't," he said fondly as he settled down wearily into the plastic chair beside Thomas's bed. "You don't owe me a thing."

Thomas's cheeks heated and he looked away towards the muted light streaming through the mint green curtains. The coffee was hot on his tongue, warming him from the inside out, and he hummed contentedly as Henry toed his trainers off, putting his feet up on the bed. They'd probably get told off if one of the nurses came to check on him but the closeness made it worth it right now; Thomas craved the human contact.

"Where's Daniel?" he asked once he'd had his fill of the coffee. Henry sighed softly, stretching out in the uncomfortable plastic chair as he rubbed at his tired face.

"He's gone to see his mum, remember? We weren't even halfway there when we heard that you were hurt so of course we came back here first." Henry looked more tired than Thomas had ever seen him. "Daniel's gone back down south now but... I figure maybe you need me more than he does. He's never listened to sense where his family are concerned."

"And I've never listened to sense at all," Thomas said dryly, raising an eyebrow when Henry let out a surprised snort of laughter. "Isn't that what you're implying?"

"Obviously," Henry grinned before he sobered. "You're going back there, aren't you? To the house…" When Thomas stayed silent, something in the dark-haired man's face seemed to cave in on itself. "It's too dangerous to go there alone, Tom. I'm not losing you again."

"It will be safer now, I think," Thomas said softly as stared down at the myriad of cuts decorating his hands. "The darkness burnt itself up after I got hurt… and besides, there's still some things I'm not willing to leave behind." Thomas saw the uncertainty in his best friend's eyes and his heart ached in his chest. "I don't think we'll be in any danger, Hal," he said reassuringly.

"Better safe than sorry," Henry muttered darkly before something softened in his eyes. "I'm almost glad Daniel's not coming back too. At least that way I won't have to worry about *both* of you."

A sliver of hurt rippled through Thomas as he thought about the fact that Daniel had left him again and Henry interpreted it easily as he reached to take the older man's hand.

"Daniel was sorry to leave without saying anything but… he didn't want to say goodbye to you," the dark-haired man admitted quietly. "Said you'd probably had enough goodbyes to last a lifetime."

"Think he was right," Thomas murmured as he settled back down on the pillows again, a sad sigh escaping him. "Are you and Daniel okay again, Hal? After everything that happened?"

Henry hesitated, his lips quirking into something that was *almost* a half-smile.

"Maybe eventually," he said in a tired sort of voice. "If we both keep trying... yeah, I think we probably will." Henry bit his lip, avoiding eye contact as he rubbed absently at a spilt drop of coffee on his jeans. "It would just be nice not to *have* to try, y'know?"

"If things could just be easy?" Thomas clarified as a heavy sigh escaped Henry. "Yeah, that would be nice."

The dark-haired man's phone chimed and he reached for it wearily, his forehead creasing into a slight frown as he read the text message.

"Daniel?" Thomas guessed but Henry shook his head slowly.

"Your mum," he replied after a long moment. "Your parents are on their way upstairs. You want me to stay?"

"No, it's okay," Thomas said firmly, wishing he was as brave as he sounded. "This is something I have to do alone."

He did not have long to wait.

His parents hadn't changed very much in the time since he'd been gone; the same clothes and greying temples, the same tired eyes that they now shared with their only son.

There was a moment of fragility when the three found themselves together again, his parents freezing as though ensnared in a spider web under the weight of Thomas's gaze.

"Morning," the youngest Barnes said evenly. "How was the drive?"

"Far too long," Diane said tearfully as she crossed the space between them, reaching to draw him into a gentle hug. The familiar smell of her perfume surrounded him and Thomas's eyes stung with tears as he clung to her, unwilling to let go. "Tommy, I've been so *worried*."

"Stop babying him," Peter snapped from where he was hovering uncomfortably by the foot of the bed. His green eyes flickered around as he took in the various monitors and the unhealthy pallor of his son's sore face, and the déjà vu Thomas felt was reflected back at him in his father's eyes as they both remembered those long weeks after the car accident.

Diane drew back a little when Peter stepped closer but it didn't scare Thomas anymore. He held his father's gaze without defiance; without belligerence or rage. Peter looked smaller these days, like the poison he carried inside was beginning to take its toll. None of his father's hatred touched Thomas anymore; not after the horrible atmosphere of the house.

Peter's venom ran off Thomas as harmlessly as water.

"Aren't you tired?" he asked quietly. "Aren't you tired of treating everybody in your life like dirt? It's why your own father couldn't stand you. Do you *really* want to push your son away too?"

Peter reeled back like Thomas had slapped him, seemingly unnerved by the fact that his son was no longer afraid of him.

"I just drove your mother halfway up the country to visit you, you ungrateful little *wretch*." He looked as though he wanted to say something ruder but had suddenly become aware that they were only separated from everyone else by a thin curtain. "I don't have to listen to this."

Peter stormed out, heading in the vague direction of the cafeteria, and Thomas watched him leave placidly, his expression mild. Diane relaxed when her husband was gone, settling down into the chair Henry had vacated and reaching for her son's hand.

A more comfortable silence grew between them, stretching like rolling green meadows and the cotton wool clouds drifting by overhead.

"I found your Book Of Shadows," Thomas said eventually, a small smile twitching his lips when Diane blushed. "That was a lovely thing to do, mum. Thank you."

"I just wanted to give you something positive to focus on," she said tenderly. "I know how worried you were about leaving, even after talking it all over with Linda, and if that could help even a little bit, it was worth parting with it."

"I think… once I come back down south again… well, maybe I'll start my own." Thomas's thoughts wandered as he considered this, already planning what he would include: the different meanings of each herb, crystal grids, the contents for different spell jars… and maybe even the bay leaf spell.

His heart melted a little in his chest as he remembered their wishes.

They had both wished that the other would finally have the chance to be happy and, as that realisation made itself apparent, he remembered again the moment when Nicholas's expression had softened as he said goodbye; the brightening of the younger man's hazel eyes as he gazed at something that Thomas couldn't see.

Nicholas's parents had been waiting for their son, hovering just out of sight, the way they should have been all along: bright and kind, full of love and light, and shining like the sun.

"I think starting your own Book Of Shadows sounds like a brilliant idea," Diane said warmly but Thomas could see the niggling doubt in her eyes and he thought he knew what had caused it. "Are you going back up there first?" she asked as a note of wariness entered her tone. "Before you come back home?"

Thomas had told her none of the fearful events that had unfolded up on Deadman's Rise but she seemed to sense it all the same. Her fingers entwined more tightly with his and she brought his hand up to her lips, pressing a soft kiss to his knuckles.

"There's something I need to do," Thomas said. "But I'll come back to London once it's all over. I promise."

Diane didn't push him for more information; didn't chastise him for potentially putting himself in danger or try to force the truth out of him. It wasn't in her nature to be cruel and that was the reason he found her so easy to be close to.

He knew he would tell her the whole truth one day – if anyone believed him unequivocally, it would be her – but he wasn't ready yet. Right now, he was still working through it himself.

"You've grown so much in the months since you left," Diane murmured, cupping his cheek gently as he rested against her palm, his bruised face softening with love. "I can see it now. How did I miss it before?"

"I'm not sure anyone else saw either," he murmured, turning his head to press a chaste kiss to her palm. "I've missed you, mum. So, *so* much."

Her pale face split into a beautiful smile as she leant forwards to draw him into another hug. It was so lovely to have her close like this - when Thomas felt calm and *sane* again (and honestly, he'd forgotten how good that felt) – that a bubble of relieved laughter escaped him as she cuddled him closer, peppering his face with kisses until he was giggling and trying to wriggle away.

"I love you," she whispered, thumbing the dampness from his bruised cheeks. "I trust you to keep yourself safe. Just… make sure you come back to me, Tommy... okay? When you're ready."

Thomas blinked back the tears that had been welling in his eyes, unsure whether they were of relief or loss.

"I love you too." He gave her a watery smile that she returned broadly. "I'll come home to you again, mum," he murmured, clinging to her once more as she pressed a firm kiss to his forehead. "I promise."

She took him once more into her arms and he had the distinct sensation of his broken heart healing in his chest.

He knew in that moment that, no matter what happened from this point on, he was finally back on the road to being okay.

For the first time since the car accident, Thomas felt like he could breathe easily again.

Chapter 27: The World Woke Up

Henry had been smoking like a chimney from the moment he led Thomas out of the hospital upon his discharge. The morning was damp with dew but the shards of blue sky visible between the wisps of cloud hinted at a brighter afternoon. Both of them were exhausted as they shuffled out of the hospital but Thomas thought that, even despite what he had suffered through himself, Henry somehow looked even worse for wear.

"You haven't been sleeping well," Thomas stated and it wasn't a question. The dark-haired man looked at him with a half-smile, cigarette almost burnt down to the filter as he rummaged around in the pocket of his denim jacket for his car keys. Henry didn't comment and Thomas's curiosity stirred. "Where've you been staying while I was in the hospital?"

Henry unlocked the car, taking a final deep drag of his cigarette before he stamped it out under his boot.

"Chase Hotel," he said, shrugging tiredly as he slipped into the seat with a cough. "Little Georgian place just off the A595. Wasn't very far away."

"Nice?" Thomas asked as he strapped his seat belt in, trying to avoid catching sight of his bruised face in the wing mirror. Henry jerked his shoulder up in a half-shrug, more focused on manoeuvring his car out of the tight parking space he'd secured that morning.

"It was close to you," he said distractedly as he turned the car onto Homewood Road. "That was all that mattered."

Thomas fell quiet as Henry began what he assumed was the considerable drive back towards Wasdale Head. It seemed that no more words were necessary and the pair of them sank into a comfortable silence beneath the rock music playing quietly on the radio as the world woke up around them.

Thomas's head was still tender but the bandages had been removed now and the stitches were easy enough to forget about under the fog of medication. Henry was looking after his painkillers for him; Thomas had pressed them wordlessly into his hands upon leaving the hospital and – despite the flicker of concern and relief mingling on the tanned man's face – Henry hadn't questioned him. That trust meant more than Thomas could put into words.

"You're definitely sure about wanting to go back to the house?" Henry asked, breaking the silence a little while later as they drove through Whitehaven in the early morning traffic. Thomas looked away from where he had been watching the passing landscape with a tired sort of curiosity. Henry was gripping the steering wheel so tightly his knuckles had whitened but there was something resigned in his face now that made him look years older.

Thomas thought that moving to Deadman's Rise had aged all of them in ways none of them could ever have imagined.

"I need to do this," Thomas answered simply. "But you don't, Hal. You can just drop me off and… I'll make my own way back. You've already done more than you need to."

"Don't be silly," Henry said dismissively, his eyes not flickering from the damp road even once. "I'm hardly going to leave now, am I? Not when it's so close to this all being over. I want to *support* you."

Thomas knew this was true up to a point; Henry had always cared about him and wanted him to succeed but Thomas had a feeling that maybe this journey was for the dark-haired man too. Maybe this was the last puzzle piece Henry needed that would enable him to believe Thomas after everything they'd been through together.

It ached a little that there was still doubt even now but the older man knew that shouldn't surprise him. It made sense that Daniel believed because he had been unlucky enough to encounter the shadowy figure in the kitchen; to spy Nicholas that day in the forest. Henry had had none of those experiences and a betrayal had been thrown into the bargain too; it only made sense that he would be craving concrete proof now.

For the first time, Thomas began to worry that perhaps gaining Henry's full trust wouldn't be possible. After all, he'd witnessed the shadowy figure burning itself away into nothing with his own eyes… and Nicholas had disappeared too, fading from sight with his parents already gone from this world.

What if Thomas dragged Henry the whole way there and there was nothing to show for it?

Maybe there was nothing Thomas could do to convince his oldest best friend at all.

God, he could barely convince *himself* over the last few days.

The events that had unfolded up at the house had been like a bad dream and, the closer they came to returning now, the more unreal everything felt.

Maybe Thomas really *had* been going mad and now his sanity was returning to him, flooding back in like the tide returning to the coast. Maybe none of it had ever happened at all.

"Where are we going?" Thomas asked when Henry turned onto Preston Street but the dark-haired man simply smiled sadly as he steered them into the Asda Supermarket nearby.

"There's some supplies we need to get before we leave Whitehaven," Henry replied mysteriously.

His words didn't make sense until he led Thomas to the area at the front of the shop containing various bouquets of flowers. Thomas was perplexed for all of three seconds before he remembered Daniel's solemn face as he detailed where Nicholas was buried and, quite jarringly, the pieces fell into place and a tear slipped down Thomas's cheek.

"Thank you for being so thoughtful, Hal," he said softly and the dark-haired man smiled, squeezing his friend's shoulder in comfort.

"Anything for you, Tommy."

Thomas stood there in silence for a long time, his tired eyes raking over the bouquets as he tried to make a decision. At last, a frustrated sigh escaped him and his shoulders slumped with disappointment. Henry slipped closer, one arm winding gently around the older man's waist.

"What's wrong?" he murmured, his cheek resting against Thomas's messy hair as they stood together. "You seem upset. Should I not have planned this?"

"No, it… it's perfect," Thomas said despairingly, rubbing the back of his neck uneasily. "I just… I want to get flowers that actually *mean* something." He bit his lip, desperately trying to remember the section detailing flower meanings in his mum's Book Of Shadows. "Nick is… he's so *important*. I want this to be special."

"What about lilies?" Henry suggested quietly as he pointed to a bunch nearby. "People usually get lilies for graves, don't they?"

Thomas frowned as he followed his best friend's gaze, feeling something troubled unravel inside him. He knew Henry was probably right about the lilies – they symbolised restored innocence after death – but something about it didn't sit quite right with Thomas. It just didn't feel like *Nicholas…* who had always felt so very alive.

"I've got it," Thomas breathed, his expression brightening as his eyes settled on an unusual bouquet nearby, the red chrysanthemum blooms and the sunshine yellow of the daffodils vibrant as he reached for them.

"Those are pretty," Henry said with mild surprise, a soft smile curving his lips. "Do they mean something special?"

"Yeah," Thomas murmured, holding the flowers close as his green eyes became suspiciously damp although Henry was kind enough not to call him out on it. The older man stroked the petals gently as he recalled their meaning.

Chrysanthemum flowers symbolised optimism, joy, and long life, and the addition of red petals conveyed love too which Thomas felt to his core. The daffodils were for rebirth, new beginnings, and eternal life.

Thomas thought they were quite fitting for Nicholas.

"They mean life," he said softly, probably hugely simplifying it as Henry sighed gently beside him. "Because I'll remember Nicholas alive."

The picturesque drive from Whitehaven to the valley of Wasdale was completed in silence.

It was a remote and beautiful place and, as Henry parked beneath an old beech tree in what seemed to be the middle of nowhere, Thomas felt a pang that they would probably never get a chance to explore it again after today. There were so many remarkable places hidden here that it felt suddenly ridiculous that he'd never tried to visit more of them before.

The River Irt cut through the valley and, from the brief local knowledge Thomas had gathered during his time in the Barn Door Shop, he knew it was winding back towards its estuary at Ravenglass.

"It's lovely here, isn't it?" Thomas said quietly, inhaling the crisp scent of approaching spring as a gentle breeze stirred the long grass growing beside the road. A bleating sound caught his attention and Thomas turned towards it, smiling a little as he noticed several lively looking sheep chewing grass behind a low stone wall nearby.

The meadows behind them were covered in purple heather as they stretched away towards the Fells and something in Thomas felt like coming home for a moment as he gazed out at the rocky peaks stretching into the sky: Yewbarrow, Kirk Fell, the Great Gable, Illgill Head, Scafell Pike, and many more.

Even after everything that had happened, it remained such a breathtaking, wonderful landscape. Thomas still thought it was the most beautiful thing he'd ever seen.

"So where *is* the church?" he asked curiously as he wrapped one arm around himself, wishing he had brought a thicker jacket. "Is it close to here?"

"Sort of," Henry said with a half-shrug. "It's so far on the outskirts of the hamlet that I figured it was probably easier to just park here instead. I heard there's a trail somewhere near Wastwater that should lead us right past Saint Olaf's and it should be a nice walk if you're feeling up to it. Don't say I never learnt anything useful in my time as a ranger, huh?"

"Never," Thomas said dryly. "A walk sounds good though. My sciatica isn't awful right now and I could do with stretching my legs after days in a hospital bed."

"Let's go then," Henry said, taking the flowers from Thomas so that his best friend could concentrate on not slipping in the mud and jarring his back again. "Follow me."

Thomas's thoughts wandered as they walked and, once again, he lapsed into silence. It seemed hard for him to concentrate today, surrounded by so much beautiful scenery after days in the hospital. Thomas felt almost as though he was seeing the Lake District with new eyes after being confronted by his parents once more.

He looked at the flowers in Henry's hand and his heart swelled in his chest a little. It didn't seem right that Nicholas was gone; that his life had been stolen from him and yet he hadn't even been granted the peace he deserved until decades later.

At least Thomas's grandpa hadn't suffered for so long, with nothing but pain and loss for company. At least his loneliness hadn't consumed him as the end approached.

Another tear rolled down his cheek and Thomas's sigh was little louder than the breeze stirring the flowers nearby.

How strange grief was… that the deeper your affection for someone, the harder you grieved for them afterwards.

Maybe that was fair enough though.

Maybe that was just love.

Slowly, Thomas became aware that Henry was guiding him with a hand on his arm, leading him over the slopes and through cattle gates with a practiced patience. The dark-haired man was whistling softly under his breath and the sound reminded Thomas of early mornings back at the house for a moment; of the birds waking with the sun and stretching their wings in preparation for flight.

"Here we are," Henry murmured, gesturing with the bouquet of flowers towards a grove of trees rising from the hillside nearby. The church behind it was sheltered by their trunks and outspread branches but Thomas could just make out the low building with its slate roof protecting the wooden door.

The air felt still and old when they stepped through the treeline, and Thomas took the flowers from Henry wordlessly as his eyes drifted towards the path leading to the graveyard. The dark-haired man gave his hand a gentle squeeze before he stepped back, leaving Thomas to walk forwards alone; Henry fortunately seemed to instinctively know that Thomas needed privacy for this.

"I'll wait for you by the gate," the younger man said softly, dimples creasing his cheeks faintly when Thomas nodded his thanks. "Take as long as you need, Tom."

He could feel Henry's eyes on his back as he skirted round the tiny church but the sensation left him when he was out of sight and Thomas let out a breath he hadn't realised he was holding. The ground was dappled with shadows as he carried on but there was something peaceful about the churchyard that made Thomas relax when he stepped into it.

"Where are you, Nick?" he murmured, the bouquet's wrapping rustling as he held it closer, almost like it would lend him strength. He felt sad as he moved between the graves but, in the end, it was easy to find.

Nicholas rested on the northern edge of the cemetery, in the shade of an elder tree which seemed fitting with what Thomas had read of folklore. Elder trees were known to be associated with witches and it felt almost as though Nicholas's mother was here, looking over him even now.

His was one of the only graves without fresh flowers and it made Thomas's pulse quicken as he stepped closer. For a moment, he simply stood there with his head bowed, unsure of what to say.

"Hello," he said lamely before giving a weak snort. "Sorry, I'm really bad at this."

Thomas knelt down carefully, wincing a little as his left leg throbbed dully, his sciatica protesting the movement.

"Hey, Nick," he said in a softer voice, carefully arranging the flowers against the weathered stone of Nicholas's grave. "This is a bit strange, isn't it? Feels sort of final." He reached out to rest his palm against the tombstone but faltered, his fingertips barely brushing it as his hand fell back down to his side again.

"I'm sorry it ended like this," Thomas whispered, a lump rising in his throat. "I wish I could've found a way to bring you back but… but you were already gone, weren't you? I guess I should just be grateful that I got to meet you at all. I mean, I fell in *love* with you. I'll *always* love you… and you loved me too, didn't you? What more could I ask of you than that?"

Thomas's trembling hand fell to the earth beneath him and he pressed his palm to it, flattening the grass as he imagined – for just a moment – that there was nothing separating them: no earth or worms; no coffin or burial shroud; no life or death… just Thomas and Nicholas again, the way it should have been.

"I wish we could've had more time," he breathed past the tears boiling over down his cheeks. He dried his eyes with the sleeve of his jacket, a sharp pain stirring through him when he read the inscription on the stone beneath Nicholas's name:

I will sleep in peace, until you come to me.

"Oh god, Nick," Thomas croaked as the sobs tore out of him. Both of his hands were pressed to the packed earth now, where Nicholas slept beneath the soil. "I love you. I've *never* loved anyone like this before. I never will again."

Thomas looked up, towards the glimmers of blue sky through the trees. A chrysalis swayed from a twig overhead and he thought of the symbolism for a moment; thought of the caterpillar inside believing the world was over right before it became a butterfly.

He thought of Nicholas and grandpa Ken, and the way losing someone from your life didn't mean losing the love you felt for them. He looked down at the flowers lying on the grave and felt the conviction flaring through him like flames.

He was always meant to come here; always meant to meet Nicholas and fall for him like this. The rightness of it had settled in Thomas's bones as he pushed himself painfully to his feet, his fingertips brushing the edge of the tombstone the way he'd combed the younger man's hair back gently just a few days previously.

"I'll come back one day," Thomas said quietly, feeling strangely numb now that all of his tears had left him. "But you're not alone anymore, are you? You're with your parents now. You'll never be lonely again."

With one last miserable look at the aged stone, Thomas turned and walked away, heading back the way he had come.

He was glad Henry had brought him here. It had felt like he was saying goodbye not just to Nicholas but to Ken too.

Thomas had always harboured resentment at the perceived abandonment of his grandpa but he realised now that there was never anything anyone could have done to change it.

Fate had claimed Ken Barnes for its own and taken him long before Thomas was ready, just like it had taken Nicholas... but Thomas was finally ready to say goodbye now; to Ken in the way he never could before, and to Nicholas in the way he had always deserved… with *love*.

Henry drew him into a tight hug when Thomas limped back over to him, taking in the older man's tear-streaked cheeks and muddy hands. There was no one else around and Thomas was grateful for that as Henry rubbed his back gently, rocking the two of them slowly beneath the trees as he held his oldest best friend close.

"Ready to go?" Henry asked after a few minutes and Thomas nodded wordlessly, gripping his hand tightly as they made their slow return to the car.

The drive back through the valley to Wasdale Head didn't take long at all and it was still breathtakingly beautiful, even now. The pair exchanged looks as the Fells opened up around them and the sun finally burnt through the clouds, and Thomas saw the hopeless longing saturating Henry's face as his dark eyes raked over the landscape.

"I'm so sorry for how things turned out," Thomas muttered, his voice still croaky from crying so much earlier. "I know how much you wanted to be a ranger."

Henry reached over to squeeze his hand but he didn't tear his gaze away from their surroundings.

"I think I'll still be a ranger somehow," the dark-haired man said softly, his dimples appearing briefly as his eyes turned faraway. "Just… maybe not here. I'll find somewhere without these bad memories."

"Then I'm glad," Thomas said seriously, his eyelashes still spiky with tears but his expression fiercely determined. "I know you're going to be fantastic, Hal. You just have to be given a chance."

The déjà vu Thomas could feel when Henry parked the car outside the Barn Door Shop was almost stifling but he felt no fear now… only weariness and the hope for a quieter life.

"I… I don't know about you but… I don't really want to sleep in that house again," Henry said and, until that moment, Thomas hadn't realised he'd been thinking the exact same thing. "How about we book in to stay at the Inn tonight, yeah? We can get our meals there too. Plus I need to remember to deliver Daniel's resignation letter to the Santon Bridge Inn. It makes more sense if we're down in the hamlet."

"Sounds like a good plan to me," Thomas said with a weak smile, unbuckling his seatbelt as he scratched carefully under his eye, trying to avoid the dark bruising there. "You gonna post the letter after lunch?"

"Probably," Henry decided as he climbed out of the car, Thomas stiffly following suit. "It's a long, *long* walk and I don't have Daniel's bike handy so we may as well drive down later after we've checked in to the Inn." The circles under Henry's eyes looked like bruises but he managed a weary smile as he eased the crumpled pack of cigarettes out of his pocket, lighting up and wandering away as he locked the car.

"You coming for a walk, Tom?" Henry called over his shoulder, his words muffled around the cigarette. Thomas shrugged, shaking his head.

"You're alright," the older man said, smiling a little. "Reckon I'll just wander round here a bit. Maybe go and see Alison. Need to tell her we're leaving anyway."

"Fair enough," Henry said but Thomas had already left, crossing the quiet street and slipping between the bollards before he let himself into the shop. The bell above the door chimed and Alison appeared, her expression of calm professionalism quickly melting into concern and fondness.

"Oh, Tom, honey!" she gasped upon seeing the state of his sore face, her worry growing when she took in the stitches under his hair and the mud caked under his fingernails. "What *happened* to you?"

Thomas just took her hand gently when she reached for him, a watery smile curving his lips.

"We're leaving tomorrow," he said softly, avoiding the question. "I'm sorry I didn't have time to work a notice period. Things have been... quite difficult recently. I feel awful for messing you around like this."

"You don't have to explain yourself, Tom," Alison said gently, her eyes so understanding that Thomas thought perhaps he *hadn't* quite cried himself out yet after all.

Her palm came to rest on his cheek gently, tilting his face this way and that as she took in the various injuries ruining his pale skin.

"I know you haven't been happy living here in a long time," Alison said gently. "It's your time to leave, pet. That's all there is to it." She softened, giving his hand a comforting squeeze. "Are you going back to the house for one last night?"

Thomas shivered before he could stop himself and the way her eyes flashed to his face then was almost *knowing*.

"No," he said firmly, thinking of the flowers he'd left in the graveyard and the noose of ivy dangling outside his window. "No, we won't."

Alison didn't press him for details but her smile was sad as she patted his bruised cheek gently.

"It was good to see you again, Tom," she said kindly and he had to swallow past the lump in his throat as he drew her into a warm hug. She'd done so much for him and he would never be able to thank her enough for that.

Thomas was so glad he'd got the chance to say goodbye.

Chapter 28: His Dying Day

Thomas woke to the smell of bacon and the warmth of sunshine on his skin. The window had been pushed open wide to let the fresh air in and Thomas basked in the comfort for a moment, at least until he rolled over and felt his sciatica give an unpleasant, threatening prickle.

Henry was sitting on the windowsill, one leg folded to his chest as his bare foot rested lightly on the carpet. He was smoking again, his mobile pressed to his ear as he murmured into it. By the softness on his face, he could only have been speaking to Daniel and Thomas relaxed a little, even despite his pain; at least *their* relationship still had the chance to flourish, even if his and Nicholas's was irredeemable now.

"- and your mum's actually getting *better*?" Henry was asking softly, his dark eyes wider with surprise as he gazed out over the Fells, painted golden in the sunrise. "Danny, that's such good news. I'm so *happy* for you. I – Oh, he *did*? Well, Jacob's always had a soft spot for you, hasn't he? Not like Adam and your dad. I'm glad he told you he missed you. That must've meant a lot."

Henry paused to listen to whatever the blond man was saying, taking a deep drag of the cigarette and sighing as his shoulders became tense.

"Tom's doing okay," he said in a wearier voice, his tone fond but undeniably apprehensive. "We're going back up there after breakfast today and then – No, I'm not planning on taking anything back with us right now. I figure we can pay a removal company to do that later, if we ever manage to actually *sell* the damn place."

There was another moment of silence and Henry let out a quiet sigh.

"I don't know," he said sadly, cradling the phone closer for a moment, like Daniel *wasn't* hundreds of miles away on the other side of the country. "Tom just wants answers I think. I only hope he can get the closure he needs… and that we both don't get killed in the attempt." Henry barked out a laugh and, dimly, Thomas heard Daniel berating him down the phone line. "I was only kidding, Danny! I'm sorry!"

Thomas's sciatica was definitely making itself known now and he let out a quiet groan as he stretched, instantly regretting the movement when pain rocketed down his leg. Henry's eyes snapped to his face and Thomas managed a tired wave, his bruised face grey with how much it hurt.

"Gotta go, Danny. Tom's awake now… but I'll call you when we're ready to leave Wasdale Head, yeah? We'll start driving back to London later today." Henry's cheeks heated suddenly and he turned away a little, looking out over the rolling fields again to where the mountains touched the sky. "I love you too, Daniel," he said softly. "More than you know."

Thomas pushed himself into an uncomfortable sitting position, raking his fingers through his hair so that it was in some semblance of control. He wanted to get it cut when he got back to London, until he'd lost the crimson streaks entirely. Maybe it was time to let his natural colour flourish again. Maybe it was time to let go.

"You hurting today?" Henry asked with a frown, his teeth worrying at his bottom lip. "Do you think you're gonna be able to make it? I know you said you wanted to walk up there but I can drive us if –"

"No, it's fine," Thomas said firmly, gritting his teeth as he got slowly to his feet. "I'll be alright in a little while." This may or may not have been true. "I'm gonna have a shower but you don't have to wait up here if you've got stuff to do first. I'll probably be slow."

"That's okay, Tom," Henry said softly, his eyes warm in the morning light. "I'll bring some breakfast back up to the room, yeah? It'll be waiting for you when you're all washed up. Then we can get going afterwards."

"Sure," Thomas said, smiling in relief. "Thank you, Hal."

The younger man was true to his word. A bacon roll and a takeaway cup of coffee were waiting for Thomas when he limped out of the bathroom, and a comforting warmth bloomed in the older man's chest as he settled down on his bed to eat. Henry was sitting nearby, dressed in jeans and a lavender-coloured sweatshirt that Thomas was fairly certain belonged to Daniel.

Thomas was so glad their friendship had survived.

The dark-haired man looked more peaceful than he'd seemed in a long time after talking to the blond man on the phone and Thomas was glad they'd got the chance to catch up. He only wished that *he* could feel so calm too but it didn't seem possible now. There was a nervous energy spreading through his veins that refused to leave.

"Ready?" Henry asked a short while later, when the conversation had died down like fire and there was nothing else holding them back. Thomas nodded, his face pale as he squared his jaw determinedly.

"Let's get this over and done with," he said, thinking back to Henry's comment earlier and trying for a smile that probably fell woefully flat. "You better bring your running trainers, Hal. Just in case we need to make a quick getaway, right?"

"You're as bad as me!" Henry said with a delighted grin. "No wonder Daniel gets so fed up of our hilarious wit. I think we have a career in stand-up comedy if my ranger thing falls through."

"Oh god," Thomas groaned, rolling his eyes skyward as he followed Henry out of the hotel room. "Don't give up your day job, Hal. Oops – too late!"

The younger man deliberately messed Thomas's hair up for that jibe but he was careful of the stitches and his face remained gentle. Thomas hummed contentedly, bumping into his best friend with his elbow as Henry loped easily down the stairs ahead of him.

"Love you, Hal," Thomas called and Henry looked back, his tired eyes crinkling as he grinned up at his best friend.

"I love you too, Tom," he said cheerfully. "Now c'mon. We've got a haunted house to visit."

"You say really stupid shit sometimes," Thomas said pointedly as he followed the younger man out into the early morning sunlight. Henry threw him a stupid wink as he gestured in the direction of the road that would lead them up to Deadman's Rise.

"It's all part of my charm," he said.

It felt like the two of them were skipping out of school together for a moment; felt like they were just fifteen years old and the world was okay again; big and exciting… an abstract concept that hadn't yet thrown everything they knew off kilter.

The walk up to the house was longer than he remembered and Thomas's sciatica protested every step taken without a cane to lean on. Their breath fogged up in the cool northern air around them but the first snowdrops of the year were already forcing their way out of the cold ground and Thomas thought again of the flower section in the Book Of Shadows for a moment as his heart softened in his chest.

Snowdrops meant new beginnings.

"You doing okay, Tom?" Henry asked anxiously when Thomas let out a particularly ragged breath, his movements laborious as his leg betrayed him yet again. He found it hard to be frustrated though; his sciatica was simply a part of life and he would have to learn to live with that.

"Yeah, almost there now anyway," Thomas grunted, gritting his teeth as his leg seared again. "The house is just round the next bend and – *Oh.*" He fell quiet, his eyes alighting on a very familiar cane resting against the low stone wall nearby. He limped towards it, his shoulders tense beneath Henry's watchful gaze.

"Is this where –?" The dark-haired man's words trailed away but Thomas nodded silently, his thumb rubbing the polished wooden handle as he swallowed audibly.

"We're close," Thomas murmured and Henry reached for his free hand wordlessly, their fingers entwining as tight as the ivy growing around the oak tree outside Thomas's window. They turned the corner together and both of them slowed to an unconscious stop.

Deadman's Rise hadn't changed a bit and, although it may have seemed foolish to expect otherwise after just a few short days, the sheer immensity of their discoveries meant that the thoroughfare seemed alien now.

The world felt so still as they stepped under cover of the trees. It was as though time had frozen almost. The decaying leaves of autumn were still visible under the dampness of the long-melted winter snow and the sunlight shone down in delicate beams between the spidery branches, illuminating dust and dew in shafts of gold.

It felt like the road was untouched by the rest of the world… like the pair of them had stumbled through a gateway into another dimension without realising it.

Thomas wondered how he'd never noticed the otherworldliness of Deadman's Rise before.

"Knowing what we know now…" Henry's voice trailed away and he shivered, wrapping his free arm around himself. "It's scary, isn't it?"

"I'm not scared," Thomas said honestly. He remembered the shadowy figure burning itself away like ink and the softer version of Nicholas's father underneath. He remembered the butterfly and the soil beneath his fingernails.

"There's nothing here that wants to hurt us. Not anymore."

Despite the older man's reassurances, Henry still hesitated and the wariness in his eyes – although definitely not unfounded – did nothing to make Thomas relax beside him. The air around them felt charged and the hairs on the back of their necks rose. Henry's fingers were tight around his.

There was absolute silence and then – quite suddenly – a clattering sound could be heard, growing louder and louder until –

A red deer darted out into the road up ahead, making them both freeze. It was beautiful, its coat shining in the light as it stared back at them, its nostrils flaring as it scented the air. Henry's hand slipped from Thomas's as he reached slowly into his pocket for his phone, his eyes wide with excitement, ever the faithful ranger even now.

A puff of breath escaped him in a thrilled gasp as he snapped a picture because, even from this distance, the deer was *so* beautiful.

It stepped gracefully across the tarmac, its cloven hooves dainty as it stepped through the shadows. Henry looked like he was about to melt into an excited puddle on the floor by now and Thomas watched him fondly, distracted for a moment at the childlike joy flooding the dark-haired man's face as he took a measured step in the direction of the deer.

It looked back at him sharply, their gazes meeting for a moment before a familiar rumbling roar sounded and the animal bounded away, crossing the road in seconds and disappearing into the undergrowth on the other side. Henry let out a little whine of disappointment, shooting Thomas a guilty look before he ran across the road too.

"I'll be just a minute, Tom!" Henry called over his shoulder, leaving the older man stranded on the pavement. "I really wanted to get a better picture – I could win the National Geographic photography competition with an opportunity like this!"

Thomas was fairly sure that this was an exaggeration but he let Henry go anyway, rolling his eyes as he stepped onto the tarmac after him. His knee ached but he figured he had time to reach the pavement before the truck had even turned the corner, let alone caused him any danger.

A shiver ran down his spine and it took Thomas a moment to realise why he suddenly felt so distressed.

He was standing where Nicholas had died; maybe even in exactly the same spot.

It sent a thrill of dread through him and Thomas shuddered as he remembered Nicholas describing his death while his imagination filled in all of the horrible details: the panicked breaths clawing out of

Nicholas as he hurtled into the road, covered in his father's blood; the crunch as the truck collided with him; the way his body broke – crumpled – *died* – even as he continued to run, chasing nothing.

Thomas's knee flared with agony and his leg folded beneath him, sending him staggering to his knees as the truck rounded the bend, almost like Thomas had been frozen in place without realising it.

A shrill ringing sound filled his ears but Thomas didn't think it had anything to do with the truck; it sounded almost like someone was screaming at him to move instead… a voice calling from so very far away and yet… it sounded *just* like –

The horn was blaring now but Thomas's leg completely gave way and he collapsed into the puddles with a winded groan, his panic flooding through him. The pain hadn't been this unexpectedly awful since that night when he'd fallen down the stairs and Thomas couldn't separate the fiery agony consuming him from the sensible adrenaline-fuelled part of his brain that wanted him to **move**.

Henry was screaming for him as he hurtled back through the trees but the underbrush was thick with thorns and Thomas watched in horror as the dark-haired man smashed down onto the pavement with a cry, his panic evident in the crackling air between them as he reached uselessly for his best friend.

Thomas wanted so badly to move – to go to his best friend and help him – but it just wasn't possible now. His sciatica was rendering him useless and the fear was settling in Thomas's aching bones, freezing him as his cane lay in the road uselessly nearby.

The truck's brakes were screeching sickeningly but the road was damp and the distance between them was shrinking by the second, and Henry would never reach him in time. Thomas knew that now.

He felt like he was watching everything through glass for a moment: the pain and fear, and the abrupt unexpected horror of it all, and the only thing he knew for sure in that moment was that he didn't want to go.

There was still so much left he wanted to do in this world.

Thomas wasn't ready to leave just yet.

He thought of all the people he'd never get a chance to say goodbye to... thought of all the people who had deserved so much *more* from him than he had ever been able to give: his best friends, his parents, his grandpa... and Nicholas.

Thomas closed his eyes as the thundering tyres sped closer, his heart forcing itself into his throat because there was nothing he could do now and –

Something hit him but not from the direction he'd been expecting.

Thomas's bruised form was lifted bodily from the road, his limp hands sliding through the puddles beneath him as he was dragged onto the curb. The truck roared past with a mere second to spare, throwing up a cloud of rainwater as the horn blared, the driver cursing out of the window.

Thomas was trembling so violently that he felt like he was going to fall apart, his arms wrapped tightly around himself as he shivered. A sob was building in his throat but before he could do much more than draw in a panicked gasp, a familiar scent washed over him and the comfort it offered was shocking.

Thomas could smell Nicholas in the air – the coolness of his skin, the way his flannel shirt was slightly damp from the rain, the pine of the forest clinging to his jeans, the laundry-detergent smell of his t-shirt, the shampoo he'd used the night before he died.

Now that Thomas knew to look for it, he realised he could feel someone else's arms wrapped around him too; a body curved safely around him as lips brushed his clammy neck. Thomas kept his eyes squeezed tightly shut, somehow aware that if he opened them then the illusion would shatter… but he could still *feel* him… like Nicholas had never left at all.

Maybe Thomas had been killed. Maybe the truck had hit him and this was his own warped version of heaven.

If it was, Thomas thought he'd be okay with it. He'd always loved Nicholas more than was healthy.

"*Tom*," a familiar voice cried but it wasn't the one he'd been hoping to hear and bitter tears welled up as he processed that it was Henry speaking.

Thomas opened his emerald eyes slowly, another shudder tearing through him as his knee ached. He was lying on the pavement, the sky above him a clear blue, the cane rolling innocently nearby. He was alone and his heart felt far too big for his chest.

Henry was stumbling towards him, his face ashen as he rubbed distractedly at a graze on his wrist. His cheeks were streaked with tears and the relief saturating his expression was outweighed only by the shocked disbelief.

"You moved!" Henry was croaking as he collapsed down onto the pavement beside his best friend. "You lifted into the air but there was no one there! What the fuck, Tom?! What the actual *fuck*?!"

Henry's terror seemed to come out of nowhere and Thomas shivered as he reached for him, pulling him down into a tight hug as the tears mingled on their cheeks.

"It was Nicholas," Thomas breathed, their foreheads touching as Henry cradled his face, apparently reassuring himself that the older man was fine. "He was here, Hal. I *felt* him."

"He saved you," Henry whispered, his eyes wide with astonishment. A tear slipped down his cheek, quickly followed by more. "I was only joking earlier when I told Daniel we might get killed," the younger man muttered suddenly, a watery smile touching his too-pale face. "Why'd you have to prove me right, arsehole?!"

"Didn't *mean* to," Thomas said gruffly, closing his eyes with relief for a moment. "You'll get big-headed if you're always right. It'll make you arrogant."

"Oh, shut up," Henry groaned but he was still hugging the older man ridiculously tightly and it took any sting from his words. "You better not scare me like that ever again. I missed turning into the new David Attenborough for you. I'll probably have nightmares for *years*."

"Oh yeah?" Thomas replied as Henry helped him painfully into a sitting position. "Join the club, mate."

It took a few minutes before either of them were ready to stand up, the rainwater soaking into their clothes as Henry stayed stubbornly beside him, his arm wrapped securely around the older man's waist. Thomas clutched his cane tightly, still trembling as the pair of them made their clumsy way down the long driveway. It reminded him of the three-legged races they used to participate in at school on Sports Day for a moment and the sudden nostalgia he felt took his breath away.

Thomas was still reeling from how *old* this memory made him feel when Henry unlocked the front door, shooting a wary glance into the shadowy hallway before he ushered his best friend safely inside. Thomas sat down heavily at the bottom of the stairs, setting the cane aside and rubbing his bruised face weakly to remove the rainwater as Henry lingered nearby, his eyes darting about nervously.

Through unspoken agreement, neither of them shut the front door - mostly because they didn't want to feel trapped here again - but Thomas already knew things were different this time. He still didn't feel as though they were alone but there was nothing malicious hanging in the air anymore. The house felt cleaner around them almost, the light purer.

The wind picked up outside and, as a handful of fallen leaves swirled across the gravel, Thomas's bedroom door creaked slowly open.

As his surprised eyes traced the unexpected movement, his heart clenched painfully in his chest.

His bedroom floor was covered in Polaroids - hundreds more than he had ever discovered before - all of them lying spread out on the wooden panels, picture-side up and spaced evenly apart. Thomas rose on weak legs, his green eyes damp with tears as he drifted unconsciously closer with Henry following him tentatively, a trembling hand covering his mouth as the younger man gazed about him in awe.

Thomas knelt down stiffly, uncaring of the pain for a moment as his fingertips skated lightly over the glossy pictures. He saw Nicholas, his parents, their house and garden, the view of the mountains. Thomas could see Nicholas playing baseball, relaxing with his friends, crouching down to pet a cat, playing on a swing set, riding his first bike, being spoon-fed baby food from a high chair, being cuddled between both of his parents.

Thomas could barely breathe past the tears and love swelling in his chest because... fuck, it was *real*.

It was all **real** and Nicholas had saved the older man's life, and Thomas could never *ever* repay him for it.

"Oh, Tom," Henry said, his voice little more than a breath as he knelt down too. One of his hands settled on Thomas's shoulder - slumped with grief and love - as he moved some of the closer Polaroids for a better look. "You can tell it's the seventies here, can't you?" His smile was soft and very sad. "They're so *happy* though, aren't they? Can't you see how much they love each other?"

Henry's fingertip was nudging a Polaroid a little further away and Thomas looked closer, a lump rising in his throat as he saw Nicholas's parents dancing together. Nicholas's mother's caramel hair was curling prettily over the flowery blouse she was wearing, her flared trousers making him smile fondly. Her husband was wrapped lovingly around her, his shirt unbuttoned at the collar, his mousy hair brushing his jaw as he tucked his chin over her shoulder, his glasses sliding down his nose.

They both looked so much like their only son that it took Thomas's breath away.

"Nick always said his dad used to be kind before they came here," he said softly, the pad of his thumb skirting the edge of the picture gently. "I guess here's the proof."

Henry made a small noise of surprise nearby as he reached out suddenly, hesitating just before he touched the Polaroid. The older man followed his gaze, shivering with misery and *longing* as he reached to pick it up.

"This is how he looked when I knew him," Thomas murmured, cradling the precious picture carefully between his palms. "This is how I'll remember him."

The Nicholas in the picture was probably eighteen or nineteen, leaning against a brick wall covered in ivy - maybe even against this very house - with his glasses sitting crookedly on his tanned face. The ever-present baseball was being tossed into the air as the picture was taken, his hazel eyes fixed on it as a grin tugged at his full lips.

Nicholas was wearing peeling trainers and an old flannel shirt, and the contentedness of his expression was something Thomas had rarely seen during their time together; only on that comfortable evening spent making wishes on bay leaves or the day they sat together on the porch as the sun rose behind the mountains.

Nicholas's bright eyes sparkled with intelligence and good humour, and absolute *life*.

Thomas had never seen the younger man look quite like that before.

Nicholas *shone*.

"I'll never forget you," Thomas whispered unthinkingly, the tears slowly beginning to slide down his cheeks as he held the picture closer. He slipped the Polaroid into his jacket pocket after a moment of hesitation and, when something that felt *almost* like the breeze gently tousled his hair, Thomas knew this was forgiven.

With the picture so close to him now, it felt as though Nicholas was beside him once more.

Henry drew the older man into a warm hug when Thomas's tears finally overwhelmed him and, as they sat there together - their sorrow, wonder, and love wrapping around the pair of them like a blanket -

Thomas knew that everything had happened as it was meant to. They had become stronger because of it.

Holding Henry so close now made their friendship feel the way it used to before they were hurt… before their lives were changed upon meeting Daniel… before the world and its hatred tried to extinguish their light.

Burying his face comfortingly in the younger man's neck, Thomas swore that he would never let anything pull them apart again.

"It feels wrong to leave the Polaroids all over the floor like this," Henry murmured when the pair of them finally parted. His dark curls were falling messily into his tear-wet eyes after the rain outside and Thomas brushed his knuckles gently over the younger man's soft cheek, his fingertip dipping into the dimple to make Henry roll his eyes fondly.

"I think you're right," Thomas said as his gaze drifted over the evidence of an entire family's history scattered on the floor around them. "But… it feels wrong to take them with us too. Maybe…" He faltered, biting his lip as he glanced back towards the hallway. "Maybe we should leave them in the living room. That's where I felt watched most. Maybe that's where they rest now."

"Good idea," Henry said, leaning forwards to gather up the pictures closest to him. Thomas did the same, both of them falling into a comfortable silence as they carefully collected the Polaroids that had been spread out so lovingly for them to view. The sheer *trust* they had been shown was an honour that Thomas would never forget; not for as long as he lived.

Daniel would be so hurt that he had missed this.

"C'mon, Hal," Thomas said softly once the dark-haired man had helped his best friend carefully to his feet. "It's almost over now."

They made their slow way into the living room together, taking in the old cracked leather sofa and the secondhand lampshade, its tassels still drifting in the breeze even now. The peace lily was alive and blooming on the coffee table once more. The goodbye note Henry had left Thomas was gone.

It was like nothing untoward had ever happened there at all and, judging by the unnerved look on the dark-haired man's face, he seemed to be thinking exactly the same thing.

Deciding not to dwell on it, Thomas reached for the Polaroids that Henry had been holding and began to sort through them until he settled on one of the entire family together. Nicholas couldn't have been more than three years old but the love in the picture was unmistakable and Thomas was sure that this was how the May family would want to be remembered.

"Do we have any pins here?" he asked and, with a slightly confused frown, Henry disappeared into the kitchen to search. While he was gone, Thomas settled the rest of the pictures neatly beside the peace lily, the waxy white petals of the flower casting strange shadows over the shiny surface of the Polaroids.

"We've got loads!" Henry called back triumphantly before he returned with a box of them, scattering a few into his best friend's waiting palm. "What are you going to do with them?"

Thomas limped towards the fireplace with the family picture held carefully in his hand. Henry was watching him curiously and the older man shot a fond glance over his shoulder for a moment before concentrating on carefully pinning the Polaroid to the wooden mantelpiece, where once upon a time the family might have hung Christmas stockings.

"I'm going to make this house look lived in, Hal," Thomas said softly, one fingertip tracing the picture tenderly. "Because it is. It always *has* been."

They spent the next few hours pinning the Polaroids to every surface they could find and, when they were finally done, it looked like a family home again, the way it has been back at the beginning.

The sheer rightness of the deed thrummed comfortingly through Thomas's ribcage like a hummingbird, filling his heart with sunlight and hope. He felt like broken pottery for a moment; all of the cracks in him sealed with gold.

When Henry squeezed his best friend's shoulder gently before murmuring that he would wait for him outside, Thomas's world righted on his axis. He saw everything as it had been, as it would be, and as it was. Most of all as it was.

The day had dawned bright and sunny through the wide living room windows, and the open front door allowed the watery light to gently fill the room.

Thomas turned to take it all in, looking past the faded grey carpet and the threadbare rug to the way the house would have been *before*, full of love and laughter and life.

He knew then what he needed to do.

Thomas had to **live**.

He would fulfill Nicholas's wish and finally be happy.

The urge struck him like a blacksmith's hammer and the resulting sparks illuminated the world around him like fireflies.

All he had to do was leave the house and keep walking until he found Henry; until they made it back to London together and reunited with Daniel; until Thomas could hug his mum again and prove that he loved her enough to keep his promise; until he could truly repair the bonds he shared with his two best friends.

Thomas would *never* stop doing everything he could to prove how much his loved ones meant to him.

That was what he had taken from this terrifying, heartwarming, unearthly experience.

That was what he would carry with him until his dying day.

Thomas was going to keep going until he felt alive again.

He *had* to.

There was no other path to take.

He left the May family's house without pain, carrying nothing but his grandpa's telescope, his mum's Book Of Shadows, Nicholas's Polaroid, and his cane tucked safely under one arm.

Thomas could feel watchful eyes on his back as he carefully descended the wooden steps but they didn't feel scary anymore. They felt *safe*.

Nicholas whispered goodbye and Thomas felt it on the breeze, ruffling his fading hair playfully and coaxing the tears from his flushed cheeks.

He was crying again but he didn't wish he was dead anymore - he had never felt *further* from it - because… god, Nicholas had *saved* him and maybe now Thomas could live for both of them.

Maybe.

He felt lighter and happier than he had been in years as he stepped down onto the driveway, emerging limping into the brightness of a beautiful almost-spring day.

He was not alone. He never had been and he never would be again.

"Hey, Tommy," Henry said softly, reaching out a hand for his best friend to take. "Let's go and find Daniel, yeah?"

Thomas entwined their fingers tightly as his heart beat golden in his chest.

He left without looking back.

Printed in Great Britain
by Amazon